WYOMING
CONFIDENTIAL

VICKI THARP

WYOMING
CONFIDENTIAL

Original Cover Design by Designs EE

ISBN 978-1-948798-26-6

✾ Created with Vellum

A friend challenged me to make them a villian. So, I did. This book is dedicated to this friend. A person who could only be bad between the pages of a work of fiction.

1
___

FORMER DEPUTY SHERIFF WYATT WOLFE LAY ON THE BENCH AT the stern of his boat. A gooey glob of cow slobber dripped on his cheek, and he couldn't drum up the enthusiasm to care. As far as bad days went, a little saliva didn't even rate. One of these days, he'd figure out a way to keep the cow off the stock pond's dock, but today wasn't that day.

A horn honked—a crisp *bonk-bonk.*

Rodriguez.

Wyatt grumbled and growled. Unless his ex-partner had come to tell him that the sheriff wanted to give him his old job back, he wasn't interested in talking. The way Rodriguez kept dropping by seeking advice on the string of murders involving sex workers was cruel—like the callous kid teasing a starving puppy with a juicy scrap of steak.

The local paper had dubbed the string of murders the 'Nightwalker murders.'

Rodriguez's Cole Haans reverberated on the dock as Wyatt struggled to sit. His head went wonky. A file folder sticking to his cheek fell away, scattering papers across his boat's rear deck and into the gaping mouth of his open engine compartment.

He caught himself on the gunwale, knocking a bottle of cheap whiskey into the hold, and spilling the last of it. *Damn.* The aroma of cheap booze wafted up and mixed with the charred undertones of burned oil.

He found the cleanest spot on his grease-stained T-shirt and wiped the cow spit off the side of his face.

Rodriguez called out from the dock's narrow gangway. "Yo!"

Wyatt glanced up, but That-A-Way, his landlord's old brindle cow. She had crazy messed up horns that both pointed to the right as if giving silent directions to go *that-a-way*, blocked Wyatt's view. He reached into a Ziploc bag and tossed her an alfalfa cube. If That-A-Way had been a dog, she would have jumped up and snagged it out of the air. But she was a cow with no eye–mouth coordination, and the cube bounced off her forehead and landed on the dock. She ducked her head and slurped it up.

"Go on," Wyatt said, shooing her away with his hands.

The bovine gave him a slow blink, ran her pointy tongue up one pink nostril, and then ambled up the dock. Rodriguez glommed onto one of the pilings to keep from being brushed off into the water.

"Jesus Christ," Rodriguez said when he'd made it to the boat. He pointed a manila envelope at Wyatt. "You're a grown-ass man. When are you going to get a real place to live?"

Wyatt flipped his ex-partner the finger and a fractional smile. "This *is* a real place. I've got water, electric, a new sewage pump for the head, and—"

"It's a relic, on a pond, in a cattle pasture, in Wyoming. If you had more than five feet of water beneath you, the boat would have sunk."

"Hey, I fixed that leak weeks ago." Wyatt held his arms out wide to encompass the whole vessel. "And Sea-Celia is forty-four feet of classic beauty."

"Right." Rodriguez eyed him over the top of his sunglasses. "I hate to break this to you, buddy, but you can put lipstick, a push-up bra, and Spanx on that pig of a boat, and she still wouldn't rate more than a two."

Wyatt ignored the comment. Some people couldn't see that beauty was more than boat hull deep. "And it's a cow pasture, not *cattle* pasture—since Evie is down to the one cow."

"I don't get it. Why doesn't the old bat ship the burger-on-a-bag-of-bones off and grind it into meat?"

Wyatt shifted his focus to a spot behind Rodriguez and said, "I don't know, why don't you ask the 'old bat' yourself?"

Cursing under his breath, Rodriguez turned. Evelyn Yates stood behind him, a glass of lemonade in each hand, beads of condensation dripping down the sides. She was a slight woman, with steel in her hunched spine, a wily spark in her faded blue eyes, and compassion in her heart. She also didn't take shit from anybody. And she was nosy. She only brought Wyatt lemonade when he had company. Thankfully, that wasn't often.

"This *old bat* thought you boys might be thirsty," Evie said.

Rodriquez made a choking noise in the back of his throat as if he'd almost swallowed his tongue.

Wyatt gave Evie a wink with his good eye as she passed him a glass.

"Your eye," Evie said, "what—"

"It's fine." At least it would be once the swelling went down.

She harrumphed as he downed the lemonade in three large gulps. Unfortunately, it wasn't enough to wash away the stale whiskey coating his tongue. Evie turned to Rodriguez. He shifted the envelope to his other hand and reached for the glass, but instead of handing it over, she brought it to her lips and took a sip.

Rodriguez huffed out a laugh and glanced away. Back when Wyatt and Rodriguez were still partners, there had been some days where it seemed like it would be easier for Rodriguez to slay dragons with a sharpened Popsicle stick than to summon proper manners.

Rodriguez met her assessing gaze. "My apologies, ma'am."

Evie eyed him the way a woman does when she's judging a man on the substance beneath the clothes. In Rodriguez's case, beneath the rumpled dress shirt and the chinos that had long lost their crease. One of her penciled-on brows rose as if surprised to find him so lacking.

But Wyatt knew better. Rodriguez could come off rude and uncaring at worst, or even ambivalent at best. But that was more smokescreen than substance. Underneath the gruff was a decent man with a tough past who'd worked his ass off to overcome it. That he enjoyed the materialistic things in life now that he could afford it, Wyatt couldn't fault him for.

She took another slow sip of the lemonade, then handed Rodriguez the glass. To Wyatt, she said, "I have some stuff in the van that needs unloading when you have a minute."

"Sure," Wyatt said, "I'll be up in a bit."

With the sun on its downward arc, the burr oak on the shoreline cast a long shadow across the boat deck. Evie turned and scooted back to her house. Rodriguez set the glass on the gunwale and stepped aboard, the boat rocking beneath his weight, then leveling out.

Wyatt slumped on the bench seat, picked up Rodriguez's ice-cold glass, and held it against his swollen eye. "I see you haven't lost your golden touch with women, Romeo."

With a nod toward Wyatt's black eye, Rodriguez said, "Apparently, you have, though."

"This was work-related. A little on-the-job training, you might say."

"What? Did your client get pissed when you showed him pictures of his wife blowing his best friend?"

"Something like that."

Why had he gone into the PI business? He hated divorce cases. He hated the cheating husbands and the vindictive wives, the slashed tires and the bruised egos, the petty fights and the hurt feelings, none of which mattered in the whole grand scheme of things.

He wanted *real* cases. The murders. The cases where he could do his job and make a substantial difference. What he *wanted* was his old job back.

Rodriguez wobbled in front of Wyatt's good eye. He couldn't tell if the boat was rocking or if the booze was still talking. Wyatt waved at Rodriguez to have a seat.

"What's up? I know you didn't drive all the way out here just to give me shit."

Rodriguez spun the captain's chair around and sat. "I have a job offer for you."

Wyatt sat up straight, his heart kicked his sternum, and the lemonade sloshed down the front of his shirt. He'd waited close to a year and a half for this news. "Day wants me back?"

Wyatt downed the rest of the lemonade and reached into the cooler beside him for a couple bottles of water. He tossed one to Rodriguez and kept the other for himself.

"Eeh," Rodriguez scrunched up his face. Wyatt knew that face. It was Rodriguez's how-do-I-spin-the-truth-into-something-positive face. "Not exactly."

Wyatt sat back. A nagging tightness clamped his chest. It shouldn't hurt so bad that Jed Day, his mentor, the Bison County Sheriff, the man who'd taken Wyatt as a petty-thieving, punk-ass teen off the streets and brought him into his house and raised him as his own, didn't want anything to do with him.

Killing Caleb Steele, an undercover agent, hadn't been Wyatt's fault.

And he had the *No Bill* from the grand jury as proof.

That-A-Way eased belly deep into the pond and munched on a mouthful of pondweeds. The ripples fanned out and sloshed against Sea-Celia's wood hull, slipping beneath her keel.

"Then what kind of job is it?" Wyatt glanced over at Rodriguez, almost afraid to hear the answer.

"Investigative work on the down-low."

"If you're trying to be funny, it's not working."

"No joke, buddy."

Wyatt reached for the whiskey bottle, forgetting it was lying empty at the bottom of his hull. For one pathetic moment, he wondered if there had been enough alcohol spilled for the bilge to pump it out. He could hold a Solo cup under the bilge port and...

No, he wasn't that desperate.

Yet.

"Who'd I be working for?"

"Sheriff Day."

The offer hit him in the gut, and the whiskey-lemonade combo surged up the back of his throat. That bilge-whiskey plan looked better and better. "Forget it. If Jed had wanted my help, he should have come to me himself... and the answer would still be no. I want my job, not someone to throw me an off-the-books bone."

Rodriguez held up his bottle of water. "Got anything stronger?"

Wyatt bumped his chin toward the open hold in front of his bare feet.

His friend's face twisted in confusion. "Since when do you store your liquor in the engine compartment?"

"Long story."

Rodriguez leaned forward, his elbows on his knees. "Look, I know things are a little rough between you and Day—"

"Rough?" Wyatt's vocal cords squeaked as they hit a register unheard since puberty. "Day and I would have to be talking for it to be *rough*. I don't know what you call all this static. This silence. This complete *bullshit*."

"Day has taken this harder than any—"

Wyatt made a noise—part growl and part grumble, all incredulity. No one had taken Caleb Steele's death harder than Wyatt except, he would imagine, Steele's wife and family.

"You've got to see it from Day's perspective, Wy. He's the freaking sheriff. Voted in, not appointed. It wouldn't look good for him to be seen talking with you."

"The grand jury cleared me. Internal Affairs cleared me. I don't see the problem." Deep down, Wyatt knew, but he wanted to see if Rodriguez was man enough to say it to his face.

"IA, the courts, they don't mean as much in a small town as the court of public opinion. And in the people's eyes, you took down one of your own."

Apparently, Rodriguez did have the balls.

"The guy was deep undercover. The DEA slipped him in, never notifying Jed and the local task force. How—" Wyatt cut himself off. This argument was nothing new. Facts don't always change a person's perception. The fucking Drug Enforcement Administration. What the hell had they been thinking?

Emotionally, Wyatt was too beat down even to raise his voice. Constantly having to defend himself, endure the stares, the whispers, the sidelong glances... It wore on a man.

But not nearly as substantially as his guilt had.

Because even though his actions that day had been justified, even though he'd played it by the book, a man, an officer, was still dead.

Forget the Solo cup for the bilge-whiskey, Wyatt would just put his mouth to the bilge spout and swallow.

Rodriguez held his hands up as if saying don't-shoot-the-messenger. "Hey, you're my friend, I've always given you the benefit of the doubt."

Wyatt laughed. Cold humor was a wicked bitch. "Fuck benefit of the doubt. You. Know. Me." He stabbed his water bottle at Rodriguez's chest for emphasis. "Probably better than anyone. There shouldn't be any doubt in your mind that I'm not a crooked cop."

"Look, that came out wrong. I know you're not dirty. *Day* knows you're not dirty."

"Yet he still fired me."

"With the elections that were coming up, you know there was a lot of pressure on Day—"

Wyatt stood and slammed the hatch closed. The deck reverberated beneath the soles of his bare feet, a catfish jumped, and That-A-Way stopped munching on pondweeds long enough to give him a baleful look and a muffled moo.

Wyatt paced the deck. From the bench seat he'd custom fitted at the stern, he crossed under the overhang of the flybridge to the captain's chair and back again. But Sea-Celia was only a forty-four-foot trawler. Three or four long strides each way, and he had to turn around again.

"Why me?" Wyatt asked as he turned toward Rodriguez again.

"If some of those rumors are true—that whoever is killing the sex workers is a dirty cop—who would be better at catching the *real* dirty cop than the one everyone *thinks* is dirty?"

Wyatt scratched at two days worth of scruff on his jaw, trying to ignore the prickle of apprehension that zinged across his scalp. Rodriguez smiled, a flash of over-bleached teeth in a clean-shaven face. That smile did nothing to soothe Wyatt's nerves.

In reality, the PI business sucked the soul out of Wyatt. And even with his expenses kept at a minimum, he wasn't earning enough in the private eye world yet to keep from dipping into his savings from time to time.

He did have a potential new client he had to meet in about an hour, but even with that, the long and short of it was, he needed the extra work. He finally stopped pacing and glanced at Rodriguez. "What's involved?"

Rodriguez flung a bulging manila envelope at him like a Frisbee. Wyatt caught it and claimed the helm chair beside Rodriguez. The chair creaked under his weight, and the cracked and yellowed white vinyl poked the back of his thighs. Mentally, he added the chair to his list of upgrades.

Wyatt pulled the papers out and glanced at the first page.

"It's a copy of the casework on the Nightwalker murders," Rodriguez said.

Wyatt glanced at Rodriguez. "This is your case."

Rodriguez nodded.

"I don't understand." Wyatt stuffed the papers back into the envelope. "I still don't see why you need me."

Rodriguez pulled a face as if he had indigestion, but Wyatt figured it was the murders that didn't sit right with his old partner rather than something he ate. Add in the fact that the sheriff wanted someone else's eyes on the case, eyes that belonged to Wyatt—and yeah, if Wyatt had had any Pepto in his first aid kit, he'd be handing the bottle over to his old partner.

"There's something we're missing," Rodriguez said. "Three sex workers dead. They all knew each other."

"Unusual for a serial killer to pick victims that aren't random."

"Exactly. Our working theory is that the women all saw something, or know something they shouldn't. We also don't know if there are other women in danger. If there are, this guy's going to strike again. The first one was killed about a month before—" Rodriguez raised his brows in a you-know gesture.

Caleb Steele. The undercover agent Wyatt had shot and killed. "Yeah, I know. That first prostitute was *my* case. I still don't know why you think I can help."

"Turns out, Steele had been working that murder from the inside. He'd told his handler shortly before he'd died that he had a strong lead."

"Which was?"

"He took that to his grave, which is why some people still wonder if you were somehow involved in the deaths."

"Yeah, yeah. Spare me all the armchair detective theories. Trust me. I've heard them all."

"Well, the killer had to be someone important enough that Steele wanted to verify his theory before he dropped any names."

"I'm still waiting for the *why me.*"

A breeze kicked up and fluttered some of the loose papers that had fallen out of Wyatt's folder that had been stuck to the side of his face. Rodriguez gathered the papers up and waved them at Wyatt. "*This* is why you."

"That's my own investigation. It has nothing to do with the Nightwalker murders."

"Yeah. Your investigation into Steele."

Wyatt shrugged. Wasn't anybody's business but his that he couldn't let Steele's death go. Wasn't anybody's business that not an hour, a minute, a second didn't go by that he didn't relive that trigger pull.

Didn't wish he could hit rewind on his life.

Didn't wish he could find a way to alleviate the guilt.

Even though to this day, he didn't doubt that Steele would have killed him if given a chance. One of the things that kept him up late into the night was the *why.*

Rodriguez scooped up the rest of the papers before they blew away and stuffed them back into the file folder and dropped it in Wyatt's lap. "Tell me why you can't let Steele's death go?"

"I'd identified myself. Steele knew I was a cop. Knew I'd shoot if he drew a weapon. So why did he draw on me?"

"Maybe he was afraid you'd figure out who he was and blow his cover."

"He was deep under. Even if I'd arrested him, his prints would have come back to his alias. Along with his fake rap sheet. So no, I don't think that's why. And who was the suit he was scuffling with that night? The guy that got away. I can't help but think that he's involved somehow."

"Or it was just what it looked like. A mugging gone bad. Or maybe all of this is connected. Maybe the rumors were right. Maybe Steele was dirty, too."

"*Too?* As in, dirty like me?"

Or *maybe* deep down, Rodriguez believed Wyatt was a bad cop.

"As in, that false rumor is what's going to be what enables *you* to dig for the answers that we can't. People see the cops, they clam up. They're scared to talk. Scared they'll be the next one killed. But you're not a cop anymore." Wyatt's harrumph didn't even slow Rodriguez down. "And in this town, a disgraced cop is on the bottom rung. The criminals are more likely to talk to you. And you can do things, get away with things that we can't."

Wyatt narrowed his eyes and injected a full dose of sarcasm into his words. "You really know how to butter a guy up. That kind of flattery, how can I say no?"

"You can't say no because as much as you publicly deny it, you want answers. And even more than answers, you want back into Day's good graces. Back into the fold and behind the thin blue line." Rodriguez stepped back, that stupid all-knowing, I-got-you-where-I-want-you smirk on his face. "And as much as you want all *that*, you want to clear your name even more."

Fuck. It chapped Wyatt's ass when Rodriguez was right.

"You don't have to give me your answer now. Read the file, think about it." Rodriguez turned to leave, then stopped and glanced back. "And fair warning, Steele's widow is on the warpath, doing her own investigation"—Rodriguez made air quotes beside his head at the word investigation—"so you'll have to deal with her, too. Who knows, maybe she has something we don't. There's some info on her in the file as well."

Steele's widow. Wyatt's gut churned. Where was that Pepto when he needed it? Probably the last person on earth he wanted to face. Wyatt slouched in the chair. He'd told himself after the shooting, that *at least* Steele hadn't had any kids. For some reason, that had been a small comfort to him. Knowing he'd taken a father away from his kids might have tipped him over the edge.

After all, he knew what it was like growing up without a father figure.

"Sleep on it," Rodriguez said, "but a chance like this isn't going to come around every day. You catch this killer, Day can put a positive spin on it, and you'll be the golden boy again."

The bifold door to Sea-Celia's bathroom stuck in the rusted track. Wyatt pulled and pushed and shoved, his head pounding from the hangover. He almost welcomed the pain. If half a bottle of whiskey gave him a hangover, he wasn't an alcoholic. Right? And it wasn't like he drank more than a beer or two here and there for the most part.

But there had been times since the shooting when the guilt hit hard, and the whiskey dulled the pain just enough.

It didn't make him a drunk.

It made him human.

Wyatt pried the bifold door open enough to squeeze through. Okay, so maybe Rodriguez had a point about finding another place to live. But besides having to stuff an extra-large frame into an extra-small toilet/shower combo, the boat suited him fine.

Besides, it was paid for, and fit his near-zero budget since Evie waived his rent in exchange for him doing odd chores. A sweet gig. He couldn't complain.

Wyatt had some extra time before he had to meet with the potential new client at Bullchips, but he still had to unload Evie's van as he'd promised. He threw on some mostly clean jeans and his last unwrinkled button-up, stepped into a pair of cowboy boots, made a mental note to drop off his clothes at the Fluff N Fold in the morning, and headed over to Evie's.

The summer sun had dipped below the horizon, but after three trips to unload the van, sweat broke out along Wyatt's hairline. His muscles ached as he carried the third computer monitor, as big as most people's television sets, into Massey's office.

"Thanks, Wy." Evie's grandson, Massey Yates, stood by his new desk, opening one of the boxes, the cuffs of his crutches looped around his forearms, and the bulk of his weight resting on the desk. "I really appreciate it."

Massey had a mild speech impairment where the consonants went soft in his mouth, but Wyatt had been around him enough that he hardly noticed anymore. Massey's slight build was a carbon copy of his grandmother's, except Massey had a mop of brown hair always in need of combing. Not because he couldn't manage with his Cerebral Palsy, but because he was too busy with his computers to bother spending time on the things that didn't matter to him.

"No problem," Wyatt said. "You need help setting them up?"

Massey eyed Wyatt's wardrobe upgrade and, though under

different circumstances, might have taken Wyatt up on the offer, Massey said, "Naw, I can get it from here."

Wyatt didn't doubt he could. The twenty-two-year-old was an expert at finding ways to prevent his CP from keeping him from doing what he wanted. It also meant Massey only asked for help when he absolutely needed it.

If Wyatt left for Bullchips now, he'd be five minutes late for his appointment. But he'd rather kiss That-A-Way full on the lips than have to listen to another client complain about their cheating significant other. "I've got a few minutes I can spare."

Massey nodded once like he was trying to play it cool, but the goofy grin gave him away.

Twenty minutes later, Massey plugged his computer into his new triple screen setup, and his eyes lit up brighter than the monitors.

"You need this many screens for gaming?" Wyatt asked.

Evie walked into the spare room Massey had turned into his office. The two-seater couch Wyatt and Massey had shared on occasion while they'd battled it out on Xbox had been shoved into a corner to make room for a desk and rolling office chair. Why hadn't anyone called to ask him to help move the furniture?

"Not for gaming," Evie said since Massey had already tuned him out as he linked the screens with his computer. "Massey got a job."

Wyatt turned to Massey. "No kidding, bro? Got tired of sponging off the old bat?"

Evie gave Wyatt a playful swipe. He earned a laugh and a middle finger from Massey.

"Who with?"

"CTS," Massey said, without taking his eyes off the monitors.

Wyatt whistled softly. "CompuTech Solutions? That's the big

leagues. Good on you, buddy. Glad to know you'll be using your hacking prowess for good instead of evil."

Evie chuckled under her breath. "You and me both."

"I heard that," Massey said.

"See you around." Wyatt got a wave from Massey and let Evie walk him out to his truck. He climbed in and buzzed his window down.

"I hope we didn't keep you too long," Evie said.

"Nothing that couldn't wait."

"It means a lot to me, to him, that you treat him like anyone else."

"He's no different. Everyone has baggage, Evie. The only difference is some people carry it on the outside. Others hide it on the inside."

———

In a back-corner booth at Bullchips Bar, Geneva Steele slammed a shot into the back of her throat. Her esophagus spasmed. Her eyes watered. She swallowed the liquid fire. Her stomach heaved, but she reached for the next shot anyway, relieved no one knew her here. Of course, dropping the weight, and cutting and dying her hair didn't hurt.

"Easy now." Geneva's best friend, Cassie, put a hand on Geneva's forearm to slow her down.

Cass's perfectly plucked brow blurred, and Geneva blinked it clear.

"You're the one who's supposed to stay sober, Gen. Wolfe, the ass-hat, is the one that's supposed to get wasted." Cassie was on her third shot, and ass-hat came out sounding like *wass*-hat.

"*Wass*-hat? Now, who's the one who's wasted?"

"I'm still sober enough to remind you this idea is epically bad. Like Lincoln going to Ford's Theatre bad."

"No one's going to get hurt. It's a roofie. And I'm only going to slip Wolfe one, maybe two. He's a big guy. He can take it, I'm sure."

"How do you expect to get a guy that big into his truck and back to his place when he's dr—"

"Can I get you ladies another drink?" The waiter turned up the wattage on his electric smile.

"Two more shots," Geneva said.

"And two coffees," Cassie added.

The waiter looked like he wanted to roll his eyes, but apparently, he was too professional for that. He chuckled. "Coming right up."

Geneva answered Cassie as if they hadn't been interrupted. "I'm not going to give him the drugs here. I'm going to wait until he takes me back to his place."

"And what if he turns you down?"

Geneva pushed up her boobs that she'd put on display behind a low-cut, skin-tight, teal top that she hoped did a hell of a lot more than bring out the green in her eyes. Geneva pasted on a saucy smile that would take a few more shots of whiskey to become real. Her hands shook, and nausea slicked the back of her throat. If Cassie knew the truth, if Cassie had any idea how she really felt, then Cassie would find a way to stop her. "I don't think he'll turn *the girls* down. Besides, it's not like he's been getting any lately anyway."

Cassie's eyes narrowed, and she angled her head and looked at Geneva as if someone had pulled the curtain away to reveal the crazy woman behind it, pulling all the strings. The woman Geneva had been hiding since her husband's funeral.

"How do you know Wolfe hasn't been getting laid?" When Geneva didn't respond, Cassie said, "*Gen?* What. Have. You. Done?" That tone questioned, encouraged trust, and demanded a response all at the same time.

Their waiter zipped from table to table, taking orders. More people streamed through the front door as the evening wore on. Bullchips hopped on Friday nights. On a postage-stamp-sized dance floor, couples swayed to the country music pouring out of the speakers.

Cassie snapped her fingers in front of Geneva's face to get her attention. "How do you know Wolfe hasn't slept with anybody? It's not like he's hard on the eyes. Everywhere he goes, the estrogen levels—"

"Those women are the gawkers. He doesn't touch them."

"The gawkers?"

"The women who want to say they slept with the man who got away with murder."

"It was an accident, honey."

A muscle in Geneva's back twinged as if the verbal knife Cassie had driven between her ribs were real. Not even Geneva's best friend believed her. Geneva cut her friend a scathing look. It didn't slice to the quick the way Cassie's words had. "Was it?"

"Caleb is buried. Don't you think it's time to let him rest?"

"Wolfe killed my husband."

"I know, but—"

"You don't get it." There was no heat behind Geneva's words. Her voice didn't break, tears didn't fall down her cheeks. Not even her sister, Becca, understood, which had only made their estrangement worse.

Geneva's determination, the *rightness* of what she was doing kept her emotions in check. The waiter delivered their coffees and shots, and Geneva wasted no time downing the whiskey. "And for your sake, Cass, I hope you never do."

Cassie glanced away, puffing out her cheeks and blowing out an audible breath. "I'm sorry. That didn't come out the way I meant it to. At all. I know how tough Caleb's death has been on you. It's been rough on all of us."

"You can leave if you want to. Give me the drugs, and you can leave."

"I'm not leaving," Cassie said. "And I'm also not letting you get away with not telling me how you know Wolfe hasn't had sex lately."

"I told you—"

"Yeah, yeah, so he doesn't pick up the gawkers. But there are plenty of other ladies in town. The only way to know that he isn't taking any of them home is if—" Cassie's hand clapped to her mouth. From behind her fingers, Cassie said, "You've been following him, haven't you?"

Geneva ducked her head, then met her friend's assessing gaze. "Yes."

"What if he'd caught you?"

"I was careful."

Cassie sat back in her chair. "Wyatt was a detective. They're trained to notice these things."

"And Caleb lived the last few months of his life deep undercover. He was always telling me how he blended in, how he kept from being seen, how he kept from getting caught. It taught me a lot."

"Do you hear yourself? You're going to get yourself hurt." Cassie stood to leave. "I've changed my mind. I don't want any part of this."

Geneva grabbed Cassie's wrist. Felt her friend's pulse hammering beneath her fingertips. *"P-Please?"* The all too familiar sting of tears painted the backs of her eyes. Geneva blinked them away, refusing to let them fall. "Don't go. Help me."

Cassie dropped back into her seat. Three guys were setting up speakers and a mic on the narrow stage near the dance floor. People brushed Geneva's table. Someone asked for one of their empty chairs. When they'd gone, Cassie leaned in and said,

"What do you expect to find at Wolfe's place? His version of *Mein Kampf*?"

"I don't know what I'll find. That's why I have to look."

"Have I told you what a bad idea this is?"

"More than once."

Cassie let out a huge breath. Geneva held hers and watched as Cassie reached into her purse and handed her a snack-sized baggie with the vial of liquid inside.

Geneva took it and stuffed it into her purse. She glanced around the bar, but no one paid them any attention. "Thank you. I know that was a lot to ask. I don't know what I would have done if you'd been caught buying this."

"It's okay. I didn't buy it."

"Then where did you get it?"

"I know people. That's a perk of being a dispatcher at the Sheriff's Office."

When Geneva just stared at her, Cassie caved. "I to it from the guy who works the evidence room at the station."

"*Cassie!* What were you thinking? If anyone finds out—"

"Relax," Cassie said, "Ever since Sheriff Day's sister moved into the Alzheimer's facility, he's been preoccupied. A lot more than a vial of rohypnol would have to be missing for him to notice."

"I hope so. But if you get caught—"

"I won't. Don't worry."

Cassie got a naughty grin on her face and swiped a lock of long blond hair behind her ear and bumped Geneva with her shoulder. "So tell me, are you really going to have sex with Wolfe?"

Geneva choked and sputtered on the sip of lukewarm coffee. Cassie patted her on the back a few times.

"Are you *nuts*?" Geneva finally managed. "Of course, I'm not going to have sex with him."

"Have you seen him?" Cassie had a predatory glint in her eye. "He's so hot I bet he tempts even the straight guys."

"Yes, I've seen him. And need I remind you I'm a widow because of that man? Just because he's hot doesn't negate what he's done."

"You admit he's hot then."

Geneva rolled her eyes. She loved Cassie, she did, but sometimes she wished her friend came fully equipped with a verbal filter.

Other times, like now, Geneva was glad there wasn't one. Cassie was the only one of her friends who didn't treat her like centuries-old crystal on the verge of shattering.

Cassie's irreverence was grounding if not gut-wrenching at times. But Cassie also refused to let Geneva dwell on Caleb's death. Cassie had cried with her. Scarfed pint after pint of ice cream with her. Even stayed the night in the early days when the grief threatened to drown her.

But the next morning, Cassie found a way to make her laugh again, using that dark, gallows humor first responders developed to harden their shell to keep them from cracking.

"If you're not going to have sex with him, do you mind if I do?"

"Yes!"

Cassie plopped her chin into her hand and pouted. "*Fiiine*. But if you hadn't noticed, it's been a while since I've gotten laid, too."

"Preaching to the choir, sister."

"At least you've been dating."

"Two first dates with two different guys is not the definition of dating."

"But you kissed the cute one. Was there tongue? Please tell me there was tongue." Cass's eyes rounded with hope like a little girl grasping for the prize at the bottom of the Cracker Jack box.

Geneva caved and said, "There was tongue, but no spark."

"Are you kidding? He's a firefighter. Have you seen that guy's chest? Those arms? He could be in one of those firemen calendars, but just him, on every page. Who needs spark when the guy looks like that?"

Geneva laughed. "I do." Then she sobered, figuratively speaking. "I don't know. Maybe I'm just not ready to date yet."

Cass gave Geneva's hand a quick squeeze. "No, honey, you just haven't met the right guy."

"What will people think? It's only been a year and a half since—"

"What people think doesn't matter, Gen. Grief has no timetable. What's right for you won't be right for someone else. I'm not saying you have to find someone now. I'm just saying don't miss out because you're not open to the possibilities. Follow your heart. It won't lead you astray."

Cass didn't give Geneva much time to digest her words before adding, "Besides, if it's been as long for Wolfe as you say, the sex could be pretty good."

Ohmygod. Geneva couldn't hold back her smile. God, she loved Cass. "Or maybe over very fast."

They both fell into a fit of giggles. Geneva blamed it on the alcohol and not the swirling anxiety.

"So, when's he supposed to be here, anyway?"

"Eight."

Cassie glanced at her cell phone. "He's late."

"Yeah, I know."

"Maybe he stood you up. Or stood up whoever you pretended you were when you set up the appointment."

The waiter slipped by and topped off their coffees.

"He'll be here." Geneva doctored her coffee with four packs of sugar. "He needs the money."

"And you know this because…?" Cassie probably knew the answer by now, but she was forcing Geneva to say it.

The heat crept up Geneva's neck, and she dropped her head into her hands. She needed to get a life… right after she figured out the real reason Caleb had been gunned down. "Because I'm a pathetic stalker," Geneva muttered into her hands.

Under the table, Cassie nudged her with the toe of her boot. "Killer ass, two o'clock."

Geneva's nerves fizzled and snapped like the fuse on a cheap firecracker. The sensation zipped up her arms and legs and centered behind her sternum where her anxiety burned bright and hot. She glanced up. Bullchips' heavy front door snapped closed behind Wolfe, like the jaws of a steel trap. No way would he escape before she got what she wanted.

He stalked over to the bar. His eyes didn't veer left or right. People didn't slap him on the back or welcome him. Some people cleared a path. Others elbowed their friends or bobbed their chins in Wolfe's direction. By the time he'd wedged his way to the bar, every soul was aware he was there.

He ordered and wrapped thick fingers around the Zonker Stout that arrived, taking advantage of the space around him by turning and leaning against the bar, his eyes now scanning, searching for Geneva. Well, not Geneva, but her imaginary alter-ego in dire need of a PI.

She let him stew for five minutes. Ten. Fifteen. When he glanced at his watch for the third time and set his empty bottle on the bar, Geneva removed her wedding band, turned to her unnaturally quiet friend, and said, "Wish me luck."

"What I wish is that you'd reconsider your crazy plan." When Geneva cut her a not-now look, Cassie added, "But I slipped a couple of condoms in your purse just in case."

Geneva manufactured a smile. "Always the optimist."

"Exactly," Cassie said as Geneva turned toward Wolfe. "That's why I kept the rest for myself."

Wolfe started tracking Geneva when she was halfway to him, his gray eyes dark beneath his brow. Sweat formed between her breasts, and her palms went damp. Until now, her contact with the loner had all been from a distance. From across a street, or the other side of a store.

Or from behind a pair of binoculars.

Then there was that one time when she'd been trying to figure out a way to get on his boat without the old lady noticing. Which was impossible. Hence *the plan*.

Wolfe's black hair was cut short. His Native American heritage unmistakable in the structure of his cheekbones, the firm set of his jaw, the straight line of his nose, the tint of his skin. The black eye confirmed what she already knew... Wolfe was trouble.

Geneva claimed the space next to him at the bar. "Can I buy you a drink?"

He considered her for a moment. His gaze dropped to her lips, then back up to her eyes. "Isn't that supposed to be my line?"

"Does that mean you're asking?"

Without taking his eyes off her, he reached for his bottle to take another swig, realized it was empty, and set it back down. His brows drew together. "Do I know you?"

Forty pounds, a haircut, and dye job ago, maybe. "No." She smiled that same guileless smile she'd used successfully at sixteen when her father had asked if the pack of cigarettes he'd found in her car were hers. "About that drink..."

"Another time maybe," he said, sounding a little disappointed. "I'm waiting for someone."

True that. She chuckled. "Aren't we all?"

The corners of his lips curved, and his expression softened.

The bartender came by, and Wolfe raised his empty and asked Geneva, "What'll you have?"

Yes! "The same." In spite of all the coffee Cassie had poured down her throat, Geneva still had a bit of a buzz going and needed to lay off the hard liquor.

When their beers arrived, they clacked bottlenecks. The way his gaze held hers, the simple act almost seemed intimate. Goosebumps raised on her arms—not the oh-shit-something-bad-is-coming kind, but the oh-shit of sexual awareness. She didn't like that, not one bit.

Especially with this man.

"So, are you meeting a friend, a girl, or..."

"A client." Wolfe glanced at his watch. Large, functional. No flash. But a man like him didn't need to flaunt expensive accessories to be noticed. "I think they're a no-show."

"Shame." She poured on the charm and sent him a sideways glance that screamed the complete opposite.

"What about you?"

She leaned into him and applied a playful smile the way some women apply cheap lipstick—thick and careless. "You asking if I'm with anyone?"

He bobbed his brows and sipped his beer.

"No," she said. "Not anymore."

She left it at that. No explanation. Not that one was needed. Her throat tightened, and when she went to wash the stricture away, the beer lodged in her throat. She pushed back the emotion. That was the thing she'd learned about grief, one second you were perfectly fine and the next—no matter how long it had been or how much you'd thought you'd healed—it smacked you in the face when you least expected it. She caught a stranglehold on her composure and swallowed hard.

He averted his gaze as if the hurt in her expression was hard for him to witness. He reached for her hand but stopped short. "I'm sorry to hear that."

Her pulse thumped once, she felt it in her neck and at her temple, as she looked at him. He had no idea who she was or what had happened to her previous relationship. It may have been the play of the dim lighting or the unexpected flash of someone's camera phone, but at that moment, he seemed... sincere.

He seemed *human*.

2

———

No doubt, Wyatt's client had stood him up. The only question was when he left Bullchips, was he leaving alone, or would he be taking the woman beside him home with him.

She wasn't his usual type. She was long and lean and... *intelligent.* You wouldn't know it by their conversation, but there was something in her assessing gaze that told him his assumption was correct. Not that he had a problem with women with brains. He preferred it. It was just that, usually, the intelligent ones were smart enough to steer clear of him.

He'd been about to reach out, to comfort her, but she didn't know him. Yet still, the urge remained. His hand rested near hers. Neatly trimmed fingernails on slender fingers. She didn't even paint clear varnish on them. No frills, much like the woman herself. He found it intriguing.

"I'm Wyatt Wo—"

"Yeah, I know who you are."

Going home alone then.

He should have known her interest was too good to be true. He pulled out his wallet and tossed a twenty on the bar to cover their beers and set his half-drunk bottle down on top of it. He stood to leave.

"Hey, where you going?"

"It's late."

"It's not even close to ten." She fished her phone out of her back pocket and handed it to him. "Here, call your mom. Maybe she'll let you stay out past your curfew."

If she'd said anything different, he would have walked away and not looked back. Instead, he sat back down, his intrigue turning to blatant interest. "How do you know who I am?"

"You're a big man, and this is a small town."

The truth, mostly, as far as he could tell.

"You're nothing like I'd expected." The way she'd made that statement, the words surprised her as much as it did him.

He scanned her features, waiting for the processor in his brain to flip through all known faces and hit on a match, like his own internal version of NCIC, the national crime information center. Usually, he was much better with faces than names, but... "What did you say your name was?"

"Cassie," she said, with only the slightest hesitation. Someone with less experience spotting evasion might have believed her. "Cassie..."

"Don't say Smith."

"Let's stick with Cassie, then."

"Tell me this, *Cassie*, if you gave me your number and I called it, would you answer?"

She thought about it. "Yes." The truth. But probably not for the same reason he was thinking.

"You want to get out of here?" she asked.

"And go where?"

She shrugged but offered no suggestions. She wasn't like any of the other women who'd wanted to climb into his bed. "There are three kinds of women who want to sleep with me. The ones who are in it for the notoriety, the ones who are in it for a cheap thrill, and the ones who want to fulfill whatever that thing is that makes women write to serial killers on death row."

If he'd surprised her, she did an impressive job of hiding it. He leaned in, his lips near her ear. No fancy perfume, just a fresh, clean scent with a hint of... *antiseptic*? Hmmm. "Which one are you?"

Heat flashed up her neck, and she took her time answering, as her gaze skimmed across the bar. The band took to the stage and began tuning their instruments. Even for a Friday night, Bullchips was so tightly packed, the bar would make a sardine claustrophobic. And once the band started their set, conversation would be impossible.

"Maybe there's a fourth category." She didn't bat her eyes or offer a flirtatious smile, which only amped up his curiosity.

He'd never contemplated the existence of a fourth category. Certainly wouldn't include his wit or charm. "What's that?"

The band started strong, and the first chords of the electric guitar assaulted his ears. Cassie yelled above the cacophony, but he had to read her lips. He caught *take me home* and *find out for yourself.*

———

"You don't have to go through with this." Cassie's voice, the *real* Cassie's voice, came through Geneva's Prius's speakers. "You can turn around before it's too late."

Geneva passed the four-way stop on the outskirts of town, Wolfe's taillights a quarter mile ahead and getting farther away as she let up on the gas while her best friend tried to talk her out of committing a crime. "Stop worrying—"

"How can I not worry?" Cassie screeched. Geneva thumbed

down the volume on her steering wheel before Cassie's pitch shattered her windshield.

"Just park down the road at that turnoff I told you about. I've got you on speed dial. I'll call if things get weird."

"You mean if he hasn't chopped you up and fed your body parts to the fish by then."

"He's not like that." *Wait, why am* I *defending* him?

"He's still a guy you don't know."

Geneva waited for that seed of an icky feeling in the pit of her stomach to bloom into a mature death flower but... nothing. Nada. Zip. Zilch. Either her sixth sense was on the fritz or, for some inexplicable reason, she believed what she'd said, that Wolfe *wasn't* like that.

Before going to the bar, she'd been prepared to hate him. She'd been prepared to rage at him. She'd been prepared to hit him. And of course, she'd been prepared to drug him.

She hadn't been prepared to feel bad for him.

When she'd told him she knew who he was, the flash of remorse that had flicked across his face before he could retreat behind a thick, impenetrable wall had frozen her breath, and the haunted eyes behind hooded lids had made her heart trip and stutter.

Wyatt Wolfe—cop killer—wasn't anything like the monster she'd expected.

Which might make him even more dangerous.

She couldn't lower her guard. She couldn't take his meek— no, that wasn't the proper word. Wyatt Wolfe was anything but meek. She couldn't tak his *beat down* demeanor for granted.

Because beat down didn't mean down and out.

Yes, she was taking a risk. But a calculated one.

"*Geneva?*" Cassie prompted.

Up ahead, Wolfe slowed and pulled into his driveway. He

stopped and waited for her to catch up. "He's turned in, Cass. Gotta go."

Geneva hung up without waiting for a reply because she feared that if she stayed on the line any longer, Cassie would find a way to talk her out of her crazy caper. She knew her scheme was not only poorly thought out, it was potentially perilous. In reality, despite all of her spying, she had no idea what kind of man Wolfe was.

But she owed it to Caleb to find the truth.

If she died trying, she could live with that.

She turned in behind Wolfe, followed him to the stock pond where he moored his boat, and parked beside him. She gathered her purse, her phone, her perseverance, and opened her car door. He held it open for her and then escorted her down the dock. A porch light clicked on at the house, but this time, Geneva had a legit, if not illegal, reason to be there.

In the dark, she found her footing. The planks of the dock were dark while the water in the pond glimmered in the light of the half-moon. The boards gave under each step, but not so much she feared falling through. Frogs croaked, crickets sang, and something splashed in the water. She'd thought it would be creepy out here at night but instead found it peaceful.

At the side of the boat, Wolfe said, "Wait here."

He jumped down into the boat and held a hand out for her. She placed her hand in his. Warm and strong and gentlemanly... *Stop it. You're supposed to be pretending to seduce him, not the other way around.*

She stepped into the boat, and even though she knew the answer, she asked, "This is where you live?"

"It is." His wary voice said he expected her to either run screaming for the hills or laugh in his face. "In all its rotting-hull, rusted-engine glory."

A light breeze kicked up, cooling her skin. Way out there in the sticks, the stars blinked in the darkness that seemed to go on for an eternity. She stepped away from him and curled her arm around a pole in the middle of the deck supporting an overhang. And because she'd had too much to drink, perhaps too much to have been driving—*what had she been thinking?*—she swung around the pole, her other arm outstretched as she watched the stars swirl around. Her legs twisted around themselves, and she stumbled, landing on the deck in an unladylike lump. "Oops."

"Easy now," he said as he reached to give her a hand up.

The heat rushed up her neck, to the tips of her ears, and to the top of her head. *Smooth, Steele, real smooth.* Her hand slipped from his, and a fit of giggles overtook her as she fell on her butt again. Her sides ached, and her breath came short and shallow. Between the alcohol and the lack of oxygen, it felt like the boat rocked and swayed beneath her.

Instead of attempting to help her up again, he plopped down beside her. She scooted back and leaned against a cushioned bench seat at the back end of the boat.

When she'd caught her breath, Wolfe leaned his head against the cushion, his eyes on the stars, his shoulder resting against hers. They sat in companionable silence, and Geneva's lids went droopy. *Stop that!* She gave herself a mental slap. She needed to wake up. She needed to get on with her plan. Cass wasn't going to wait all night. Well, she would, but Geneva didn't want to make her do that.

Wolfe broke the silence. "Why are you really here?"

Adrenaline spiked in her veins, and warmth flooded her system, and suddenly, she wasn't so sleepy anymore.

She couldn't tell him the truth, but she could tell him a version of it. "It seemed like a good idea at the time."

"And now?"

She still had an objective. She hadn't come this far to go home a failure. "Nothing's changed."

He shifted toward her, cupped his hand to her cheek. His intentions sparked in his eyes as he lowered his head. Geneva slammed her lids closed and waited for his lips to touch hers, for the revulsion to boil in her belly, and the bile to build at the back of her throat.

His breath brushed against her lips, and he whispered, "You good?"

She nodded once, her throat tight, unable to speak. She'd kissed a man since Caleb. But if she kept kissing other men, would she forget the feel of Caleb's lips on hers? Would she forget his touch, his gentleness, or the way Caleb had always made her feel safe and wanted and cherished and—

"Look at me," Wolfe said.

Geneva smelled the hops on his breath as they shared the same air. She didn't want to look. Didn't want the reminder of what she was about to do. All she wanted was to open her eyes and see Caleb there, not the man who'd taken him from her. Her throat clogged, and her heart thumped in triple time as if it could outrun her stupidity.

Cassie was right.

She had no business being here.

"*Cass?*" Hearing her friend's name tumble from Wyatt's mouth popped her eyes open. The moonlight reflected off his cheekbones and shined in his eyes where his concern burned even brighter. "You okay?"

She nodded again, and his thumb brushed across her bottom lip. This time she didn't close her eyes as he dipped his head. After all, if she was going to make the biggest mistake of her life, she should do it with her eyes wide open.

———

Wyatt's lips brushed against Cassie's. Just a touch, a taste, a test. He wanted more, but he forced himself to pull away. He didn't know why this woman was different or why he'd taken her back to his boat when so many others had lied and tried.

And even though she hadn't been completely honest with him, there was a rawness to her honesty that tugged at his heart. Whatever had happened in her previous relationship had scarred her. If he could get his hands on the bastard that had hurt her, he'd—

"You didn't have to stop." Her voice wavered, and the hand she'd looped around the back of his neck trembled.

He started with the truth. "It's been a long time."

"I know." Her eyes rounded as if a state secret had slipped through her lips.

He pulled back so he could see her face more clearly. "What do you mean, 'you know'?"

"I meant it's been a long time for me as well." A flinch of a lie, a flicker of truth. A warning bell clanged in the back of Wyatt's head, but his libido threw a wet blanket over it to muffle the sound.

He didn't exactly like that she wasn't candid with him, but he had his own secrets, so he understood. He didn't owe her any explanations, and she owed him none as well. She wasn't his wife or his fiancée or even his girlfriend.

She was his one-night stand.

Since when does a serial monogamist have one-night stands?

Since his life took a nose dive off a high cliff at low tide.

Since he'd hit bottom and couldn't find a way to climb out.

Since no one but the depraved and desperate wanted anything to do with him.

He kissed her again. Nipped gently at her lip when she didn't respond. She opened her mouth for him. Tentative. Her tongue tracing his. Beer on her breath. Angling his head, he took the kiss deeper, his hand grazing the side of her face and slipping down to her neck, to the thrum of her pulse that matched the pounding in his ears, in his groin.

He scooped her up and pulled her across his lap. She squeaked in surprise, then straddled him before settling back into the kiss. Reaching down, he adjusted himself, palmed her... *wow, amazing ass...* and snugged her up against him. She groaned, then froze.

He pulled back and held her at arm's length. Her breath hitched a couple of times, and it wasn't from being turned on.

She'd come on to *him* at the bar. She'd followed *him* home.

Had they gotten their signals crossed? "Something wrong?"

She closed her eyes and breathed in through her nose and out through her mouth. Her breathing evened out. When she looked at him, she said, "No. Nothing's wrong." She sucked in another breath and held it and held it and... held it. She blew it out. "That's the problem."

Huh? "Look, we don't have to do this."

"No, it's not that, it's..." She scooted off his lap and sat beside him again. "I liked it. More than I'd expected. More than I'd wanted. More than I should."

"I feel like I'm missing something here."

She hid her face in her hands, then scrubbed them over her cheeks. When she straightened, she bobbed her chin toward the cabin. "You have anything to drink in there?"

"There are a couple of beers in the fridge, but if you have to get blitzed to have sex, then let's call it off. I don't think my ego could take it." He forced a laugh because he hadn't been totally kidding.

She nodded twice then said, "Okay," more to herself than to him, as if she'd talked herself into something. His ego was gonna be battered and bruised and blue by the time this night ended.

She stood and headed for the cabin, taking her purse with her.

"Lights are on the right as you go down the steps," he said.

She stumbled on the second step, caught herself on the railing, and slapped at the wall until a light came on. Wyatt tilted his head back and stared past the overhang at the stars and out into infinity, wondering how the hell his life's path had gotten so convoluted.

Maybe convoluted wasn't the right word. More like his life's path had been pulled out from beneath him like some slick magic trick that had the universe and everyone in it laughing their ever-loving asses off.

Hardy-har-har. Everyone, that was, but him.

He didn't know how long he'd sat there, only that his ass cheeks had gone flat. He stood and rubbed the circulation back into his glutes and headed for the cabin to see what was taking Cassie *Not-Smith* so long. Maybe she'd crawled out through the forward hatch and abandoned ship while she'd had the chance.

Intelligent, like he'd thought.

Ducking his head inside, he saw her in the galley, her back to him as she zipped her purse. He braced his hands on the top of the bulkhead, swung down, and landed with a light *thud* on the scarred teak flooring.

She spun around, skittish as a two-day-old colt in front of a wolf's den.

"Find everything?" he asked.

"Yeah, I was just headed up." She wiped her hands on her jeans, and something silver, no larger than the nail on his pinky finger, fluttered to the floor. She picked up the beers. He reached for the closest one, but she shifted at the last second and handed him the other one.

That alarm bell in the back of his head clanked and echoed as he led the way out.

"Hang on," she said, from the second step up, "I forgot my

purse." She turned to step back down, teetered, and caught herself.

There was only the one handrail, so Wyatt reached out and plucked the beer from her hand so she could hold on and not do a header down the stairs. He didn't have the insurance for that. She hesitated, glanced at the hand holding her beer then went back for her purse.

"I'll meet you topside," he said, the bell in his head clanging so loud that his ears rang. He glanced at the bottles in his hands. The one in his left hand, the one she'd kept for herself, had a fingernail-sized bite of the silver label missing in the top right corner, and he realized what he'd seen fall to the floor in the galley.

He didn't know if he was paranoid or observant or lucky as hell, but he switched the bottles and scraped the corner of the label off the other bottle with his thumbnail. The torn labels didn't exactly match, but in the dark, it was close enough. He didn't know what she'd put in the beer, or what she was after, but as he handed her the beer, the one she thought was untainted, he *did* know he'd soon find out.

3

Geneva sat down on the deck of the boat with her back against the cushioned bench, her knees against her chest to hide the fact her heart was about to bounce out of it. She chalked her nervousness up to the crime she'd committed. It was her first, so she figured the anxiety wasn't expected.

She'd been careful to take the beer from his left hand, but as she brought the bottle to her lips, she did a quick check of the label to make sure they hadn't been inadvertently switched. The corner was gone. *Phew.* Wolfe was a big man, so she'd decided not to take any chances and gave him all of the Rohypnol in the vial. No telling what would happen to her if she ingested that amount of the drug.

She'd texted Cassie with an update while in the galley, but hearing from her didn't seem to calm Cassie much.

Now to get Wyatt talking and drinking before Cassie couldn't take the waiting anymore and came storming down the dock to the unwanted rescue.

Wolfe settled in beside her. The heat from his body only added to the heat index of the warm Wyoming night.

Motioning between the two of them, indicating the abrupt

ending to their makeout session, she said, "Sorry about all that. I don't know what's wrong with me."

He took two long swallows of his beer, draining the volume by a third. At this rate, Geneva would be back on the road in thirty minutes, tops. Wouldn't that make Cassie happy? The tension in her belly eased, and she took a sip of her beer.

"No apologies. Still have feelings for your ex?"

She took a full swig, sloshed it around in her cheeks, then swallowed. "Yes."

"Wanna talk about it?"

She choked on her next sip and wiped her mouth with the back of her hand. "I don't think that's such a good idea. Isn't that the number one thing the dating site gurus say not to talk about on your first date?"

"Dating sites? You on CowboyOnly.com or something?"

She choked on a laugh and beer sputtered out of her mouth.

He reached out and swiped the drop from her chin. "This isn't a first date. It's a hookup, so I don't think the dating rules apply."

She considered him for a moment. Watched him lick the drop of beer off the pad of his thumb. She took another fortifying sip, sloshing the beer around in the bottle. Almost empty. *Oops. How did that happen?* What she told him would be irrelevant. It wasn't like she had anything to lose.

After all, she was trying to get her hands on his files, not in his pants.

"There's not much to tell. I thought everything was going fine. Then one day, he left for work, and he didn't come home. No goodbye. No closure."

"No calls, no texts, no notes?"

"Nothing."

He downed the last of his beer. It wouldn't be long now until the drug took effect and she could search his boat and get out of there with him none the wiser.

He slumped lower so that the back of his head rested on the cushion. Did his eyes look heavy?

"If he was willing to do that to you, the bastard didn't deserve you."

She finished off her beer and almost choked on the irony of having this conversation with the man who'd stolen Caleb from her. Her chest tightened, but she drew strength from her confidence that she was doing the right thing. Even if her methods were a little unorthodox, and a tad illegal. Caleb would be proud of her. He'd be sweating out the details the way Cassie was, but he would be proud. And she was *so* close. She couldn't back out now.

"Why do you say that?" she asked. "You know nothing about me besides the fact that I hit on a stranger at a bar and followed him home. I could have deserved it for all you know."

"No." He didn't raise his voice, but the quiet conviction with which he said the word hit her as hard as if he had. "You didn't."

She glanced up at him, and he looked at her with an earnestness that made her chest even tighter. After four years of marriage, had Caleb ever had that degree of unfounded belief in her?

Wyatt stripped her now empty bottle from her hand and set it aside, taking her hand in his. "What I know is that you loved him, that you still love him. And if he couldn't see that, if he didn't know what a lucky man he was to find that, then he's the undeserving fool."

Fool. The word cut, and she caught herself before she lashed out. She had to remember Wolfe didn't know who she was. He was trying to be supportive, not hurtful. She had to stay in character. "You wouldn't say that if you knew the whole story."

Wolfe harrumphed. "Enlighten me then."

"I'd rather not." Her words had come out little more than a whisper because it would have taken too much energy to say them any louder. She was tired. It was getting late. And by the way the boat rolled beneath her even though there were no waves on the pond, she realized she'd had one beer too many. If that drug didn't hurry up and knock Wolfe out, then she'd be the one passed out.

Her eyes fluttered closed, her head lulled to the side, and she jerked awake, her eyes landing on the bottle of beer in his hand. The bottle of beer with a torn label. *Wait!* She reached out and grabbed for her bottle, but her hand came up empty. She reached again and knocked it on its side. It rolled away, and she crawled after it, finally catching up to it when it plinked to a stop against the support pole.

She fumbled with the bottle, her fingers forgetting how to hold something cylindrical. Giving up, she trapped the bottle between her two palms. Light spilled onto the deck from the open cabin door. Her eyes weren't deceiving her. Her label was also torn. Her arms shook and collapsed beneath her, her cheek kissing the rough deck.

Her eyes landed on Wyatt, still sitting against the cushion, his arm draped over an upturned knee, the twitch of a smile on his face.

"Wolfe," she croaked out, "what have you done?"

GENEVA CAME TO AND STARED AT THE CEILING OF WHAT SHE suspected was the forward berth of Wolfe's boat. In the bow? Is that what they called the front? An air conditioner hummed overhead, spewing cold air and the occasional drop of condensation onto her pillow. She listened for sounds indicating Wolfe was near, but no sounds came from inside the cabin, only the muffled moo of a cow somewhere outside.

She peeked beneath the covers. Her clothes were still on. She wiggled her toes. Her boots were off as if Wolfe had tucked her into bed after a bender. Did he have any idea she'd tried to drug him? That her plan had backfired?

The events from the night before lay fuzzy in her mind. *Cassie!* Had she given up? Was she still sitting out there waiting for her call? Was she about to call the sheriff?

Geneva rolled out of bed, stood on wobbly legs, and balanced herself with a hand on the cupboards that hung above a small sink. Her head still swirled as if she'd gone through a full wash cycle set on *agitate.*

Her seasick stomach roiled, and bile slicked the back of her throat. *Uh oh!* She made a mad dash for the bathroom, which consisted of a lot of tripping and stumbling and cussing and— the bi-fold door stuck. She fell on her knees and shoved her head through the narrow opening, but that was as close to the toilet as she could get before she heaved up everything she'd eaten in the past month, which wasn't much considering she hadn't had much of an appetite since Caleb's death.

She coughed and sputtered and spit. When her stomach showed a modicum of mercy, she rolled onto her back and sank against the wall, her breath coming in harsh pants. A hand towel appeared in front of her, and a drop of water fell and landed on her thigh. She tilted her head. Wolfe stood above her, with an expression that on Caleb would have been disappointment.

She probably deserved that. After all, she'd followed Wyatt home and, if the fact that her clothes were still on was any indication, they hadn't had sex. He waggled the towel, and she took it and wiped her mouth. When she'd finished, he took the towel, and replaced it with a glass of water.

"Rinse and spit," he said, indicating the floor of the bathroom behind her.

Heat rose up her neck and turned her cheeks to fire. Slosh, spit, repeat. The stench of her vomit filled her nostrils and made her stomach turn. *Not again!* She tamped down on the nausea, refusing to puke in front of this man.

When she'd finished rinsing out her mouth, he hauled her to her feet and plopped her on the end of a bench seat that wrapped around a table. Without a word, he turned back to the bathroom, one of those toilet/shower space savers with the drain in the floor, and turned on the water and hosed away the evidence of her not-so-well-thought-out night.

"Have you seen my phone?" she asked.

"Yeah." He turned off the water and wrangled the door closed, but he didn't elaborate any further. He wore a pair of cargo shorts and a wife-beater so wrinkled that he must have found it balled up in the corner of one of his drawers. Annoyance rolled off of him in giant, crashing waves.

"Nice boat," she said, trying to stay in character and ignore his aggravation.

He leaned against the stove and crossed his arms over his chest. The edge of his lips now tipping more toward amused than annoyed. "That's all you have to say after last night? Nice boat?" He raised a dark brow at her that dared her to elaborate.

"It still needs work, but it has good bones, and—" That wasn't what he'd meant at all. "And sorry about last night?" She posed it as a question. She wasn't quite sure what grievance he wanted an apology for.

"Which part?"

"The no sex? The passing out? The vomiting in your bathroom? Though technically, that was this morning." She glanced through the open cabin door and saw a pillow and a thin blanket laid on the bench at the rear of the boat. "For making you sleep outside?"

"That it?"

She racked her brain. Besides the almost drugging? "I think that about covers it."

Again, that flash of disappointment that hardened his features and dulled his eyes. It poked her temper. He didn't know her well enough to be disappointed in her. Cassie or Caleb, maybe, but not him.

"If you could just point me in the direction of my boots and my phone, I'll be getting out of your hair."

He hitched a thumb over his shoulder toward the door. "Boots are on the deck." He pulled her phone from the rear pocket of his shorts, and set it on the table in front of her.

She snapped it up, anxious to update Cassie and let her know she didn't have to call out the Coast Guard, the National Guard, and the Bison County Sheriff's Office. She thumbed through her text messages.

One from her saying: *Go home. Everything's cool. I'll call in the morning.*

From Cassie: *Does he know?*

From her: *He does now.*

The details of the night before came back to her in snippets, but Geneva knew she hadn't sent those texts.

Wolfe.

Adrenaline dumped into her system. Her veins heated and burned as her heart hummed, and blood blasted through her system. She flicked a glance up at Wolfe, not daring to look him straight in the eye. "Um..."

Instead of the fury she'd expected, his expression remained enigmatic. "I took the liberty of replying to your friend after you passed out last night." A blip of a smile. It wasn't real. "Wouldn't want your friend to worry, *Cassie.*"

Oh, shit.

He turned, poured a mug of coffee, and set it in front of her. He fixed one for himself and scooted onto the bench across from her. She reached for the sugar bowl on the table and mindlessly scooped the sugar into her mug spoonful after spoonful. Stirred. Sipped. Sputtered. *Too sweet.*

"Good?" he asked with that maddening arch to his brow. He knew damn well it wasn't.

She pushed the mug away. "Just how I like it."

"Who are you?"

"Cass—"

He made a noise in the back of his throat somewhere between a game show buzzer and don't-lie-to-me. "Try again. Remember, I've seen your texts. And just a little tip from a deputy—"

"*Former* deputy."

He tilted his head in acceptance of the truth. "*Former* deputy, to civilian. If you're going to text incriminating evidence, you should delete them after. Anyone half-decent in computer forensics could still retrieve them, but the average Joe, like me, would have had no clue."

He picked up her phone and typed in her four-number password—Yeah. One, two, three, four was kind of obvious, and easy to remember. He scrolled through her texts.

"You: *u get the rx?*" He glanced up at her. "'Rx' meaning prescription, or in this case shorthand for drugs, I'm assuming."

She didn't reply.

He turned his attention back to her phone. "Cassie replies— the *real* Cassie, I might add," he said with a flick of his eyes toward her. "*Yep c u at the bar.*"

He dropped her phone on the table, reached for the manila envelope beside him, and pulled out a stack of papers. He flipped through them until he found the one he was searching for. He glanced at it one last time before shifting his gaze to her. "Let me make this easy for you."

He turned the sheet around and laid it in front of her. Some kind of police report it looked like. With her picture. Her *recent* picture. And her name, her real name, underneath. The blood drained from her face, and if she had a mirror right then, she knew she'd be as white as the underbelly of a flounder. Unfortunately, when the blood left her face, it took the red blood cells in her brain along with it. Her head went all wonkified, and it fell against the hand she'd propped on the table.

"Rohypnol?" he asked.

Slowly, she nodded, her eyes focused on the photo of her. In it, her skin tone looked sallow, her cheeks a tad too pronounced, her hair in a messy bun on the top of her head. It wasn't flattering.

Jesus. Your brain must be oxygen-deprived if you're worried about a bad photo. Why not worry about the fact that there is a police file with your picture in it.

She didn't know what the hell was going on, but the fact that she was screwed crossed her mind.

"Where did you get the drugs? Or should I say, where did your friend get the drugs?"

"I'm going to have to plead the fifth on that."

He snorted. "Funny." Though his tone implied the opposite. "This isn't court. This is you and me on a boat on a pond."

Her stomach dropped so low she'd need a submarine to find it. She glanced around. No knives, no guns, nothing she could use as a weapon. And with him between her and the door, she didn't kid herself that she could blast past him without getting caught. And Wyatt obviously worked out, whereas she tried hard not to.

"So, are you going to kill me now?"

Whatever he'd expected her to say, it wasn't what had come out of her mouth. He sat back and stared at her. "Seriously?"

Yeah, seriously. Geneva shrugged.

"I don't need that kind of headache."

It wasn't a promise not to harm her, but she figured it was as close to one as she was going to get. A few stray oxygenated red blood cells crept into her brain, and the dizziness dissipated.

"Am I free to go?"

"This isn't the Sheriff's Office. And as you so kindly pointed out, I'm not a deputy. No one's going to stop you."

She slid her phone into her back pocket and padded toward the stairs in her sock feet, giving him as wide a berth as she could in the confines of the cabin just in case he changed his mind about letting her leave.

She had her foot on the step when he said, "There wasn't a client last night, was there?"

SWEAT STREAMED OFF THE TIP OF WYATT'S NOSE AS HE HOSED down the open engine compartment. He'd retrieved the empty bottle and rescued three sheets of his research into Caleb Steele from the spilled booze and leaking oil, and hung the sheets of paper from a clothesline strung beneath his hardtop. They fluttered behind him in the breeze.

Geneva freaking *Steele.*

On his boat.

In his arms.

In his bed.

Well, the *in his bed* part didn't really count since he slept on the bench at the stern, but still. It showed how screwed up in the head he was right now not to have recognized her. Though in his defense, she looked nothing like the woman he'd seen from a distance at the cemetery all those months ago when she'd buried her husband. She'd cut and colored her hair. Lost a bunch of weight.

The weight loss? Yeah, not unexpected when your husband was killed in the line of duty.

Thank God they hadn't had sex. Hell, he would have gladly taken the drug himself if it meant he didn't sleep with the widow of the man he'd killed.

There had to be a special corner of hell for men who would take advantage of a woman like that. His own corner of hell was bad enough.

In the pit of Wyatt's stomach sat this *thing*, this knot of... of... what, he didn't know. But it was weighty and relentless, making it near impossible for him to think. What had Steele's widow been thinking? She'd known who *he* was. She'd admitted that much at the bar. He would have understood if she'd wanted him dead.

But she hadn't come to kill him.

Just drug him.

Why?

Should have asked her while you had the chance, brainiac.

Yeah, well, his brain had stripped a few gears when he'd stumbled across her picture in the paperwork Rodriguez had given him. If only he'd glanced through the file before he'd hit the bar. Then he would have been prepared.

But the encounter hadn't been a total loss. Geneva Steele wanted something from him. Something worth the risk of drugging him. That gave him an advantage.

He put away the wash-down hose, turned on his bilge, and pulled his cell phone out of the pocket of his shorts. He punched Rodriguez's name on his favorites list. It rang and rang and rang. He was about to hang up when Rodriguez's "Yo!" came over the line.

"It's me."

Rodriguez chuckled. The smug son of a bitch. He knew why Wyatt was calling. "Decided to take Day up on his offer?"

"How's this going to work?"

"You go through me. I'll be your handler. Your only point of contact. It's common knowledge you and I are still friends, no one seeing us together would get suspicious."

"What about Day?"

"He wants plausible deniability if this thing goes sideways. Plus, everyone knows you two haven't exactly been on good terms since the shooting."

"You think?" Wyatt huffed a laugh, slathering it in sarcasm. "So basically, it's my bare balls hanging out there."

"I've got your back. Besides, do you have a better plan for getting off Day's shit list? Or have you decided you like the odd pot-shots from pissed-off clients?"

"Fuck you," Wyatt said, unable to drum up any heat to put behind the words. "I'll call when I've had a chance to digest the file."

Before Wyatt could hang up, Rodriguez asked, "What changed your mind?"

No way would Wyatt tell Rodriguez about being duped and almost drugged by Geneva Steele. Best friend or not, after Rodriguez had laughed his ass off, he'd never let Wyatt live the near mishap down.

"Suffice it to say, last night's meeting with my potential client didn't go at all as I'd expected."

SIX HOURS AWAY FROM STARTING A DOUBLE SHIFT AT THE FIRE station, Geneva had a hard time keeping her eyes open and her thoughts clear, even after sleeping like the dead.

Despite Cassie filling her full of coffee and caffeine and calories, her head pounded and her body felt as drained as if she were already ten hours into a bitch of a shift.

"Call in sick," Cassie told Geneva, "you'll be no good to anyone on that ambulance, and you know it."

Geneva huddled in the corner of the couch in her den, the lights low, the shades drawn, a warm mug of the nectar-of-the-gods warming her hands. "You're right." She hated to admit her stupidity. Not only had she been the one who'd ended up drugged, she hadn't even managed to get any useful intel from Wolfe.

Except that he was an exceptional kisser.

Though that information seemed of little practical use.

Cassie grabbed Geneva's phone and pulled up the fire station's number and handed it back to Geneva. Geneva trapped the phone between her cheek and the back of the couch, the muscles in her neck too tired to do anything as taxing as holding her head up. When the station chief came on the line, Geneva made her excuses, though she really couldn't afford to miss work.

Good thing she wasn't eating much these days, or else she might have to take Cassie up on her offer to move in and be her roommate. Not that Geneva didn't love Cassie. It was that Geneva needed her alone time. Time to decompress from work. Time to learn to be alone again.

Time to plot and plan and scheme.

"Don't take this the wrong way, Gen, but I don't think this obsession with Caleb's death is healthy."

"Maybe. But I've come this far. I'm not going to stop now. After the first sex worker, Alexa Martinez, was killed, Caleb discovered something, and I can't help but think that whatever he found out got him killed."

How Wolfe fit into all that, Geneva hadn't a clue. That's why she was kicking herself about the night before. Or at least she would be if she'd had enough energy.

The silence dragged on, except for the light slurp as Geneva sipped at her coffee and the faint *tink, tink, tink* as Cassie tapped a fingernail against the side of her mug.

"You had me scared to death," Cassie said. "I was so close to coming and getting you. Then I got your text."

"Wolfe's text."

"Which explains a lot. I couldn't understand why you'd decided to spend the night..." A light brightened in Cassie's eyes. "Well, I mean, he's hot, so I could *imagine*, but—"

"It wasn't like that."

"How do you know? You were passed out for most of it."

"Ha, ha." But Geneva found a sliver of a smile. "As far as I can tell, he tucked me into his bed. Alone. And slept out in the open at the back of the boat."

"Chivalrous...for a kil—"

Geneva cut her a look as sharp as a scalpel, though Cassie's sarcasm said she didn't think Wyatt was a killer. And for some reason, after her encounter with Wolfe, she had a hard time thinking of him as one, either.

He hadn't taken advantage of her.

Never threatened her—even after discovering she'd tried to drug him.

He'd had every right to be pissed, every right to take that out on her, but he hadn't. She couldn't reconcile *that* man with the one she'd built up in her mind, the one who'd made her a widow.

Wyatt Wolfe wasn't the monster in the closet. And she didn't quite know what to do with that discovery.

"So," Cassie said, the playful tone back in her voice. "Not even a peck on the cheek?"

"I didn't say that."

"*No!*" The word tumbled out of Cassie's mouth hardly more than a whisper as if she'd had no air in her lungs to force it out. "Spill," Cassie ordered, recovering quick. Her tone hard, emphatic. Not to be ignored.

"I was there under the pretense of seducing him, so that involved a little kissing."

"A little tongue?"

"A lady doesn't kiss and tell."

Cassie huffed out an indignant breath. "Since when? And don't feed me that 'lady' crap, I knew you during your slut phase in high school."

"I'm pretty sure that was *your* slut phase. I lived vicariously through you if you'll recall."

Cassie waved her off as if Geneva shouldn't sweat the details. "How was it?" But the soft way she'd asked it, Cassie wasn't asking how Wolfe kissed, she was asking how Geneva felt about it. After all, the last man she'd kissed—*really* kissed since she couldn't count the firefighter with no spark—had been her husband.

Until the night before, she hadn't taken her wedding ring off since before Caleb had died. Geneva twisted the diamond inlaid band on her finger. She'd felt naked without it, but since she'd slipped it back on that morning, the band hadn't quite fit right either.

Or maybe it was her and not the ring that wasn't the same anymore.

As scared as she'd been, kissing Wolfe had been part of her plan.

Enjoying it hadn't been.

Outside, a car door slammed, but Geneva thought nothing of it. Her next-door neighbor worked from home and was always coming and going at all hours of the day.

Bam! Bam! Bam! The front door shook in its frame. "Geneva Steele!"

He'll huff, and he'll puff, and he—

"Don't look now," Cassie said. "But I think there's a Wolfe at your door."

"Ignore him. He'll go away."

Bam! Bam! Bam! "I know you're in there. I'm not leaving until you open the door."

Cassie called out, "Go away, or we'll call the sheriff."

Wolfe chuckled, a low, feral grumble that resonated through the door. "I think that's a great idea."

Shit. Geneva went to get up, but Cassie said, "Stay here. I'll send him away."

4

Steele's front door opened, and a small woman with blond hair—two-fisting a fire poker that rested on her shoulder—met Wyatt at the threshold. "What do you want?"

He leaned a shoulder against the doorjamb. "I don't know, Cass, maybe to find out why your friend was hell-bent on drugging me last night for starters."

Her eyes narrowed. "How did you know my name?"

"Lucky guess." With a quick grab, he plucked the poker from her hands, tossed it behind him, and started forward.

"She's not here. Go away." Cassie pushed and shoved against his chest, her sock covered feet slipping and sliding on the wood floor.

"Would you stop?" He could have overpowered her, but brute strength wasn't the answer here. "I can see her from here."

"Cass, let him in." Geneva sat crumpled on her couch, her cheek resting against the back cushion.

Cassie pointed a purple fingernail at him and said, "If you touch one hair on her head—"

"You'll what? Call the sheriff, the way you threatened a minute ago? If I'm not mistaken, I'm not the one who got drugs for a friend, and I'm not the one who tried to slip someone a roofie."

She sucked in a breath and slapped a hand over her mouth. "You know about that?"

Wyatt smiled, all teeth and fangs and glaring certainty. Cassie wasn't cut out for a life of crime. Not when she had one of those expressive faces that showed exactly what she was thinking. And *Oh shit*, pretty much summed up her thoughts.

He brushed past her and stood in front of Caleb's widow. That thing in the pit of his stomach worked overtime, twisting his guts into teeny, tiny knots. "Ms. Steele, we need to talk."

She rolled her head on the cushion so she could meet his gaze, but didn't bother raising her head. "What's with the *Ms. Steele*?"

In light of everything, somehow, it felt wrong calling her Geneva. "Call it manners."

Her lips formed a tired smile. "It's Geneva. You've had your hands on my ass and your tongue down my throat. I think we've graduated to a first name basis."

Heat pricked the back of his neck, as his hands and his tongue begged for a repeat. His brain, his *guilt*, overrode that thought and promptly dumped Geneva into the—not the *friend zone* because they weren't friends—but the not-on-your-life zone. Then he threw up razor wire and barricades, and anything else he could think of that would keep her confined to that tiny space.

Just his luck, the first woman who'd piqued his interest in a long time was the one woman he couldn't have. He tore his gaze from hers before he mentally threw a thick blanket over the razor wire and scaled it. "You got any more of that coffee?"

She bobbed her head, indicating somewhere behind her. He headed that way. From behind him, Cassie hissed at Geneva, "You need me to stay? Two against one. Just in case?"

"I heard that," he called from the kitchen as he opened cupboard after cupboard, searching for a coffee mug.

He found one, poured himself a cup, and leaned back against the counter. Geneva joined him and fell into one of the kitchen chairs. He refilled her mug. Cassie came in, and he held up the pot.

"No, I don't want any coffee," Cassie said. "I'm like a United Nations observer. I'm here to make sure no one gets hurt."

"I'm not the enemy here."

"*Cass.* Don't you have to get to work?" Geneva asked.

Cassie glanced at the clock on the oven. Frowned. "I'm not leaving—"

"Go." Geneva mixed about a cup of sugar into her coffee and took a sip.

Cassie was protective. He admired that in a friend. Everyone needed someone in their life that had their back no matter what. Rodriguez was that friend for him.

Perhaps his only friend.

But this was going to be a long day if he had to maneuver around Geneva's UN pit bull all morning. So he decided to shoot the elephant sitting in the middle of the room. "If I'd wanted to hurt her, I had plenty of opportunities last night."

The hard set expression on Cassie's face never wavered, so he considered throwing in an apology. He *was* sorry a man was dead. He *wasn't* sorry he'd defended himself, but his throat got tight anyway. Though he was talking to Cassie, he looked Geneva in the eye. "The last thing I want to do is cause her any more pain than I already have."

Geneva blinked rapidly and sniffed. *Awh, hell.* He hadn't meant to make her cry.

"Sweetie," Cassie came around the table, her arms extended to draw Geneva in for an embrace.

Geneva held up her hand to fend Cassie off. "I'll be fine, Cass. Go to work. I think Wolfe and I have a lot to talk about."

"If you're sure?"

"Positive."

Wyatt waited while Geneva walked Cassie out. When she returned, he took the seat across from her. "Why did you try to drug me?"

"Going straight for the jugular?"

He admired her spunk. "I just want the truth."

"How do I know you're not one of the bad guys?" She had a sad, ironic twist to her lips.

It impressed him how she managed not to dwell on her grief, not hammer him with the fact he was responsible for that, and focus on the conversation. "What do you do for a living?"

"Does it matter?"

"Humor me."

"Paramedic."

That explained her ability to compartmentalize her emotions and focus on her objective. "I should have known."

That earned him a genuine smile that flashed in her green eyes. Her shoulders relaxed, and she sat back.

"I was working the night Caleb died. My partner and I were on a call. A child had fallen into a pond. We were ten minutes into the resuscitation when we got a pulse. Then my captain drives up with someone to relieve me and drove me to the hospital. But I was too late." She laid her story out in a dry monotone, like something the teacher had made her memorize for a grade.

It wasn't that Geneva was cold and unfeeling. Wyatt understood the detachment. You couldn't always jump headfirst into that kind of emotional riptide and expect to survive.

"The kid made it through," she said, "so that was good." She sipped her coffee, grimaced. It had to be going cold. "But you didn't ask me that, did you?"

He shrugged. He had no intention of pushing her. This wasn't an interrogation. And something told him she was the kind that pushed back against pressure, not caved under it.

"The Nightwalker murders. While Caleb was undercover, he came across some information related to the case. After that, he'd been on edge. Nervous. Couldn't sleep. He didn't tell me what, only that he had compelling information but needed confirmation before he could do anything about it. You shot him the next day. I thought…" She glanced up from her mug and met his eye. "I thought you killed him to shut him up. And I wanted to search your place, hoping I could find the reason why."

"And now? You still believe I killed him to silence him?"

She shrugged. "I'm not sure what I believe anymore."

"So why the drugs? Why not slip on board when I wasn't around?"

"Your landlady is always home. I couldn't get to your boat without getting past her first."

Ballsy move. "Your plan almost worked."

"That's like saying I almost didn't get pregnant."

Wyatt sat back. A little honesty on his part might go a long way. There was a good chance they each had information that could help the other out. "I have a file on Steele," he admitted. "That night…"

Adrenaline seeped into his system. One drop. Two. His scalp tingled, and sweat broke out on his brow. Despite what the therapists said, for him, the telling never got any easier.

"That night, I was headed home after dinner with friends. Took a shortcut through an alley to get to my truck. Saw two men. A guy in a suit arguing with what looked like one of the local street thugs—who turned out to be your husband. It got physical between them. Your husband threw a punch. I pulled my weapon, announced who I was, told them to put their hands behind their heads."

Wyatt rotated the mug in his hand. Around and around. Still in disbelief at what had happened next. Caleb had been a *freaking* cop. He of all people knew not to draw a weapon in that situation. He would have known what would happen. "Your husband started to raise his hands. Then the suit said something to him. And Stee—your husband, went for his gun. I told him to stop, to drop the weapon. He froze. Then he raised his gun again and..." He let the rest of the sentence drift off. She knew the rest. It wasn't like he had to spell it out for her.

"It was caught by a security camera. That's why you weren't charged."

Wyatt nodded. "You saw it?"

"No." Quick. Fast. Absolute. She fiddled with the handle of the mug. "Why would he draw on you?" When she looked up, red rimmed Geneva's eyes, and her face had gone blotchy, but her voice remained mostly steady. "That doesn't make any sense."

"That's why I haven't been able to reconcile the shooting in my mind. I could have arrested him without it blowing his cover, so I don't think that would be a reason. Something else had to have been motivating him."

"Who was the guy in the suit?"

"He ran when I fired. The sheriff's department hasn't been able to identify him." Wyatt swallowed back the rest of the cold coffee and suppressed a shudder as it slid down. "Now, about those drugs."

"You going to call the sheriff on me?"

"I think you got what was coming to you. At least on the attempted drugging part." Wyatt blew out a breath. "That's still some serious shit, but I'd rather know where Cassie got the drugs. I can try to keep both of your names out of it, but no promises."

She considered his words. "How do I know this isn't a trick?"

"I guess you'll have to trust me."

Her lips twisted in an ironic smile as she tried to brush her fingers through her hair, but they caught in a knot. Her knee started bouncing, and finally, the nerves overtook her, and she started pacing her kitchen.

She boosted herself up on the counter, then hopped back off again. "Okay, fine."

Wyatt rubbed a hand over his mouth to hide the smile he couldn't quite contain. Geneva was even worse at this criminal thing than her friend was. Good thing the Dynamic Duo wasn't trying to make a serious go at working the wrong side of the law or else they'd probably find themselves on an episode of Stupid Criminal Tricks.

"Cass knows a guy at the Sheriff's Office who works the evidence room. She traded for the drugs."

Wyatt narrowed his eyes. "What did she trade?"

"She sexted him a boob shot."

"You're kidding me, right? You're telling me a deputy sheriff willingly risked not only his career but being brought up on charges, for a photo of some chick's boobs when he could go to a porn site for free and get essentially the same thing?"

Geneva raised her hands in a who-knows gesture. "But did you see them? They're pretty spectacular, if you ask me, so yeah. I'm not too surprised. And this guy has been panting after her for a while, so there is that."

Things certainly had changed since he'd worked there. "Cassie's quite the friend."

"Yeah, she is." Geneva rubbed her hands down her face and looked at him over the tips of her fingers. "I don't want her getting into trouble. You can't tell anyone it was Cassie. She could lose her job at dispatch, and it wasn't even her idea, and I was the one who talked her into it, and she's my best friend, and all I wanted—" All of her sentences ran together, and her face went red with the need to take a breath.

"Whoa, whoa, whoa. Easy now." Wyatt came out of his chair and reached out for her, but she lightly batted his hand away.

"No. Don't touch me." Her breath hitched, and she swiped at her cheek.

Damn. Wyatt hadn't meant to make her cry.

She sank against the counter, her face hidden in her hands, sobbing. It was like she'd been holding on by the tips of her fingernails until her strength gave out. Tumbling was unavoidable. It had only been a question of when. Eventually, something had to give.

He stood beside her, fists in his pockets to keep from putting an arm around her shoulder. He knew her meltdown wasn't just about him knowing how Cassie had gotten the drugs for her, or Geneva's fear of police reprisal. This little meltdown felt a whole lot bigger than that.

The guilt of taking the life of a fellow officer had left a dark smudge on his psyche, and on his soul. It didn't matter that the shooting had been justified or that no criminal charges had been filed. Standing there in the man's kitchen, watching Steele's widow go to pieces and knowing he had a part in that, only made the smudge darker and wider and more encompassing. His chest constricted, and every shallow breath burned.

GENEVA'S CRYING JAG SLOWED. SHE PEEKED THROUGH A CRACK IN her fingers. Wolfe stood beside her. Inches away. Head bowed. She had to give him bonus points for not bolting like a rabbit at the first sign of trouble.

"Sorry," she said as she swiped at the moisture on her cheeks.

He turned her toward him. She ducked her head and hid her face with her hands. He tried to tug them away. "You don't want to do that," she said. "Trust me on this."

"Look at me."

Good God, no. Heat crept into her face. She'd hated crying in front of Caleb, and she'd been married to him. "No. I'm an ugly crier."

His short bark of laughter echoed in her kitchen. "What the hell does that mean?"

"It's like those movies with Julia Roberts when she cries, only worse. I even get that vein that pops out on my forehead, and my face is splotchy and red, and—"

He pulled her hands away, and she didn't have the strength to fight him. With a finger under her chin, he lifted her eyes to his. "Ack!" He pulled a face as if the Creature from the Black Lagoon stared back at him.

"See!" She tried to cover her face again, but he wouldn't let her.

"I was kidding. Come on, look at me."

She looked up. Wyatt's gaze roamed over her face, from her eyes to her nose to the ugly vein on her forehead to her lips that felt chapped from all the boo-hooing.

"You want to know what I see?" he asked.

This could be bad. "Hit me with it."

"I see a woman who is strong and determined and willing to do whatever it takes to do right by a man that she loved. In my book, there's nothing ugly about that."

She sniffed and swallowed hard. The backs of her eyes stung. He was going to make her cry again. "I hate you," she said, but it was hard to put any force behind the words.

"Excuse me?" He didn't sound offended. He almost sounded amused.

She didn't know how to explain it to herself, much less to

him. In those early months after Caleb's death, her grief, her anger had built Wolfe up into this horrible person who had destroyed her world. But now that the cloying mental fog of grief had lifted, she could see clearer now. Even though she'd tried to drug him, he'd been gentle and kind and patient and understanding.

Was he playing her to get something he wanted?

Maybe.

But she didn't think so.

They weren't friends, not by a long shot, but if what he said was true, if he had a file on Caleb, if he'd been trying to dig beneath the surface in search of the truth, then maybe, if nothing else, they were looking for the same answers.

She stepped away, needing some space. "I mean, I did hate you. Or should hate you." He settled against the counter, his boots crossed at the ankles, his hands resting on the counter behind him. "You were the Big Bad. The destroyer of my perfect little universe but now... now I see that you're just a man, not a monster."

"I really am sor—"

"Don't." She pressed her palms over her ears. She didn't want to hear the words. "You may not be the man I thought you were, but I don't know if I can ever accept your apology or forgive you for what you've done. Maybe someday. But not today."

———

THAT-A-WAY STOOD ON THE DOCK BESIDE HIS BOAT AND MOO-ED, her hot breath wafting over Wyatt, stinking of partially digested hay and grass. Her ear flicked at a fly, and she nudged Wyatt's arm. He handed her an alfalfa cube along with a peppermint from his pocket. The mint could only help.

He lowered his sunglasses and settled onto the bench seat at the back of his trawler. In front of him, he'd set up a folding table and laid out the reports from the envelope Rodriguez had given him. The breeze kicked up, and Wyatt reached into the bag of treats and laid alfalfa cubes in the center of each pile as a paperweight.

When That-A-Way realized no more cubes were coming her way, she lowered herself onto the moving pad he'd set out on the dock, rested her chin on the gunwale, and gave each nostril a quick swipe with her pointed pink tongue.

Evie had once told Wyatt how That-A-Way used to mother strays and orphans. Not that Wyatt needed another mother. Yet despite That-A-Way's halitosis, she wasn't a half-bad companion. She didn't complain if he drank too much or stayed out late or even that he only stocked the two basic food groups in his mini-fridge—beer and hot sauce. An unconventional partnership, but —That-A-Way blew out a heavy sigh, and her eyes rolled into the back of her head—it worked.

He turned his attention back to the reports. He'd been the lead detective when the first woman—now linked to the Night-walker murders—had been killed. Before he'd been relieved of duty after Steele's shooting. Rodriguez and a junior detective at the Bison County Sheriff's Office had been reassigned the cases after the second and third women had been murdered.

Reading over his old entries from the murder book took Wyatt straight back to the primary scene. The body had been found about a hundred and fifty yards from a highway pullout, at the mouth of a creek swollen with spring runoff. A creek that dumped into the Snake River.

A photographer taking sunrise shots through a telescopic lens had spotted one of the victim's exposed butt cheeks hidden in a thick patch of grass at the river's edge with blowflies blanketing the bloated body.

The state medical examiner, the ME, had attributed the post-mortem abrasions on the skin to a stiff bristle brush as if the perpetrator had scrubbed the body clean. Traces of dish soap found on the body supported that theory. The fingernails had also been trimmed back to the quick.

Not only was the suspect smart, but the killer had also been methodical about ridding the body of as much trace evidence as possible. Whatever evidence may have been missed, the creek had taken care of the rest.

The victim had benn sexually assaulted, but no semen found, so the ME assumed a condom had been used. Death by asphyxiation—a man's leather belt still around the woman's neck.

About the only clue they had on their suspect was that the perpetrator had a thirty-six-inch waist, based on the hole-wear pattern on the belt. That, and the guy could afford to spend about eighty bucks on a belt. The rolling at the top edges of the leather suggested the user had a bit of a belly.

If the belt belonged to the suspect and wasn't a weapon of opportunity.

Wyatt couldn't ignore that possibility since the ability to carry dead weight a hundred and fifty yards over rough terrain at night meant the suspect either had help, or he was reasonably fit.

Which didn't jibe with the overweight perp hypothesis.

So, basically, they'd had jack shit to go on.

And the best part—and by *best* he meant the part that had his fellow deputies, and even his sheriff, eying him with veiled suspicion—was that a white pickup had been ticketed for parking at the day-use-only pullout four nights before the body had been found.

A pickup that had been stolen.

A pickup that had been claimed, cleaned, and immediately

sold to pay the District Attorney, the DA's, fees for a series of forged checks.

A pickup that had belonged to his cousin.

Didn't matter that Wyatt hadn't had any contact with his cousin in four years—if you counted turning and walking the other direction when he'd spotted Jasper at yet another fucked up and failed family reunion as contact.

But the hint of impropriety had stuck to him like hot gum on a shoe—he'd gotten most of it off, but a tiny bit remained.

At the time of Steele's shooting, though, not only had he and Rodriguez not had a suspect, they'd had no viable leads.

And now two more women were dead.

The low grumble of Rodriguez's black Dodge Challenger woke That-A-Way. She stretched her neck, burped up a wad of cud, and started chewing. Rodriguez walked down the dock, dressed in black slacks, a black polo, and matte black shades. A Beretta on his hip and a badge on his belt. From the look of him, Rodriguez belonged in the city, not beneath the shadow of the Rockies.

Rodriguez stepped over the cow's rump, grabbed the edge of Sea-Celia's hardtop, and swung down into the boat. He waved a hand in the general direction of the cow. "You know this isn't normal, right?"

Much like the rest of my life. "Have a seat."

Rodriguez unfolded a red deck chair and brushed the leaves out of the crease.

As Rodriguez's ass landed in the seat, Wyatt said, "Someone is using the evidence room as his personal pharmaceutical dispensary. Jed know about that?"

"He's looking into it. How did you hear about that?"

"I could tell you, but then I'd have to kill you."

"Cute," Rodriguez said, but the near snarl of his upper lip said otherwise. "No, seriously."

"I'd rather not say at the moment."

"I'm your ex-partner. Your best friend. If you can't tell me, who—"

"I made a promise to keep the person's name out of it. At least for now. Besides, you know about it, so what does it matter?"

Rodriguez bobbed his brows in a point-taken gesture, then helped himself to a bottle of water from the cooler stashed beneath the table. He twisted the lid and took a long drag. Rodriguez pointed at the case files with his water bottle. "Anything jump out at you?"

"Just got started. Why don't you give me the Cliffies on the other two murders? I can slog through the reports and get the details later."

"It will be quick. Like the first one you investigated, we have little physical evidence and no witnesses tying anyone to the murders. The second and third victims were believed to have been picked up off the street, like the first. But I haven't been able to confirm that. And like the first, both bodies were dumped in wilderness areas close enough to a road, but far enough away that wildlife predation made our jobs tougher."

That-A-Way stood and nosed Rodriguez on his shoulder, leaving a smear of cow slobber on his sleeve. "Jesus Christ." Rodriguez wiped it away, but that only made his hand slobbery, too.

Wyatt barked out a laugh. If he could have high-fived a cow, he would have. He tossed Rodriguez a mostly clean hand towel he kept around for that purpose. "She just wants an alfalfa cube."

Rodriguez grabbed a handful of cubes from the bag and tossed them up the dock in ever-increasing distances like a reverse breadcrumb trail. That-A-Way gave Rodriguez a baleful look before ambling up the dock after the treats. She was proud, but not *that* proud.

After rinsing his hands over the side of the boat, Rodriguez leaned a hip on the gunwale. "That's seriously messed up."

"Be nice, or she'll put a horn through one of your tires. Or Evie will put a bullet through them. Those are two females you don't want to foul hook, trust me." But Wyatt didn't want to talk about the women in his life. "About the case. You were saying?"

"One victim was strangled with hands. The other with a plastic bag, the ME believes. No defensive wounds to speak of."

"Usually, a serial killer picks one method of killing and sticks with it. And I saw something that said the victims knew each other," Wyatt said. "That's unusual, too."

"This isn't New York City. It wouldn't be strange that someone targeting sex workers would stumble across victims that knew each other."

Maybe. "What about copycat killings?"

"The detail about the bodies being scrubbed down and the fingernails cut back has never been made public, so unless the copycat knew the real killer, that's unlikely."

Rodriguez's phone *bleeped,* and he pulled it out of his pocket for a quick check. "That's Day. He wants me back at the station for a briefing with city officials and the senator, for fuck's sake. How do they expect me to do my job if they don't let me go out and do it?

"Your senator? Senator Lambert?"

Rodriguez climbed out of the trawler, rocking it on its moorings. "Just because Lambert was a close friend of my father's doesn't make him *mine.*" Rodriguez's tone came out more annoyed than his normal reverence when referring to Larson Lambert. Lambert was more than a family friend.

The senator had been as significant of an influence on Rodriguez's life as Jed Day had been on Wyatt's. In that way, he and Rodriguez were a lot alike. Only Wyatt's father didn't own fancy cars or multi-million-dollar homes or hob-nob with celebrities and politicians.

Wyatt's lasting legacy from his father was his propensity to drink.

"What's with the tone?" Wyatt asked. "I thought you and Lambert were close."

"We are, but when three murders happen near the hometown of a tough-on-crime senator who's throwing his hat in for the next presidential bid, the pressure gets a little intense."

"What about calling in the FBI?"

"Day—and when I say Day, I mean Senator Lambert—wants the local boys to have the coup. But I'm afraid if we don't get these murders solved soon, more women might turn up dead, and we may not have a choice."

Rodriguez turned to leave, and Wyatt said, "You really think Lambert could be president someday?"

"He's got a good track record and that kiss-the-babies charm the public gobbles up like Pez. Plus, he has the money and the party backing. I figure he's got as good a shot as anybody."

"So, he gets the presidency, and you end up as a trusted adviser at the White House?"

Rodriguez ducked his head and chuckled. "Would that be so farfetched?"

Wyatt thought about that. Washington would suit Rodriguez better than Wyoming. Wyatt suppressed a shudder. *D.C.* Wyatt would rather slather his balls with honey and be staked out over an anthill. "Better you than me, buddy. Besides, I don't think they'd allow a bovine on the South Lawn."

5

AFTER ALL THE TIME GENEVA HAD PLOTTED AND PLANNED FOR ways to get on Wyatt's boat, it was surreal to drive up to his dock in broad daylight. She parked next to a black Challenger and grabbed Caleb's journal from the passenger seat. She'd found the journal and Caleb's spare set of keys at the back of the bottom drawer of the rolling tool chest in the garage where she kept the hand-held pruners. Pruning had always been her job. Caleb hadn't had the patience for it.

Which begged the question: If Caleb been hiding his journal from her, why put it in the *one* drawer in the tool chest she was most likely to go through? And if he'd wanted her to find it, why not put it someplace it wouldn't have taken more than a year after his death for her to find, like in the freezer next to the ice cream?

She'd have found it *really* fast then.

Now, she had more questions than answers—including which lock did the old key on her husband's spare key ring go to? It reminded her of an old barrel key for locks from years gone by. She'd checked every lock at the house. The shed in her back yard. Nada.

As she walked down the dock, a man headed her way. All dressed in black, like a young, metrosexual Johnny Cash.

She couldn't be certain with the dark shades, but she thought the guy cut her a look.

"Ms. Steele," he said as he came abreast. He had a smug look on his face. He'd wanted her to know that he knew who she was. She half expected him to point two fingers at his eyes and then point them at her in the universal sign for I'm-watching-you. Did he know she'd been stalking Wolfe?

She inclined her head. Thanks to her stalk—*ahem, research* —she knew who he was, too. "Detective Rodriguez."

A corner of his lips twitched. If he'd been an infant, everyone would have blamed it on a pinch of gas and not called it a smile.

Wolfe glanced up as she approached. The crease between his brows eased. If she hadn't tried to drug him the night before, she might have thought him glad to see her.

"Permission to come aboard, skipper?"

He snorted out a laugh. "Do I need to call in a drug dog and have you searched first?"

She deserved that. "I'm clean. Promise."

He waved her on board, and she jumped in. "If you're busy working, I could come back."

"'S okay." He leaned back, took a long drink from his water bottle, "I didn't expect to see you again today. What's up?"

"Can I be honest?"

"Sure. Save me from having to break out the truth serum."

She probably deserved that, too. "I'm not exactly sure why I'm here. But I found this journal not too long ago, and I couldn't get anywhere with it." She waggled the leatherbound notebook and plopped it on Wolfe's makeshift desk. "It belonged to Caleb. The Sheriff's Office considers his case closed. We both want to get to the bottom of his death for our own reasons, so maybe together we can do that."

"Kind of an I'll-show-you-mine if you-show-me-yours?"

"In a way."

"Does that mean we're friends?"

Geneva hesitated. "Allies, maybe."

She looked at him then, his expression open and relaxed, with a hint of amusement in those gray eyes of his. Not as if he thought this whole thing was funny but as if he were able to see the irony and, she supposed, a bit of rueful humor in their situation.

"I don't get you," she said.

"How's that?"

"I tried to drug you last night. Why aren't you yelling at me, or cussing me out?"

"Would that help?"

"I don't know. I could understand it at least. What I don't understand is why you don't hate me right now."

"Hate is a powerful word."

It was. It took so much mental energy to feed that beast, and she was tired. So damn tired. Of the hating, the loathing, the planning, the scheming.

Wolfe was not the heartless killer she'd painted with a black brush. He was just a man.

She blew out a breath and let some of the negative energy she'd nursed and fostered toward Wolfe go free. When she breathed in again, that constant tension in her chest had eased a fraction, and the air she breathed in seemed fresher, clearer, cleaner.

Was it all behind her?

Not by a long shot. But it felt as if she'd ripped the dirty bandage off a festering wound, and now it could finally get some air and start to heal.

He picked up the journal. "What have we got?"

"I don't know. It's in some sort of code or shorthand. I can't make any sense of it."

He opened the journal and patted the cushion next to him. She didn't budge. He glanced back up at her. "I'm not going to bite."

Still, she hesitated. Less than twenty-four hours ago, she'd been making out with him. And it had only been roughly eight hours since she'd climbed out of his bed.

The amusement slipped from his face. "Seriously, Geneva. I'm not going to hurt you."

She could hear Caleb's voice clearly in her mind—*Suck it up, buttercup.*

She forced a smile as embarrassment burned up her cheeks. Wyatt might have taken her hesitation as fear—but if he'd wanted to hurt her, he'd had plenty of opportunities to do that. No, she wasn't *afraid,* she was *aware.*

Which was even scarier.

And having Caleb's voice in her head while she stood in front of a man she'd enjoyed kissing, despite the circumstances, felt all kinds of wrong.

She could have kissed the firefighter in a drought-ravaged forest, and there wouldn't have been any concerns about starting a raging forest fire. But with Wolfe, Smokey the Bear might have needed an extra-large fire extinguisher.

Or maybe one of those tanker planes loaded with fire retardant.

His attention dropped back to the journal as if letting her make up her mind without any undue pressure. *Don't be stupid.* It would be easier to go over the journal together if they were sitting close. So, she took her husband's advice and sucked it up.

"When did he go undercover?" Wolfe scooted over, making room as she slid in next to him.

"He took the assignment a couple months before he died. I'd had a bad feeling about it all along. But he loved undercover work. He felt like that was what he was meant to do. Where he could make the most impact."

Wolfe looked at her then. *Really* looked at her. He set the journal down and made a circular motion with his index finger, indicating her face. "What's with all that?"

"I don't know what you're talking about."

"The detachment. Every time you talk about Steele, your voice and your expression go flat, as if android Geneva has been turned on and the real Geneva has been switched off. Did he hurt you?"

Geneva shook her head, surprised by the question and but by the way his hand had fisted on the table as if he'd deck Caleb if he hadn't already killed him. She didn't know what to make of that. "What? No. Nothing like that."

"Then what?"

Just because she no longer hated Wolfe, didn't mean she wanted him crawling around inside her head, but for some reason, "It's the only way I can deal," slipped out. "I know it sounds callous, but if I think about him, I think about how lucky I was to have him, to love him. Then I think of what we shared and what we'll miss. And then... a-and then..." Tears pricked the back of her eyes, and her throat shrank to the diameter of a coffee stirrer straw.

He wrapped an arm around her shoulders and held her against his side. It should have felt so wrong to be comforted by him, but for some reason, it didn't. He cleared his throat. "It's okay to cry." His voice had grown tight. "And it's okay to feel."

It's okay to feel.

That's what she'd been doing for far too long now—feeling sad and hopeless and distraught and sorry for herself. But now more than ever before, as the grief eased, as her brain re-engaged, as she started to... not forget—because that would never happen—but as she started to move forward with her new reality, this overwhelming sense of determination boiled up from her marrow.

She swiped at the tears that dared escape, and as she sat up straight, Wolfe's arm dropped to his side.

"I've done nothing but feel for the past year and a half," she said. "Now it's time to do something. And now more than ever, I'm determined to find out why he drew on you and the truth behind my husband's death."

He gave her a short nod and a wink. His smile was similar to the one Caleb used to give her when he was proud of her. Her heart bumped a beat of acknowledgment. She paged through Caleb's journal until they found a date from around the time her husband had gone undercover.

Anticipation made her heart beat faster. Could Wolfe figure out Caleb's shorthand? Maybe it was something that would only make sense to someone in law enforcement. Wolfe thumbed through the pages. Past the chart of numbers and associated initials. Past listed times and location names, stopping on the last page of the journal from a couple of days before Caleb had died—*Sent recording to the pack leader*. Then the word *mistake*, in all caps, written diagonally across the page, several times larger than everything else he'd written and he'd underlined it three times and added an exclamation point.

"What recording was he talking about?" she asked.

"No clue," Wolfe said. "You didn't find anything?"

"No. Nothing at the house."

"What about in his belongings from work? Did they pack up his desk and drop everything off?"

The box. She'd completely forgotten about the box. Geneva's vision blurred and dark spots flickered in her peripheral vision.

Wolfe rubbed a hand down her back and said, "Take a breath before you pass out."

She sucked in a breath, blew it out, and drew in another

and another. "There's a box," she said. "Caleb's captain delivered it a week after Caleb's death. I shoved it in the back of my closet."

"What was in it?"

Maybe something that could help them. "I have no idea."

———

Wyatt couldn't believe his ears. Not the sound of the crickets singing in the grass or the croak of the bullfrog or the slow rhythmic snapping of stems as That-A-Way stripped mouthful after mouthful of grass and chomped it between her molars. No, what he couldn't believe was that Geneva had a box of Steele's belongings and hadn't even opened it. The possible ramifications for the investigation were enormous. "It could hold the missing piece we've been looking for."

"Wouldn't his supervisor at the DEA have kept anything case related?"

"More than likely," Wyatt admitted, "but you never know. They might have missed something."

After learning Steele had been investigating the Alexa Martinez's murder from his own angle, Wyatt's gut told him that the answers he sought with regards to Steele were tied up with the Nightwalker murders. Wouldn't that chap Rodriguez's ass if Wyatt got this thing sorted within a couple days of being handed the case? He could practically feel the slaps on his back as he was welcomed back into the fold, and all of his doubters and detractors wanting to buy him a beer.

"I think one of us should take a look." Wyatt tried sounding nonchalant. He mostly pulled it off, more because Geneva was still in disbelief that she'd blocked the box from her mind than any brilliant acting skills on his part. "I can do it if you don't want to."

"No," she said. Wyatt feared she'd deny him any access to her husband's personal effects. "I want to do this."

Wyatt nodded. If nothing else, being a detective had taught him the benefits of backing off and letting the scene play out.

"But you can tag along if you'd like." The way she'd offered the invitation, it was as if she could take his help or leave it, but that hollow look in her eyes told him she could use the backup.

"Sure." He thumbed back through the journal's pages. Nothing Caleb had written made much sense. Then he spotted the words *pack leader* again as well as *white pickup—sold!*

Cold sweat formed along his spine. Wyatt checked the date —a week after he'd started his investigation into Alexa's death. A week before he'd killed Steele.

Pack leader... wolf... *Wolfe.* It wasn't such a stretch. How had Steele found out about his connection to the stolen vehicle? Wolfe wasn't that rare of a name in Wyoming. Plus, his cousin lived in a different town. Few people even knew he and Jasper were related. But Steele had figured it out before anyone else had. *Nice work.*

"What is it?" Geneva asked. "You find something?"

He kept his hand over the words *pack leader*, he pointed to the entry about the truck. He'd just started to gain her trust. If she connected him to the stolen pick-up, she might get the wrong idea about him. Like his former friends and colleagues had. "The Martinez murder was initially my case."

"Now the papers are saying there's a serial killer out there."

"Possibly," Wyatt allowed. "But it's more complicated than that, and I find it interesting that your..." He almost said husband. He had a hard time calling Steele her husband. It reminded him too much of what he'd taken from her. "That Steele had written notes about the case. He wasn't even involved in the investigation."

"But he was undercover investigating drug dealing through a

prostitution ring. He never told me much, only that he came across some information about the murder while working his case."

The more Wyatt thought about it, the more it made him itch to dive into that box she had stuffed into the back of her closet.

"I don't know how it ties in, though. And the rest of this—" Wyatt waved a hand at the journal pages, "is a bunch of gibberish right now. Unless we can find some a key that tells us what these initials stand for and what these numbers are related too, we don't have much to go on."

"I've got something else," Geneva said.

He found it intriguing how quickly he'd made the switch from thinking of her as Steele's widow to thinking of her by her first name.

Probably because of the whole tongue down her throat and hands on her ass thing.

Don't deny it.

Shit.

He rubbed his palms down the legs of his shorts, trying to wipe away the feel of her from his hands, from his mind. "What's that?"

She tugged at the gold chain around her neck that disappeared beneath the collar of her shirt and pulled it over her head. From the end of the chain dangled one of those antique-looking keys you'd expect to find in the padlock of great-great grandmother's steamer trunk stuck up in someone's attic for untold decades.

He took it from her, the metal warm from her skin, and did his best not to think about how amazing she'd felt in his arms. Blood sped to his groin, and he draped his other arm over his lap to cover his arousal.

So much for not thinking about it.

"Haven't figured out what it goes to yet. He'd attached it to his spare set of car keys and placed it in the drawer with the journal."

"Last time I saw a key like that was at a flea market."

"Same here. I have no idea where Caleb got it, when he got it, or what it goes to. Nothing at our house, that's for sure."

"An old padlock or safe, maybe?" He laid it on the table next to a stack of papers. Then he thought of another possibility. "Or a safety deposit box."

"I'd wondered the same thing. I checked with our bank, but all of their keys are modern."

Wyatt checked his watch. Almost four. "I know a guy that might be able to help us figure it out. If we hurry, we might be able to make it before he closes."

"What do you want to do with the journal?"

"I'd like to keep it for a while if that's okay with you. Maybe if I stare at it enough, I'll be able to figure something out."

She rubbed her hand over the cover as if it were some priceless ancient document she couldn't let leave her sight. And in some ways, Wyatt figured it was. Something handwritten from Steele probably meant the world to her.

"I promise to take good care of it," Wyatt added, for what his word was worth.

Geneva didn't immediately answer, her fingertip tracing the letter C embossed on the leather cover. He glanced out and found That-A-Way on the other side of the pond, having munched her way around, the sun angling toward the cutting edges of the Rockies in the distance.

Geneva picked up the journal and hugged it to her chest, then held it out to him. "Okay," she said at last. "But I want it back."

"Scout's honor." He held up the hand sign for the Boy Scouts. Not that he'd ever been a Boy Scout. But he'd always wanted to be one. Rodriguez had been one. Funny how Wyatt's father had found enough money for the booze but never enough money for scouting. "I'll find a safe place for it, and then we can go see what we can find out about your key."

She nodded, even as it looked like she wanted to change her mind. He trod down the steps to his cabin, expecting her to call out and take the journal back, but she didn't. Wyatt admired her for that.

He stuffed the journal behind a false panel in the storage compartment beneath the bed in his berth, then dropped the mattress and rumpled covers back down.

Grabbing his car keys off the hook, he climbed out of the cabin and emerged onto the deck. "I'll drive," she said as she spotted the keys in his hand. "Or, we can take two cars."

So maybe she didn't trust him as much as he'd thought.

Just because Geneva's opinion of Wyatt Wolfe had shifted, didn't mean she was ready to relinquish all control. She sucked in a breath, prepared for an argument, or at least to have to spout a list of valid reasons why she should drive, but Wolfe tossed his keys back into the cabin where they slid across the top of the table and landed on the bench seat. "Fine by me."

Wyatt held out his hand to help her onto the dock, but she didn't like how his touch made her want more. Wolfe wasn't a man to depend on. He was a man to tolerate until she got to the truth.

She scrambled out of the boat under her own power. If she'd annoyed him with the slight, it didn't show. They rounded his truck, and he came up short when he saw her dark blue Prius.

He groaned. "If you'd told me you drove a soup-can-on-wheels, I would have taken my truck."

"No one is sticking a gun to your head. I can always follow you."

He glanced over his shoulder, rechecked his watch and sighed like a man who couldn't believe he was about to walk willingly through Dante's circles of hell.

She beeped the car unlocked. "It's not that bad," she said as she climbed in.

He opened the passenger side door, buzzed the seat all the way back, and folded himself into it like an origami crane. One shoulder brushed against the window. The other brushed against hers. She pressed the engine start button and cranked up the air conditioning. Why was it so warm in there?

"Seriously, a push button to start?" He grumbled as she backed out and headed down the driveway.

She ignored the question and asked one of her own. "Where to?"

"Murdock," he said. "Eastside."

"Isn't that the—"

"Bad part of town? Yeah. Lefty's services aren't needed as much on the good side of town."

"Lefty?" she said. "Let me guess. He's missing his right arm?" She was only half kidding.

"You would think," Wolfe said. "But no. He was *left* holding the bag, so to speak, on a burglary gone bad. Spent nine years in prison on a rash of charges. The nickname stuck."

"What does he do now?"

"Locksmith."

"Don't you need a license for that?"

"He's not official, but he keeps his nose clean and flies under the radar."

Geneva laughed. "I guess that's a great line of work for a burglar."

"Reformed burglar."

"You seriously believe that?"

"With this guy? Yeah, I do."

She braked for the four-way stop not far up the road from Wolfe's place and accelerated up the road, the engine whining as it spooled up.

"Jesus, how many gerbils you got under the hood anyway?"

Geneva patted the car's dash. "Be nice, or you'll hurt his feelings."

"*His* feelings? Your car is a guy?"

"What's wrong with that? Men refer to boats as she. I can refer to my car as a he."

"Poor puny bastard," Wolfe said. "He probably got beat up by the Tundras on the assembly line."

"Well, this 'poor puny bastard' kicks ass and takes names when it comes to sneaking up on people. I bet your diesel couldn't get within a mile of someone without being heard."

He cut her an inquisitive look. "How close did you get to my boat without me knowing?"

Oops. Well, it wasn't like it was a secret anymore. "I got past the house one night. Then a light came on in one of the rooms. It was pitch black out. My headlights were off. I know there was no way anyone had heard me, but as I waited for the light to go off, I came to my senses. Or chickened out. Still not sure which."

He didn't grumble or growl or get mad. He laughed. Who was this man? "I wouldn't call a woman who'd go home with a stranger and try to roofie him a chicken."

She slapped a hand over her face and drew it down. "Are you ever going to let me live that down? It wasn't my proudest moment."

"Great story to tell the grandkids."

Geneva slammed on the brakes. Good thing no one was behind them. "Grandkids?" she squeaked.

"Relax." He made a get-going motion with his hand. "It's just an expression."

If it was just an expression, why had the awkward factor jumped from zero to sixty in less than a second? She didn't know what to say after that. Apparently, he didn't either.

When she pulled onto the main drag in Murdock, she passed the bank, the sandwich shop, and the three pawn shops before Wolfe said, "Turn right at the next stop sign."

She turned and continued down that road, and then another and another until the cute, touristy Wyoming town turned seedy and dirty—boarded-up buildings, weedy vacant lots, and people wandering the streets. She never ventured to that part of town alone. The loiterers gave her car the once over.

Her car didn't belong here.

She didn't belong here.

Toto, we're not in Kansas anymore.

Maybe she should have let Wolfe drive. Being an ex-deputy, he was probably better at the fast driving and evasive maneuvering nonsense in case they needed to make a quick getaway.

"It's okay," he said. "The area's not that bad."

Geneva's fingers cramped from gripping her steering wheel so tight, and an ache settled deep into the taut muscles along her spine. "Not that bad? There are sex workers on every corner."

He pointed up the road. "Not that one."

She chuckled, some of the tension leaving her body. "That makes me feel *so* much better."

Wolfe pointed to an empty street-side parking spot up the road. "Pull in there."

She parked, and they got out under the watchful eye of a scrawny teen standing on the corner. He had short-cropped hair, wore Wranglers with a Skoal ring on the back pocket, and a T-shirt that said *Porn Star Academy—Head instructor.* A wad of tobacco bulged his lower lip even though he couldn't have been any older than fourteen.

The kid's eyes went from her to the Prius to Wolfe. Over his shoulder, the kid said something to someone around the corner and out of sight. Two more teens appeared, their shoulders back and their chests puffed out.

One of the new teens was older, heavy-set, with a mangy splotch of stubble across his fleshy jowls. "Hey, pretty Mom—"

Wolfe stepped in front of her, clamping a large hand on the big kid's shoulder, his thumb on some sort of pressure point if the grimace on the kid's face gave any indication. "You don't want to finish that sentence." Wolfe spoke in a calm, conversational tone, the same one he'd probably use to order a meal at a diner. But the kid shut up.

Wolfe released the pressure but didn't remove his hand. Porn Star spat a wad of tobacco and stepped forward. "Hey, man, get your—"

With a cutting look, Wolfe silenced Porn Star. Then Wolfe reached into his back pocket and pulled a twenty out of his wallet and stuffed it into the breast pocket of the big kid's shirt. Wolfe pointed to her Prius. "You get twenty more if that car is as pristine when we return as it is now. A dove so much as shits on it, you clean it up, got me?"

By the way the big kid swallowed hard and nodded, the money had been unnecessary. Not having Wolfe's hand on his shoulder was payment enough. Wolfe patted the kid on the cheek. "Good man." He eyed the other two punks. "Gentlemen," he said as he took Geneva's hand and pulled her away with him.

"You didn't have to do that. I'm sure my car would have been fi—"

"This street isn't nicknamed Stripper Street because of the adult club on the corner. It's because a car on this street can be stripped to the frame faster than a flock of vultures through roadkill."

"Aren't you putting them in danger by having them watch out for my car? What if they tried to stop the thieves—"

"Sweetheart," he said as he steered her toward a shop front and opened the door for her. "They are the thieves."

———

Wyatt ushered Geneva into Lefty's locksmith shop. He hadn't seen Lefty in close to ten years, but Wyatt had kept unofficial tabs on him since the man had been released from prison. From what Wyatt knew, most of Lefty's business was mobile, so there wasn't much to the shop. Two gun safes almost as tall as he was, a display of padlocks hanging on the wall. A key-making machine. An open door to a back room. All of it fit into a space no bigger than Sea-Celia's back deck.

He had to turn sideways to edge between Geneva and the dust-covered gun safe. People around that part of town tended to have their guns out in the open withing easy reach, not locked up in some safe where you'd be dead before you could get it open. "You in here, Lefty?"

Something crashed and shattered in the back room, and a rash of profanity followed. Geneva glanced at him. He shrugged. "Hey," Wyatt said again.

"Yeah, yeah," came the grumble of a male voice from the back. "Keep your freaking pants—"

Lefty came out of the backroom, wiping what looked like soda from the front of his shirt. The man drew up short when he saw Wyatt. The rag dropped from Lefty's hand and, for a guy named Lefty, he had one hell of a right hook.

A solid fist hit Wyatt on the left side of his jaw. His head snapped back, and in the time it took him to regain his footing,

Wyatt wondered what kind of job he needed to get that didn't involve fists flying at his face. Maybe a barista at a coffee shop.

On second thought. Probably nothing more dangerous than a caffeine addict awaiting his next fix.

Lefty shook the sting from his hand and held it to his chest, rubbing his sore knuckles. Served the bastard right.

"Oh my God, what is wrong with you?" Geneva gave Lefty a shove and got in his face. "What did Wyatt ever do to you to deserve that?"

Despite the sucker punch, Wyatt couldn't help the stupid grin that slid across his face when he looked at her. Geneva rounded on Wyatt. "Why are you looking at me all goofy like I gave you a calf for Christmas?"

"That's the first time you called me by my first name." Jesus that sounded even stupider aloud. He tried to ditch the smile, but it didn't work. Instead, he rubbed at his sore jaw and ran his tongue along his teeth. At least none of them were loose.

Whatever retort was on her lips died. She stared at him as if deciding what size straitjacket would fit him best. Then she shook her head and raised her brows at Lefty, letting him know her question to him hadn't been rhetorical.

Lefty pointed at Wyatt. "Fucker sent me to prison for nine years."

"You sent yourself. I'm just the one who arrested you."

Lefty harrumphed, but the flash of anger had fallen away as he reached out a hand. Wyatt shook it, pulling him in and slapping Lefty on the back in a one-arm hug. Wyatt looked the ex-burglar up and down. The man had filled out from the lanky nineteen-year-old, adding muscles from his years in the prison yard, perhaps. But he was clean-cut, with clear eyes. Must have gotten sober while on the inside. Damn if it wasn't good to see Lefty doing so well.

"Besides, if it hadn't been for me speaking up at your probation hearing," Wyatt said, "you'd still be stamping out license plates for the foreseeable future."

"I was in a mustang program. I trained wild horses. Do inmates even make license plates anymore?"

Wyatt shrugged. "Hell if I know."

"I hate to break up old home week, boys," Geneva said, emphasizing boys until the 's' buzzed in her mouth. "But—"

"Not like you don't have the time," Wyatt crossed his arms over his chest. "Your next shift isn't until—"

She turned, slowly, with her hands on her hips, her feet planted wide, and the flash of fire in her eyes tugged at his groin. He mentally sent his dick a *down boy* command.

"How do you know when I work next?"

He shrugged. "Detective," he said by way of answering.

"Ex," she threw back.

"Yeah, yeah." He frowned. "Show Lefty the key."

Geneva tugged on the chain around her neck. The key popped free from between her breasts, and Wyatt tried not to think about how close he'd come the night before to having his face planted between them.

Tried real hard.

Failed.

After all, Rodriguez had been the Boy Scout. Not him.

Maybe he needed to rethink the whole serial monogamy thing and dive into the deep end of one-night stands with his eyes open, and his arms wide. Anything to wipe away the memory of having Geneva's body in his hands. Of all the people on this earth he did *not* need to get involved with, it was Caleb Steele's widow.

Geneva handed the key over, and Lefty said, "What's this go to?"

Wyatt rubbed at his jaw again. Damn, the kid must have

been wrestling horses, not training them, to develop that kind of power. "That's what we were hoping you could tell us."

"Where did you get it?"

"It was my late husband's."

Lefty glanced at Geneva and then back at Wyatt before concentrating on the key. "Haven't seen anything quite like this. It's got a number stamped on the barrel, so I'm thinking a locker in a public space."

"Like a gym or something?" Geneva asked, turning her attention to Wyatt. "Any gyms or YMCAs around here?"

"Not with that kind of locker," Lefty said. "This thing is probably over a hundred and fifty years old. No gyms or YMCAs around here back then. Especially in these parts. You sure it goes to something, and isn't just a memento?"

"Maybe," Geneva said, sounding disheartened as Lefty handed it back. She slipped it over her head, tucking the key beneath her shirt with a frown.

"Sorry I couldn't be more help," Lefty said.

"Thanks anyway."

Lefty glanced up at Wyatt and scrutinized his face. Wyatt's jaw still throbbed, and the corner of his lip had started to swell. "Sorry about that. No hard feelings?"

"As long as you've got it all out of your system. If not, there's a boxing gym a couple of towns over," Wyatt said.

Lefty rubbed at his red knuckles and flexed and extended his fingers as if making sure everything still worked. "I'm good." Then he bobbed his chin at Wyatt's face, and he knew Lefty had shifted focus to his healing black eye. "Though maybe I could teach you how to block a blow."

"Hard to block a sucker punch."

"Ever consider another line of work?"

No. Not really. Even after the shooting, if Wyatt had had the chance to return to the department, he'd have done it in a heartbeat.

Was doing it.

There had been no question in his mind when Rodriguez had come to him with the proposal for him to work on the case that he'd do it. He'd just wanted his ex-partner, and Jed especially, to sweat it out a bit.

Wyatt wasn't sure he liked what that said about him, but he'd have time to analyze his feelings and motivations later.

Or he could hopefully just earn his old job back and finally move on with his life. Yeah. That sounded way better.

Wyatt gave Lefty a genuine smile. "It's good to see you on the outside."

They headed out the door. Wyatt was anxious to get back to Geneva's Prius. The promise of forty dollars for *not* doing their job would only hold the teens off for so long before they decided to disappear with his twenty *and* the car. Though seriously, it was a Prius. Who would want to strip that?

The kids and the car were where they'd left them. Wyatt forked over the other twenty as promised, and he and Geneva were on their way.

"Where to?" Geneva zipped under a stoplight as it slid from yellow to red, and hit a pothole in the road hard and fast enough that his head hit the roof.

"Easy now." He braced a hand on the roof. "This isn't the Indy 500."

"Sorry. I'll feel better when we get out of here and..."

He was only half-listening to her when he spotted a woman on the next corner. She was short and curvy, and just what he needed right now. "Stop."

Geneva glanced over at him, looking as if she thought he'd completely lost his mind.

"Pull over. Now."

She dove into a spot past a fire hydrant. "What?"

"That woman," Wyatt said as he popped the door release.

Geneva glanced in the passenger-side mirror at the woman they'd passed. "She's kinda hot if you're into that sort of thing," she said. "You thinking of graduating from one-night stands to sex workers?"

He sent her a baleful look. "For the record, I don't think last night counts as a one-night stand."

Before he could get the door open, there came a knock on his window. He found the button and buzzed the glass down. "Hey, what's up, Sot—"

"Sugar," the woman said, her upper lip curling up for a fraction of a second. "People call me Sugar."

Wyatt glanced around. There wasn't a soul on this block. There weren't even any cars driving by, so definitely no one to overhear him, but he appreciated the fact Sugar wanted to keep her cover.

Wyatt turned to *Sugar*, aka DEA Special Agent Maria Soto. "You got a minute?"

6

WHEN GENEVA WOKE UP THAT MORNING, NEVER IN HER WILDEST dreams had she thought she'd be picking up a hooker later that day. The woman lifted up on Geneva's rear passenger door handle. Geneva glanced at Wolfe, and he gave her a quick nod. She pressed the unlock button.

Then again, never in her wildest dreams had she thought she'd wake up in Wolfe's bed either.

Either her dreams were too tame, or her life had become too wild.

The woman slipped into the backseat, her perfume hitting Geneva like a floral slap to the face with an undertone so prickly she almost smelled the thorns.

"Drive," the woman said. "First right. Second left. Then turn in at the motel."

Yeah. Geneva's dreams were definitely too tame. What did that say about her imagination?

Geneva pulled out and followed Sugar's instructions. Sugar didn't say anything. Wyatt didn't say anything. So Geneva didn't say anything. Had Wolfe suddenly decided he had an itch that he couldn't wait to scratch?

Unlikely.

Did he know someone from back in the day that might be able to give him some information? A confidential informant?

Probably.

The whole not saying anything lasted until they'd pulled into a parking spot at the motel.

"Play along," Sugar said.

They climbed out of the car, and Sugar latched onto Wolfe on her way to open the door to her motel room. There had been some groping on Sugar's part along the way. And some kissing. With tongue. Geneva wasn't involved in the groping and the tongue, and she was happy about that.

Mostly.

Though by the spark in Sugar's eyes, maybe Geneva had missed out on something. As soon as they stumbled through the door, Sugar kicked the door closed and released Wolfe back into the wild... ehr... the room.

"Damn, Wolfe," Sugar waved a hand in front of her face as if her internal temperature had redlined. "The way you kiss, you could make a nun give up the habit. If I didn't have my sights set on someone else..." She let the rest of the sentence dangle out there between them. Naked, unafraid, and unabashed. "What's up, dude? Or are you just trying to blow my cover?"

Cover?

Wyatt winced and plopped onto the bed, his legs straddling the corner. "My bad."

Sugar flipped a hand toward Geneva. The woman didn't look pleased. "And who's this?"

"Geneva Steele," Geneva said.

Sugar shot Wolfe a look. Wolfe gave her a tight nod. When Sugar looked back at Geneva, Sugar's demeanor had changed. The irritation had drained from her body, and her dark eyes softened. The woman held out her hand to Geneva and said,

"Agent Maria Soto, DEA. I'm sorry for your loss. Steele was a good man."

Suddenly the air got too thin. Or maybe the mold spores in the dank, damp room had coated the inside of Geneva's lungs. Her breath got thick, and spots flashed in her peripheral vision. She didn't even bother clearing her throat before she spoke. "Y-you knew my husband?"

"Our paths had crossed a couple of times. A few years back when we were on a joint task force together in Rock Springs."

A softness in the agent's eyes made Geneva think that she had known her husband more than in passing. Not that Geneva suspected there was anything personal between the two, but perhaps there had been more to their undercover activities than the agent could elaborate on.

Agent Soto turned her attention back to Wolfe. "I've got johns to meet, drugs to buy, and bad guys to take down. What do you need?"

"I've got some questions about the Nightwalker murders," Wolfe said.

Agent Soto toed out of her scuffed high heels and plopped into one of the chairs at the round table under the window. She worked her thumb into her instep. "Is this official business?"

Something flicked across Wolfe's face that on Caleb would have been frustration. Wolfe released a heavy breath. "You know it isn't."

"I'm DEA. Not homicide. I'm not the one you need to talk to."

"But you're on the streets. You know the local sex workers. With three murders in this area, I'm sure there's a lot of talk."

"I haven't been undercover in this capacity for very long. A couple of months. Though, I've heard a lot of rumors. From what I've been able to determine, there are many unfounded claims and flat-out untruths. The pimps are using the murders as a scare tactic to get the independent women under their belts… so to speak."

"Anything helpful in the rumors?"

Agent Soto shrugged and glanced at Geneva then back at Wyatt as if she had something to say but wasn't comfortable saying it around her. "I can sit in the car," Geneva offered. She'd rather stay, not entirely confident Wolfe would fill her in, but she could find a way around that. The most important thing was that they got as much information as they could.

"Whatever you have to say, Soto, you can say in front of her."

Soto scrunched her face, glanced at Geneva, and said, "Some are saying there's a cover-up with the murders. That law enforcement is directly involved."

"No," Wolfe said. "I was lead on Alexa's murder. There were few leads, yes. But no cover-up."

Instead of Soto's expression relaxing with this firsthand information, Soto's eyes narrowed. "Some of the rumors say that you were involved in the cover-up."

Wolfe barked out a laugh.

"No, seriously," Soto said.

Geneva's heart skipped a beat, faltered, stuttered, and steadied out. Was that why Caleb had drawn on Wolfe? Was the man in front of her, the man who could have hurt her when he'd had the chance, a dirty cop?

She started to rethink her decision to team up with Wolfe. Was he trying to find out what she knew to see if she, too, had to be eliminated? She had no desire to be his or anyone else's next victim.

Geneva must have done a poor job of hiding her emotions because Wolfe turned his piercing gray eyes on her. "It's not true."

He seemed sincere. Very believable. But then again, if it were true, if he was part of a cover-up, it wasn't like he'd admit it in front of her and a DEA agent. But she wasn't going to sit there like a scared little rabbit and not ask questions either. "In what way is it rumored that Wolfe's involved?"

Those gray eyes didn't waver. "So now I'm 'Wolfe' again? What happened to 'Wyatt'?"

Geneva met his hard gaze straight on. "That was a mistake. I'm not here to make friends, Wolfe. I'm here for answers."

"I like this girl," Soto said. "I think you should keep her."

"I'm not his." Geneva wanted to make that *perfectly* clear. To Soto, to Wolfe.

To herself.

"In what way did you hear Wolfe was involved?" Geneva repeated.

"Nothing specific. Or actionable. If there had been, someone higher up would have taken action."

Geneva didn't know if she believed that. But Soto seemed convinced. "Or maybe," Geneva said, "someone higher up is involved, covering for him."

Wolfe scrubbed his hands down his face. His black eye had started to yellow around the edges, while the fresh bruise on his jaw continued to darken. "Even if you don't believe me, it would be nearly impossible for a massive law enforcement cover-up to remain quiet. Someone would find out. Someone would talk."

Instead of making her feel better, Wolfe's statement made her feel worse. Her stomach rolled, and acid etched a burning trail up her esophagus.

She'd felt so sick all morning between the alcohol and the Rohypnol that she'd hardly had anything to eat, but that had little to do with her nausea and everything to do with the fact that Wolfe might actually be the monster she'd originally thought him to be. "Maybe my husband tried to talk. Maybe my husband was silenced."

Wyatt had already denied any involvement in a cover-up. He refused to repeat it over and over and over again. Geneva wiped her palms on the thighs of her jeans and wouldn't look him in the eye.

What little headway he'd made in the trust department lay in shards at his feet. He figured the only thing that kept Geneva from running and getting as far away from him as possible was her determination to get to the bottom of Steele's death.

"Give me a name," Wyatt said to Soto. "Someone I can talk to." He locked eyes with Geneva. "So I can find the truth about what happened to your husband."

Soto hiked up her spandex-wrapped rack, but her breasts still threatened to spill out. As good as she looked in the dress, if you asked Wyatt, Soto pulled off the Kevlar vest and thigh holster even better.

"Desiree Sweet." Soto gave up the name at last. "I'm assuming that's her street name and not her real name."

Wyatt nodded. "I brought her into questioning. Didn't get anything out of her."

"She hangs at that biker bar outside Murdock. *Cruisers*. And I heard she rents a room at the Delight Inn in Alpine when family or friends have had enough of her and kick her off their couches."

"Delight Inn?" Geneva's brain must have re-engaged.

"Bring your HAZMAT suit if you dare. The Delight Inn makes this place look like The Ritz."

"What do you know about Desiree?" Wyatt asked.

"She's unreliable and only looks out for numero uno. Will tell you exactly what you want to hear as long as it suits her and then changes her story to fit whatever crazy-ass agenda that pops into what's left of her drug-addled brain. The DA has already lost a case she was a witness to."

Soto stood and slipped her feet into her heels. Apparently, she'd said all she was going to say. Wolfe stood, too, and held the door open for Geneva. Geneva crossed the threshold, and Soto said, "For what it's worth, Wolfe. I believe you."

His next breath came sweeter. He nodded in reply. "Appreciate that." Before he could get out the door, she whispered, "You two make sure to look extra satisfied as you leave. I have a reputation to protect."

———

WOLFE CLOSED AGENT SOTO'S MOTEL ROOM DOOR BEHIND HIM and leaned against the jamb, a strange expression on his face. Not guilt. Resignation? Like he'd already decided how Geneva felt about him and didn't think there was much he could do to change her mind. He probably wasn't entirely wrong.

"Go on," he said. "I'll have a friend come pick me up and take me home. I can tell what Sot—" He glanced around as if making sure no one was within earshot. "I can tell what Sugar said has made you uncomfortable. I can do this alone."

Were those the words of a man who meant her harm? Or was he *that* good? *Shiiit.* Geneva rubbed at her temples, trying to ease the headache that had settled somewhere behind her eyes —sharp, stabbing pains as if a miniature demon was using her optic nerve as a dartboard. Her brain told her she would be a fool to trust Wolfe. Her gut told her he was the key to the answers she sought.

The key to what she wanted most.

She opened her mouth to answer, still undecided what she was going to say when Wyatt's phone buzzed. He looked at the screen, and a crease formed between his dark brows. "I need to take this."

Wolfe didn't wait for her to respond. Instead, he answered and pressed the phone to his ear. "What's up?"

Her cue to leave. At least she would avoid the awkwardness of her telling him that he needed to call for a ride.

That's what you were going to tell him, right?

Right. And if she didn't say it aloud, then maybe she could get away with the lie.

Geneva climbed into the car, started the engine—no growl of a motor in a Prius. The car was so quiet she had to check the display panel to make sure it was on. Something she was still getting used to.

Pressing the car into reverse, she glanced at Wolfe one last time before backing. He scrubbed the fingers of his free hand through his hair, his palm cradling the back of his head. His face went slack, his eyes lost focus, and he lost two shades of color. She knew that look. She'd seen it day after day, emergency after emergency, on the faces of the people she met on the worst days of their lives.

Geneva tapped the *Park* button and scrambled out of the car.

"I'm on the way," he said, then ended the call.

"What's wrong?"

He startled as if he hadn't even realized she was still there, but then his brain must have popped the clutch and dropped into gear. He slipped his phone into his pocket. "That was Massey, my landlord's grandson. Evie was in a car accident and was life-flighted to the trauma hospital in Idaho Falls." He glanced at her car, then back at her. "Can I get a lift back to my truck?"

Like with any emergency, she shoved any thoughts for her safety aside and acted. "I'll drive you to the hospital. Your truck is in the opposite direction."

Relief flashed across his face. Wolfe gave her a curt nod of thanks and headed for the passenger seat.

They made the drive to the hospital in silence. Except for the five or six times Wolfe asked if her car could go any faster. No. No. And still no. Already she sped through the twists and turns of the mountain roads, zipping by cars and trucks, the streaming silver ribbon of guardrail flashing past like a live version of Mario Kart.

She'd always hated that game.

She'd always crashed.

Geneva eased up on the gas.

"Why are you slowing down?"

"You won't do Evie or Massey any good if I get you killed before we get there."

"Pull over. I'll drive." His right knee jackhammered, the heel of his boot tap, tap, tapping against her plastic floor mat, the worry rolling off him, wave after wave after wave.

A dark chuckle escaped her. "Not on your life."

He muttered something under his breath. Probably best she hadn't heard. Ten minutes later, she zipped beneath the covered circular drive in front of the emergency room. Wolfe popped his seatbelt and jumped out before she'd come to a complete stop.

Fifteen minutes later, after driving down row after row of the packed hospital parking lot, she found a spot. Jogging to the emergency room, the doors swished open in front of her. Almost every seat in the waiting area was taken. A baby cried. A couple of young kids sat in a corner fighting over building blocks at a play table. A triage nurse called someone back for evaluation. And Wolfe...

"I need you to take me back there. Now." Wolfe leaned over the reception desk, frustration and anger painting his complexion red. Last time Geneva had had a patient that color, he'd stroked out.

The receptionist blinked at Wolfe, her face a bland mask, waiting for him to calm down. The woman could give Job lessons on patience. Wolfe apparently wasn't the first irate person to yell at her. Probably not the first that day. Or that hour.

Geneva walked over and laid a hand on his arm. "Come on. You know she can't let you back there." He shrugged his arm free but followed her as she stepped away.

"What are you doing here?"

"I drove you, remember?"

"You don't need to stay." He turned away from her and found a seat.

Geneva crossed her arms and planted herself in front of him. He may not think he needed her, but he was wrong.

"Seriously," he said.

"Why are you trying to get rid of me?"

He didn't answer.

"If nothing else, you'll need a ride home."

He looked at her, then glanced around the waiting room, noticing the lack of seating. He stood. "Sit," he ordered.

She would have argued, but damn if the effects of the crazy night and the long day hadn't crept up on her and yanked away the last shreds of her dwindling energy. She plopped into his vacated seat, the air in the cushion whooshing out.

"Coffee?" he asked.

She blew out a breath, and some of the tension drained. "That would be—"

The double doors to the emergency hall opened, and one of the emergency room nurses strode out. *Jacob*. Geneva jumped up and grabbed Wolfe's hand and dragged him along behind her.

"Jacob!" Geneva waved at the nurse. As a paramedic, she'd brought enough patients to the trauma center that she'd gotten to know much of the staff. She pulled Jacob in for a quick hug and didn't waste any time on other pleasantries. "I need your help."

Jacob's smile faded, and his eyes went serious. "Name it."

She pulled Wolfe forward and released his hand. "My friend's landlady—"

"Evie Yates," Wolfe supplied.

"Evie Yates was recently life-flighted in. Car accident... Elk Creek?" Geneva turned to Wolfe for confirmation.

Wolfe nodded. "That's what it sounded like."

"Yeah. A bed opened up in ICU. They just sent her up. That's all I know. Wasn't my patient."

Geneva tossed Jacob an award-winning pretty-please smile. "Can you get us up there? Besides her grandson, Wolfe is all Ms. Yates has." She didn't know if it were true, but Jacob was a good egg. He'd forgive a little fibbery.

"I'd really appreciate it," Wolfe added. He didn't beg. He wasn't that type of man, but Wolfe's concern for his landlady was palpable.

And admirable.

Before she had a chance to contemplate that revelation, Jacob said, "You know this is against the regulations."

She leaned in and under her breath, said. "So was the time I..." She whispered the remainder into his ear.

"Touché." Jacob gave Geneva a sheepish smile. "Follow me."

———

ALL WYATT COULD THINK AS HE FOLLOWED THE NURSE AND Geneva down the hallway to ICU was what a lucky bastard Caleb Steele had been to marry a woman like Geneva. No matter what her conflicted opinion of him was, when he'd needed help, she hadn't hesitated to step in. That could have been the emergency responder in her, but Wyatt suspected that was who she was at the core.

And when she could have dumped him at the door of the emergency room, she hadn't. And when the opportunity came to help even more, even if it meant bending the rules, she jumped in again.

Lucky, lucky, bastard.

The ICU consisted of a nursing station with a series of beds laid out in the shape of a U around the station with divider curtains in between each bed for a modicum of privacy. The ends remained open to allow the nurses to monitor the patients. Jacob pointed. "Fourth bed on the right." He started to back out of the ICU and said, "If anyone asks who let you in, you forget my name."

"Thank you!" Geneva said. "I owe you one."

Wyatt stuck out his hand, and Jacob shook it. "Appreciate the help."

When Jacob disappeared, Wyatt stepped toward the beds. The smell of disinfectant hung like a thick fog in the air, tickling the back of his throat. He covered his mouth with the inside of his elbow and coughed. An ICU nurse brushed by, chart in hand. Various machines beep, beep, beeped—a discordant low-level cacophony that set his teeth on edge.

An alarm sounded, coming from one of the beds to their left, and several people in scrubs rushed over. His heart tripped, and his steps faltered. Geneva took his hand again and led him to Evie's bed. Massey glanced up from the chair he'd been sitting in and scrambled to his feet, his crutches catching on the chair legs. Wyatt put a hand out and steadied him before pulling him in for a hug.

A crutch hit the back of his leg as one of Massey's arms came around his waist. "Jesus, Mass." Wyatt took Massey by the shoulders and held him at arm's length. "What the hell happened?"

"A truck ran a red light, clipped the rear of our van, and spun her into oncoming traffic. The paramedics said if she'd been driving anything smaller, the crash might not have been s-survivable."

"Jesus." Wyatt didn't know what else to say. And with what felt like Evie's wrecked van sitting on his chest, it was hard enough to breathe, much less talk.

Geneva stepped up and offered her hand to Massey. "I'm Geneva Steele, I'm a fr—I'm..." She glanced at Wyatt as if not sure what to call herself. She didn't trust him, so he figured the 'friend' label didn't fit. "I'm with him. How is she?"

Massey shook Geneva's hand and turned his attention to his grandmother. "She's hanging in there."

The skin around Evie's eyes was puffy and already turning black, her nose red and bandaged. Traces of dried blood crusted around her nostrils.

She had a tube down her throat, and a ventilator forced air into her lungs with a bellows, her chest rising and falling beneath the light-weight blanket. Her heart monitor beeped. The rate seemed fast to Wyatt, but steady, as clear fluid dripped into the back of her left hand through the IV catheter.

"She couldn't breathe on her own. They're keeping her sedated, and they're taking her for an MRI shortly to evaluate her lungs and check for brain bleeds." Red rimmed Massey's glassy eyes, and his breath shuddered out then in.

"She's a tough old coot," Wyatt said. "She'll be back home, driving you batty in no time."

Massey leaned heavily on his crutches, and a sad smile flittered across his lips. "I sure as hell hope so."

"Hey, what are you two doing in here?" A heavyset nurse came up behind them, her brown hair tied back in a bun so tight it negated her need for a facelift. "Shoo." She made a waving motion with her hands.

Massey's brows went up. "Busted."

Wyatt clapped him on the shoulder. "Anything I can do for you?"

"Nothing to do now but wait. Thanks for coming. I didn't know who else to call."

"Get in touch if you need anything. I'll take care of everything at the ranch until you get back."

"Go," the nurse said, "before I kick you all out."

They left ICU. As Massey said, there wasn't much they could do, but Wyatt wouldn't have felt right not coming to check on Evie.

When they made it back to Geneva's car, he collapsed into her passenger seat and tipped his head against the headrest. Seeing Evie with his own eyes, even as beat up as she was, made it easier for him to breathe as if a wrecker had lifted that hunk of twisted metal off his chest.

Since his fallout with Day, besides Rodriguez, who was like a brother, Evie and Massey were the only other people he considered family. And if that wasn't a kick in the gut, he didn't know what was.

Geneva closed her door, shoved the fob into the dashboard slot, and pressed the start button. Something flashed on the display, but other than that, he couldn't tell it had started. Give him a good engine grumble any day. He'd gladly pay the premium for the extra gas.

She pulled out of the parking lot, and the next thing he knew, her car bumped over the cattle guard at the front of Evie's property and jerked him awake.

Geneva yawned and held a hand over her mouth as she parked beside his truck. "We're here." She glanced over at him. "Oh, you're awake."

He scrubbed a hand down his face. He couldn't believe he'd passed out like that. "Yeah, that cattle guard needs a little work."

With his head on the headrest, he popped his seatbelt and reached for the door handle, but possessed neither the strength nor the will to open it.

"You okay?" she asked.

He rolled his head to the side and looked at her. Thought a moment. In the green glow of the dash lights, she held his gaze, like she wanted to know the truth and not hear hollow platitudes.

Like she might give a damn.

He dug deep for the truth. "As long as she comes home, I will be."

"I'm sorry about earlier," she said. "I shouldn't have let what Soto said about the rumors get to me." Geneva was quiet a moment. "They *are* just rumors, aren't they?"

"It doesn't matter what I say. Words don't matter. You know nothing about me."

Her nose scrunched as if she wasn't sure how to break the bad news. "You'd be surprised what you can google."

"Does Google tell you what kind of man I am? Does it tell you about the time the sheriff pulled me off the streets as a troubled teen and made me one of his own?"

Shut up. Shut. The. Fuck. Up.

But it was as if he'd taken a pickaxe to the bottom of the Grand Coulee Dam, the gush of words too strong to stop. "Does it tell you how hard I worked to put my past behind me?" His chest tightened, and even though it took effort to talk, it didn't slow him down, it only increased his volume,. "Does it tell you how I wish every damn day that I hadn't had to take that shot?"

Different emotions flickered across Geneva's face. Surprise. Horror. Disbelief. Guilt. She sucked in a slow, thoughtful breath. Her cheeks puffed out. She held it. One heartbeat, two. She blew it out. "I didn't know."

"No. Don't look at me like that." Wyatt shook his head and

shouldered out of the car, his legs and body stiff from being folded into the front seat. She got out, too. "I'm not an injured animal you have to rescue off the street."

He couldn't look at her any longer. The pity in her eyes shone bright, even in the dark. He turned toward the dock and over his shoulder said, "Thanks for the ride."

"Wait," Geneva called out after him, but no, he couldn't wait. He needed to get on his boat. He needed to get away from her before he said anything else.

Gravel crunched beneath her shoes as she jogged up behind him. "Damn it, would you wait?"

He upped his pace, the wooden dock planks sounding hollow beneath his boots. She caught up with him. Grabbed his arm. "Wyatt, wait."

Wyatt.

He stopped. His back to her, his eyes focused on the way the moonlight knifed through the pond with Evie's dark house beyond. The 'old bat' had better fight.

"I owe you an apology."

"You owe me nothing. If you don't mind, it's been a long day." He tugged his arm free and stepped onto Sea-Celia's deck. The boat swayed beneath his feet, and the displaced water gave her hull a light slap.

He'd made it to his cabin door when he heard the *thump* behind him, and the deck swayed again. He turned. "Did you listen to your husband any better than me?"

She planted her hands on her hips. "What do you think?"

Wyatt shook his head, too tired to hold back the faint smile. "Poor bastard."

"Hey!" she said, though he caught the edge of a smile. Then she sobered and waved a hand toward the bank where she'd parked her Prius. "You can't dump all that shit in my lap and not let me respond."

"What's there to say?"

"Maybe that you're right?"

"That's not something a woman has ever told me before." He leaned against the bulkhead. "This should be good. Want a beer?"

"No. I want to say what I have to say."

He held out his hand in invitation for her to talk.

"You were right when you said words don't matter. They don't. Actions do. And so far, what I've seen is a man who is willing to drop everything to meet his friend at the hospital even though there's nothing he can do to make it any better.

"I see a man who offers to help where he can. I see a man who stores alfalfa cubes on his boat and puts a blanket on the dock, so an old cow has a soft place to lay. I see a man who, instead of getting mad, offered me a wet rag when I puked on his floor. I see a man who, like me, is searching for the truth..." Her voice quieted, and if she hadn't stepped closer, he wouldn't have heard her. "What I think I see... is *you*."

That wrecked van settled on his chest again. He swallowed hard.

"Truce?" she asked.

He reached out and cupped her cheek. He had no plan, beyond a need to touch. Her skin soft and warm against his. Then his lips brushed hers—nearly, barely, hardly there.

His body, her body, *their* bodies on autopilot as her lips parted, and she eased into him. He brushed his tongue against hers, just a taste.

His dick hardened.

Her thigh raked against the inside of his.

He pulled back, his heart *tha-da-dumping* against his sternum, in a heavy, steady rhythm settling into his bones like a good bass line you couldn't get out of your head. He traced her bottom lip with the pad of his thumb. "Truce."

7

―――――

DESPITE THE CHILLY MORNING, SWEAT DRIPPED DOWN WYATT'S spine as he stripped the shavings from the second horse stall in the barn. The horses were out in the small paddock munching on their bowls of feed. When he finished with the barn, he'd turn them out and let them roam the fifteen-acre horse pasture. With Evie in the hospital, Massey wouldn't have time to ride anytime soon.

A fine mist of sawdust clouded the air, thick with the smell of pine and urine. He dumped the last wheelbarrow of used shavings and headed back into the barn as Rodriguez pulled into the ranch. Wyatt waved, and Rodriguez drove over to the barn.

Rodriguez climbed out of the car, his badge on his belt catching the sun. He frowned at the rubber band wrapped newspaper in his right hand and tossed it to Wyatt.

This couldn't be good. Wyatt caught it and pulled the rubber band free. Above the fold on the front page was a not-so-flattering picture of Day. He'd lost weight. His hair needed a trim. And he sported a shadow of gray stubble on his usually clean-shaven face.

The headline read: *Complicit or Incompetent?* Then below that in smaller type: *A small town not-so-cozy mystery. Who is getting away with murder?*

Fuck.

"There's chum in the water, the sharks are circling, and Day just got shoved overboard." Rodriguez rubbed at the muscles at the back of his neck. "You got anything for me yet?"

"You're kidding me, right?"

Rodriguez shrugged. Wyatt re-bundled the newspaper, threw it into the empty wheelbarrow, and headed back into the barn, Rodriguez heeling like a well-trained border collie. Picking up a bag of shavings, he tossed one to Rodriguez, who caught it with a grunt. Wyatt picked up one in each hand and carried them into the stall. Rodriguez dropped the bag at his feet.

As Wyatt pulled out his pocket knife and sliced through the bag, Rodriguez said, "Day's a little anxious for results."

Anxious for results.

Wyatt's temper flared, and he threw the knife. It tumbled end over end and spudded into the bag at Rodriguez's feet. Rodriguez didn't jump. They both knew that if Wyatt had wanted to hit him with the knife, he could have.

"Maybe Jed should have thought about that before firing my ass."

"That's not fair."

Wyatt rounded on Rodriguez. "What's not fair is getting canned when the shooting was ruled justified." Wyatt tapped Rodriguez in the center of his chest with his finger.

Rodriguez's eyes went dark, and Wyatt knew, despite the slacks and the button-down dress shirt Rodriguez wore, his friend was a second away from trying to toss Wyatt on his ass.

Let him try. "What's not fair is Jed not having my back."

Rodriguez crossed his arms over his chest. Wyatt had a good

five inches and thirty pounds on him, but Rodriguez was a scrappy fucker who fought dirty. They'd been in enough scrapes as teens for Wyatt to know.

"He's under a lot of pressure."

"If you're so worried about the pressure, why don't you talk to your buddy the senator and tell him to back off?"

Rodriguez's lip curled up. "You know dealing with Lambert doesn't work that way. He's results-driven and doesn't let his foot off the gas until someone waves the checkered flag."

"Or maybe one of these days, the bastard is going to crash."

Rodriguez laughed. "You know Lambert better than that."

What was more frustrating than the fact that Lambert could use his considerable power and influence to get his way was the fact that Rodriguez was right.

Rodriguez bent over, sliced the shaving's bag open, and dumped it in the stall. A mushroom cloud of shavings dust billowed up. Wyatt coughed. Rodriguez sneezed, wiping his nose with a handkerchief from his back pocket. A *handkerchief*, seriously? Probably monogrammed— definitely a city boy.

Rodriguez sneezed again and again. Wyatt followed him out of the barn to the fresh air, walking him back to his car.

"Sweet Jesus," Rodriguez said, "What the hell are you doing mucking stalls, anyways? I thought that CP kid liked to clean them as a part of his physical therapy."

"What the fuck, Rod? The kid *has* CP. He *isn't* CP." Wyatt shook his head. Sometimes the shit that came out of Rodriguez's mouth made him sound like a cold bastard. "And the kid's name is Massey."

"I know."

"Then use it. Massey has enough going on in his life without having to deal with your shit, too."

Rodriguez raised his hands. "Ease up, man. I didn't mean anything by it. Not like I would have said it to his face."

To Wyatt, somehow, that only made what Rodriguez had said that much worse.

"What's eating you anyway?"

"Evie was in a car accident last night. She's in ICU in Idaho Falls."

"The old bat?"

"You're such an asshole sometimes." Wyatt grabbed the newspaper out of the wheelbarrow and left Rodriguez by his car. Wouldn't do Wyatt any good to be arrested for assaulting a deputy.

"What about the case?" Rodriguez called out. At least Rodriguez was smart enough not to follow Wyatt.

He didn't have the patience to tell Rodriguez about Desiree, or even Steele's journal. Besides, he didn't want anyone getting their hopes up until he had something more concrete. Turning, Wyatt said, "Tell Jed I'll send an update when I have something."

It was late afternoon the next day when Geneva parked beside Wolfe's truck and climbed out of her Prius. She double-checked her ankle holster and readjusted the leg of her jeans to make sure Caleb's old backup gun was covered. It wasn't that she didn't trust Wyatt—after staying up half the night thinking about their last kiss, it was tough to keep thinking of him as Wolfe.

Then why the gun?

Okay, so despite what she'd told Wyatt yesterday, despite the kiss, she would be stupid not to take precautions. Even though Caleb had taught her some basic self-defense, Wyatt was a big man, with his own defense training. He could no doubt over-power her if he wanted to. The gun, well, the gun tipped the scales more toward the center.

She popped her trunk and retrieved the box and headed for the dock. Off to her left, the cow with the crazy horns lifted her head, sniffing the air. A mouthful of grass stuck out on either side of her muzzle. She chewed, then returned to grazing.

"Knock, knock," Geneva called out as she approached the boat.

Wyatt ducked out of the cabin, tugging a T-shirt on over his head. It fit snug around his torso and settled around his hips. He wore athletic shorts and jogging shoes. He clipped his phone into an armband and laid the cord of his wireless earbuds around his neck.

"Sorry," she said. "Did I catch you at a bad time?"

"I've got a few minutes." He bumped his chin toward the box in her hands. "What's that?"

"The box from my closet. The one Caleb's captain brought me."

Wyatt's brows went up, and he reached out to take it from her. "What did you find?"

She hopped into the boat. "I haven't opened it yet."

"Want a beer?"

"Got anything stronger?"

"Not anymore."

"Beer it is then."

He handed her the box back and pulled a couple of iced-down beers from a cooler on the deck. "Fridge runs warm."

"Aren't you worried about food poisoning?"

He slipped the beers into a couple of koozies he had lying around. "Hasn't killed me yet."

She went to put the box on the folding table he had at the back of the boat, but files and papers and Caleb's journal covered the top, so she set the box on the deck and sat down beside it, using the bench seat as a backrest. He sat beside her, handed her a beer, and draped his arm over his bent knee.

She opened the beer and stared at the box. Was the key to Caleb's death inside that box? Had she had the answers all these months and hadn't known it? Wyatt handed her a pocket knife. It trembled in her hand.

"Want me to open it?" he asked.

"I got it." She set her beer aside and poked the tip of the blade between the cardboard flaps. Her stomach swirled, then the bottom fell out, stealing her breath with it. She panted, her breath whooshing in and out, yet none of the oxygen made it to her brain. The knife in her hand, shaking, shaking.

Wyatt's steady hand came down over hers. The ridges on the knife handle pressed against her flesh. "You've got this," he said. Then he drew their joined hands down the length of the box.

He closed and set the knife aside, and his hand came to rest on her shoulder, his thumb kneading the taut muscles in her neck. He didn't push her to go any faster than she was comfortable.

Maybe that's why she'd never opened the box. She couldn't face the task alone, and while Cassie had volunteered to help way back when, her friend would have grown impatient and tackled the box herself.

Not Wyatt.

He sipped his beer. His thumb bumping up and down three vertebrae in her neck. She reached for her beer and downed half a bottle of liquid courage. What the—*Light* beer? That wasn't going to do any good.

But the therapist she'd seen a few times after Caleb's death had explained how numbing herself with drugs and alcohol wasn't the answer. Allowing herself to feel the emotion, acknowledging it, no matter how painful, would be best.

Geneva downed the rest of the beer. What the hell did that guy know? He'd only looked about ten years old and had that spark in his eyes of someone who hadn't lost anything in his life more significant than a pet goldfish.

With trembling fingers, she opened first one flap and then the other. Blindly reaching inside, she came out with a picture frame. Her and Caleb on their honeymoon in front of Old Faithful. She ran a thumb down Caleb's face and his forced smile.

Wyatt took the picture from her and looked at the two of them. "He doesn't look very happy."

"We'd just had our first fight. I don't even remember what it was about now." They'd stayed mad through dinner and then... she smiled, and just thinking about that night made her stomach float.

"That sucks," Wyatt said.

She grinned up at him. "Not really. Caleb was the king of make-up sex."

Wyatt huffed out a laugh. "I didn't expect that to come out of your mouth, but then again, considering your track record, maybe I should have."

"Hey." She set the picture aside. "My coming on to you was part of my plan. Besides, you have to give me credit, it almost worked."

"What would you have done if I hadn't taken you home with me?" A flash of humor lit his gray eyes. "Or better yet, what if I hadn't switched the drinks?" He glanced at her lips, his thumb now tracing light circles on her arm. "Would you have taken advantage of me?"

She tucked her knees up to her chest and was about to answer him when his gaze went to her ankle. He reached over and hiked up her pant leg.

"You got a license for that?" His tone lost all its playfulness as if she'd kicked the cute puppy that just wanted to have fun.

Adrenaline dropped into her system with a sizzle, like coffee on a hot burner. Her heart skipped into a faster rhythm, and heat ran out to the tips of her fingers and back again. There was only one answer. Her mouth went dry. She could really use another beer. "You don't need one in Wyoming."

He nodded once. She hadn't told him anything he didn't already know. He sipped his beer, and she waited for him to get angry. To get indignant. Instead, what she got was an even, "You know how to use it?"

"Caleb taught me."

"What about self-defense?"

"That too."

"Good on him." Wyatt peeled back one of the box's flaps. "What else you got in there?"

Wyatt and Geneva sifted through the rest of Steele's box of stuff. A few mementos, but nothing vital to the investigation. Though with the key Geneva had around her neck, he figured if there was anything out there that Steele had found, then it was hidden behind a lock somewhere and not in a box that had been stored in the back of a closet.

The night before, Wyatt had racked his brain, trying to think of a public location with lockers as Lefty had described. But he'd come up blank.

Geneva put all of Steele's belongings back in the box. As the sun set, a chill crept into the air. Wyatt got up and turned on the deck lights. He'd have to get his run in early the next morning.

"What's this?" Geneva asked.

She stood by his make-shift desk, scanning the front page of the paper Rodriguez had brought and held it up. "Do you think there's truth to this?"

No way would he tell her how Day had wanted him to investigate the murders on his own, out of the purview of the rest of the department. If someone from law enforcement were responsible for the murders as the rumors suggested, the fewer people who know why he wanted the information, the better.

But he had a hard time lying to her.

So he answered with the truth. "I sure as hell hope not."

She went to toss the paper onto the table when the "Living" section of the paper fell out. The section with all the advice columns and recipes and other useless—

"This is it!" She held up the front page of the section in question.

The headline read: *Murdock Stagecoach Station Set for Demolition.*

"That is what?"

She yanked the old key from beneath her blue blouse. "A public station. A hundred and fifty years old. Give or take."

Wyatt snagged the paper, laid it on the table, and skimmed the article. *Ho-ly shi-it.* "That's only about twenty minutes from here."

"We need to go. Now."

"Now? It's not set for demolition for three more days. We should scope the place out. There will be fencing around it and—"

She pointed to the top right corner of the page. "This paper is from two days ago."

They needed to go. Now.

Pages and files and photographs littered the top of the table. He had just begun getting the piles to where he could make sense of them. If he picked them all up now, it would take him forever to get it back the way he wanted them. "Cover the table with the tarp." He pointed to the blue tarp folded up on the deck by the helm. "And throw the cooler on top, so everything doesn't blow away. I'll go change."

A few minutes later, he returned, tucking his Glock into the holster at his hip and settling the tail of his shirt over the top of it. It wasn't that he expected trouble. It was that after so many years as a law enforcement officer, an LEO, he didn't feel right without it.

He grabbed his wallet and his keys. "I'm driving."

Unlike before, she didn't hesitate or argue. By the time they drove out to the old stagecoach station in Murdock, darkness had settled except for the glow of the nearly full moon behind a gray cloud. It was the type of spooky, bright moon you'd want for a Halloween night. But when you were trying to sneak around and go unnoticed, it wasn't ideal.

He pulled into a parking space on the far side of Murdock's community park away from the stagecoach station. They got out and kept to the gravel path amongst the towering ponderosa pines. Where there were large gaps in the trees, they held hands like a couple enjoying a nighttime stroll.

At the site, they skirted around the perimeter of the demolition fence. Wyatt counted two armed guards on opposite sides of the site. The pucker factor ratcheted up a notch.

"Guards?" Geneva whispered. "Who would want to go in there anyway?"

He leaned over and whispered in her ear. "You mean besides us?"

She gave him one of those that's-beside-the-point faces. The face nearly identical to the one his father used to give him when Wyatt told him they needed to spend what little money they had on food, not booze.

Her hand dampened in his, and her breathing shallowed out. "I guess they don't want any of the preservationists sneaking in and chaining themselves to the building like the article talked about."

"If you're nervous about getting caught, you can wait in the truck."

"Nervous?" She stifled a laugh, but he heard the strain in her voice. "After the felony I tried to commit the other night, what's a little trespassing added on?"

Despite the fact he could be minutes away from getting arrested, he smiled. Rodriguez would laugh his ass off if Wyatt got caught. Day would bolt the metaphorical door he'd already slammed in Wyatt's face. But if that building held information they could use in the investigation, he wouldn't allow a wrecking ball to bury it.

"That's my girl," he said.

She stiffened.

"Sorry. I didn't mean... you're not... that was a figure of speech. I—"

She placed a hand on his chest. It shut him up. "It's all right. Caleb used to—" She dropped her hand and her gaze, then glanced back up, with glassy eyes and a tumultuous smile. "It's fine."

Shit. Shit. Shit.

After he yanked his size eleven boot out of his mouth, they sneaked through the trees until they came to an area where the fencing skirted the tree line. He held on to Geneva's hand to make sure she didn't fall behind.

Is that the only reason?

Maybe not, but he didn't have time to do a deep dive into his motivations.

Approaching from the tree line remained their best bet for a concealed entry. It was also where the company had skimped on the quality of the fence and, more importantly, their quality of assembly. One of the poles of the chain link had been cemented into a five-gallon bucket.

All he'd have to do was shift the bucket until there was a gap large enough for them to slip through. He shifted the bucket, and the chain links rattled, making a racket that echoed through the quiet night.

A flashlight clicked on, and Wyatt shoved Geneva behind some brush. They peeked through the branches as a guard waved the light over the fence. From the direction the guard had come from, he wouldn't notice the gap unless he came to investigate.

"Crap," Geneva hissed. "He's coming closer."

Wyatt shifted his weight. His boot slipped on a rock. Then a cat screeched and darted out from the bushes beside them. It bolted for the chain link, tried to scale it, fell, tried again. Fell. The chain link scraping and rattling and drawing the attention of the other guard.

"What's over there?" the second guard asked.

The first guard clicked off his flashlight. "Fucking cat scared the piss out of me."

The second guard laughed. "Pussy."

The first guard playfully shoved his colleague as they turned and walked the other way.

Wyatt dropped to his knees. "That was close." Geneva glanced over at him, a massive grin on her face. What the—?

"But fun."

Wyatt shook his head. "I think that roofie did something to your brain. You're not quite right."

She swatted him on the bicep and jerked her chin toward the fence. "Go. Before they decide to come back."

He stood and placed her hand against his lower back. "I want to feel your hand there the entire time. I don't want to have to take my eyes off where we're going to make sure I don't lose you."

"Got it. I'll be harder to shake than the plague."

She... she was having *fun*. Definitely drug-addled.

They moved from the tree line, through the gap in the fence, to the cover of a metal dumpster then to a mountain of construction debris. Wyatt climbed onto the platform that hadn't had any steps for as long as he could remember. He held out his hand and helped Geneva up.

With his back to the outside wall of the station, he reached out and wrapped his fingers around a doorknob. It rattled but didn't turn. Locked. Figured.

He peered through the window in the door and saw straight through the building. The two guards sat out front on a couple of tree stumps, passing a cigarette between them.

With the moon to Wyatt and Geneva's back, if they made it inside the building and the guards looked over, he and Geneva would be silhouetted by the moonlight. He could already hear Rodriguez's amused cackle in his ears as Wyatt got arrested. Fucker.

Crouching down, they skirted across the back of the building to where one of the window panes had been broken out. With the impending demolition, no one had bothered boarding it up with plywood.

He stepped over the sill, his boots crunching on the glass underfoot. Geneva climbed in after him, only taking her hand off of him long enough to get through.

From where they stood, the guards couldn't see them, which also meant they couldn't see the guards. Wyatt didn't like the idea that the guards could come from behind and discover them. The skin between his shoulder blades itched, much like it had the night he'd seen Steele scuffle with the man in the suit.

Geneva ran her hand over the bank of locker doors beside them, many of them with their keys still in the lock. She blew out a breath of amazement. This could be the right place.

"What was the number on the key?" he whispered.

"One hundred and fifteen."

"One what?"

"One fifteen." Geneva sucked in a breath and slapped a hand over her mouth.

"What's wrong?"

"One fifteen. January fifteenth. Our w-wedding day."

Jesus. Wyatt reached out and pulled her against him, wrapping her in his arms. She tucked her face against his chest and shuddered.

He pressed a kiss to the top of her head. She smelled of pine and clear skies and something vibrant. Something that spoke to him on a base level.

She swiped a hand across her cheek and sniffed. "Sorry," she mumbled as she stepped away.

He squeezed her hand but didn't let go. "Let's see what old Caleb saved for you. What do you say?"

She nodded, swiped at her face again, taking in a cleansing breath. They worked their way from one bank of lockers to the next, the numbers increasing, but not fast enough.

They came to the end of the bank of lockers. A wide hallway linked the front of the building to the rear and separated the banks of lockers. There was no way to get to the other side without passing through the middle.

The middle that had a straight shot view to the guards.

The middle that creaked with each step they took.

The middle that had holes in the floor where the rain from the caved-in roof had poured in year after year after year.

Wyatt stole a glance at the guards. Then they tiptoed across the hall as fast as they could. What boards that didn't grunt and groan under their weight felt soft underfoot, the wood fibers rotten. He angled his feet so that they fell across the width of several boards instead of lining up along the length of one to help distribute his weight.

They made it across without being seen, then Wyatt's foot hit a bad board, and it broke with a silence-shattering crack. They froze, the lockers plastered against their backs.

As long as the guards didn't walk too far to one side and get the angle on them, they wouldn't be seen.

Two flashlights clicked on, the beams of light scanning through the building and over the wood floor. Back and forth. Back. Back. Then the lights shined on the ceiling. Where was that old tomcat when they needed him?

The flashlights clicked off, pitching them back into near darkness.

Geneva wasn't smiling anymore.

———

GENEVA'S EYES READJUSTED TO THE DARKNESS INSIDE THE OLD stagecoach station. Wyatt's lips moved, but blood whooshed past her ears louder than Tower Falls during the spring runoff, and she couldn't hear what he said.

Instead of talking louder, he leaned closer. "Let's find that locker and get the hell out of here."

He'd get no argument from her. She turned and scanned the bank of lockers, but the way the moon shone, she had to brush her fingers over the raised locker numbers and read them like braille.

The locker in front of her was 114. She moved her hand down one, her finger tracing over the one, the one, and the five. The *whoosh* behind her eardrums got louder, and her pulse kicked at her temples. "Got it."

Wyatt moved beside her as she pulled the necklace over her head. She fumbled with the key a few times. Wyatt didn't say anything, but the hurry-the-hell-up vibe radiating off him worsened her fumbling.

She slapped the key into his hand. "You do it."

In Wyatt's steady hands, the key slid straight in and, after a turn, the locker opened. She reached inside. The lockers were surprisingly large. Probably would hold a couple backpacks or a small suitcase, but all this one held was a thumb drive.

"That's it?" Wyatt asked.

She handed it to him. "Yes."

He reached in and checked for himself. "Nothing."

Like I said. Geneva would have rolled her eyes, but it was dark, and they didn't have that kind of time to waste. She pulled the key from the lock and slipped it over her head.

Glass crunched behind them. She froze. Wyatt spun and reached a hand to his hip, and she knew he'd put a palm on his gun.

Before she could turn, a man said, "Hands where we can see them."

The blood rushing behind her ears went silent. Had her heart stopped? Every creak of the floorboards, every tinkle of the glass, seemed amplified. Was that Wyatt's heart she heard pounding?

Wait. No. That was hers. It hadn't stopped after all.

She raised her hands. More crunching. The second guard must have stepped over the sill. In her peripheral vision, Wyatt raised his hands and slid one step, then two, away from her.

"Stop right there," the first guard said. "Lady, turn around."

"Do what he says." Wyatt's firm, calm tone said he had control, not the guards.

Geneva turned.

The two guards stepped closer, weapons drawn, the glass crunching under their feet until they'd stepped clear of the broken window. The guard nearest to them was bald and built. The other guy was just as big, but his belly was about three fast-food trips away from spilling over his belt. The gun shook in his hand.

This wasn't Shit Creek. This was Shit River. As long and wide as the Amazon.

Then Geneva threw her head back and laughed, grabbing her stomach for dramatic effect. She sneaked a glance at Wyatt. His jaw had gone slack, and he clearly thought she'd lost her mind. Maybe she had. But if she didn't do something, they'd both be arrested.

Baldy stepped closer, Belly glanced from her to Baldy and back again.

"Oh, wow." Geneva slapped a hand to her chest as if she were trying to catch her breath. "For a second there, I thought you two were real."

Belly lowered his gun.

Baldy didn't. "Miss, you need to keep your hands raised where I can see them."

"Wow, these guys are good. They don't even break character." She turned to Wyatt and said, "Oh, honey, this is the best prank our friends have ever played."

"Sweetheart, this is no prank." Wyatt's voice held a warning, but there was something in the way he looked at her that told her he was up to speed on her plan. "I told you this was a bad idea."

"Wait," Geneva looked at Wyatt then back at Baldy. "You two aren't actors?"

Baldy shook his head but holstered his gun. He thumbed a mic pinned at his shoulder. "Dispatch, this is A one-five, we have a—"

"No, no, no," Geneva held out her hands in front of her. "This is all a big misunderstanding. Please. We'll leave. It was all supposed to be part of the scavenger hunt."

His radio squawked. "Dispatch. Repeat."

Geneva stepped closer to Baldy with her hands clasped to

her chest as if she were pleading. "Please, please, please. This wasn't how this was supposed to go. We'll leave."

Belly chose that moment to speak. "What kind of scavenger hunt?"

Geneva stepped over to Wyatt and gripped his hand. He was playing along, but he still had a bit of a what-the-fuck face going on. "For our engagement party." She glanced up at Wyatt. "Show them, honey."

Wyatt held out the thumb drive. Wiggled his hand so they could see.

"Dispatch to A one-five," the radio squawked, "Repeat."

Baldy thumbed the mic again. "A one-five, cancel the call, dispatch." Baldy let his thumb off the mic, and to her and Wyatt said, "For the moment. Talk."

"Our friends are throwing us an engagement party, and they hid this thumb drive and said if we didn't find it and return to the party in two hours, they would release a copy of the contents on social media." Geneva scrunched up her face to show how bad that would be. "I don't want my mom to see that."

"What is it?" Belly asked. Baldy cut him a look, but he must have been curious enough himself because he turned his attention back to her and waited for her answer.

"Uh..." She drew a blank, glanced over her shoulder at Wyatt in a panic.

Wyatt cleared his throat. "It's a sex tape."

Brilliant. "Of us. With a... uh... *friend.*" Geneva said. "So, you can see why we wouldn't want it released, even if it is pretty hot."

"How do we know you're telling the truth?" Belly said.

Wyatt shook his head and added a pretty convincing self-deprecating chuckle. "Because you can't make this shit up." He stepped forward and held out the thumb drive. "But if you want to see for yourself, go ahead."

Belly brightened, almost eager. Probably the kind of guy

who had all of the free porn websites bookmarked on his browser bar. He reached for the thumb drive, but Baldy batted his hand away. "We don't have a computer."

"The audio might still play if you have a USB slot in the car stereo." Geneva took it from Wyatt and held it out to Baldy. "Of course, it will just be the sounds of, you know, grunts and groans and—"

"And screams," Wyatt added.

So helpful.

In a bad stage whisper Wyatt said to Belly, "She's a screamer. Loud, but…"

She whacked Wyatt on the arm. "I'm *not* a screamer."

"We can place bets, let these guys listen and be the judge." He turned his attention back to the guards. "What do you say, boys?"

"How much time do we have left, honey?" Geneva asked.

Wyatt pressed a button on his watch. The face lit. "Twenty minutes."

Geneva hissed in a breath as if that wasn't a very long time. "Where's your patrol car, we can—"

"Go," Baldy said. "Get out of here."

Geneva screeched and clapped her hands with joy. She wasn't acting. "You two are the best sports." She grabbed Wyatt's hand and pulled him toward the window. "Come on, honey, if we run, we can just make it in time."

They passed both of the guards. Baldy's hands on his hips as he watched them leave. Any second, Geneva feared he'd change his mind. Belly just had one of those blank expressions on his face like his frontal lobe had been zapped and was waiting for it to reboot.

They'd made it through the broken window when Baldy said, "Lady, you have some fucked up friends."

Geneva grinned back at him. "I know. Aren't they the best?"

8

———

In Geneva's den, Wyatt sank onto the couch beside her. It was one of those butter-soft leather couches that once you sat down, you never wanted to crawl out of again.

Or maybe that was his fatigue talking, grumbling, complaining. He definitely needed to get some sleep or lay off the adrenaline spikes for a day or so.

Her laptop sat on the coffee table at his feet, an audio file cued up. But for some reason, neither one had hit play yet.

"I could sleep for a week." Geneva was sitting in the corner of the couch, shoes off, her legs tucked beneath her, a cup of decaf in her hand. She held her hand out in front of him. It shook as if she were going through detox. "I can't stop shaking."

"It's the adrenaline."

"Let me see your hands."

He laid his mug on the coffee table and held out both of his hands. Steady. Maybe he should have been a surgeon. Probably less blood and guts and gore than homicide.

"Caleb was like that," she said. "Cool under pressure. I guess you would have to be to work undercover."

"It's not for everyone," Wyatt allowed. "But from what I've

heard, your husb—" Why was it so hard for him to call Steele by his first name?

Because then it's real.

And *personal.*

"From what I've heard, *Caleb* had been very good at his job," Wyatt said. "Got a lot of bad guys off our streets. But yeah, not everyone could have done his job. Takes a special kind of person to live a double life and not take the bad home to bed with him."

"How do you know he didn't?"

Something he felt more than knew. Wyatt shrugged, but by the way her brows rose, the question hadn't been rhetorical. He searched for the words for something he couldn't explain. "I see it in your eyes and the way you look at the world. You've been through a lot, lost a lot, but you aren't jaded or cynical. You still believe in right. You still believe in justice."

"You don't think we'll get to the truth." Her voice came out small, and it wasn't a question.

"I think there's a good chance we won't. It's already been a long time. Memories fade. People have a way of moving away or disappearing."

Her hesitant smile came out sincere. "Thank you."

"For what?"

"For being honest. For not telling me what you think I wanted to hear. But most of all, thank you for talking about Caleb. People are afraid to bring him up. Afraid it will remind me."

She took a sip of her coffee, then rested the side of her head on her hand on the back of the couch. "But the reality is, I don't have to be reminded. Every fiber, every cell, every atom of my being is acutely aware he's gone. But at least if people talk about him, I know he's not forgotten."

"Trust me." Wyatt held her gaze. As much as killing Steele twisted his guts and made his days long and his nights even longer, he couldn't hide this simple truth from her. "I'll never forget."

For several long seconds, Geneva refused to look away. Felt like minutes. Then something shifted in her eyes. A spark that hadn't been there before.

"I'm a screamer, huh?"

It took Wyatt a second to catch on, the same way it had back at the stagecoach station. But Wyatt was quick on the uptake, especially if it helped him jump out of the emotional fire. She was so damn strong.

Wyatt chuckled, shaking his head. "You just look like the type is all."

"Screamers are a type?" Her lips scrunched, fighting the smile. She sat up straighter. "This ought to be good. Enlighten me, detective."

This can not end well. "You're a very determined, passionate woman. It's the passionate ones, the fiery ones, who tend to be more vocal."

"Complaint?"

"Observation."

"This from the man who hasn't gotten laid in—"

He cut her a look, all fine-honed, serrated edges. "What do you know about my sex life?"

"Google." She set her mug on the coffee table, but Wyatt saw the move as an excuse to break eye contact. "We talked about that already."

She got up, and he caught her wrist and sat her back down. "Google my ass. Spill."

"*Shit.*"

Uh-huh. Geneva still looked like she wanted to bolt, so Wyatt kept a tight grip on her wrist. Her pulse thumped beneath his fingertips.

"I may or may not have been watching you for a bit."

"A bit?"

"A while."

He narrowed his eyes.

She blew out an exasperated breath. "Months. Went to the bars, watched. Many prospective women, many practically throwing themselves at you. But you always left alone."

Jesus Christ. He dropped her arm and stood, stepping away and then came back. "Do you always stalk men?"

She stood. "Not *men*. You."

"Why?"

"I—" She closed her mouth. Opened it. Closed it. "I might have been a little obsessed with the man who'd killed my husband. I wanted to know everything about you. So I followed and watched and researched. In my mind, you were the key to finding out more about Caleb's death."

She backed away, putting the couch between her and him. "And if there had been a way to find new evidence that would have gotten you recharged in the shooting, I would have."

The air in Geneva's house clogged his lungs—stuffy, old, unbreathable. He wanted to throw open every window, throw open every door, or run out the back and straight up the side of the Rockies, to the crisp, clean air, someplace, somewhere, he could take a long, deep breath and finally breathe again. "Dangerous game. I could have been—"

"You could have been what? A killer?"

He had no response for that.

"I knew what I was getting myself into, what you were." She paused and deflated. "At least I thought I did."

Hands on his hips, he stood straighter, ready for her to shoot him with both barrels. "And what am I?"

"Not at all what I'd expected." The way she said it made it sound like a good thing, yet she almost seemed saddened by the realization. She offered a tight, apologetic smile and ducked her head.

He came around the couch, tipped her chin up so he could see her face. Her frizzled hair stuck out from her head from their escapades earlier that night, smudges darkened the skin under her eyes, and a hollowness lay beneath her cheeks. When was the last time she'd had anything to eat? Hell, when was the last time *he'd* had anything to eat?

"And tonight? When you told that cockamamie story about a scavenger hunt, did you know what you were getting yourself into then?"

"That story saved our asses. What were you going to do? Shoot your way out?"

She had one of those *Ah-hah!* gleams in her eyes, as if she knew that had been precisely what he'd been thinking. He might have thought it—didn't mean he would have done it. No, if she hadn't come up with that story, they would probably be cooling their heels in a cell down at the Sheriff's Office. *Still.*

"That was stupid," he said. "And riveting and reckless and..."

"And?"

He glanced at her lips, brushed his thumb over her chin and along the edge of her jaw. "And hot as hell."

Like the other times he'd kissed her, he shoved all thoughts of her husband from his mind. He didn't need the reminder that if he hadn't taken that shot, he wouldn't be standing there in her living room, kissing her, tasting her.

Her hand came up to his chest. She didn't push him away. Instead, she fisted her hand in his shirt and stood on her toes, taking the kiss deeper. He slid his hands down her arms, then dropped them to her hips, his erection pressing against his zipper, against her.

If he felt so damn guilty, why couldn't he stop?

He laughed at himself. Maybe for the same reason Vegas

would never run short of gamblers, drug dealers and sex workers would never be out of a job, and the prisons would never be empty—just because something made you *feel* guilty, didn't mean you didn't do it anyway.

The house phone rang and rang, but he angled his head and took the kiss deeper. He pressed her back against the couch, one firm, sleek thigh locked between his. A click. The answering machine picked up.

You've reached the Steele residence...

Geneva froze. The voice echoed through the kitchen. A strong voice. A protective voice.

Her husband's voice.

She broke the kiss but didn't move away. Wyatt wrapped his arms around her shoulders, placed a chaste kiss at her temple, then rested his forehead against hers.

She didn't deny the attraction. She didn't come out and say kissing Wyatt was wrong. But the way she sagged against him, kissing him, being with him, wasn't easy either.

Cassie left a message for Geneva to call. When she'd hung up, the near silence drifted on and on. A car door slammed outside. One of the fluorescent fixtures in her kitchen buzzed. Her breath became, jagged and ragged and raw.

He tucked her under his arm and led her toward the kitchen. "Come on," he said, "let's get some food in you before you collapse."

"I'm not hungry."

"You need to eat."

He pulled out one of the kitchen chairs and sat her in it. She had goosebumps on her arms, so he filled another coffee cup and set it in front of her, though he suspected her chill came from so deep inside, the coffee could never touch it.

He made quick work of dinner. Amazed at how much easier it was to prepare a meal when you had more than a square foot of counter space. In no time, he plunked down a bowl of chicken noodle soup fresh from a can and a grilled cheese sandwich in front of her.

He commandeered the chair across from her and tucked into his food. She ate in silence, but the important thing was that she ate. All of it.

When she'd slurped the last noodle, and had eaten the grilled cheese down to the crust, she pushed the bowl and plate away. "That was probably the best grilled cheese I've ever had. What's the secret?"

"Feeding a half-starved woman. I could have soaked alfalfa cubes in water, and you would have thought it was good."

The tension around her eyes eased, and her cheeks rounded with her smile. "Thanks."

"It wasn't entirely altruistic." He picked up their dishes and loaded them in the dishwasher before turning back to her. "Alfalfa cubes were starting to sound good to me, too." He walked around the table and held his hand out to her. "You ready to see what's on the thumb drive?"

She took his hand. "Lead the way."

———

WITH HER FREE HAND, GENEVA REACHED OVER AND PRESSED PLAY on her laptop. She sat on the edge of the couch, her other hand still in Wyatt's, not knowing what she'd hear in the audio file. The cheese from the sandwich curdled in her belly. Nausea swirled, and saliva pooled in her mouth. She swallowed hard, trying to keep everything down.

As the audio started to play, hisses and pops came through the speakers as well as road noise from cars driving by, the giggles and shouts of children playing, the hollow bounce of a basketball, the clunk and metallic swish of a chain-link basketball net. It felt as if they were sitting in a park somewhere watching the world go by.

Wyatt extracted her hand from his, shook the blood back into his fingers and folded her hand between his palms.

"Look, Desiree, word on the street is you know something about the murders." Caleb. The quality of the recording was muffled and scratchy as if Caleb had had the recording device in his pocket, and it had recorded the scrape and rub of his clothes as he moved. But Geneva would recognize her husband's voice anywhere.

"What do you care anyway? You a cop or somethin'?" a woman said, her voice thick and raspy as if she needed a good cough to clear her throat.

"Do I look like a cop?" He hadn't. When he'd gone undercover, Caleb had let his hair and beard grow long and scraggly. Pierced one of his ears. He'd bought his wardrobe from the second-hand store and would wear the same shirt and jeans a few days in a row. He'd get mad when Geneva got tired of the funk and stink and washed his clothes. *"Alexa was one of my best girls."*

"There are more girls where she came from."

"Not that can make me the money she did." The voice was Caleb's, but that cold, callous tone was not her husband. Caleb had been warm and generous and—

"All I know is you talk, you the next one they find dead."

"You be my girl. I can protect you."

"You can't protect me from the cops."

"I know people. You tell me what you know. I get them, and you got nothin' to worry about."

The recording whirred on. A car honked. A mother yelled at her kid. Geneva leaned forward, straining to hear.

Wyatt placed a hand on her shoulder and gave her neck a gentle squeeze. "Breathe, Gen."

She blew out her breath and sucked in another and another until the dots disappeared from her vision.

"There's two more who's seen it. Two more that's gonna get themselves killed if people talk. I'm not talkin'. Whorin's not an easy life, but that don't mean I wanna die. You can't protect me from these people. They're too powerful, and the cops are just their mad dogs they keep on a chain."

"Are you one of them who's seen it for themselves?"

There was a long pause. More scraping and scuffling as Caleb shifted. A dog barked, and a kid laughed.

"What do you know about bad cops?" Caleb changed his tactic.

"I know they take advantage. Wheneva they can. That detective, Wolfe, he pulled me in. Said he wanted to ask me about Alexa. She's the first who got herself killed. When I tell him I know nothing, he grabs me here and here..."

There was no indication where 'here and here' were on her body, but by her tone, she wasn't talking about her hands. Geneva's stomach took the express elevator to the basement. Wyatt stopped touching her, resting his forearms on his knees, leaning forward as if he got close enough he could see what was happening.

"I'm a whore. I ain't sayin' I'm not. But that don't give him no right to touch me there. But he's got the power."

"You report it?" Caleb sounded less like a pimp and more like a cop, but Desiree didn't seem to notice.

"Who you gonna report it to when Wolfe's the sheriff's pet?"

"Hey, woman," another man's voice. Loud, angry. *"What you doin' talking to him? You think he goin' ta treat you betta than me?"*

Desiree said something unintelligible. Caleb cussed, then the recording went silent. They searched, but there were no other recordings on the thumb drive.

Geneva scooted over one cushion, putting distance between her and Wyatt. "That true? What Desiree said?"

Wyatt didn't pretend not to know what she was asking. His head hung between his shoulders, and for a moment, he looked… defeated. When he glanced up, his gray eyes had darkened to charcoal, then to flint. "I interviewed her. I never touched her." His gaze didn't waver.

Truth or practiced lie?

He didn't elaborate. He also didn't beg or plead for her to believe him. He let his words sit out there. Stark. Naked. Powerful in their brevity. Then he stood and smiled, but it was rueful and wry. "All interviews are videoed. I could prove it to you if I still had carte blanche access to the investigation."

Deseree's claim didn't fit with the description of the man in front of Geneva. This was a man who didn't push when she'd backed away after he'd kissed her. This was a man who could have taken advantage of her when she'd drugged herself. Instead, he'd tucked her into bed and slept out under the stars.

Was that the kind of man who would inappropriately touch a woman he was interviewing, especially when all interviews were videoed?

"You know what? It's getting late. I think I should leave." He grabbed his keys off the coffee table and headed for her door. He had it partway open when she caught up to him.

"Wyatt, wait."

He stopped but didn't turn to look at her. The muscle in his jaw working double overtime.

She wanted to tell him she believed him, but her hesitation had hurt him, saying so now would make her seem insincere, so instead, she said, "My car. It's still at your place."

WYATT PULLED UP BESIDE GENEVA'S PRIUS AND SHIFTED HIS TRUCK into park, still stewing. *What do you expect? You killed her husband for Christ's sake. That automatically dumps you down to the bottom of the* Most Trustworthy People List *right there.*

"Wyatt." Her voice came out quiet. He knew what she was going to say. Didn't want to hear it. "I believe you."

Mostly. He could still hear the hint of doubt in her voice. She *wanted* to believe him. He believed *that.* "Save it, Gen." He popped the latch on his door and shouldered his way out.

She scrambled out her side. "I don't think you're that kind of man."

"Maybe," he said. "But it took you a while to figure it out."

"That's not fair."

Wyatt came up short. Her distrust was valid. Didn't make it hurt any less. "You're right." He rubbed the tight muscles at the back of his neck. "That wasn't fair. Life's not fair." Then he looked her in the eye, his throat tight when he said, "But I suppose you know that already."

"Clearly." For a moment, she looked at him like all she wanted to do was step into his arms, to find some kind of comfort from someone. *Anyone.* Instead, she wrapped her arms around herself. "When do you want to talk to Desiree? That's the next step, isn't it?"

"It's late. We both could use the sleep. We can talk about this in the morning."

She started backing toward her car. "You're taking me with you." Part question, part statement.

"Probably better if I go alone."

"Desiree already doesn't trust you. She may be more willing to talk if I'm there."

He hated to concede the point, but Geneva was probably right. He backed toward the dock, unwilling to make any promises that he couldn't keep. "I'll call you."

Wyatt hit the dock and glanced over at Evie's house. The lights remained off, no van in the driveway because the wrecker had hauled it away from the accident. He pulled his cell phone from his pocket and dialed Massey to check on Evie. The call went straight to voicemail, so he left a message to call back.

He detoured to the barn as Geneva's taillights bumped over the cattle guard and turned back toward town. The horses were off in the big pasture, their heads popping up when he turned on the barn lights. That-A-Way was nowhere around, so he bypassed the alfalfa bin. He checked the water trough and called it good.

Thirty minutes later, he was showered and laying in the front berth, a cool breeze blowing through the open hatch. Crickets did their thing, That-A-Way moo-ed, and somewhere far off a pack of coyotes yipped and yodeled. He pounded his pillow into shape and shifted to his side, the boat rocking gently beneath him.

Closing his eyes, he tried to put the day behind him. They'd made some progress on the case—maybe not progress, but they'd found a couple of promising leads. Priority number one in the morning was tracking down Desiree. She hadn't admitted to Steele that she'd witnessed anything that would put her in danger, but her silence had been telling.

He understood her reluctance to talk, but the reality was if Desiree had seen something, telling Wyatt what she knew could save a life.

Could save *her* life.

He burrowed his head into his pillow, and Geneva's scent wafted up. She'd been right there. In his bed. Lithe and lean and —a heaviness settled in his groin, and he groaned in frustration.

No point in wanting what he couldn't have.

Then why do you keep kissing her?

Good question. The honest answer, the only answer, was because he could.

Because she let him.

Because he wanted her.

And it had nothing to do with his recent rash of celibacy that she was kind enough to point out to him. Well, maybe a little, but if all he'd wanted was a warm body in his bed, he could have had his pick long ago.

He laid there for fifteen long, interminable minutes. He knew that because he had a direct line of sight to the clock in the galley mounted to the right of the cabin door. The second-hand tick, tick, ticking away, the swing of the arm slow and steady.

Wyatt sat up. If he couldn't sleep, he might as well work the case. A drop of water hit his head. Then another. Rain pattered on his deck, on the bow. A breeze kicked up, and Wyatt closed the forward hatch and made a beeline for his improvised desk at the stern.

The tarp should keep the papers dry, but with the wind, he wasn't willing to take any chances. He threw on some shorts and barefooted it outside. Between the tarp and the papers, he had a fight getting everything inside without losing anything over the side.

Finally, he stacked the papers on his too small kitchen table and wrestled the tarp into roughly a square shape and tucked it away beneath the helm. The breeze kept the mosquitoes down, so he left his cabin door open and set to work.

Because the papers were now in a disorganized stack on his table, he took out Steele's journal and tried to make sense of it.

The next hour sped by in a blur of dates and initials. Some numbers Wyatt figured were dollar amounts. But the shitter of it was, he had no way of telling if they pertained to Steele's under-cover case or what Steele had been investigating alongside what had turned into the Nightwalker murders.

His eyes kept returning to the words *pack leader*. No doubt in Wyatt's mind, Steele had been referring to him. But why? Had

Steele suspected Wyatt's involvement because of how slowly the case had progressed?

And that line on the page, *tapes to pack leader*, followed by the word *mistake*. Had he been referring to the audio file on the thumb drive? Had Steele sent Wyatt a copy? He racked his brain. If they'd received anything pertinent, it would have been listed as evidence.

He grabbed a stack of the police reports and went searching for the evidence list. After thirty frustrating minutes of sifting through pages of reports, he'd found the list. But no listing for any kind of audio or video existed, so whatever Caleb and sent into the investigation wasn't officially in the police files. He continued looking through all the documents Rodreguez had supplied him, branching out into the Internal Affairs, IA, investigation into his shooting of Steele. On that evidence list, the only recordings mentioned was the security footage pulled from the bank across the street from where Steele had been shot.

But he hadn't seen that footage.

He'd already been placed on administrative leave by the time that video had been obtained.

Wyatt plucked a lukewarm beer out of his cooler. All the ice had melted. He popped the top anyway. Took a sip. Wretched. Spat it out.

Fuck.

He shook the beer off his hands, pulled off his shirt and dried the paperwork, the seat, the floor, then tossed the shirt onto the wet deck and let the rain take care of the rest.

He needed answers, not more questions.

Picking up his cell phone, he punched Rodriguez's number from his favorites list. His list of one.

Wyatt had deleted Day's number months ago.

He put his phone on speaker and reached into his refrigerator for a bottle of water. Not much colder than the beer had been. Maybe Geneva had a point about setting himself up for food poisoning.

The phone rang and rang as he scanned the food in his fridge. A half-used bottle of mustard and some lunch meat and cheese with mold. He tossed the meat and the cheese and left the mustard.

Ring, ring. Where the hell was Ro—

"What the ever-loving fuck, Wolfe? It's one in the morning." Rodriguez's breath came in quick pants, and Wyatt heard a woman complaining on the other end. "Can't this wait until morning?"

"Quick question."

"Hang on, baby." That, Wolfe figured, was not directed at him. "Don't you ever sleep?" *That*, Wolfe decided, was.

Not for a long time now. "Did you take in any tapes, disks, or thumb drives related to the Nightwalker murders?"

Wyatt heard a door closing, muffling the woman's voice. Rodriguez said, "What did you find?"

"Geneva found her husband's journal and—"

"Geneva, is it?" The smile in Rodriguez's voice grated Wyatt's nerves.

It isn't like that. Well, it *was*. But no, it really wasn't. And if it was, he wouldn't tell Rodriguez, even if they were best friends.

"That's her name." Wyatt rubbed his forehead, at the headache that had crept in with the uncertainty and fatigue. "Steele's journal indicates he might have sent tapes to the investigation."

The other end of the line went eerily quiet. Wyatt glanced down at his phone's display, but the connection hadn't dropped. "Rod?"

"Yeah." Rodriguez's sigh carried over the line. "Yeah. He'd sent a thumb drive of a recorded conversation."

Wyatt stopped rubbing his temples. Not wonder why Steele

had triple underlined the word 'mistake' in his journal. Steele had thought Wyatt had received it and buried it. "Why didn't you tell me? I was the lead fucking investigator. That was my case. And why isn't it in the evidence log?"

"Whoa, whoa, whoa. Slow down, hoss."

Wyatt paced the length of his galley. Three steps up. Three steps back. "When did you get it?"

"About a week before…"

…you killed Steele. Rodriguez didn't need to say it.

"That was that day you were out, helping that CP—"

Wyatt snarled.

"That day you were helping Massey move back in with his grandmother."

"That still doesn't explain why you didn't tell me." Wyatt's patience stretched to the max. Taut. Ready to snap.

"I didn't tell you because it didn't contain any significant information. And it…"

"And it what?"

"It implicated you for sexual harassment during an interview following Alexa Martinez's murder."

"Let me guess. Desiree."

Again, the silence. "How did you know?"

"Doesn't matter. What did you do with it?"

The silence dragged on. "Look, Wy—"

"That was *evidence.*" Rodriguez had disappeared it. As much as Wyatt knew the sky was blue, he knew Rodriguez had tampered with evidence. A tiny hole opened up in Wyatt's chest. A small rent. A tear. So much for Rodriguez being the perfect Boy Scout.

"Fuck, Wyatt. If anyone else had taken in that thumb drive and listened to it, you could have been brought up on charges." Rodriguez spoke in a gruff whisper as if trying not to be overheard. "I did it to *protect* you."

"I don't need protection, Rod, not then. Not now. I didn't sexually harass Desiree. You can pull up my interview video and see for yourself."

"I did. Or at least I tried. Buddy, that video isn't there."

What the hell was going on at the station? "What about the evidence log?"

"The log is there. The video is gone. Without it, it's a he said, she said kind of deal. I was going to tell you, then the shooting happened, and you were off the case and under the magnifying glass. At that point, it could have only hurt you."

"What if what she says is true? What if someone higher up is covering up the murder?"

"You don't really believe that, do you?"

Wyatt didn't know what to believe anymore. "The video is missing. Something is going on."

"Misfiled or misplaced tapes are a far cry from a cover-up."

"Don't forget the drugs running out of the evidence room. I doubt there's a connection, but either way, problems in the evidence room can have far-reaching consequences to all of the cases."

"You don't think I know that?"

"You need to tell Jed about the thumb drive. First thing in the morning."

"Are you fucking nuts? Your ass is already in a sling."

"Maybe, but it would be better if he heard it from us than someone else, or God forbid, an investigator from Internal Affairs."

Rodriguez grumbled, but Wyatt took that to mean it would get done. Rodriguez would get a slap on the wrist, but probably not much more as long as IA didn't get involved.

Wyatt stepped out onto the deck, under the protection of his hardtop. The rain had turned to mist, and the wind gusted and blew the moisture against him, dampening his skin. But he was too pissed for it to chill him. "What about Desiree? What did she have to say when you talked to her?"

"I didn't. If there wasn't a thumb drive, then there's no connection to her. No reason to question her."

"But there was a thumb drive. *And* a reason to question her. What if something she knows could have solved the case?"

"She's an addict and a whore. With a reputation of saying anything to the cops that she thinks they want to hear."

"Desiree had no clue Steele was a cop. For all she knew, he was a pimp, like he'd pretended to be." Wyatt really couldn't believe this conversation. *I did it to protect you.* Rodriguez was loyal. Wyatt would give him that, but a line had been crossed. "Rodriguez, you messed up."

Rodriguez blew out a long breath. "Yeah. I get that now. Give me a couple of days. I'll get it cleaned up with Day."

"You don't, buddy, I will."

———

Geneva's head knocked against the driver's side window of her Prius, knocking her awake. *Ouch.* She rubbed at her temple and glanced at the clock on her dash. One-twenty-one in the morning.

Maybe Wyatt had gone to bed.

After leaving his place, she'd waited about twenty minutes before she drove back by and parked down the road in the drive to someone's lower field. She had a perfect, unobstructed view of his boat. He hadn't budged since she'd left, although a light glowed in his cabin. Her head fell forward, and she shook herself awake.

Sleep. She needed sleep. As she reached to press the start button, she caught a flash of light out of the corner of her eye. Headlights. *Where are you going, Wyatt?*

She started her car, waited for him to pull onto the main road, and followed with her headlights off. The moon cast just enough light that she could make out the reflective stripes down the center of the road, and Wyatt's truck illuminated the way ahead of them. Like the other times, if her luck held, he wouldn't notice her following him.

She followed him into Alpine. She'd finally had to slow down on the windy roads and turn her headlights on to keep from driving off the side of the road or crash into the foothills. Up ahead, Wyatt pulled into the parking lot of the Delight Inn. The motel Agent Soto had told them Desiree liked to hole up.

She drove past the motel's reception and parked along the street. For a count of thirty, she closed her eyes and waited until she figured Wyatt had had time to climb out of his truck and head into the motel's office. She didn't want him to see her until the last second and give him a chance to try and talk her into going home. Though the thought of climbing into her bed, even if it was without Caleb, sounded glorious right then.

Knock, knock, knock.

Geneva slapped a hand over her mouth to stifle the scream, her heart rate spiking as the whoosh of blood poured past her eardrums.

She buzzed her window down. "You scared the h—"

"What are you doing here?" He placed his hands on her door sill, the blood blanching from his fingertips.

"Same thing you are."

One finger tapped the sill. His expression stuck somewhere between I-should-give-you-a-spanking and Lord-give-me-strength. Not one of his more flattering faces. And that vessel pulsing at the base of his throat couldn't be good.

She opened the door and buzzed her window up, careful to lock the door behind her. This road wasn't Stripper Street, but

Stripper Street's slightly more upscale kissing cousin. Emphasis on the slightly.

"You said you wouldn't go without me."

"*You* said not to go without you. *I* said I'd call you in the morning."

She glared at him. He crossed his arms and glared back. The mist fell, dampening her clothes. "We going to stand out here and argue all night, or are we gonna find some answers?"

His expression didn't shift much. Just when Geneva thought he would choose 'argue,' he said, "Come on, we haven't got all night."

Clasping a hand around her bicep, he led her back to his truck, yanked open the driver's side door, and handed her inside. She scooted across the bench seat, making room for him. He climbed in after her and eased the door closed, his irritation filling the space between them.

The parking lot was less than a third full. Wyatt had reversed into a spot on the last row, between a work truck and a panel van, away from the yellowed street light. Through the rain-spotted windshield, they had a view of the entire row of rooms.

The Delight Inn might have been something special in the early sixties, but over the years, it had lost most of its charm and all of its polish. Two stories tall. Fifteen rooms wide. Bars on the open windows. No air conditioning.

A soda machine flickered at the end of the row near the door to the office. Geneva half expected the machine to blink off, and Jason and Freddy to walk out, all masked up and weapons at the ready.

She still had her gun strapped to her ankle but wasn't convinced she could use it on anything but a paper target. "You brought your gun, right?"

He gave her an even look. "I left it on the boat. I figured

Desiree would be jumpy enough with me knocking on her door without going in there armed."

"That's why I wanted to come with you. So she wouldn't be so scared."

Wyatt sighed. It was one of those you-have-a-point sighs.

"Which room is hers?" Wyatt changed the subject.

Okay. She'd bite. Wyatt's dash clock said it was two in the morning, so still working hours for a sex worker, she figured. She scanned the rooms. Three rooms had lights on. One on the second floor. Two on the first—one in the middle, one on the end.

"That one." Geneva pointed to the one on the end on the first floor. "Two cars out front, hers and a john's. Windows closed, where the others are open." She cut him a sly look. "Maybe she's a screamer."

He huffed out a laugh, and the tension inside the truck ramped down from DEFCON 1. The way his features softened when he looked at her, she might have even moved down a spot on his Shit List.

"Bingo," Wyatt said, with a bump of his chin toward the room in question.

The motel room door opened, and a man stumbled out, threading his belt through the loops of his pants. A woman leaned her shoulder against the jamb, her head resting against the wood. A thin negligee brushed her legs mid-thigh. She had a full figure with long dark hair in a braid that snaked over her shoulder and down to her waist. She toyed with the bound end.

"You sure that's her?"

"Positive." Wyatt popped his door as the john climbed into his car and backed out of his slot. Geneva's door was too close to the van beside her, so she slipped out Wyatt's side.

He jogged over to Desiree's door, and Geneva ran after him, wiping her sweaty palms on her jeans, her sneakers slapped against the wet asphalt. Wyatt knocked like the big bad wolf coming to huff and puff and blow the door down.

The door swung open and banged against the opposite wall. "I told you I ain't your—"

Wyatt caught the door on the backswing, one massive paw on the meat of the door. Desiree swallowed the rest of her tirade, frozen by Wyatt's carnivorous stare.

She choked, then found her voice. "*You.*" She grabbed for the door, but Wyatt shoved his way past her, and Geneva followed in his tracks, closing the door with the heel of her shoe so Desiree couldn't escape.

Musk and body odor skunked the stuffy room like biological napalm. Geneva almost gagged.

Desiree backed away, knocking a lamp off the waist-high dresser. The bed caught her on the backside of her knees, and she collapsed onto the mattress. Her negligee rode up. She didn't bother to tug it down.

Wyatt picked up the lamp with slow, deliberate movements, and set it back to rights as if his composure was as thin as cheap veneer. Then he focused on Desiree. "Why did you accuse me of sexual harassment?"

9

____

WHY DID YOU ACCUSE ME OF SEXUAL HARASSMENT? WYATT'S question echoed in his mind as he grabbed a pair of gold-colored pants and a blue sequined top off the floor and tossed them to Desiree. "Get dressed."

This wasn't how he'd wanted this talk to go. He'd wanted to be calm, to earn Desiree's trust, maybe find some common ground so that he could get her to open up to him. But something snapped when he'd seen her, and instead, the question had shot from his mouth, and he couldn't take it back.

Which didn't make any sense, because, in truth, he hadn't been all that worried about the accusation. He hadn't done it, and if someone looked hard enough, he felt confident the interview video with Desiree would be found and prove the accusation unfounded.

But it was all about perception.

Besides Rodriguez, nobody knew Desiree had accused him.

Geneva knows.

And there lay Wyatt's answer.

A radioactive truth bomb he feared setting off. After years and years of not giving a damn what anyone thought of him besides Day and Rodriguez, another person's opinion of him mattered.

Geneva's opinion mattered.

A lot.

"You can't take me in. You ain't no cop no more."

Good news travels. "I'm not taking you in. We want—"

Jesus Christ. Wyatt turned his back as Desiree stripped out of the negligee and put on her clothes. He stared at the grimey wall. "We just want to talk."

A few moments later, she said, "You can turn around. What's the matter, you ain't never seen no naked woman before?"

At the moment, there was only one woman he wished to see naked. He glanced at Geneva and the tips of his ears heated.

To Geneva, Desiree said, "Sister, you need to take your man and—

"Answer the question."

Geneva's face flushed, the embarrassment settling into her cheeks—a sexy, spicy red.

A heaviness settled in his groin, and he tore his gaze from her and filed his body's reaction under *Things Not To Think About While Conducting Interviews.* He leaned back against the rickety motel room dresser and crossed his arms over his chest.

Geneva stood near the door. Partly as a physical barrier to the outside, but by the way her face had squished up as she'd entered the room, mostly he figured she feared letting anything in the room touch her.

As it was, the grimy, threadbare carpet and the pervasive stench of unwashed bodies and stale sex made his nose wrinkle and his skin crawl. If he hadn't been concerned people might overhear their conversation, he would have opened the window.

"It don't matter. Nobody there gonna listen to no whore anyways."

"Meaning?"

"That you and everyone like you look out for your own first. Problem? It ain't our concern. Complaint? File away. We's just gonna throw it away anyway. Cop do something wrong? We gonna cover it up."

"The Sheriff's Office is there to help you," Geneva said.

"The sheriff's there to help *you*." Desiree said the word *you* the way most people spit out a cuss word. "You and your privileged, skinny white ass."

Geneva huffed out an exasperated breath. "You're white, too."

"But—" Desiree waved both hands down her body from head to toe. "I ain't privileged. Unless you call fucking and sucking cock for a living a privilege."

"You're wrong." Wyatt wrestled for control of the conversation. "You make an accusation like that, it gets tossed to the sheriff, and to Internal Affairs."

Only as he said those words, he knew *he* was wrong. She'd made the accusation. Even if she hadn't known Steele was a cop when she'd said it, Steele had turned in the recording. Yet the accusation never made it to Day.

Or IA.

The accusation had stopped at Rodriguez.

I was protecting you.

Jesus Christ, the dumb ass. Wyatt hadn't needed Rodriguez's misguided protection. He hadn't done anything wrong.

But that only begged the question. How many times had something like that happened before? How many times had one of his colleagues done what Rodriguez had, what they thought was right to protect their partner? Or someone else in the department? What lengths would someone go to? Misfile reports? Steal evidence from the evidence room?

Cover up a murder?

No, someone had misplaced the video of his interview with

Desiree. He could hardly believe anything else. Besides, stealing that interview tape could only hurt Wyatt. Not help him. But even if the video had been taken or destroyed, covering up a murder was a long, long, *long* way from a little evidence tampering.

"If I make that complaint, the next thing I know, I'd be gettin' busted every time I step out on a corner." Desiree picked at her long, flashy red nails. She didn't have much of a drawl, but her cadence put her growing up south of the bible belt. Alabama or Mississippi, perhaps. "A workin' girl ain't got no time for that. Besides, I never woulda said nothin' if I'd known that man was a cop."

Desiree fell silent. Wyatt glanced at Geneva, who covered a yawn with her hand. Yeah. It was way past time to wrap this up. The accusation wasn't what he'd come here to talk about anyway.

"It was a shame." Desiree looked at Geneva. "When I'd heard."

"That he was killed?" The words sounded hollow as they fell from Geneva's mouth.

Desiree cut a scathing look at Wyatt. "That he was a cop."

Right before his eyes, Geneva deflated. One second she was three dimensional. The next... flat.

"Treated his women right. I thought about switchin' and goin' with him and then..." She shrugged like it didn't matter. That *Steele* hadn't mattered. "I shoulda known somethin' was up. Ain't no pimp 'round here treat their women that nice."

They were getting nowhere fast, so Wyatt came out and asked what he wanted to know. "What do you know about the Nightwalker murders?"

"Just as much as anyone. Word on the street, some suit gets his kinks strangling women, and then one time it goes too far, and the cops cover it up."

Kinks? Word on the street or firsthand information?

He looked at Desiree. *Really* looked at her. With her fair complexion, she might actually be a blond, but with the fine lines around her eyes, the bottle brunette might have been covering up some gray. She was large breasted, with a belly pooch and full hips—Marilyn Monroe plus an extra ten pounds, and minus all the glamour.

The Nightwalker victims had all been different races. The first, Alexa Martinez, had been Hispanic. The second woman, black. The third, caucasian. They had all known each other. But the other thing they had in common was their body type—all full-figured women with more curves than a road through a mountain pass.

Did the killer have a thing for full-figured women?

"Why do you keep saying cover-up?" Wyatt asked.

"No arrests. When there be that many witnesses and—"

"You were there." His statement made the most sense.

"N-no," Desiree shook her head and scooted farther away on the bed. "I's—"

"We can help you," Geneva dropped to her knees at the foot of the bed, and took Desiree's shaking hands in hers. "The sheriff can protect you."

Geneva glanced over her shoulder at Wyatt for confirmation.

He kept his voice low, shooting for a soothing and trustworthy tone. "Desiree, tell us what happened. I'll find a way to keep you safe, even if I have to guard you myself."

He meant every word. If there was a bad cop or cops out there, he'd find a way to take him or them down.

Tears brimmed in Desiree's eyes, and she swiped them away. "There's this man. He likes lots of women at one time. Like an orgy, but he's the only guy there. Likes curvy women. Always curvy. But he has a kinda straight kink if ya know what I mean."

Wyatt had no freaking idea what she was talking about. By

the *say-what?* expression on Geneva's face, she was lost, too. "Enlighten us."

"No blowjobs. No oral sex of any kind. On him or on the women. And only vanilla sex."

"Vanilla sex?" Geneva's voice went up in pitch.

"Missionary position. Always."

"I see the straight. I don't see the kink," Wyatt said.

"He's into breathplay. He likes to choke you out, watch you turn blue. Only way he gets off."

"You let him choke you?" Geneva couldn't hide her surprise.

"He pays extra," Desiree said as if that explained it all.

Sick bastard. "That night. What happened?"

"Most girls wake up in a few seconds or a minute. Only this time, Alexa didn't wake up."

"This guy have a name?"

"Not that we know. We always just called him The Suit, cuz that's what he always wears. Expensive ones, too. He don't even take them off for sex, he unzips and—" She made a thrusting motion with her hand.

"Would you recognize him if you saw a picture?"

"He always wore a mask."

Of course, he did.

"Besides, when you're high, you don't notice the little things if you know what I mean."

"How many witnesses?"

"Five of us. Two now."

By *us*, he assumed she meant sex workers. "Anyone else?"

"The Suit's driver. He picks us up, drops us back off... after. Don't know his name, neither."

"He wear a mask, too?" Wyatt tried hard to bank his building frustration and keep it out of his voice. It wasn't Desiree's fault The Suit was extremely cautious.

"No, but we only saw his eyes in the rearview."

Geneva got up off her knees and braved sitting on the side of the bed next to Desiree. Geneva may have to burn those clothes later. "Where did he take you?"

"Somewhere in the mountains. There was this cabin, but I don't know where. The driver would pick us up in this panel van off the corner of Twisted Pine and Eighth in Murdock. No seats, no windows. All we could see out of the windshield had been trees and more trees."

An eyewitness that saw nothing. This perp was smart. "How long of a drive out of Murdock?"

"I wasn't lookin' at my watch."

Wyatt pinched the bridge of his nose. "Hazard a guess."

"Fifteen minutes, maybe twenty."

"Would you recognize The Suit's voice?"

She shrugged. "It was like most other voices, but he'd talk down to us like we was no better than a stray dog. Like we was lucky he fucked us."

"Bastard," Geneva ground out.

"Maybe," Desiree said, "But like I said. He paid well." Desiree stood as if concluding the interview. "We done here?"

Wyatt stood. "One last thing. Who else was with you that night?"

Desiree hesitated. "I guess it doesn't matter much, no one seen her in months." Desiree's voice lost all emotion, like someone who'd given up. "She probably dead like the others, only no one's found the body. Girl that goes by the name of Candy Lane."

Wyatt reached into his wallet and started to pull out some twenties, but Desiree refused the money. "I don't want your money. I want you to catch this guy, so I don't have to look over my shoulder every day of my life. This life is hard enough without havin' to worry about that."

He didn't know where he could stash Desiree on his boat,

but he wanted her safe. "Then come with me, until we can get protection arranged."

Desiree scoffed. "And stay where? On your boat?"

"How did you—"

"There's only one person in these parts who lives on a boat on a pond. That's you. Everybody knows it."

"She could stay at my house."

"Nuh-uh," Desiree said. "I got appointments tonight I can't afford to miss."

"Hang tight, then," Wyatt said. "As soon as I can arrange protection, we'll come back for you."

She laughed. It was short and sad. "Good luck," she said. "Most like, I'm already dead."

———

Wyatt followed Geneva home and waited until she'd made it safely inside before making the ten-minute drive to Evie's ranch in six.

Being sleep-deprived, he had difficulty wrapping his head around what he'd learned tonight. The first order of business was catching up with Rodriguez and getting protection for Desiree. The second was sleep—wait that was the first. The third... something niggled in the back of his brain, but the fogginess in his head obscured it. He needed sleep and lots of it.

He pulled into Evie's drive, and Massey's horses came galloping up to greet him, stopping shy of the cattle guard. Wyatt groaned. Had he forgotten to lock one of the gates? He checked his phone for messages. And why the hell hadn't Massey called or texted him back?

He parked and climbed out. The horses surrounded him, looking for a handout. That-A-Way let out a muffled moo, and Wyatt glanced toward the pond and...

His boat.

He shoo-ed the horses away and jogged down the dock. His boat had drifted to the middle of the pond. He inspected the dock lines by the light of his phone—their ends neatly cut.

The hair rose on the back of Wyatt's neck, and cold fingers of dread skittered up his spine.

Fuck.

He glanced longingly at Massey's house, at the spare bed he knew was there, but he didn't have a key. Someone had always been home in the past. Reaching down, he sloshed his hand through the water and cursed under his breath.

Not ice water, but damn close since the pond was spring fed.

Before he went to retrieve his boat, he put the horses up. Fortunately, no fences were down. Only a gate had been opened. Back at the dock, he hesitated before stripping down to his boxer-briefs and diving in at a shallow angle since the pond wasn't very deep.

He came up, gasping for breath. *Ho-ly shiiit* that water was cold! With long, fluid strokes, he swam for the bow rope, and then he tied the frayed end back on itself, forming a loop he could put over one shoulder and swim it back to the dock. He quickly scribbled *repair engine* on his long mental list of things Sea-Celia needed to have fixed. Before, it hadn't seemed like a priority.

He kicked and stroked, and stroked and kicked. His breath coming fast and hard, yet the dock only seemed to be getting farther away. Finally, like an underpowered freight train, he slowly gathered momentum. His muscles burned, and he gulped water a few times, coughing and sputtering and wheezing.

Then his foot touched ground, landing in a patch of pondweeds and slippery muck that squished between his toes. *Perfect.* This night couldn't possibly get any better.

Step by frigid step, he hauled Sea-Celia toward the dock, his teeth chattering despite the physical effort. He placed his palms on the dock and tried to haul himself up, his triceps burning. He fell on one elbow but caught himself, throwing a leg over and pulling himself up.

Wyatt rolled onto his back, water cascading off of his body, his chest heaving, his breath coming in large, gulps. A shiver overtook him, and his cold, lactic acid filled muscles started to cramp.

Rolling to his stomach, he gathered his legs beneath him and stood, his quads quaking and his arms shaking.

He tied up his boat the best he could with what remained of the dock lines, then jumped on board—*Ouch!* His foot landed on something sharp, and he stumbled to his knees, the scent of stale beer slapping him in the face.

Biceps quivering, he sat on his haunches. The folding deck chairs and table were twisted and broke. The top ripped off his cooler, bottled water, and punctured cans of beer littered the deck.

He crawled over the mess and flicked on the cabin lights, but nothing happened—his battery must be drained. He reached into the glovebox in the console by the helm, pulled out a flashlight and turned it on.

Inside the cabin, he flashed the light around. His stomach twisted into a square knot. The cabin's interior made the deck look ready for a *Boating World* photoshoot.

Someone had gutted his cushions, as well as his mattress, which now filled the floor space in the galley, mustard smeared all over it. His table had been set upside down on his stove and partially burned. Probably the only thing that had kept his entire boat from going up in flames was the fact he'd neglected to refill his propane tank.

Every nook, every cranny, every shelf and cupboard, and

cubby had been emptied and the contents thrown around. His port side window—busted. Stepping down, he squished in water from the shower that had been left to run. The paperwork from the cases strewn everywhere, mixed in with his soaking wet clothes.

He clambered over the debris and made his way to the berth. Putting the flashlight in his mouth, he pulled off the top leading to the hidden storage where he'd stashed Steele's journal. His frigid fingers fumbled with the secret catch, then popped it open. Steele's journal lay there, unharmed. He closed his eyes and ran his hand over the leather cover, his knotted stomach loosening a fraction.

This wasn't just Steele's journal or potential leads.

This was Geneva's connection to her husband. Something that spoke to her from beyond the grave—and she'd entrusted it to him.

Tucking the journal under his arm, he maneuvered through the galley, back out onto the deck, then onto the dock. He stripped off his wet underwear, tugged his dry clothes over his damp skin, and headed for his truck.

He drove through the tiny town of Elk Creek, fully intending to drive into Murdock and find a hotel for the night, but at the flashing red light by the diner, his truck turned left on its own accord, and he found himself in front of Geneva's house not long after.

He threw the truck into park, his diesel chug, chugging at idle. What a fucking mess. He scrubbed his hands over his face, and his lids scratched over his dry eyes like eighty-grit sandpaper. He needed sleep but somehow needed Geneva more. Not just her body. *Her.*

Why?

Hell if he knew.

But wanting her wasn't fair to her. Was their attraction

mutual? He'd have to say yes. That didn't mean they should act on it. And despite her attraction to him, he was also aware of the way she looked at him sometimes, as if she couldn't reconcile him with the man she'd built up in her mind.

And late at night, he often wondered which he was, the man or the monster.

Probably best for both of them that he kept as much distance between them as possible. He reached for the shifter as Geneva's porch light kicked on.

———

HEADLIGHTS FLASHED ACROSS GENEVA'S FRONT WINDOW AS SHE sat in the dark on her couch, a pillow in her lap, a light blanket around her shoulders. As much as she'd wanted—needed—sleep, it refused to come.

The heavy chug of a diesel engine vibrated her front window. She waited for it to pass. When it didn't, she padded over to her front door and peered through one of the sidelights. *Wyatt.*

He sat staring out his front windshield, scrubbing his hands over his face. The street light a few houses away cast a soft light into his cab. He looked so... so... *lost.*

Like you.

Wyatt reached forward like he was going to shift into gear and leave. For reasons she couldn't or wouldn't try to explain, she didn't want him to go. She turned on the front porch light.

Is this what you want? You'll only open yourself up for more hurt. Do you expect to gain something fulfilling from the person who—

She squeezed her temples with the heels of her hands. She wasn't looking for a happily ever after. Those were fairy tales. She wasn't even looking for a relationship. All she wanted was to feel connected to life again. Maybe Wyatt was, too. And maybe between her grief and his guilt, they could help each other find the people they used to be before a bad decision, and a 7.5-gram piece of lead had wrecked that for the both of them.

She opened the front door and stepped onto the porch.

He killed the engine and stared at her through his window. She waited for a count of twenty, but he didn't move.

She went back inside, leaving the door open—a silent invitation into her home.

Into her life.

A minute or so later, there came a soft knock on her open door.

"Come in." She climbed off the couch and met him in the entryway.

He closed the door behind him and leaned against it, Caleb's journal in his hand. The porch light shining through the side windows cast his face in shadows. But even then, the exhaustion sat heavy on his features as if life had knocked him back, and it was taking all of his sapped strength not to collapse.

Taking his hand, she led him to the couch, turned on the floor lamp, and sat on the coffee table across from him. Pale-faced, his eyes unfocused, his hair damp, his feet bare. "Evie?"

He shook his head.

"Then what's wrong?"

He blew out a long breath and told her. About the horses being let out, about the cold swim, about someone ransacking his boat.

"Who would have done that?" she asked.

"No idea. But according to Desiree, everyone knows where I live. So that narrows it down." He added a hefty helping of sarcasm at the end.

"Did you report it?"

"I will. Nothing that can't wait until morning, though. I just…

I just need to get some rest." He glanced around. Saw her pillow and her blanket on the couch. "Couldn't sleep?"

She shook her head. "Sometimes, I lay in my bed, and I think I can still smell him. Sometimes it's comforting. Sometimes it's confining. Sometimes..." She shrugged. Sometimes the grief grew all too consuming.

He reached out, and she let him pull her to the couch beside him. He settled into the corner and tucked her under his arm, snugging her against him. As she rested her head on his shoulder, the irony wasn't lost on her that she was drawing comfort from the man who'd caused all her pain.

Maybe not all.

He killed—

He killed a man who'd drawn on him.

Still.

A man who damn well knew better.

The tight constriction around her heart eased, allowing a frisson of anger to slip in. Anger at Caleb. Anger at her husband's culpability in his own death. Why? Why had Caleb drawn on Wyatt? "Can I ask you a question?"

Wyatt clipped off the light and kissed the top of her head. "Get some sleep, Gen. You can ask me whatever you want in the morning."

Morning came too quick. The light skirted around the shades. Geneva shifted, pushing up from the couch—

"*Oomph*," Wyatt grunted and clasped his hand around her wrist, lifting the pressure off his abdomen.

She sank back against him. "Sorry."

Trapped between the back of the couch and his body, her legs entwined with his, his arm around her back, she had no way out. She put a hand to his ribs and rocked him. "Come on, time to get up."

"Don't wanna," he grumbled, but he opened his eyes and gazed down at her. "Did you sleep well?"

"Yeah. You?"

"Yeah," he said, almost sounding surprised, "I did."

"Are you going to get up?"

He threw his free arm over his eyes to block out the light. "Let's lay here a few more minutes. The day's not going anywhere."

No. It wasn't. Geneva snuggled against Wyatt and closed her eyes, sinking into his warmth. He hadn't showered after he'd come over the night before, and she caught a musty whiff of pond water on his skin.

Wyatt's finger found bare skin, and he traced lazy circles on her hip beneath her nightshirt. She shifted again, her thigh brushing against his erection.

He stiffened, and his finger stilled. "Sorry, don't mind that... it's..."

She chuckled. "It's okay. I've lived with a man. I know that morning chub doesn't necessarily mean anything."

He lifted his arm, uncovering his eyes, and looked down at her. His hand moved from her hip and spanned her lower back. "Not always, but sometimes... other times..."

His gaze heated and slipped down to her lips.

"Other times, what?"

He shifted her until she lay on top of him, their bodies aligned, his 'other times' pressed snuggly against her lower abdomen. Blood pooled at her core, and she welcomed the old familiar heaviness of arousal.

"Other times—" His voice had gone gruff, like ground glass and granite. "It means *I want you*."

Goosebumps ghosted up her arms. It had been a long time

since anyone had wanted her. Not that she'd been ready to be intimate with anyone before now. Caleb's death had sent her into the no-fly-zone for relationships, that barren wasteland where even when the time seemed right, few prospective men dared enter.

Except Wyatt.

She pressed a kiss to his lips, then nipped his chin, his jaw. He tilted his head back, giving her access to the tender flesh of his neck. His whiskers pricked her skin, and his hands roamed over her back and buttocks. Then he held tight and ground against her.

Her heart rate climbed up desire's steep ramp—a slow, insidious chug, building heat, building speed, building excitement.

With his hands on her ribs, he shifted her higher, until their faces were level, deepening the kiss, his thumbs tracing the soft curve beneath each breast.

With a grunt, and a fast move, he reversed their positions, and he lay partially above her on the couch, resting his weight on his arms.

He settled between her legs, his erection tight against the thin cotton of her sleep shorts. She pressed against him, feeling free and wanton and wanted. Shifting his weight to one arm, he traced a finger over the lettering on her shirt. *Boston*. His finger followed each letter, over the humps and bumps of her breasts, over the sensitive tips of her nipples, and the deep valley in between.

"You a Sox fan?"

She almost said yes, but she didn't want to lie to Wyatt, even a white one. With Caleb's death between them, it seemed imperative that she tell the truth. "Caleb was."

The light in Wyatt's eyes dimmed, and he rubbed a hand over her heart and pressed a kiss there. Her throat clogged, and her breath caught.

She appreciated Wyatt's humanity. His willingness to dive in, to embrace and acknowledge what hurt her the most, and not turn his back and pretend the pain didn't exist.

Then the shine returned, and his lips twitched with mischievous intent. "Think we can ditch the shirt?"

No doubt, he wanted to see her bare, but in his gray eyes, she saw the other question he posed. Could she let Caleb go for this moment so that nothing marred the space between them?

No guilt.

No grief.

No ghosts.

She nodded her head and swallowed the lump in her throat. She could do that. For *this* moment.

Sitting up, he relieved her of her shirt. She lay back down, and he ran his fingers across her collarbone, to the dip at the base of her neck, down, down, between her breasts, his fingers separating, then cupping her.

Geneva arched into his hand, and he sucked in a breath. He squeezed and kneaded, and lowered his head, tongue lashing out. Need flashed and sparked, sending tingling tendrils down her arms and legs until they ricocheted back and gathered low in her belly.

She struggled with his shirt until he grabbed the back of it with one hand and yanked it over his head and slung it against the wall. She ruffled her fingers through the smattering of hair on his chest, over the slabs of muscle, the rippled ridges of his abdominal muscles that quivered beneath her touch.

He took her mouth with his, and she parted her lips, another open invitation. He didn't bust in and claim the homestead like she thought he would. Instead, he came and went, little tastes, little tries.

Sampling.

Savoring.

She had other ideas. Starting with his cock in her hand and then...

Geneva fumbled with the button on his jeans. His breathing kicked up a notch, and he broke the kiss and started working his way from the corner of her mouth, to the edge of her jaw, to nibble the tender flap of her earlobe, his hand caressing her breast, teasing the nipple taut.

"Finally," she said as his button popped free. She made quick work of the zipper. His erection sprang free, into her hand and...

"Holy moly," she managed as she wrapped her fingers around his thickness, "I never took you as the type to go commando."

Wyatt chuckled, the sound vibrating in her chest, and dampening her panties. "Out of necessity, not choice. I promise."

From base to tip, she gave him one long stroke. He made a sound in the back of his throat, part growl, part howl, all feral.

His hand locked on her wrist. "Are you sure you know what you're doing?"

She served up a saucy smile. "If you have to ask that, then maybe I'm not doing it right."

Have you thought this step through? That's what he'd *really* asked.

She hadn't.

Didn't want to.

This morning, this *minute*, all she wanted was to feel something other than grief and frustration and sadness and anger and pain. Would she regret it when they finished?

Only one way to find out.

She nipped at his chin on the downward stroke, his whiskers clicking lightly against her teeth. He stilled. His breath shallow, his eyes closed tight against the pleasure. Then she brushed her thumb over his slit, the slick pre-cum moistening her skin.

He hissed in a breath, "No, you're definitely doing it right."

But instead of thrusting into her hand, he rolled away.

"Hey, where are you—"

He stood and grabbed the waistband of her sleep shorts, and stripped them off her body. His jeans went flying next, her eyes darting between his legs a second before he dropped down on his knees.

He didn't touch her at first, his gaze embarking on a long, slow, sensuous journey from the tip of her head to the bottom of her toes. Everywhere his eyes lingered, her skin heated. From her nipples to her navel to her—

She slapped her hands over her pubic area.

His brows furrowed. "What's wrong?"

"I haven't shaved down there since..." She winced at how long it had been. When had she started letting herself go? Points for her for remembering to shave her underarms and legs the day before. "It's been a while. Obviously." She started to sit up. "Maybe this isn't such a good—"

He planted a hand in the middle of her chest and laid her back down. "Move your hands."

When she didn't comply, he moved them for her, then spanned his hand across her, running his fingers through the soft hair. "Do you think that because you haven't shaved down there that that's going to make me not want to touch you, to taste you?"

Heat gathered beneath his hand, and her cheeks caught fire. "It's a little wild and woolly down there."

"Sweetheart, I've always liked my sex a little on the wild side."

Her heart rate kicked up, not in fear, in anticipation. Caleb always had—

He cupped her, bringing her back to the present, one finger sliding through her slickness, parting her lips. "I've never understood men who like everything trimmed and tamed." He nibbled on the point of her hip bone and licked the sting away, the pad of his thumb brushing over her clit.

Ohsweetbabyjesus.

Her hips surged up, seeking the pressure and the pleasure and the promise.

He parted her legs, pressing kisses against the sensitive flesh of her inner thigh and worked his way up, up—

Ring-ring, ring-ring. Geneva stiffened. Wyatt growled. *Ring-ring, ring-ring.*

Wyatt ignored it.

"Don't you need to get that?"

"No. That's Rodriguez," Wyatt said. "If it's important, he'll call back."

It rang once more, and the phone forwarded the call to voicemail. Wyatt grinned. "See? Now, where were we?"

She'd hoped the question was rhetorical. She arched against his hand, but he didn't move. His eyes turned flint gray and cunning. "Bastard," she hissed out, trying to keep the laugh out of her voice. "You're going to make me answer, aren't you?"

A smug grin turned his lips. Less of the-cat-who-ate-the-canary, more like the-wolf-in-sheep's-clothing—no, make that the-wolf-in-*no*-clothing.

Fine. If Wyatt demanded an answer, he'd get one. At this point, he could almost name his price. "You were just about to—

Ring-ring, ring-ring.

Wyatt muttered a long stream of curses and dug through the pile of clothes until he found his pants and his phone. She scooted over, and he sat on the couch beside her, his hand rubbing up and down the inside of her leg.

Ring-ri— "Man, what the fu—"

All of Wyatt's muscles went taut as he listened to Rodriguez on the other end of the phone. "What channel?"

Geneva scrambled off the couch and grabbed the remote off

the end table next to Caleb's recliner. By the time she turned around, Wyatt had already hung up and was sliding one leg into his jeans.

She clicked the power button for Caleb's flatscreen. "What channel?"

"Any of them."

"*...details are sketchy...*" A news reporter stood in front of a dilapidated motel, a ribbon of bright yellow crime scene tape flapping in the breeze behind her. "*But sources inside the Sheriff's Office who wish to remain anonymous because they don't have the authority to speak, have confirmed the identity of the murder victim as a local sex worker named Desiree...*"

10

———

Wyatt waved a hand in front of Geneva's face, her sights fixed on another dimension, far, far away.

She refocused on him and swiped away the nervous sweat that had broken out on her upper lip. "No, no. We were just there."

He pulled her to the couch and made her sit before she fell, handing over her shorts and finding her shirt against the near wall. She held the clothes in her lap, oblivious to her nakedness.

On the TV screen, Rodriguez worked in the background directing a man and a woman as they donned booties and gloves. The woman picked up a camera and entered the motel room.

"I don't understand," she said. "We were just there a few hours ago. How could... how could..."

Wyatt muted the report and took Caleb's Boston T-shirt out of her hands, pulled it over her head, and threaded her arms through. Then he had her step into her shorts. She managed to grab the waistband and pull them up herself.

"Coffee?" Wyatt asked as he headed to the kitchen.

Geneva tore her attention away from the unfolding report. "What?"

"Coffee?"

"Yes. Please." She followed. Her steps faltered, her legs looking wonky and weak. She plopped onto the kitchen chair. Wyatt prepped the coffee maker and pressed start.

"We should have made her come with us," Geneva said, her voice reed-thin, a mere husk of its usual vibrancy.

He rubbed his hands down his face and glanced over at her. The shadows under her eyes had deepened. Whatever respite their few hours of sleep had offered, the tragic news negated. "She was an adult. We couldn't force her to leave with us."

"Do you think the same person who killed the other three killed her?"

"If you're a person overly concerned about job safety, sex work as a career choice should be crossed off the list." His voice thickened as anger and frustration vied neck and neck in a close race to the finish line. Unease churned in his gut. "She could have had problems with her pimp, with a competitor with a vendetta, she could have overdosed, or a john could have been rough."

Geneva accepted the steaming mug of coffee he offered. "But you don't believe that."

He sat across from her. "Not for one minute."

"What do we do?"

"Nothing we can do. At least not for Desiree. So we let Rodriguez and the rest of the department do their job. There is one more witness out there. We need to find the killer before he finds her."

"How do we do that?"

"Keep on like we've been doing. Ask questions. Pour over the case files. Try to decipher the journal."

"If I could have deciphered the journal, I wouldn't have brought it to you."

He took a sip of the coffee, winced at the double-strength brew, though the jolt of caffeine hit his brain and gave it a jump start. "Go over it again. Go through the box from his office again, go through his things in the house. There has to be a key or a clue that will bust this thing wide open."

"What are you going to do?"

"Try to get a hold of Massey. Computers are his thing. If we can't find the killer, maybe we can locate the last witness. If she has an e-trail out there, credit cards, social media, cell service provider, he can find it. Plus, I have the boat I need to make livable."

He also had a hunch.

It had been brewing on the back burner in his brain, a slow simmer that, now that the coffee had kicked in, started to boil. Something about Desiree's description of the man who'd hired the five prostitutes had hit a chord with him. It could be nothing, so he didn't want to bring it up until he had something more concrete. "Call you tonight?"

"I have a shift tonight."

"The morning, then." Wyatt swallowed back the last of his coffee, rinsed his mug and set it in the sink. He turned.

She was right behind him. "Thank you for last night and—"

"Don't thank me. You're the one who took me in. I'm the grateful one."

He took her wrists and tugged her to him, settling her hands behind his back. Leaning in, he kissed her lips. Wanting to take it deeper, wanting more than he felt she was prepared to give.

Something more than just her body.

He pulled back, brushed unruly hair away from her face, and smoothed the creases in her brow with the pad of his thumb. He knew she was hurting and in disbelief about

Desiree's murder, knew she had to be wondering, like he was, if their visit to the motel had somehow led to her death.

He couldn't stand the idea of leaving her with her spirits so low, so he tried for a little humor. "Now, if you want to thank me for this morning..." He let the sentence trail off, his dick pressing against the rough denim of his jeans at the memory of how he'd been minutes, seconds away from being balls deep in that incredible woman before Rodriguez had rudely interrupted.

Her cheeks pinked, and a sly, sexy grin slid across her face. "Skipper, you'll have to do a whole hell of a lot more than rev me up if you want my undying gratitude."

He cupped her cheeks and pressed a firm kiss to her lips, breathing her in.

He was about to tell her to pick a time and place, but when he let her go, her smile fell away. It wasn't regret he saw in her eyes, but something much worse. *Resignation.* "Look, we don't have to pretend this is anything it isn't. We don't have to force the issue," she said.

"Did this morning feel forced to you? Nobody held a gun to my head."

She winced at the reference, but he wasn't going to back down on this, even though everything in his brain told him any involvement with Steele's widow beyond the professional bordered on the insane. In that case, bring on the padded room, because he was going to need it.

"Anyone hold a gun to yours?"

"No." The tension around her eyes eased.

"Okay." He kissed her on the forehead, then tapped his finger against her temple. "Then stay out of your head."

———

LATE AFTERNOON HAD HIT BY THE TIME WYATT HAD GIVEN THE

Sheriff's Office his vandalism report and returned from the hospital in Idaho Falls after taking Massey not only a change of clothes but his laptop. Wyatt also gave him Candy Lane's name. Too bad, he hadn't known about the hidden house key in the barn the night before.

And miss the glorious sight of seeing Geneva naked? Of having your hands on her, your mouth on her?

Okay, so not knowing about the key had turned into the icing on top of the turd cake that had been his never-ending night.

And seeing Evie at the hospital, awake and off the ventilator, and finding out she could be moved to a hospital closer to the ranch in a day or two, had put a charge in his step the caffeine hadn't.

He checked on the horses and That-A-Way, who followed him back to the dock, a day short on her alfalfa cube rations. He laid a few cubes on the dock, then stretched her moving pad across the bow of the boat to dry out from the rain.

Stepping aboard felt like he'd crossed into some post-apocalyptic parallel universe. It was his Sea-Celia. But at the same time, it wasn't. Vandals had violated her chill vibe.

He broke out the heavy-duty trash bags and started the cleanup process. What was too big for the bags, like the mattress, the bench cushions, and his scorched dining table, he wrestled onto the dock and into the back of his truck.

He strung para-cord in zig-zags under the hardtop and clipped the sodden case file pages up so they could dry. The stagnant water in the cabin, trapped by all the debris, had already attracted flies. They buzzed and dived and generally made clean up hell.

But Sea-Celia was afloat, so he couldn't complain too much. If he'd had more propane, the whole boat could have gone up in flames and ended up at the bottom of the pond.

After he cleaned the cabin and the galley, he found some leather work gloves and cleaned the broken glass out of the port window frame and started duct-taping a garbage bag over the gaping hole from the outside.

That-A-Way nudged him, leaving a green slime trail of alfalfa slobber on his forearm. "Go away. I'm all out of cubes."

That-A-Way stuck a pointy tongue up one wet nostril and then the other and belched up a mouthful of cow cud. Wyatt choked on her exhaust and made a mental note to buy more peppermints the next time he went to the store.

Rodriguez pulled in, and Wyatt shoo-ed That-A-Way up the dock. Climbing back into the boat, he pulled two beers out of the new cooler he'd picked up on the way back from the hospital.

"Redecorating?" Rodriguez asked, glancing around at the heaps of bulging trash bags on the dock and page after page of police reports dangling from beneath the hardtop like a string of banners. It looked like Sea-Celia had become the victim of an overzealous party planner.

Wyatt twisted the top off a bottle and handed it up to Rodriguez. "I'm calling the look Blight and Squalor. It'll be all the rage next year."

Rodriguez's sunglasses reflected the boat and the calm water of the pond. "I heard at the station you'd had some problems. Who'd you piss off this time?"

"Wish I knew."

"They get anything?"

Bile spiked the back of Wyatt's throat, and he spat over the side of the boat. "My gun."

"You report it?"

"I'm not an idiot."

"What about your backup?"

"At the gunsmith. Bad firing pin."

Rodriguez swung down into the boat, looked around for a place to sit. Wyatt offered the captain's chair, probably the only seating surface the vandals hadn't damaged. He leaned against the hardtop's support pole. His feet ached, his biceps griped every time he lifted his beer, and if he didn't get his underwear out of the wash soon, his jeans would rub his crotch raw.

"Do you think it was him?" Wyatt didn't have to explain to Rodriguez that he was talking about the Nightwalker killer.

"That's my guess. She was strangled like the others. No digital bruising on the victim's neck this time. He used a lamp cord." Rodriguez eyed Wyatt from behind his sunglasses.

"But she wasn't dumped like the others."

"Maybe something spooked him off, and he didn't get the chance to move the body."

Wyatt couldn't see his friend's eyes behind the reflective lenses, but the heat from that gaze scorched him just the same. Rodriguez tipped the bottle back and took a long swallow, but his eyes never wavered. He had a way about him that would make a priest want to confess all his sins.

You couldn't be partnered with a man like Rodriguez for very long and not witness suspects and perps fry under that laser focus. But in all the years they'd been friends, Rodriguez had never wielded that weapon on him.

Then Wyatt realized the truth.

Rodriguez wasn't here to visit, or get advice. Wasn't there to pick Wyatt's brain and strategize about the investigation. He wanted something else. That knot in Wyatt's belly tightened around his stomach, one hitch, two, and a third for good measure.

Wyatt crossed his feet at the ankles and held his arms out wide in an expansive invitation. "What did you come here to say?" He'd tried to keep his tone non-confrontational, but by the way Rodriguez paused, the bottle halfway to his lips, Wyatt hadn't pulled it off.

"You know I think of you as a brother. Even after everything that happened last year, I stood by you."

The knot around Wyatt's stomach cinched down as if each end were held by fighting factions in a life and death game of tug of war. "Whatever you have to say, spit it the fuck out."

Rodriguez laid his bottle on the console of the bridge right above the throttle controls, his movements slow and precise, as if he needed the extra time to figure out how he was going to say what he'd come there to say. He took his sunglasses off and met Wyatt's glare. "Where were you between the hours of—"

Wyatt barked out a laugh, the tension easing from his belly. "Good one, asshole."

Rodriguez crossed his arms over his chest. "No joke."

"*Jesus Christ.*" Wyatt paced the rear deck as the anger built, as a whole year and a half of frustrations and veiled accusations and outright lies ignited the fury inside him. He rounded on Rodriguez. "You *know* me."

"Better than anyone."

"And yet you come here, come on Evie's property, come on my boat and accuse me—"

Rodriguez held up his hands. "Hang on now. I didn't accuse you of anything."

Wyatt snorted out a bitter, rotten laugh. "Ah, my friend, you did."

"I'm doing my job, Wy. That comes first. You know that. At least you used to."

"Fine," Wyatt spat, though in no way was he okay with any of it. At least being with Geneva gave him an alibi. "Ask your questions."

"Where were you last night between the hours of ten pm and four am?"

"With Geneva, for most of it."

"You with anyone else?"

Fuck, this is going to look bad. "Desiree."

Rodriguez didn't even flinch, he just reclaimed his beer and polished off the last sip. "Yeah. I know."

Wyatt did a double-take. "What do you mean, you know?" The setting sun hit him in the eyes, and he had to step beneath the hardtop to block the glare. He still hadn't found his sunglasses.

"Found your prints in the motel."

"Results back that fast?"

"With Senator Lambert pushing, Day was able to cut to the front of the line at the lab."

Great.

"You didn't even ask where they found your prints."

"Does it matter?" When Rodriguez didn't answer, Wyatt played into the game. "Okay. Where did you find my prints?"

"On the murder weapon." Again, that focus. A focus meant to break the innocent and shatter the guilty. But Wyatt knew how to play this game.

"Yeah, I already told you I was there. With Geneva. You can ask her. Desiree knocked the lamp over. I picked it up and put it back on the dresser. We talked. We left. Desiree was very much alive at the time." Wyatt grabbed another beer. Didn't bother offering one to Rodriguez. He wasn't exactly up for playing host.

"What did Desiree say?"

Wyatt wanted to tell Rodriguez to go fuck himself. But that wouldn't help get Wyatt back at the department. Only doing the job Day had assigned would. "Nothing too helpful. Four women witnessed a john asphyxiate Alexa Martinez. Apparently, it was an accident."

"How is strangulation an accident?"

"When the john is kinky as shit and needs to choke his sex partner out to get his rocks off."

Rodriguez muttered under his breath. Something along the lines of *sick fuck.* "Did she know who the guy was?"

"No." Wyatt leaned back against the gunwale, his fury easing. The beer and his sheer exhaustion might have played a part in that, as well as the realization that it didn't appear as if Rodriguez was going to drag him off in cuffs. *Yet.* "They never saw his face. Only his driver's eyes in the van's rearview mirror."

"Anything else useful?"

"By Desiree's count, there's one more witness out there."

Rodriguez didn't look surprised. Then again, Rodriguez used to hold his own in the departmental Friday night poker games. "Who is she?"

"Woman by the name of Candy Lane. Desiree said no one has seen or heard from her in a few months. Desiree figured she was dead, and no one has found her body yet."

Rodriguez's poker face slipped for an instant, and Wyatt saw the stress and the strain and the toll these murders had taken on his friend.

Wyatt didn't want to bring up any more bad news, but this was information he couldn't sit on. "I think you have a leak at the Sheriff's Office. Or maybe the killer is one of our own. Maybe the rumors are true."

"What makes you say that?"

"It's too big of a coincidence that after I tell you about Desiree that she's killed within hours."

"I didn't tell anyone at the station. No one knew but me."

Well, shit.

"Could you have been followed to the motel?" Rodriguez asked.

"No, I'm very car—"

Geneva followed you. Last night and *on many other nights. And you never noticed. Never suspected. If Geneva could do it, somebody else could have, too.*

Nausea roiled in his belly, worse than that time his grandfather had taken him offshore in Sea-Celia as the storm had rolled in, and the waves had tossed the boat around like a bathtub toy.

Wyatt braced his hands on the side of the boat and spat out the sticky saliva that pooled in his mouth. When he was confident he wasn't going to toss his lunch, he said, "I could have been."

"You need to find that last witness."

No shit. "What the hell do you think I've been doing these past few days? Sitting on my ass, knitting sweaters for squirrels?"

"Yeah, yeah, I get it. You've been working hard. We've all been working hard."

As late as it was, Wyatt still had a lot to do before he called it a night. The mosquitoes came out and started dive-bombing him. He swatted them away. "That it?"

Rodriguez dumped his empty into the cooler as if he were about to leave. "I still need a timeline of your whereabouts last night."

Wyatt chewed on his anger, but Rodriguez wouldn't leave without an answer. He gave his friend the rundown, including the approximately two hours he'd spent dealing with his boat that he had no alibi for unless he could bribe That-A-Way into talking.

"You going to cuff me and take me in?"

"Don't be an ass. You know I had to ask."

"What did Jed say about the prints?"

Rodriguez looked away, finding sudden fascination in That-A-Way's ruminations. He put his shades back on even though dusk had hit, and the sun had dipped behind the Rockies. He looked back up at Wyatt. "I haven't told him yet."

"I'd like to be there when you do."

"Only the lab tech and I know about the fingerprint match. And I plan on keeping it that way. For now, at least."

"You can't keep that type of information to yourself. Let me go with you. I can expl—"

Rodriguez laughed. "For a kid who lived on the streets, you've always had that surprising streak of naivete." Wyatt narrowed his eyes in warning, but either Rodriguez didn't notice it with his sunglasses on, or he ignored it. "What do you think Day will do when he finds this out?"

"I can explain." Wyatt didn't bother hiding his anger or his frustration as his words came out low and tight.

"No, Wy. You can't. If Day finds out, he'll slap the cuffs on you himself, and you'd be read your rights. And being the smart guy you are, you'd keep your damn mouth shut and not say a word until you had a lawyer present.

"In the meantime, our killer would be out there, and another woman's life would be in imminent danger." Rodriguez clapped a hand on Wyatt's shoulder. "Brother, I need you on the streets, not rotting in a jail cell."

Rodriguez was both right and wrong, and lord help him, Wyatt wanted this bastard caught as much as Rodriguez did. Maybe even more.

"Look," Rodriguez removed his sunglasses so Wyatt could see his eyes. "I *know* you didn't do this."

"Jed finds out you kept this from him, and it could end your career."

"Then let's hope like hell he doesn't find out. At least not until we catch the real killer." Rodriguez clapped him on the shoulder again and climbed onto the dock.

"Hey," Wyatt called out. Rodriguez stopped and turned back. "Thanks. For not hauling me in."

"Just find that woman. And fast." Rodriguez smiled that charming smile the women found hard to resist, and Wyatt found annoying. Rodriguez pointed a finger at Wyatt like a rock star does to the drummer during a solo. "You're family. I'll always have your back."

———

AT FOUR IN THE AFTERNOON, GENEVA PUT THE COFFEE ON. IT WAS morning for her after getting some sleep and recovering from her night shift. It had been one of those crazy nights where they'd fielded call after call. The ones that got your heart revving and your brain spinning.

She'd come home, stumbled through the door, and dropped the box of Caleb's belongings in the entryway, the contents spilling out. The frame with the picture of her and Caleb had tumbled out, the glass shattering on her tile, and she'd been too exhausted to clean it up.

Pouring a cup of coffee, she headed to the entryway with a broom and dustpan in hand. She set the mug aside and started sweeping up the shards while avoiding focusing on Caleb's belongings.

It had almost been cathartic going through Caleb's things when Wyatt had been with her, but she knew if she went through them now, she'd lose it.

Maybe because her raw emotions hovered millimeters beneath the surface after hearing about Desiree's death. She feared if her feelings broke the surface, it would rip through her thin shell the way that iceberg did to the Titanic.

She stepped forward, and a tiny shard stabbed the underside of her foot. "Damn it!" She threw the broom aside and hopped around on one foot while she tried to pick the glass out. Then her other foot landed on another piece of glass, and Geneva stumbled against the wall.

"Stupid glass," she ground out, as she slid down the wall, the tears threatening to fall. She blinked them back, but then her gaze fell on the picture of her and Caleb. Her smile had been so big, so excited for the future she and Caleb would share.

But like the glass, life was so fragile.

Her chest constricted, and her heart hammered against her sternum, a frantic, pulse-pounding beat that bloodied and bruised. She pulled the picture free of the frame, her thumb brushing across Caleb's sweet face. And her delicate shell, shattered as she clutched the photo to her chest.

The tears came, and they rolled down her cheeks as silent sobs racked her body.

Why? Why did you draw on Wyatt?

She curled up on the floor, lost in the blackness, the bleakness of her grief. She didn't know for how long she laid there, but the coffee pot beeped as it shut off. Finally, the tears slowed, and her breath evened out. She dried her eyes with the hem of Caleb's Boston shirt she'd worn to bed.

She set the picture aside and pulled one foot onto her lap and then the other, plucking out the shards of glass and dropping them into the dustpan. A folded up piece of yellow legal paper caught her eye. It must have been behind the picture in the frame. Carefully, she unfolded it, finding Caleb's writing scribbled across it. She lost her breath again, then closed her eyes and concentrated on her breathing. In and out. Slow and steady. The constriction in her chest and the pounding at her temple eased.

As her brain re-engaged, a tingle of nervous excitement skittered along her nerves. She opened her eyes again and looked at the paper.

Initials.

Names.

Was this the key to the journal they'd been looking for?

She crawled away from the tile until she was clear of the

glass. Row after row. Name after name. There had to have been twenty or thirty of them.

She didn't recognize *all* of the names. But she recognized many. Prominent doctors, lawyers, city officials, members of law enforcement, a firefighter from her station, a senator.

She grabbed her now cold coffee and sucked it down and made a beeline for her bedroom to get dressed, leaving the mess behind. She didn't have time to clean up. This was something she had to show Wyatt. Now.

Twenty minutes later, she pulled into Evie's ranch. Wyatt had left his truck parked by the dock, but she didn't see him anywhere.

"Wyatt?" she called out as she half-walked, half-jogged down the dock. "Are you—"

Wyatt poked his head out of the cabin, his shirt off, his jeans low on his hips, the top button undone, and a slow smile spreading across his face. Her steps faltered. Not because the sight of him made her think of hot mouths and shallow breaths, but because of the *whomp,* the soul hit, of that smile.

The smile that said *I'm interested.*

The smile that said *I want.*

It left a slow buzz burning in her system. It had been a very long time since someone had smiled at her that way.

"I've got something to show you." She didn't wait for an invitation to board. With a hand on the hardtop, she swung down, landing a few feet from him. She pulled the piece of paper out from between the pages of Caleb's journal and waved it in his face.

He buttoned his jeans and took it from her. "What's this?"

"I think it's the key to the journal."

"Come on in," he said as he retreated into the cabin.

The interior smelled like a combination of bleach, Fabreze, and laundry detergent. He grabbed an armful of clothes off one of the bench seats in the galley and carried them to the forward berth. He returned, pulling a T-shirt over his head.

"Sit here." He pointed to one of the benches where he'd laid a folded up blanket over the exposed wood as a makeshift cushion. He sat next to her, bumping her over with his hip. He braced his bare feet on the bench across from them, using his knees as a table for Caleb's journal.

They skimmed through. Page after page. Aligning initials to names and names to dates. Though it remained unclear what the dates referred to.

When finished, there remained initials they couldn't associate with any names.

"I think we should focus on the dates and initials around the time of the first murder," Geneva said.

"Agreed." They turned to the appropriate pages. "All the sets of initials are in threes. And the last two letters of each set correspond to each individual's first and last names. But what does the first initial stand for?"

Geneva glanced from the journal to the key and back to the journal again. "Look at this. Robert Green. That's Bobby, one of the guys from the fire house. There's an F in front of his initials."

Wyatt nodded his head as he scanned down the list, a smile coming to his face as realization set in. "And here. Dave McMahon. He has a D in front of his initials. He's a deputy at the Sheriff's Office."

"That's the guy that has the crush on Cassie."

"This guy, with a C in front of his name, is a city councilman."

"But what do the dates mean?" Geneva's brain hurt as her caffeine levels dipped so low it entered the danger zone. If she were a fighter plane, they'd be sending out a distress call for an emergency in-air refuel. "You got any coffee?"

"At the house. I brought Massey home this afternoon. They moved Evie to the hospital in Alpine."

"She's doing better then?"

Wyatt tore his attention away from the journal and focused on her. His black eye had faded considerably, and the tension around his eyes had eased. "Much. Might be back home within the week."

She patted his upturned knee. "That's such good news. I know that must be such a relief to you and Massey."

He closed the journal and placed a hand over hers and gave it a quick squeeze but didn't let go. "It is." He tossed the journal to the other bench and stood, pulling her up with him.

He offered up a tired smile, but it faltered.

Voicing the concern that had rattled around in her head since the news report the morning before, she said, "Do you think it's our fault? Desiree? Did we lead her killer to her?"

No quick denial. No reassurances that Geneva's idea was ludicrous. Wyatt took a step back and pulled her with him as he leaned against the counter, and settled her between his legs. "I sure hope not. She hadn't gone into hiding, but if the rumors are true, that the Nightwalker murders are a cover-up for the accidental one, for Alexa's, then why wasn't Desiree killed weeks or months ago? Why now? What's different?"

Geneva's throat tightened. "B-besides us going to see her?"

Wyatt pressed his forehead to hers, his fingers working the sore muscles at the base of her neck. She groaned softly at the perfect mix of pain and pleasure. She tilted her head back, leaning into the gentle massage. As her head lolled from side to side, it wasn't lost on her that Wyatt hadn't answered her question. It hadn't entirely been rhetorical.

He stopped his ministrations all too soon. "Come on," he said. "I could use some coffee, too."

At the cabin stairs, he slipped his feet into flip-flops and tugged her along behind him. That-A-Way greeted them at the foot of the dock. Wyatt stopped and gave the cow a good scratching behind the withers.

The more she got to know Wyatt, the more she saw his gentle side and his kind nature, the more she believed in his inherent goodness.

And the more she believed that if he could have done anything to keep from shooting Caleb, he would have.

Geneva reached up and swirled her fingers through the bovine's cowlick on her forehead, then edged her fingers up and scratched her behind the ears. That-A-Way's eyelids twitched as she leaned into Geneva's hand. "I think she's more dog than cow."

"Agreed. I'm pretty sure if she could figure out a way to get on the boat, she'd crawl into my bed." Wyatt gave the cow one last pat, and they continued up to the house.

He knocked on the door with two hard raps then let himself in. "It's me," he called out, "just getting some coffee."

Massey made some sort of acknowledgment that Geneva couldn't quite make out, but then again, she was focused on Wyatt's promise of caffeine.

They washed cow hair and grime off their hands. Wyatt pulled out two regular mugs and a travel mug and filled them from the pot. "Massey drinks his coffee like it's a competitive sport," Wyatt said by way of explanation as to why there was a full pot of coffee going late in the afternoon.

"My kind of guy," Geneva said as she accepted the full mug.

"I do have a girlfriend," came a voice from behind her. She and Wyatt both turned. Massey rolled into the kitchen in his wheelchair, a crooked, wicked smile on his face. "But it's not that serious yet, so if you're interested, now's the time to speak up."

Wyatt cut him a look as he filled the travel mug. "She's too old for you."

Geneva sputtered out a laugh. "Too old?"

Massey scoffed. "And *you're* too old for her."

Wyatt handed him the full travel mug. "That zit cream I bought you seems to be working."

Massey grinned. "At least I have my whole life ahead of me. I'm not scraping and clawing as I slide into middle age."

"Middle age, my ass." Wyatt blew on his coffee.

Geneva sneaked a peek at said ass. It was a fine one.

When she glanced over at Massey, he had a smug caught-ya smile on his face. Heat sprinted up to her cheeks as she tipped her mug to her mouth. Ugh. Where was that sugar?

"You okay?" Wyatt sobered and gave a short chin bob toward Massey's wheelchair.

"Just a little stiff and sore and tired. The chair's easier than the crutches when I get this way."

"Need me to call the physical therapist? With your van totaled, I bet they'd come to you."

"I already have my grandmother on my case. I don't need to hear it from you, too." Massey glowered, but it lacked any real heat. "But I called. The therapist can come out the day after tomorrow."

"Call them back. I can take you in the morning."

Massey blew out a breath as he neared what looked like the limit of his patience. "The day after tomorrow is *fine*. Stop fussing."

"I'm just trying to look out for you."

"I appreciate that dude, I do, but I'm a grown-ass man. I can look after myself."

Wyatt raised his free hand in surrender. "You have anything for me?"

"Something. Don't know exactly what yet." Massey stuffed the travel mug between his thighs and maneuvered out of the kitchen. Over his shoulder, he called out, "Follow me."

———

GENEVA SAT IN A ROLLING DESK CHAIR ON ONE SIDE OF MASSEY while Wyatt sat in a chair on the other. She had one eye on the bank of three large monitors that sat on the over-sized desk, and one eye on the muted television mounted on the wall above.

On the bank of monitors, Massey attempted to enhance the grainy security footage from the night Wyatt's boat had been vandalized. Slow going didn't even begin to describe it. Glaciers moved faster.

On the television, Vanna White uncovered the letter M and then the letter G. Geneva solved the puzzle in her head. "Trumped-up charge."

"What?" Wyatt glanced at her over the top of Massey's head.

"Sorry." She grimaced and pointed to the screen. "I solved the puzzle."

Wyatt turned his attention back to the monitor without comment, but she thought she detected an eye roll. She considered going back to the boat to get Caleb's journal so she could continue where she and Wyatt had left off, but with the growing darkness, she didn't want to walk back alone.

The gameshow ended, and after a set of commercials, the evening news began. "Wyatt," she said, "Isn't that Detective Rodriguez?"

Detective Rodriguez stood at a podium. Behind him stood flag poles and men with gray hair and grim expressions.

"Turn it up." Wyatt sat back and crossed his arms over his chest.

Massey handed her the remote without glancing up.

"...this is early in an ongoing investigation, and we have limited information we can tell you at this time." Detective Rodriguez tugged at the collar of his shirt. His face a little red. Either his collar was too tight, or the reporters gave him hives.

A reporter raised their hand and waited for Rodriguez to call on them. *"Detective, our sources say you have a suspect. When can we expect an arr—"*

Rodreguez's upper lip flashed upward, though he mostly masked his irritation that there had been a leak of departmental information. *"As I said, this is an ongoing investigation, and I can't divulge that information at this time."* The detective backed away from the podium. Reporters continued to hurl questions at him as he retreated.

Sheriff Day stepped up, giving assurances to the public that his office was doing everything they could to track down the killer. After a commercial break, the news report cut to Senator Lambert and his wife as they climbed out of their limo, a bodyguard on either side them.

The senator waved with his left hand—always the left, Geneva noticed, since that exposé last year that told how he'd lost his pinky finger during the Gulf War—at the crowd gathering at the press conference where he was expected to announce his bid for the upcoming presidential election.

The senator's wife was a petite, thin thing, who wore a look of disdain on her face the way Geneva wore her favorite T-shirt —all day, every day.

Like the other times she'd seen the senator on TV, he'd dressed in the finest suits tailored for a man who'd gone a little soft around the middle, a light gray pinstripe in deference to the building heat of summer.

It wasn't the color, so much as the exceptional fit and the way it cloaked him like a second skin that fascinated her. Not as if Lambert would *feel* naked without it, but as if he would *be* naked without it, figuratively, that was. "Who wants to bet this guy fucks with his clothes on?"

Don't be crass.

Too late, Mom.

Geneva cringed and took another sip of life's elixir. Massey barked out a laugh, though he didn't look up from the videographic magic he was performing. Wyatt got this funny look on his face that shifted from surprise to *WTF*, to an eye-widening *holy shit*.

"What?" Geneva asked. She swiped a hand across her nose when he continued to stare at her. What? Did she have a booger hanging out of her nose?

He stood, waves of frenetic energy wafting off him, his expression finally settling on this complete look of disbelief.

Massey must have felt the energy shift as well because he rolled his wheelchair around to face Wyatt. "What? What is it?"

"The other night when we were talking to Desiree, she said the guy who hired them—as Gen so nicely put it—fucked with his suit on."

"You think the Nightwalker killer is Senator Lambert?" Massey shook his head in disbelief. "The guy who champions women-centric legislation, the guy who prosecuted and won more sex crime cases than any other District Attorney in the history of our state?"

Wyatt cut him a look. "You sound like you should wear a sign saying, *This has been a paid promotional ad by Citizens for Larson Lambert*."

Massey raised his hands. "Whatever, dude. I'm just saying you've got the wrong guy."

"Maybe not the Nightwalker killer, but maybe he's the guy who strangled Alexa Martinez," Wyatt said.

Turning back to his monitors, Massey said, "I don't see it."

Wyatt leaned a shoulder against the wall and scratched his head as if trying to reconcile Massey's thoughts with his own. "You could be right. Look at his wife. Definitely not full-figured like all the women The Suit guy seems so fond of."

"Yeah, but look at his wife." Geneva paused the news and

pointed at the senator's wife on the screen. "She's all buttoned up. *Vanilla.* A no blowjob, no oral sex, missionary only, kind of vanilla."

Massey clicked away on the video enhancing program he was working on but added, "She's so uptight, she could probably eat coal and shit diamonds."

"Those women were the exact opposite of his wife," Wyatt said.

"Curvier women could be his true preference," Geneva said. "But the sex sounds the same. You think *that's* his kink? You think Lambert sees his wife beneath him when he's having sex with these women, and that by choking them, he's taking out his sexual frustration on his wife?"

"I don't know." Wyatt pinched the bridge of his nose. "I'm sure having vanilla sex doesn't turn you into a killer. There have to be millions of people out there that have perfectly wonderful vanilla sex and are happy to have it."

"I'm sure there are, too. But just because *they* are, doesn't mean *Lambert* is."

"Check this out." Massey bobbed his chin toward his center monitor. "You're not going to believe it."

11

WYATT LEANED AGAINST MASSEY'S DESK AND WATCHED THE
monitors over his friend's shoulder. The motion active light on
the corner of Evie's house had burned out a couple weeks before
his boat had been vandalized. According to the security footage,
about twenty minutes after Wyatt had left for the Delight Inn, a
car had driven by the camera.

Before Massey had manipulated the footage, all they had
seen was a dark mass pass by the house. Now, after Massey's
wizardly work, they had an identifiable image.

Anger seeped into Wyatt's system as he watched the sheriff's
deputy's car drive past. The newer department cars were black,
which had made it more difficult for Massey to finesse the
footage, but the moonlight reflected off the side of the car—a
flash of chrome from the driver's side spotlight, the sheriff's
department logo in reflective black paint on the door.

"Son of a bitch," Wyatt muttered.

Who did you piss off?

Rodriguez's words came back to him. After shooting Steele,
the flak and the backlash he'd received from fellow officers, at

not only his but neighboring departments, had been swift and often brutal.

People he'd considered friends not only refused to return his calls, but they also had sent hate-filled letters, glared, or bumped his shoulder in the halls. A couple times, they'd almost come to blows.

After Internal Affairs cleared him of any wrongdoing, instead of everything improving like he'd thought it would, things went south. Still, he'd prefer the scrutiny of his peers to the drudgery of the PI business.

"Can you trace the vehicle?" Geneva asked.

"If we can get a plate or a unit number off the rear."

"I think you're out of luck," Massey said. "I've already looked at the footage of them leaving. The moon had shifted, making the lighting much worse. Plus, the angle was wrong to get a clean shot of the plates. But I'll keep working on it."

"Do you think the vandalism is related to the Nightwalker murders?" Geneva asked.

"More likely goes back to Caleb's shooting. All the case files Rodriguez had given me had been damaged, but not taken. Besides, it's not like I couldn't get another copy, so I don't believe that was the motive. And with as much stuff as they tore up, it seemed brutally personal." And if that's the case, if it's a personal vendetta, the suspect list could stretch for miles.

Truth was, in relative terms, the lasting damage to Sea-Celia had been minimal, and no one would die if the perpetrators got away with the vandalism. The murders were a more pressing matter.

During the televised press conference, the reporters had hammered Rodriguez. Day and the rest of the department had to be feeling the squeeze. That Wyatt still cared at all about what happened to Day after the way Wyatt had been treated grated on him. But that didn't change the way he felt deep down.

They needed to find the murderer, and if they couldn't do that, they needed to find the last witness before she became the next victim. "What about Candy Lane, any luck tracking her down? Or the owners of cabin properties within the radius I gave you?"

Massey cut his eyes to Wyatt. "Dude, you know there's, like, one of me, right?"

"I figured you'd have some super-spook-wanna-be program running in the background that would pop up with the information we needed."

"What kind of TV shows you been watching?" Massey chuckled. "You two get out of here and let me work. I'm gonna find what you need, Wyatt, but it'll take time."

Wyatt blew out a breath. "Yeah, sure. Fine." He glanced over at Geneva. "Ready to go?"

Already back to work, Massey held out his travel mug to Wyatt. Wyatt made a fresh pot, refilled the travel mug, and left Massey to do his job.

On Massey's stoop, That-A-Way had bedded down for the night. She opened one eye as they stepped over the top of her, then fell back asleep.

This was the time of year Wyatt loved most in Wyoming. The days warm but not scorching, the nights cool and pleasant. A bat swooped and flitted by overhead, and an owl hooted from somewhere near the barn.

Geneva walked beside him, their shoulders brushing every third or fourth step. "So if the killer were Senator Lambert, how would we prove it?"

"I think there are two killers."

"Two?"

"It makes the most sense. If Lambert was responsible for the first death, I believe it was accidental. Like Desiree said."

"And the others?"

"Like the rumors say. Cover up. What better way to keep not only the department scrambling and overtaxed, but also set us chasing after a ghost while they systematically get rid of witnesses."

"Who would do that? Who would kill for Lambert?"

"Answer that, and you solved the case. Lambert has the money to hire the best."

"Or it could be someone who has as much to lose as Lambert does. His wife? She strikes me as the wizard behind the curtain kind of person."

"I like the way you think." A dry twig cracked beneath Wyatt's foot as they walked. "It's no secret her family money funded Lambert's senatorial bid. And now the run for president? It'll be like the senatorial run, only on mega doses of steroids and with the associated astronomical costs.

"If word got out that Lambert hired sex workers for his own private orgy, had an asphyxiation kink, *and oops, oh, by the way, I accidentally choked out a woman*? I don't think that would fly with Lambert's father-in-law, or law enforcement, or the voters. If he's the man responsible, he, and his family, has a hell of a lot to lose."

Wyatt reached out and twined his fingers with hers. He thought back to the news report, back to the vanilla sex assumptions, back to the other night at Geneva's. What they'd started had been anything but vanilla. What they'd shared held the promise of spice, and held an excitement that suited him like—

Suit.

We called him The Suit. That's what Desiree had said.

Which was the same name he'd given the POI, person of interest, he'd seen with Steele the night of the shooting. The Suit.

"Ouch." Geneva wiggled her hand. "Lighten up on the grip. I promise not to run off."

"Sorry." He dropped her hand, and she shook the feeling back into her fingers. "I just thought of something."

He needed to call Rodriguez, he needed—

Geneva snapped her fingers in front of his face. "You mind filling me in?"

"The security tape."

"Massey said he didn't have any hopes—"

"No, the bank security video on the night of the shooting. The guy in the alley with Ste—Caleb." Saying Caleb's name out loud made it feel that much more personal. *Steele* was a fellow officer but a man he hadn't known. *Caleb* was Geneva's husband. A well-loved man. A man who had made her happy. A man who did his job well. A man who tried to right a wrong the only way he knew how. Wyatt's stomach shrank two sizes.

Wyatt cleared his throat. "The guy in the suit. What if the guy in the suit was Lambert?"

"How can we prove that? Even if we could get past Lambert's personal assistant and bodyguards, it's not like we can walk up to him and ask if he was in the alley that night."

"Maybe there's something on the security tape from Caleb's shooting."

"I want to see it," Geneva said.

"That's not a good idea." He went to retake her hand, but she backed away. He caught her wrist before she fell off into the pond. "Think about what you're saying."

"I wasn't ready before, but now...n-now I need to see it for myself."

He dropped her wrist and cupped her cheek. She didn't pull away. In the low light, her eyes glistened, but her cheeks remained dry. Her breath came in short, quick, silent gasps. All he wanted to do was take the pain away. To go back to that day.

Knowing what he knew now, having lived with the gnawing guilt, knowing her, getting to know Caleb through her eyes, he liked to think things would turn out different. If he had to do it all over again...

He might not take that shot.

She stared at the ground.

"Look at me." Her gaze came up, a halting fraction at a time as if she fought it the entire way, but her curiosity won out. He said, "You don't want that image in your head for the rest of your life."

"Maybe," she said, her voice as empty as if all emotion had poured out of her. "But it's my choice to make."

"I'm sorr—"

She shut him up with a finger to his lips and an almost imperceptible shake of her head. He swallowed audibly, the backs of his eyes pricked. He held out his hands, a silent plea of *what do you want me to say?*

How could he even begin to make amends?

Instead of retreating further, she stepped into his arms, and he tucked her under his chin, holding her tight against his chest. She wrapped her arms low around his waist, and they rocked.

A few minutes later, she made a strange snuffling noise, and despite the somber mood, his lips twitched up. "Did you just sniff me?"

She laughed. Short. Shaky. But real. Wyatt's heart tumbled. How could he not fall for a woman like her?

Fall?

What the hell was he doing?

"Maybe," she said. "Is that weird?"

He took a half step back and ran his hands down her arms until he'd captured her wrists. "And?" No way this would wind up good.

"You smell like cow and alfalfa and pond."

He laughed and wrapped an arm around her shoulder, and they started walking toward the dock. "That bad, huh?"

"Actually..." She shook her head as if she couldn't believe the direction her mind had gone. "I kinda like it."

That tumbling heart? Yeah, it tumbled some more. Further down that path, past interest, past attraction, gaining quickly on total infatuation.

But this wasn't an easy path. Up ahead were sticks and stones and prickers and briars and things that go bump in the night.

If he were smart—

Wyatt shut that thought down. No one had ever accused him of being Einstein. So why start now?

"Come on," he said as he took her hand and led her down the dock. "I've got a phone call to make."

Wyatt settled Geneva into Sea-Celia's cabin and stepped out onto the dock to call Rodriguez. The call connected, and Wyatt said, "You got a minute?"

"Hang on a second." Rodriguez gave out instructions then came back on the line. Wyatt must have caught him still at the station. "Been meaning to call you. Things have been stupid crazy."

Wyatt knew how difficult the first few days and weeks were after a murder. Murdock wasn't a big town. The sheriff's department didn't have the manpower that some of the bigger cities had to handle those kinds of cases. Which meant you worked long hours, on short sleep. And in a town of that size, all eyes were on you. The pressure could be tremendous, but damn if Wyatt didn't miss it. "Kind of late for you to still be at the office."

"No kidding. Day called in the Feds. They're expected here sometime tomorrow. I need to make sure all the evidence is logged correctly, and the murder books are up to date."

"Any breakthroughs?"

"Besides my best friend's prints on the murder weapon?"

"Christ, Rodriguez. You've got to tell them. Let them bring me in."

"I can't—" Rodriguez cut out again, and all Wyatt caught were muffled words. When Rodriguez came back on the line, he'd lowered his voice, yet there was a distinct echo. "I can't let you do that yet."

"You in the head?"

"It's a fucking madhouse out there. Only place I can get a little privacy."

"Please don't flush."

"Can you be serious a minute?"

Wyatt held his tongue. Rodriguez always lost all sense of humor after about twenty-eight hours with no sleep. By Wyatt's calculation, Rodriguez was closing in on thirty.

"I'm cock deep in this case, my partner is so young he's barely housebroken, and Day's riding my ass like the lead jockey in the Donkey Derby. I don't need—" Wyatt heard a thump. Someone cursed. "Occupied!" Rodriguez hollered out.

Wyatt paced up and down the dock while he waited for Rodriguez to get back on the line. One of the boards sagged every time his foot went across it. He made a mental note to replace the board. He added it to his list right below *find last remaining witness* and *find the murderer*.

"Where was I? Oh, yeah. I don't need you sitting in the interrogation room until the Feds decide they've got the wrong man. I need you out there finding our last witness."

"I don't want you getting canned because you covered for me."

"Let me worry about that. Though with the Feds coming in, I might not be able to hold back that tidbit about you for much longer."

"I'm a big boy. I can handle the Feds. What I need from you, though, is a copy of that security tape from the bank across the street from the alley the night of Steele's shooting."

Silence.

"Hello? Hello?" Wyatt checked his phone, but he still had two bars. "Rodriguez?"

"Yeah, sorry, bro. That's a no go. Day needs you concentrating on the—"

"I think it could be connected."

"There's nothing there. The best guys at the state lab have tried to enhance the footage. Besides, my and Day's asses are on the line enough by providing you the case files. I take that tape out of the evidence room, and we've got a paper trail we have to explain. Drop it. It's a dead end."

Like hell. "Yeah, fine."

"Anything else?"

Wyatt considered telling Rodriguez his suspicion that someone in the department was responsible for the vandalism of his boat, but it wasn't anything that couldn't wait. And Wyatt's suspicions about Lambert? Well, he planned on keeping that nifty piece of info under strict lock-down until he had something other than conjecture to back up his suspicions. As close as Rodriguez was to Lambert, it would take more than an accusation he pulled out of his ass for Rodriguez to drink Wyatt's Kool-Aid and be a convert. "No. Nothing else. I'll call you if I find anything."

They said their goodbyes. And despite Rodriguez's assurances that the tape of Steele's shooting held nothing relevant, Wyatt needed to confirm it for himself. The state boys may be good. But he doubted they were *Massey* good.

Now all he had to do was figure out how to get his hands on that tape.

———

During the vandalism, the light fixture over the galley table had been damaged, and the remaining light over the sink made reading Caleb's entries difficult. Geneva held the journal at an angle to catch the light.

The words blurred, went clear, then blurred again. She rubbed her eyes. But that only made her vision worse.

Scanning the journal, she saw the reference to 'pack leader' mentioned several times, and then it clicked. *Wolfe.* Wyatt had to have made the connection already.

Several pinpoints of evidence pointed to Wyatt. Hinting that, somehow, he might be involved. Had Caleb suspected Wyatt was the killer? Had Caleb thought Wyatt was onto Caleb's suspicions? Had Caleb thought Wyatt was out to silence him? Was that why Caleb had shot at Wyatt?

Geneva fisted both hands in her hair and tugged. *Caleb, what were you thinking?*

No answer came. No magical beam of light pointing to the answer on the page, no goosebumps, no nudge, no hint, no voice from beyond the grave.

If anything, she felt more distant and disconnected from Caleb than she'd ever had in the time since his death. There had been so much going on in his life she'd never known about. A part of him she'd never been privy to.

She closed the journal and rested her head on the back of the seat—the hard, now un-cushioned seat. Wyatt was outside on the phone with his ex-partner about the security tape from the shooting. What should have been a short conversation was taking a lot longer than she'd anticipated.

In front of her, the dark berth invited her, even without the mattress. If she could lay down for a few minutes, then she would be ready to go again when Wyatt returned.

She stood and gathered up the blankets he'd laid on the bench seats and made a pallet in the berth, fluffing up a thick winter jacket as a pillow. She curled up on her side, Wyatt's voice and a cool breeze drifting through the open hatch.

The pallet of blankets couldn't mask the hardness of the wood beneath, but she wasn't planning on staying there all night. As her skin cooled, goosebumps erupted on her arms. She grabbed one of Wyatt's flannel shirts and snuggled under it.

The boat rocked gently, and there came a soft thud as Wyatt landed in the galley. She started to sit up.

"Don't get up." He laid a staying hand on her knee and crawled onto the pallet beside her, groaning as he settled onto his back. "Christ, this feels good."

"It's late. I should be getting back to the house."

"There's no rush." He reached out and scooped up an armful of clean clothes, fashioned a pillow for himself, and rolled onto his side to face her. "When do you have to work again?"

"In the morning. I pulled the six to six shift. Is Rodriguez going to give you the security tape?"

Wyatt made a face. The ambient light coming from the galley was enough to see that Wyatt's expression wasn't a pleasant one. "No. Says there's nothing there. That he doesn't want to leave a paper trail by getting it out of the evidence room."

Geneva had an deliciously bad idea. She smiled. With a little help, it might work. "What if we could get it without leaving a paper trail?"

A slow grin slid across his face. "That's my girl," he said. "Always thinking."

My girl. Caleb used to call her that. *How's my girl, thatta girl, there's my girl.* That elephant that always seemed to be in the room between her and Wyatt jumped on her chest, and all the air in her lungs wheezed out.

"Hey, hey, now." Wyatt placed a finger under her chin and forced her to look at him. "What did I do?"

"Nothing." She sniffed, tried to smile, but the edges of her lips turned down instead. Then she said the one thing that worried her the most. "Do you think it will ever get to the point where Caleb isn't between us?"

She waved her hand to dismiss her words. "Wait, scratch that. I know there isn't an *us*. I didn't mean it like that."

He brought his lips to hers. To shut her up? To get her out of her head? A touch of full lips. A gentle slide. He pulled back. "You want there to be an us?" His voice came out a low rumble as he brushed the pad of his thumb across her lower lip.

Did she?

Did she dare?

She skimmed her tongue across his flesh, feeling the faint ridges of his thumbprint. He hissed in a breath. His jaw clenched.

He cupped the back of her neck and drew her to him, slanting a kiss across her mouth. His tongue flicking in, finding hers. Rising up, he rolled her onto her back, deepening the kiss. He tasted of Massey's nuclear-strength coffee.

Her girly bits tingled, her heart thumped, her mind whirred.

Are you really going to have sex with him?

Cassie's words from that first night came back to haunt her. Geneva pressed a hand against Wyatt's chest, and he pulled back, their breath blowing hot and fast. "Maybe this isn't such a good idea."

He leaned on one arm, brushing the hair off her forehead and smoothing the furrow between her brows. "You know, you may be right."

Wait, what? She was? "I am?"

He shifted, giving her more space. "I don't want to take advantage—"

"Advantage? Are you kidding me? We're two grown, consenting adults. Do you think I don't know my mind? That I don't know what I'm doing?"

"I—"

"If you don't like me, if you aren't attracted or interested, say the word." Maybe she'd read this all wrong. Maybe this thing, this attraction she thought they shared was all in her head.

"No. I like you." Simple. Direct. No hesitation.

She smiled. Relief. "I like you, too. Maybe more than I should." And the fact that she was now trying to convince him to have sex wasn't lost on her. Did she have this thing all figured out?

Not by a long shot.

But that didn't keep her from wanting him.

Then he tapped a finger to her temple and gave her a knowing nod. "You're thinking too much again."

"A minute ago, you liked the way I thought."

"This is different."

"How so?"

"This thinking is irrational."

She rose up on her elbows as a hint of anger seeped in. "*This* should be good."

"You're wondering what people will say, what they'll think if you're seen with me. Tell me... are you worried what they'll think if you're fucking me?" Anger now. Palpable. Not at her. At how the town had treated him. At how the town had turned their back on him.

She got that. He sucked in a deep breath and blew it out. Wyatt didn't seem like he was finished, so she waited him out.

"I don't think the real problem is out there." He pressed his palm over her heart. "It's in here. What do *you* think?"

The damned thing was, he'd hit the bullseye.

Cassie would clap her hands and tell Geneva to have a nice ride. The townspeople and the rest of her friends and co-workers were a different matter. They would judge her. They knew the story.

But they don't know Wyatt.

And God help her, she had loved Caleb, *still* loved Caleb, but no matter how much she'd loved her husband, no matter how much she wished things had turned out differently, Caleb was gone, and he wasn't coming back.

Are you worried what they'll think if you're fucking me?

Nerves zinged, and blood pooled between her legs. And if Wyatt thought he'd shock her by his coarse words, he didn't know her very well.

They hadn't shocked her.

It had the opposite effect. It had turned her on. "I think for the first time, in a very long time, I'm interested. I think I like that you bring a spark into my dark world."

His nostrils flared as he sucked in a breath. She sat up and held out a shaky left hand. One of the diamonds on her flat gold wedding band caught the light.

She slipped the ring off her finger and placed the band on a narrow wood shelf next to a flashlight. The last time she'd taken her ring off was at the bar when she'd tried to pick up Wyatt.

"You sure about this?" he asked.

"You chickening out on me?"

He huffed out a laugh and tried to ease her down with him.

"Hold your horses, skipper." She caught the hem of his shirt and pulled it over his head, tossing it out of the berth. "Now, lose the pants."

He eyed her for a second as if waiting for the punchline to a bad joke. She raised a brow. She wasn't kidding.

Wyatt shucked his pants, the bend of his legs hiding his erection.

"That was fast."

"I'm a genius. A beautiful woman tells me to lose my pants, I lose them."

She cocked her head. "Is that your kink? Are ropes and cuffs and slings too tame for you? You gotta be a genius in bed?"

His teeth flashed in the light. "This is going to be fun."

Wyatt stretched out, folding his hands behind his head. Watching her watch him. One thing about Wyatt, he wasn't shy. Geneva let her gaze travel up his legs, savoring the long journey. Up past his meaty calves, to his thick, muscular thighs, the thatch of dark hair at the juncture of his legs.

His cock.

It bounced once when brushed by her gaze. Her stomach clenched. Bigger and broader than Caleb. Not that Caleb had ever been lacking in that department.

"So?" Wyatt drew out the word, and Geneva detected humor mixed with the heat. "How do I compare?" When she glanced up, his confidence appeared unshaken.

Geneva's cheeks flashed hot. "That obvious?"

"I could get a tape measure if you want to get scientific."

Her hands itched to grab him, to brush her fingertips all over those muscles and enticing dips and valleys across his abdomen. She straddled his thighs and ran her palms over the points of his hips, higher to his tan line, then downward again. His stomach muscles quivered.

"You know, I've never been much of a numbers gal. I'm more a fan of empirical, *hands-on* research."

"I think—"

She took him in her hand. His breath caught. His eyes closed. His hands fisting in the blanket. He was warm and soft and hard all at the same time.

With a light stroke, she skimmed her fingers up his shaft.

His whole body went rigid, his eyes blazing and locking on hers. "What's the verdict?"

She trailed a fingernail over the ridge, her thumb brushing across the tip, over the drop of pre-cum. Without breaking his gaze, she brought her thumb to her lips and tasted him. "So far, results look promising, but a good scientist always conducts more than one study."

She continued her ministrations with both hands, going from the tip to the base.

"Better, more reliable data?" His voice went low and hoarse.

"Exactly."

She shifted, her feet dangling off the end of the berth, and took him into her mouth. Hissing in a breath, he palmed the back of her head as his fell back.

"*Jesus fucking Christ,*" he ground out, the low growl of words reverberated in the small space.

She took him deep and deeper. He thrust up, his fingers threading through her hair and tugging gently. The salty taste of him coated her tongue, the back of her throat. He smelled of musk and pond and the fresh outdoors.

When she came up for air, he guided her up, aligning her body with his. His hands gripped her ass, and he thrust against her pelvis as his mouth crashed into hers, his tongue questing, jousting, invading.

She broke the kiss long enough to yank her top over her head and strip off her bra. There would be time later for a slow seduction, right that minute she wanted skin on slick skin. Flesh against delicious flesh.

She wanted this man inside her.

Her heart thrummed, and the blood rushed past her ears, drowning out the sounds of her heavy breathing. In the tight space, she wrestled out of her pants, her panties already wet.

"Mind if I'm on top?"

"Does anyone ever answer no to that question?"

"Not if they're smart."

Grinning up at her, he settled her over his pelvis, his erection flat against his belly. She rubbed up against him, slick and eager, his hands at her hips, his fingers pressing into her flesh.

"Sweetheart, I'll take you whatever way you'll have me. Top or bottom, up, down, or sideways. Whatever floats your boat."

He slid his hands up her abdomen, cupping her breasts and giving her nipples a slight pinch before starting a slow slide back down.

"Nice to have opt—"

His thumb brushed her clit, and she surged into the pressure. Whatever she was going to say vanished from her brain, her nerves going haywire, the sinfully sweet pleasure building.

Now, only one word came to mind. "Condom?"

The hand doing delicious things to her clit disappeared, and she huffed her displeasure.

"Impatient." By the smug grin, it hadn't been a complaint.

He reached into a cubby until he came up with a foil package. She ground against him. He needed to hurry.

He ripped the package open with his teeth, and she grabbed it from him. A soft growl of pleasure escaped him as she slid the condom down and sheathed him.

Geneva rose into position, the tip of him at her slick and ready entrance, the broad head pressing against her. And as much as she wanted this, as much as she wanted Wyatt, she hesitated as all those useless, helpless, hopeless things people always say after losing a spouse flooded her mind.

It's time to move on.

Caleb would want you to be happy.

It doesn't mean you love Caleb any less.

———

WYATT LAY THERE, GENEVA POISED OVER THE TOP OF HIM, THE TIP of him pressed intimately against her, her slim hips in his hands. He wanted to plunge upward, to bury himself balls deep, to take, to possess. And he'd thought she'd wanted that, too.

Seconds before, she'd been the eager one pressing him back, having him strip, taking him into her mouth. Now, she hesitated, her eyes searching his face.

She didn't ask what he was feeling, what he was thinking. He was thankful for that because he didn't want to lie. He didn't want to tell her how it felt like he was about to take something he had no right to. That he was about to experience something only her husband should have been allowed.

"We quit right now," he offered. "Or take this slow."

She hesitated, then her contemplative expression shifted, and a sly, sexy smile slid across her lips. "Fuck slow."

In one smooth motion, she sheathed him, and his mind blanked like someone had tripped over the power cord to his brain. She gripped him. Warm and slick and tight and—

His breath caught.

"You still with me?" Through the blood pounding in his ears, her words drifted down, like an angel the sex gods had sent from high above.

"Yeah," he managed, though the word came out thin, strangled.

Then she started to move. Slow and steady at first, and then the tempo increased as she braced her hands on his chest. He met her stroke for stroke, his hands on her hips, driving her down, driving himself deeper. The zipper from his jacket poked him in the back, but he ignored it.

In the tight space of the boat's berth, the heat built and the sounds of flesh slapping flesh echoed. The musk of their sex and the smell of her on him was intoxicating. Wyatt slid his hands up her torso as sweat slicked her skin. He palmed her breasts, her nipples pebbling beneath the light brush of his thumbs.

His orgasm built, and the tight tingling at the base of his spine had his hands going back down to her hips. He wanted to turn her over, to drive, to pound into her, but there had been a reason she'd wanted to be on top. So he buried the urge, and himself, deeper with each downward stroke.

Her control wavered as her breaths came fast and frantic, her breasts bouncing, her eyes closed, her hands braced behind her on his thighs. He slid his thumb over her clit, and she arched, grinding against his hand as she held on.

"Sweet... Jesus," she moaned. "Right there."

Her words brought a smile to his lips as he worked the tight, slick bud, enticing, and inciting an internal riot. His balls tightened. He was seconds away. "Come on, baby."

Her breath came in short pants, and she reached down and pressed his hand tighter against her, her eyes squeezed shut.

He stilled.

Was she fucking *him* or her dead husband?

"Look at me," he said, the words barely a whisper. She shook her head, but he insisted. "Geneva, look at me."

She ground against him, her eyes fluttering open, her focus loose before zeroing in on him. For some reason, he needed to be sure she knew who lay beneath her. That it was him she fucked and not her husband's ghost.

"I see *you*," she said as if reading his thoughts. "I feel *you*."

He hugged her to him, looping his hands around her shoulders and driving harder as he crushed his mouth to hers. Their tongues dueling, fighting the memories, slaying the phantom that had no business lingering between them. Then he reached a hand between them and pushed her over pleasure's hot, sharp edge.

And just so she knew, just so there wouldn't be any doubt, he said, "I see you, t—"

Her muscles clamped down around him as her orgasm hit, stealing his voice and his thoughts and his control. He gripped her hips and pounded into her. Once. Twice. He came. Hot and hard and erratic. She milked him dry.

Spent and spineless, she lay over the top of him as aftershocks shook her body.

They lay there, catching their breath until he started going soft. He pulled out and took care of the condom, then laid flat out on the pallet, and snugged her up against him. Geneva threw a leg across his hips, and he absently ran his hand along the length of her muscled calf and up to her knee.

She hissed in a breath between her teeth and jerked her leg away. "Ouch."

"What?" He sat up and tapped the light above him.

She laid back, her hands behind her head, knees bent. Abrasions ran across the cap of each knee. Red and raw from the thin layer of blankets over the wood deck of the berth beneath them.

"Tell me, Doc," she said. "Am I going to live?"

"It will be touch and go," he teased, "but with the right treatment and physical therapy, you could be good as new in no time."

She leaned up and braced herself on her elbows. "Physical therapy?"

"Of the sweaty, sex variety."

"Uh-huh." She looked him up and down with an eye of appreciation. And damn if he didn't start getting hard again. "That's how I got into this mess to begin with. It would only happen again."

"Trust me," he said as he pressed his lips to hers. "We have plenty of other options to explore. If you're game."

She looped a hand behind his head and pulled him in for another kiss. He tasted himself on her tongue, and he broke the kiss before he took her again. "You okay, Gen?"

He wasn't talking about her knees.

He wasn't even talking about the sex.

He was talking about Caleb.

She sucked in a deep breath and held it for a long while.

Then her cheeks puffed out as she released the pent-up air. "I think so." Her voice rose at the end, so it came out more as a question than a statement.

"You wish you could take it back?"

She traced a hand absently over her lower belly, and he tried not to think about how much he liked her hands there. "No. I'm a big girl. I knew what I was doing. What about you? How's it feel to be the first to fuck the widow?"

He stiffened. *So, not as okay as she thought she was.* He didn't need the reminder, but her lashing out at him had more to do with how much she hurt inside, and how she was processing everything, than him.

But also, he didn't like the crude way that she'd referred to what they'd shared as fucking. What they'd shared hadn't been base. It hadn't been vulgar. It had been bewitching.

He held her chin and looked her in the eye when he said, "For what it's worth, that was more than fucking. At least it was for me."

He climbed out of the birth, turning his back on her, not waiting for her response. "Hold tight. I'll get some Band-Aids for you."

Naked, he searched the head and then the cupboards above where the table should be before finding the first-aid kit stuffed behind the plastic food storage containers in the galley. He sifted through the box and found what he needed. Over his shoulder, he glanced at her. She was curled up on her side, her head resting on her arm, watching him.

"What?" he said as he brought the supplies back to their makeshift bed.

"You're beautiful." There was a note of surprise in her voice.

He smiled at that. No one had ever described him that way before. "Isn't that supposed to be my line?"

"It's not in the way you look." When he sat, she brushed her fingertips over his flank. "Though I have no complaints there." Then she placed her hand over his heart and said, "It's what's in here that continues to amaze me."

He took her hand and kissed her palm. "When this is over…"

He let the rest of the sentence drop because he saw the insanity of the direction his thoughts had taken. When this case was over, when they'd found the Nightwalker killer, when they'd found the man with Caleb the night Wyatt had shot him, when they'd discovered what Caleb had been investigating, the reality was, nothing will have changed.

Wyatt would forever be the man who'd killed her husband, and she would forever be the widow. Whatever there was between them had no future.

"When this is over… what?" she asked.

He opened the disinfectant and started cleaning her wounds. "It will be nice for things to get back to normal."

"Sure." Her expression soured, and she reached over and pulled on his blue flannel shirt and buttoned it up to her neck. The temperature in the cabin seemed to plummet though the breeze hadn't picked up.

Back to normal.

His words lay heavy in the air. He wanted to take them back because they weren't the truth.

Wrapping a blanket around her lower half, she moved to the bench seat in the kitchen. She settled into the corner and hugged her arms around her knees. "Speaking of getting this thing over with… want to hear my idea about how to get that security tape?"

He threw on a pair of shorts commando-style since all his underwear seemed to have gone AWOL when he wasn't looking.

Geneva didn't seem too happy with him, so sat across from her and gave her some space, bracing his feet on the bench beside her. "What is this diabolical plan of yours?"

"We borrow the tape from the evidence room."

His head popped up, and he choked on the bark of laughter. She didn't crack a smile. She wasn't kidding. He narrowed his eyes and said, "Define 'borrow.'"

"The classical definition. We take and use for a short period of time, and then we give it back."

"Great idea," he said, though his words leaned heavily on the sarcasm scale. "Except for the whole issue of it being in a sealed bag, in a locked evidence room, at the Sheriff's Office."

"Where my friend Cassie works the night shift at dispatch."

Wyatt sat back, and his feet fell to the floor. He couldn't believe he was going to ask the next question with a straight face. "And how would she get in?"

"She wouldn't. You would. Or rather, we would. After she gets you the key."

"Who would be stupid enough to give her the key to the evidence room?"

"Deputy Dave McMahon," she said. "Not only does he have a crush on Cassie, but Cass has always had a light touch. Her freshman year of high school she had some juvie charges for pickpocketing expunged from her record in her freshman year of high school. With a bit of a distraction, she could snag the key, and he would never know. What do you think?"

Wyatt scrubbed his hands over his face. There was so much at risk. For them. For Cassie. One little mistake. One little slip-up and one of them, or all of them, were going to jail. But without Rodriguez's cooperation, he didn't see where they had much choice. "I think we gotta try."

12

THE NEXT MORNING, GENEVA ARRIVED EARLY FOR HER SHIFT AT the fire station and walked next door to the Sheriff's Office to talk to Cassie when she came off her shift at dispatch.

Anxiety gnawed in Geneva's gut as she knocked on the open door of the dispatch room. She had to keep reminding herself to relax her clenched fists.

Cassie was sitting in front of a bank of monitors and talking to one of the deputies on the radio. She turned at Geneva's knock and gave her a bright smile. Cassie's replacement showed up, and Geneva waited until Cassie finished the call and the shift change.

Before Cassie could ask her what she was doing there, Geneva said, "I need a favor."

"Anything. What do you—" Cassie cut off when she glanced at Geneva. Cassie's eyes darted to Geneva's fists, then back to her face. Geneva's jaw muscles hurt, and her molars were at serious risk of being crushed under the pressure.

"What is it? What has that bastard done?"

"Wait. What? No. It isn't anything like that."

"Then what is it?"

Geneva opened her mouth to answer, but Cassie latched onto Geneva's bicep and said, "Hold that thought."

Cassie ushered Geneva out the back door of the department where everyone usually went to grab a smoke. Fortunately, this early in the morning, she and Cassie were all alone. Before the door closed, Cassie caught it and peeled a piece of duct tape off the inside edge of the door and placed it over the door latch to keep them from being locked out.

"Nifty system," Geneva said. "Doesn't seem too secure."

"Yeah, well, we had to come up with something because everyone kept locking themselves out when they came out here. So spill. If it isn't Wolfe, what is it?"

"I need you to help us break into the evidence room."

Instead of a gasp of shock, instead of indignation and a 'hell no,' Cassie's grin went wide, and she said, "Now you're talking."

God, Geneva loved that woman. But her own smile slipped from her face when she said, "Think about it first. You could lose your job. Or worse, end up in jail."

"Answer me one question."

"What's that?"

"Is this important? Is this something that will help you? Help answer questions about Caleb?"

"Yes. We believe so."

"Then, I'm in."

Geneva's radio shoulder squawked. Someone at the fire station was looking for her. "I gotta go," Geneva said. "Seriously, think about it and meet me at my place when I get off work and give me your answer."

"I'm not going to change it."

Geneva hugged her and thanked the fates that had plopped a surly Cassie next to her their first day of freshman health class.

They parted, and Geneva had almost made it to the corner

of the building when Cassie called out. "Hey, you might need this."

Cassie waved something small in the air. Geneva glanced down at the front of her uniform where her ID badge should be. How? When? Cassie jogged over and handed it to her, and gave her a wink. "I've still got the touch."

The next twelve hours passed excruciatingly slow. On a day where all Geneva wanted was a lot of calls to make her day go by faster, she had a dud of a day. One call. To the diner. It turned out the guy had indigestion, not a heart attack. Good for the guy. Bad for her.

She'd passed the time cleaning an already clean ambulance, organizing well-organized drawers and cabinets, but mostly she spent the day watching the clock. As soon as the little hand had hit the six and the big hand had hit the twelve, she scrammed. No hanging with the crew after hours, no shooting the shit. Just *ding* and she was gone.

She made a quick stop at the diner for a to-go dinner. If Cassie was going to take such a huge risk for her, then the least she could do was feed her.

Arriving at home, she dumped the food on the kitchen counter, then scrambled to finish cleaning up the mess in the hallway before Cassie came over.

"Knock, knock," Cassie called out as she opened the front door.

"In the kitchen." Geneva pulled paper plates out of the cabinet and removed the Styrofoam containers of food out of the plastic bag.

Cassie laid her purse over the back of the chair and went for the utensils and napkins. She glanced at the three plates Geneva had pulled out and said, "We expecting company, or are you eating for two?"

"Wyatt is going to join us, but he's running a little late."

"Ooooh," Cassie shoved aside the samples of marble, paint, and cabinet doors that had been floating around the kitchen for the past year and a half, and opened one of the containers of food. "So it's Wyatt now, huh?"

"It seemed awkward to keep calling him Wolfe."

"Why? Is Wyatt easier to scream when you climax?"

Geneva pelted Cassie with a french fry as embarrassment heated Geneva's cheeks. "It's not like that."

Geneva sat and dished her chicken fried steak onto her plate, the ends of the meat hanging over the edge. She added the gravy, salt and pepper, and scooped out the mashed potatoes.

Cassie bit into her club sandwich. "Oh, my God." The words came out sounding more like omyagawd due to the mouthful of food. She chewed fast and swallowed hard and washed it down with her soda. "Liar!"

"Who's a liar?" Wyatt asked as he stepped into the kitchen.

Geneva slapped a hand over her chest to keep her heart from jumping out and escaping to the next county. "You scared me. I didn't hear you come in."

"Coffee?" he asked as he headed for the half-filled pot.

"That's old," Geneva said, "I can make more if you like."

"I can manage." He dumped the old coffee and rinsed the pot. Over his shoulder, he repeated, "Who's lying?"

"Gen."

Cassie bumped into Wyatt as she got up and retrieved the coffee mugs out of the cabinet. Geneva noticed she had that same mischievous look on her face she'd had right before she'd sneaked into the boys' locker room in high school and swiped all the clothes while the football team was showering.

"Gen?" But Wyatt was too focused on the coffee to give Cassie his full attention.

"Don't say it," Geneva warned, even though, after all the

years of knowing her friend, she knew Cassie was deaf to that tone.

Wyatt turned, leaned back against the counter, and crossed his arms over his chest. "Don't say what?"

Cassie returned to her seat. "Geneva was just telling me how she prefers to call you Wyatt instead of Wolfe when you make her come."

Sweat broke out on Geneva's forehead, and she wanted to crawl under the table and hide. Wyatt glanced from the stupid grin on Cassie's face to the mortified grimace on Geneva's.

Then his attention went back to Cassie, a brow raised. "Did she now?"

The coffee maker beeped, and Geneva jumped up to fill the mug for him, unable to sit still any longer. "Sit down," she told him. "I'll get the coffee."

He sat across from her, foregoing the paper plate and tearing the lid off his spaghetti and meatballs. He dug in with his fork and mumbled his thanks around a bite of pasta when she set the mug of coffee down in front of him.

"What else did she tell you?" Wyatt didn't even have the good grace to blush, and if Geneva wasn't mistaken, there was a hint of a smile on his face.

"*Nothing*," Geneva said. "I didn't even tell her *that* thing."

Cassie shrugged. "No. But you would have, eventually."

"You're not helping."

For the next few minutes, talking fell away as they filled their bellies. Wyatt fiddled with the decorator samples on the corner of the table and picked out a mint green paint chip, a piece of a white shaker cabinet, and the white marble with black flecks. "These three," Wyatt said as he pushed the samples toward her.

Geneva's chicken fried steak did a slow roll in her stomach. Those had been her favorites, but she and Caleb had gone around and around. Her choice had been the complete opposite of what Caleb had wanted. And since he'd done most of the cooking, she'd decided to give in and let him choose what he wanted.

But she'd never gotten the chance to tell him.

Now she was stuck.

Stuck with the old cabinets where the doors wouldn't close, with the yellow countertops with the chipped laminate at the corners, with the dingy white walls. Stuck between what she wanted and honoring what Caleb would have liked.

"Caleb wanted the other," Geneva said.

Wyatt wiped his mouth. The apology in his eyes again, but she shook her head. A dark expression flashed across his face, but it wasn't aimed at her.

He tossed the napkin on top of the last bite of meatball and began busing all the throwaways. He dumped the utensils in the sink and poured himself a second cup of coffee.

"So," Wyatt said as he boosted himself up on the counter. "Did Geneva tell you her idea?"

"A little," Cassie allowed. "You need in the evidence room. Once to take what you need. Once to put it back."

He looked Cassie up and down as if he could assess her abilities from across the room. "Think you can get us in?"

"I know I can."

Geneva turned her chair so she could see Cassie and Wyatt at the same time. "The smokers routinely tape over the latch on the back door so they can get back into the building. I thought when the time comes, that's how we could gain access."

"And with the evidence room off that back hallway," Cassie added, "there's less chance someone will bump into you. And at night, many times, I'm the only one at the Sheriff's Office unless a deputy is doing paperwork or processing an arrest."

Geneva frowned. "And all the more likely that you'll be accused of the theft."

"I'll make sure I'm logged into my station at whatever time you choose. Trust me, even if they had reason to suspect me, I would have a bulletproof alibi."

Breaking into the evidence room was starting to feel like a horrible idea. A low-level buzz hummed along Geneva's nerves, and she got up and opened the dishwasher beneath where Wyatt sat and started loading the utensils and the past couple days of dirty dishes. "The security cameras will be a problem for us though."

"Whoa," Wyatt said, "There's no *us*. There's me. I'm going in. You're going to be with Massey."

"Massey doesn't need a babysitter."

"No, but he needs someone on lookout. Someone to watch over his shoulder while he makes a copy of the tape."

Geneva stifled a grumble. She didn't like the idea of Wyatt taking all the risk. She finished loading the dishwasher and turned to Cassie. "Any way you can shut off the security cameras?"

"Not from dispatch."

"I was afraid of that."

"It'll be okay, Gen." Wyatt's placating tone grated. It felt like he was patting her like a dog, telling her the thunder wouldn't hurt her. "I'll get in, get out, without anyone the wiser. If it's the same old system they had when I was there, they only keep the video for twenty-four hours before the files are overwritten. We get past that first day, and we're golden."

The plan started coming together, but Geneva still had concerns. "What about the evidence bag? We open that, and someone is going to know it's been compromised."

"That's mine and Massey's department. I have evidence bags and sealing tape from when I worked with the department. Massey has a portable scanner wand and printer. I spoke with him earlier. He's confident he can recreate the chain of custody label for the bag. It should pass a cursory inspection at least."

Cassie stood and rubbed her hands together like the consummate evil scientist right before she unleashes evil onto the world. "Now, all we have to do is pick a time."

They conferred about their schedules. In three nights, when Cassie would be working and Geneva would be off, Deputy Dave McMahon from the evidence room would be coming off day shift around the time Cassie went on.

"So, how are you going to get the key from him?" Wyatt asked.

Cassie reached into her purse and tossed Wyatt the wallet she'd swiped off him while he'd made the coffee. "The same way I got that off you. With ease."

Wyatt let out a long, low whistle of appreciation. "*That* is impressive. I bet the city of Murdock is glad you gave up your life of crime."

"Now I only use my powers in the fight against the forces of evil," Cassie said, channeling superhero mode. She shouldered her purse and started to back out of the kitchen. "I've got to head out. Thanks for dinner," she told Geneva. "And the next time I see you, you'll have to tell me if Wolfe's as good in bed as the rumors say he is."

"*Cassie!*" Geneva hissed out, but the only answer was the front door clicking closed.

She reached down and closed the dishwasher door. "I'm sorry," she started, unable to meet his eyes. "I really didn't—"

Wyatt took her hand and pulled her between his legs. He lifted her chin with a finger and locked eyes with her. A smile tipped his lips when he said, "If I had known I had more than one woman I had to satisfy, I would have taken more care last night."

Wyatt wrapped Geneva's arms around his waist as he sat on the kitchen counter, enjoying the mortification on her face.

"I didn't tell her anything about... about us." Geneva's cheeks burned bright. "That's just Cass. She doesn't mean anything by what she says."

"Relax," Wyatt said. "I was giving you a hard time. I know the type, full of bluster and bullshit. She only wanted to get a rise out of me. It was all in good fun."

"You're not mad?" The fact that she seemed surprised by the idea that he didn't feel like he had to take Cassie's ribbing out on her made his chest ache.

"No. I'm not mad."

The tension in her shoulders eased, and her lips plumped back up. He couldn't keep his eyes off her mouth. Kneading the muscles at the base of her neck, he pressed a kiss to her lips and said, "You should have stayed over last night. I missed you in my bed."

"I'm pretty sure Massey didn't say you could crash at his place, imagining you would hook up with strange women at his house."

"Probably not," he allowed, "but he likes you. He wouldn't have a problem with you being there. Besides, the only woman I want to hook up with is you. It's not like I'd planned on tacking up an 'open for business' sign above the bedroom door."

"Still." She ran her hands up his thighs and stopped at his belt buckle. His heart faltered a beat then skipped ahead. "You could stay here."

He almost would have preferred Massey's place, or the boat, or the barn, or just about anywhere else *but* Caleb's house. Caleb's *bed*. Wyatt had already put the man in the grave and screwed the man's wife. He wasn't going to further insult Caleb's memory by taking her in the man's very own bed.

He wasn't that much of a rat bastard.

"As much as I'd love to stay," he lied, "I'm meeting with a client tonight."

"After, then?" Hope lit her eyes that he didn't want to crush, but as much as he wanted to be with her that night, he couldn't forget he still had a job to do.

"It'll probably run late. How about we meet up tomorrow night after your shift? I'll buy you a real dinner."

She pulled a half-step away and asked. "This client you're meeting, do they have anything to do with what we're working on?"

"No."

One word.

One lie.

No hesitation.

Funny that he'd found it easier to lie to her than to tell her the truth, that he was meeting with Candy's old pimp and didn't want her to come because not only was it not safe, he didn't want her anywhere near that scumbag. He only wanted to protect her.

She wouldn't see it that way.

She leveled a steady, assessing gaze on him. "It bothers me that I can't tell whether or not you're lying."

"You're just going to have to trust me." Maybe he should have been the officer deep undercover, the one telling all the lies. They seemed to be rolling off his tongue easy enough, even if they made his chest tight and his conscience shoot him a big fat middle finger.

She took his hand and pulled him off the counter. "Dinner then."

Dressed in casual clothes—jeans and a cotton top with her

hair pulled back in a ponytail—she shouldn't have looked so sexy. But he knew what she hid beneath the layers. Knew what awaited him. Knew what he was missing.

He hugged her to him and brought his mouth down on hers, loving the way she sank against him—all softness and steel. She smelled of hometown cooking with a hint of work-related disinfectant.

As the kiss deepened, he started walking her backward out of the kitchen. He was going to be late if he didn't get a move on, but he couldn't force himself to break the kiss. She nipped at his lower lip, his chin. She shoved him back against the refrigerator, straddled one of his legs, and rubbed up against him.

One of her hands squeezed him through his fly, and when he was about to say screw it all and haul her to Caleb's bed, she gave him one last nip. Between heavy breaths, she said, "Be sure you save room for dessert."

He smiled wide. He was a damn lucky bastard. "Noted."

Taking him by the hand, she tugged him along to the front entry, where a series of glossy black and white photos of Geneva and Caleb hung on the wall. He held back and took a moment, looking from one to the next to the next.

In all of them, Geneva was smiling or laughing. Big genuine smiles and belly laughs. Her on Caleb's shoulders. Them dancing at their wedding. Them on a rocky outcropping near the top of the world.

The one thing that rang true in all of them—Caleb had made her happy.

Fingers linked with his, Geneva leaned against his arm. "He was a good man. I think you would have liked him."

"I think so, too." That's what made what he was starting with her so damn difficult. Like he was stabbing a friend in the back after they'd already called dibs.

———

GENEVA KNEW WYATT WAS LYING FROM THE MOMENT THE WORDS had left his mouth. He hadn't hesitated. He hadn't flinched. He hadn't looked away. But she'd *known*. The same way she'd known the times when Caleb had lied to her.

Standing in her doorway, she hadn't been able to look him in the eye when she told him he needed to get going. Deep down, she knew he was trying to protect her. In that way, he was so much like Caleb.

Was she mad about the deceit? Hell yeah. Was she going to sit at home and cry and whine? Hell no.

She was going to follow him.

She had just as much at stake as he had, maybe more.

Practically shoving him out the door, she grabbed her purse and her car keys and threw on a pair of sneakers then watched as his taillights disappeared down her street.

She ran to her car, her tires skidding on the road as she stomped on the gas to try and catch up. She patted her Prius on the dash. "Good boy, Mino."

They rolled into Murdock about fifteen minutes later, the traffic heavy for a weeknight. From the abundance of white shoe polish on the vehicle windows, one of the local youth baseball leagues had a tournament.

All the cars made following Wyatt that much easier. She kept her Prius tucked between an older Chevy single cab pickup and a beater of a purple Impala with shiny spinner rims and skinny bald tires. Four cars ahead, over the top of the Impala, she kept her eye on the third brake light on the back of Wyatt's extended cab.

Wyatt turned off the main drag, headed toward the sleazy part of town. She followed, her fingers drumming on the steering wheel to the *James Bond* theme song playing in her head. "What aren't you telling me, Wyatt?"

Traffic got lighter as they drove from the part of town where she got calls for heart attacks and little old ladies with broken hips, to the streets where she got calls for knife wounds and bullet holes and crackheads who'd OD'd.

They ended up back on Fifth Street. AKA Stripper Street. Wyatt parked at a corner, and Geneva cut in behind a Lexus, its axles up on blocks, its tires stripped off. Geneva glanced around. Someone in the alley stopped digging through the dumpster long enough to give her a stare, then went back to his search.

At the corner up ahead, the vapor light cast a yellow glow on a group of four women. Their heels were high, their cleavage low, and their skirts short. Agent Soto broke off, her ass kicked out like an elbow as she leaned through Wyatt's passenger window.

Soto hopped in, and they were off again. Five minutes and seven turns later, Wyatt dropped Soto at another corner, and she started the long trek back to where she'd come from.

Geneva had no choice but to drive by, hoping Soto wouldn't recognize her. But Soto was a sharp woman. The agent spotted her car, her laser gaze following her progress down the street. Geneva gave her a weak wave and put a finger to her lips in a silent plea not to squeal on her. Soto shook her head and started walking again.

Phew.

She turned the corner on the dark, narrow side street where Wyatt had turned and slammed on her brakes, Wyatt's knees inches from her front bumper, his hands on his hips, his face murderous.

For half a second, she considered throwing Mino into reverse and getting the hell out of there, but running away wouldn't solve anything.

He bumped the meat of his fist on her window, and she buzzed it down. Fresh air rushed in, which was a good thing because sweat bubbled on her upper lip.

"Hey," she said.

"I don't appreciate being followed."

"Yeah? Well, I don't appreciate your lies."

He looked away and stared down the street. Running a hand over a day's growth of stubble, he looked back down at her. "It's for your protection."

"Don't feed me—"

"Gen... *please.*" His voice dropped, and his tone changed from detective mode to something much, much more intimate. "I need you to leave. I need you to let me do this alone. I promise I'll tell you all about it tomorrow."

"What are you doing here?"

"I'm meeting with a guy named Scout. He used to be Candy's pimp. Soto said he's back in town, hanging at the warehouse at the end of the block. I thought I'd see if he's heard from her."

The air grew still, and her car started to get stuffy. Idling, her car went into battery mode and ran nearly silent. A cat snarled and hissed in a nearby alley, and the sound of a tin can bouncing and rolling down the asphalt came from the same direction.

In the distance, headlights zipped by on a cross street two blocks down. She couldn't see anyone out on the street, but the back of her neck prickled with apprehension. She glanced at the top of the nearby buildings. Nobody looked down from the edge, but she couldn't shake the feeling of being watched.

"Please," he said again.

She stared into his gray eyes that had gone to pewter in the illumination of her green dashboard lights. If she pressed, if she insisted, she had the feeling he would give in, but there was something about the way he'd asked that had her saying, "Be careful, I don't want to—"

Lose you, too.

But he wasn't hers. Not by a long shot.

"Just promise me you'll be careful," she said.

"Done," he replied a little too quick. He leaned through the window and pressed a kiss to her lips.

"Call me when you get home?"

A slow, smug smile spread across his face. "Worried about me, baby?"

"Just call me." She shifted into drive and buzzed up her window, catching the hint of a swagger in the sway of his shoulders as he straightened and backed away. She didn't need to feed his ego. He clearly already knew the answer to his question.

———

WYATT STRODE DOWN THE MIDDLE OF THE STREET, GAZE SHIFTING side to side searching for the eyes he knew watched the warehouse. He spotted one set slumped against the doorway of a boarded-up two-pump service station, a man with dirty blankets and a couple of crumpled beer cans nearby.

But the real drunks only glance up long enough to make sure you mean them no harm, they don't follow your progress down the street. They don't whistle a warning. They don't jump from the top of one building to the next.

He had to hand it to Scout. The pimp had these couple of blocks sewn up tighter than the drawstring on a pirate's purse.

Walking past his truck, he shoved the driver's door closed that he'd left it open in his rush to cut Geneva off. At least this time he'd caught her tailing him.

He didn't bother to lock his truck. Locks didn't keep people like these out of vehicles. He stepped to the front door of the warehouse. The door was old. The locks were new. The original door had been glass, but someone had screwed plywood to the inside, protecting the spiderweb of cracked glass and blocking his view to the interior. He pounded on the door frame.

Seconds later, movement flashed behind a hole cut in the plywood at eye level, but no one answered the door.

He pounded again. Like a monkey on his back, apprehension settled into the spot between his shoulder blades, chattering in his ear. A warning. He glanced behind him, expecting to find someone standing there, but the street remained clear.

Again he pounded. "Scout. Open the damn door."

More movement behind the peephole, then a key turned in the lock, and the door opened a fraction. Wyatt had to look up to see the guy's face. He had a mangy beard almost down to his bare chest and mustard stuck near the corner of his mouth.

"What do you want?"

Wyatt leaned a shoulder against the opposite side door jamb, acting relaxed. He wasn't. He didn't cross his boots at the ankles. He wanted to be able to move fast and not trip all over his feet if he had to. "What does any guy want from a pimp?"

The Beard just stared at him. Wyatt stared back and raised a brow.

"The girls are on the street, not here."

"Not the one I want."

The Beard went to close the door, and Wyatt shoved a heavy boot against it. "Just do me a favor and get Scout."

"Let him in," a pre-pubescent sounding voice from inside said.

The Beard stepped back, and Wyatt opened the door wide. The front part of the warehouse had been partitioned off into an office or display area at one time, the wood-paneled walls cracked and damaged. Three camping style fuel lanterns flickered and hissed as they dangled from the mold and water-stained dropped ceiling. Scout sat in a rickety chair at a card-board table with one corner propped up on a stack of boxes.

At least Wyatt had assumed the man was Scout. Soto had said to find the skinny kid who looked like he helped old ladies across the street to earn his merit badge.

The kid at the table fit the bill. A shock of white-blond hair, neatly parted and combed. Short-sleeved plaid dress shirt buttoned up to his neck. Tan Dockers an inch or two too short for his long legs.

"Detective Wolfe," Scout said.

The Beard pulled a gun from the small of his back and leveled it at Wyatt's chest. "What're the cops doing here?"

Wyatt didn't move.

"Hey, man, chill," came a voice from a dark corner. A man stood. Wyatt hadn't even seen him sitting there. "He ain't a cop no more."

A short but strong, wiry man stepped into the light. Wyatt knew the man was strong because he'd had to wrestle his ass to the ground to arrest him on drug charges five years before. Bastard almost got the best of him.

"Jonah." Wyatt cut the Beard a quick look and stepped inside. The Beard kept the gun in hand but pointed it at the floor. "Nice to see you on the outside. I would have thought three years in prison would have taught you to keep your nose clean."

Jonah put his hands up, palms out. "Nothing illegal about having a beer with a couple of old friends."

So far, only the trespassing part was against the law. Oh, and the bags of weed on the table. And Wyatt was confident the white powder on the small mirror wasn't flour, and the digital scale wasn't there to help them bake the perfect cake.

But he couldn't care less about the drugs.

After all, as Jonah so delicately put it, he wasn't a cop anymore. Scout must have done some homework to have recognized Wyatt's face, but not enough to know he was no longer with the sheriff's department.

"Close the door," Scout said to the Beard before holding his hand out to the chair at the table across from him. "Have a seat, detec—Mr. Wolfe."

Moths buzzed the lantern hanging above the table. Wyatt pulled the chair away to give him maneuvering room if he needed it and folded himself into the chair. The legs wiggled under his weight.

"So, no longer with the Sheriff's Office?" Scout lit a Marlboro with a *Scooby Doo* lighter, the tip of the cigarette glowing bright red as he inhaled.

Wyatt wasn't about to hash out his employment history with a pimp. "I'm looking for one of your women."

"Like my friend said, they're all on the corner. And if they're not, give them an hour, and they'll be back."

"Not this one. I'm looking for Candy Lane."

Scout exhaled and disappeared behind a cloud of smoke. The kid didn't look cool. He looked like a twelve-year-old who'd swiped his mother's cigarettes on a dare. But Soto had warned Wyatt not to let Scout's child-like innocent look fool him.

He wasn't a kid.

He most certainly wasn't innocent.

"You and everybody else in this town," Scout said.

"Like who?"

"Johns for one."

"And for another?"

Scout just shrugged and sucked in another lungful of carcinogens.

"Still sounds like a cop," the Beard grumbled from a worn-out sofa shoved into the far corner of the room.

"He ain't. He's a private dick," Jonah said. "He's the one who killed that cop last year."

Jonah turned his attention back to Wyatt. "Thought for a while there, we might share a cell."

"I bet you would have liked that."

Jonah shrugged. "I got nothin' against you, man."

"The fucker sent you to jail," the Beard groused.

"He's the only motherfucker who treated me with any respect. He just did his job. Like I did mine. I got no hard feelin's." Then to Wyatt, he said, "I guess you and me being roomies wasn't in the cards."

"Guess not." Wyatt turned his attention back to Scout. "The woman?"

"Why you want to know?"

Scout squinted through another cloud of smoke but held Wyatt's gaze. Nothing short of full honesty would get Wyatt what he wanted. He leaned forward and said, "She could be the key to clearing my conscience."

Scout considered that as he stubbed out the last of his cigarette on the top of an old beer can and stuffed the butt through the hole. "I heard she lit off for a waitress job in Jackson Hole. Considering what's been going on around here, she thought getting off the streets would be safer."

"Where?"

Scout tried to light another cigarette, but the Scooby lighter spat and sparked and gave up the ghost. Scout replaced the cigarette in the carton and shoved them into the breast pocket of his shirt. Wyatt expected to see a pocket protector and maybe a scientific calculator, but sadly, no.

"The Bull Moose. Off the main drag," Scout said.

"Nah, man, it was the Caribou Cafe." That from Jonah.

"Both you dickheads are wrong," came a grumble from the couch. "It's the Moose Lodge."

Jonah tipped his head toward the Beard. "What he said."

"We done here?" Scout asked.

Wyatt nodded and headed toward the door. Jonah followed him out. High above, the heavy *whomp, whomp, whomp,* of one of the task force helicopters cut the relative quiet of the night, its searchlight skimming the area ahead of it.

The warehouse door closed, and Wyatt held his hand out to Jonah. "Thanks for the help."

Jonah shook it.

"If you ever decide to give up the life of crime, give me a call."

A sheepish smile crossed the man's face. "If you ever quit thinking like a cop, give me one."

Wyatt clapped him on the shoulder and headed back to his truck. He pulled the door open, and the helicopter's spotlight lit him up. Holding his hand up to his eyes to shade them, he wondered if this is what it felt like right before you were abducted by aliens.

Then the light shifted and continued down the street. As the spots cleared from his eyes, and his vision readjusted to the dark, he caught a flash of light in the alley—the shine of chrome. What the?

Wyatt strode down the street to the alley. An engine started, and a car shifted into gear, but instead of the tires squealing as the car pulled away, the tinted window quietly rolled down.

Wyatt didn't bother hiding his irritation. "You following me?"

Rodriguez shifted his Challenger into park. "It's called back up."

"I don't remember requesting any."

"I was driving home and checked your location." Rodriguez held up his phone with the locator app pulled up that they'd used back when they'd been partners to help keep track of each other. "This isn't the best part of town for a guy like you to be by yourself."

"A guy like me?"

"A deputy."

"Ex-deputy."

"You're still my friend, still more of a partner than that sniveling little shit they saddled me with."

Wyatt laughed. "Sucks to be you. Now get the hell out of here. You know they got eyes everywhere, right? Hard for me to do this on the down-low if you don't stay off my ass."

"Find out anything useful?"

"Not so much." Wyatt wanted to check into Scout's information further before he hassled Rodriguez with it. His friend's plate already overflowed with dead bodies and Feds. "I'll let you know when I have something solid."

Rodriguez's tie hung loose, the top two buttons of his shirt lay undone with wrinkles creasing the front of it as if he'd slept in his clothes the past two nights. "You look like twice-baked roadkill. Go home and get some sleep."

"Roger that." Rodriguez shifted into gear. "Watch your back."

13

———

A light tap to the bottom of Geneva's boot woke her from a sound sleep. Geneva opened her eyes.

Wyatt was squatting down in front of her. "What are you doing here?" He held out a hand and helped her to her feet. "Didn't trust me to call you when I got home?"

That-A-Way, who she'd used as a pillow and body warmer, raised her head and belched as Geneva stood and rubbed the flatness out of her ass from being on the ground for so long. "I —" She hated to admit this, hated that it made her feel weak with the admission. Time to woman up. "I didn't want to be alone."

"So, you thought you'd drive all the way out here and get cozy with Evie's cow?"

"I thought you'd have been back by the time I got here. And then you weren't, and I didn't want to knock on the door and wake Massey."

Wyatt glanced at his watch. "It's just after midnight. Trust me, he's awake."

He placed a hand on her hip and went in for a kiss. She rose on her toes and met him half-way. His tongue brushed her lips, and she held onto his shoulders and opened for him, not quite understanding what it was about this man she couldn't get enough of.

She broke the kiss before one or both of them ended up naked in the front yard with an ancient bovine for an audience. Would that be considered animal cruelty? "Do you really think Massey won't mind that I'm here? I can go home if it's going to be a problem."

"Stay. I'm sure it'll be fine."

They stepped around That-A-Way, and Wyatt used Massey's spare key on the front door. Massey was rolling into the kitchen with his travel mug between his legs. The coffee pot beeped.

"Hey." Massey glanced up and rolled on past.

"Hey," Geneva and Wyatt said.

Wyatt took her hand and started tugging her down the hall toward the guest room. Over his shoulder, he said, "Geneva's spending the night."

"Sure," came the reply from the kitchen.

"You got anything for me yet?"

"No."

"Eek," Geneva whispered. "He doesn't sound too happy."

"And asking me every fifteen fucking seconds if I have anything doesn't make it go any faster," he hollered back at them.

Wyatt chuckled. Low and warm, his affection for Massey bottled up in the sound. He held his bedroom door open for her as Massey wheeled down the hall toward them.

"Got a tip," Wyatt said. "On Candy Lane. Jackson Hole. Waitress at the Bull Moose, or Caribou Café, or Moose Lodge. Something like that."

"On it," Massey said as he started the turn into his office.

"And Massey?" Massey caught the wheels with his hands and looked back at Wyatt. "Thanks, buddy."

"No worries, dude."

Wyatt closed the door and turned toward Geneva.

"You got a lead on Candy?"

"Who knows if it's good or if she's still there, but it's a start. Now that Massey has a general area to look, he can narrow his search."

"Then what?" Geneva asked as Wyatt backed her toward the bed. The look in his eyes said he had more important things on his mind than their case. She didn't think he was thinking farther ahead than the next couple of seconds when he'd get his hands on her.

She appreciated his singular focus.

The backs of her legs hit the mattress, and she plopped down. Wyatt kicked out of his boots and tore off his shirt. "Then we go talk to her."

She placed a staying hand on his bare chest, wanted to scrunch her fingers through the thin mat of hair, but she still had a thread of a coherent thought in her head that didn't have to do with what it was going to feel like having Wyatt's hands and mouth on her. "You're not leaving me behind this time."

"Don't you have work?" He kneeled in front of her and slipped one boot off her foot and then the other. "Scoot up."

He nodded toward the head of the bed, and she scooted herself backward until her feet no longer hung over the edge. Wyatt followed. If he had been a real wolf, the hungry, feral way he concentrated on her would have made her pee her pants. Wyatt wanted to eat her up.

But in the best way.

Geneva smiled. "I can always find someone to cover my shift for tomorrow, if he finds anything."

He crawled up the bed until he hovered over her, his hands on either side of her head, his knees flanking her thighs.

Snaking a hand into the back pocket of her jeans, he pulled

out her cell phone and handed it to her. "I think you should make those arrangements now."

He leaned in, nipped along her jawline, and whispered in her ear. "Because regardless of what Massey finds, six in the morning is going to come way too early with what I have planned for you."

She quickly thumbed a text to a fellow paramedic who had been scrounging for extra shifts so he could afford a down payment on a house he had his eye on. Her phone made a whooshing sound as the text sent.

Wyatt grabbed the phone and tossed it over his shoulder.

"Hey!" She bopped him on his arm with feigned annoyance. The floor had carpet, and her phone had one of those bullet and nuclear blast-proof cases. He couldn't hurt it.

He settled beside her, resting his head in his hand as he looked down at her. "No distractions." His fingers slid beneath the hem of her shirt and brushed across her abdomen. Her muscles fluttered and heat pooled low in her belly.

He kissed his way across her collarbone. Hot, open-mouth kisses that zinged her nerves, sending goosebumps skittering to the top of her head. "Just you and me and—"

Bam, bam, bam!

Geneva startled. Wyatt cursed. Massey called through the door, "Dude, I think I found something."

Wyatt pressed his forehead to hers. "Wait here. I'll kill him, dispose of the body, and—"

"*Dude!*"

"Yeah, yeah, keep your pants on," Wyatt groused.

Geneva rolled out from beneath him and straightened her shirt and ran fingers through her hair. Wyatt opened the door and tugged on his shirt.

Massey was already back at his bank of computers by the time they padded into the room in their sock feet. On the far right screen was a mugshot of a woman, her hair unkempt, her eyes dull, her lids half-mast. On the left screen, a picture of the same woman with a man about twice her age, but she had a genuine smile on her face and luster in her eyes.

Massey pointed to the screen on the right. "This was seven months ago. Arrested in Teton County on drug possession charges and prostitution. With reduced charges, she ended up serving about four months in jail."

Then he pointed to the screen on the left. "This is her a week ago with a cattle rancher outside Jackson Hole. Pulled this photo out of the special section of the Jackson Hole Daily from a cattleman's ball."

Wyatt said, "That's a bit of a step up from working a street corner."

"No, kidding." Massey pointed to the middle screen, where he had several social media sites open. "I ran facial recognition software on her friends and acquaintances' social media pages, and I got the pop in the newspaper of all places."

"Facial recognition software?" Geneva asked.

Massey smiled. "Don't ask. At least not in front of a deputy."

"Former deputy," Wyatt corrected.

Then Massey pulled up new information on the middle screen. "She's going by the name of Candace Cartwell now."

"A little more respectable sounding than Candy Lane," Geneva said.

"Did you find out where she's living?" Wyatt settled into the chair beside Massey.

"Nothing rented in her name. But Mr. Cattleman rented a unit at the Cedar Creek condos a month ago."

Geneva whistled. "Wow. Cedar Creek? I've heard of about that place. No way she could afford the rent at that place on a waitress's income."

Massey pulled up the condo complex's web page. The

complex had first-rate facilities and a doorman and a concierge. You could combine hers and Wyatt's salaries, and they still couldn't afford that place.

Yours and Wyatt's, huh?

Her inner voice chuckled. It was just an observation. It wasn't like they were *together*, together. Or that she thought their relationship was anything more than what it was—a distraction.

A damn fine distraction. "Shoosh."

Wyatt said, "What?"

Shit. "Nothing. I was just... nothing." She tossed him a wan smile and changed the subject. "You think Mr. Cattleman is her sugar daddy?"

Wyatt settled back in the chair. "Or maybe he likes having a place in town, and it has nothing to do with Candace at all. She could have been a paid escort for the cattleman's event for all we know. Closer to her usual MO."

Massey pinned the addressed to the complex, as well as the three places Candace may work and send it to Wyatt and Geneva's phones.

Reaching over, Massey shut his computer down and tucked his travel mug between his legs. "I'm going to bed. And just FYI, the house is old and the insulation in the walls is thin. Take it for what it's worth."

Heat slowly burned up Geneva's neck, not stopping until it reached her cheeks. Wyatt grinned. With a wave over his shoulder, Massey wheeled out of the room.

"I don't trust that look on your face," Geneva said.

"What look?"

"The one that's not so innocent. The one that says you wanna test the noise dampening capabilities of those walls."

"Empirical research. Besides, I can be quiet. It's you I'm worried about."

"Me?" Geneva squeaked.

Standing, Wyatt spanned her waist with his hands and lifted. She wrapped her legs around him, locking her ankles behind his back and her arms around his neck as he carried her to the bedroom.

"Last time you almost had the coyotes howling along with you."

She laughed. "You're such a liar."

They bumped their way into his room. Her feet hit the jamb. His shoulder hit the door, and he stumbled his way to the bed and dropped her on her back. He leaned over and kissed her— all heat and promise and primal need.

Her heart went haywire, and her stomach started that slow, hitching ride up the steep slope of a roller coaster. And all she wanted to do was hold on for the thrill of the sweet ride.

"Hold that thought," he said as he closed and locked the door.

He turned out the light, dumping them into complete darkness.

First came a thump. "Ouch. Damn it," he grumbled. Then more thumps near the far wall as he stumbled over their boots.

Then came the muffled *whump* of his clothing hitting the carpet. Then his hand caught one of her ankles and then the other, and he slowly ran his hands up her shins and knees and thighs. The end of the bed dipped under his weight, his hands stopping at the button of her jeans.

"You good?" he asked before continuing.

"As long as you aren't planning on stopping there."

He chuckled. "Not even close."

He reached over her, and there were two soft plops on the bedside table. Protection, she figured. A man who plans ahead. Another check in the pro column.

Then he was back, straddling her hips with his knees, his weight settling on her thighs. She ghosted her fingertips up his muscled quads, the hair shifting under her touch. As her thumbs reached the juncture where his legs joined his body, his breath drew in on a prolonged hiss.

"Stop right there," he said. He wasn't entirely convincing, but she stopped anyway.

"What's wrong?"

"You're not naked."

She shucked her shirt and bra and slung them across the room. Then she fumbled with the button on her jeans. Playfully, he knocked her hands aside and undid her pants.

"Lift your hips."

She did, and he stripped her jeans and panties off. Somehow, in the near-total darkness, she felt more exposed, more vulnerable, as if all their barriers had been torn away, and only their raw, true selves remained.

"Roll over," Wyatt's disembodied voice said from somewhere above. "And hands stretched out above your head."

Thrumming heat coursed through her, and her stomach hitched a notch higher on the roller coaster rails. The tension, the anticipation building, building.

"Oooh, deputy." She pitched her voice to damsel-in-distress. "Am I under arrest?"

Wyatt's warm chuckle washed over her, raising goosebumps on her arms. He settled his legs between hers and laid over the top of her, his chest to her back, his erection pressed tight against the juncture of her thighs, his weight pinning her to the soft mattress.

She wiggled against him. He groaned and pressed her harder into the sheets. "You're going to have to quit fighting, ma'am. Or I'll be forced to take you into custody." He ran his hands up the length of her sides, over her shoulders and down her arms, linking their fingers and grinding against her.

She arched her back, but when she tried to press back

against him, the devilish man raised his pelvis. "You're a cruel, cruel man, deputy."

He nibbled the crest of her ear, his warm breath brushing against her skin as he whispered, "It's your first offense. Maybe I'll have mercy on you."

He rose and rested on his haunches behind her, his fingers trailing down the trough of her spine, bump, by bump, by bump until they came to the cleft at the top of her ass. He palmed her cheeks and gave them a firm squeeze, his thumbs sliding between her legs, dipping into the wetness that gathered there. She arched up and pressed against his thumbs.

She wanted more, needed more.

"Sweet baby Jesus." His words came like a long-lost prayer. There was a nip on the globe of one cheek, her heart rate spiked and blood swooshed past her ears as he licked the sweet sting away.

She ground her pelvis into the mattress, searching for relief.

"Uh, uh, uh," Wyatt warned. He threaded his arm beneath her and lifted her ass into the air, her head down. She stilled, on new sexual ground.

But the way her blood simmered, her stomach swirled, and her girly bits sang, experimentation was definitely a turn-on.

"Right there," Wyatt said. Even on her knees, his reverent tone made her feel wanted and empowered and celebrated.

He shifted behind her, his thumbs parting her lips, his tongue tangling in her folds. A moan escaped her as his hands kneaded her flesh. His tongue working strange and wondrous magic on her body.

Click, click, click, up the rails, her arousal climbed higher and higher.

She rocked back, his tongue impaling, her limbs shaking. "Now, Wyatt."

"You in a hurry, sweetheart?"

Her breath came faster, and instead of answering, she reached a hand to the nightstand and felt around until she found one of the condoms. She tore the corner with her teeth and handed it to him.

One last lick and he disappeared, but he returned in mere seconds, pressing against her, his cock slipping between her thighs and bumping her clit. She sucked in a breath and reached between her legs, trapping him there. He surged, and his hand smoothed over both ass cheeks then up the length of her spine.

She wanted him inside her. Wanted the pounding, wanted the pleasure. She guided him into position. With one arm wrapped around her waist, he buried himself to his balls.

He guided her torso upright until she sat atop his thighs, her back to his chest, his hands twinning up both sides of her body, over her ribs and breasts until he looped them over her shoulders and rammed her tight against him. Full and fuller.

His breath came hot and quick on the back of her neck. He smelled of fresh Wyoming air with a hint of stale cigarettes, reminding her of the danger he'd been in. It should have dulled her need, but with an ironic twist, the peril only sharpened her drive.

He rained kisses down her neck to the tip of her shoulders, his hands roving, roaming over her body, squeezing her breasts and teasing her nipples. She rocked her hips back and forth, creating a terrible, sweet friction that pulled harsh, quick pants from her lungs.

"That's it, swee—" Wyatt's voice faltered, and his teeth teased her flesh. "Damn, you feel so good."

In the complete darkness, Geneva's senses heightened. She felt the puffs of Wyatt's breath on her skin, the tickle of his chest hair on her back, the scrape of his whiskers on her neck, the damp flick of his tongue on the curve of her ear.

Musk filled the air, and from outside the bedroom door

came the whir of Massey's tires on the wood floor as he passed by on his way to the kitchen. But Geneva was beyond caring how loud she was or if Massey overheard. Her body *clickity-clacked* to the tippy top, teetering on that precipice.

All she cared about was this moment.

This man.

More than she wanted to. More than she ever thought possible.

He gave her strength without overpowering.

He gave her purpose without losing sight of her past.

He gave himself without demands.

Reaching around her, he rubbed tight circles around her clit, and she pressed against his hand.

Almost. Almost.

Then she shot down the other side. She could practically feel the rush of wind in her face, the blur of the drop as everything rushed by, her stomach plummeting, her body shuddering.

And he gives you orgasms without fail.

"*Fuuuck,*" Wyatt ground out on a huff of air as he nipped her shoulder.

When she caught that first fast freewheeling curve after the descent, Wyatt eased her to her hands and knees, his hands on her hips as he pounded into her from behind. She met him stroke for stroke, the pressure, the friction, building again.

As she tumbled down that last steep slope, the one that made her want to throw her hands up and ride screaming into the station, Wyatt groaned, as his strokes became erratic. He pumped one last time, long and deep.

He pulsed within her, and her arms quivered and gave way. Wyatt collapsed on top of her, their bodies sweat-slicked and sated.

They lay there joined for the time it took to pay off their

oxygen debt. Wyatt rolled off her, trashed the condom, then stretched out beside her, his hand skimming across her skin, down her back, to the dip of her pelvis, to the curve of her ass. Long, gentle, soothing strokes. If she were a cat, she'd start purring.

She folded her arms and rested her head on her hands. He pressed light, tender kisses on the ball of her shoulder. "Do you think we kept Massey up?"

"Do we really care?"

"Not in the slightest." He squeezed one globe and then the other. "Jesus, I love your ass."

She turned, and he found her lips with his, their tongues lazily exploring, knowing that the treasure had already been plundered but reliving the taking in the aftermath.

"How's that for fucking the widow?" Wyatt asked.

She barked a laugh and rolled to her side. "God, I love—" she caught herself before *you* slipped out. Because she most certainly didn't. "Your macabre sense of humor," she substituted.

His hand stilled at the small of her back, before resuming its trail up her spine.

"It *is* rather dark," he said, and she knew he meant his humor and not the room. There was a note of caution in his tone as if he'd suddenly stepped into a minefield blindfolded and didn't know which way to step.

"I get it. Being a paramedic, it's difficult to survive without it." And really, *I love you*? What was up with that? Did she? Love him?

She'd come to admire his integrity and his sense of honor, the way Evie and Massey were so much a part of his life, even the way he tossed alfalfa cubes to an old cow who claimed him as one of the herd.

More importantly, she loved the way he treated her like an equal. Loved the way he worshiped her body. Loved his playful side in bed, as well as the way he pushed her beyond her comfort zone, beyond her limits.

But love *him*? Nah. Loving two amazing men in a lifetime seemed like more than she deserved.

———

Tonight was the night.

For once, Geneva was glad she didn't have a pet, something to worry about in case she and Wyatt got caught, and their asses landed in the Bison County jail.

Their trip up to Jackson Hole had been a bigger bust than when she and Cassie had stuffed their bras their freshman year and tried to get the senior football guys interested.

While she and Wyatt had made the hour drive to Jackson Hole and found Candy, or rather Candace, coming off the lunch shift at the Caribou Cafe, she had even less helpful information than Desiree had.

Yes, she witnessed the strangulation. No, she didn't know who the man was. More importantly, she didn't care. She'd left that life behind. Found herself a new gig. No, she didn't want protection. How would she explain that to the new man paying her rent? Thank you kindly, and get out of my life.

So, Geneva and Wyatt did just that.

Geneva pulled into the parking lot at the Sheriff's Office, talking to Wyatt on her hands-free.

In the cup holder, her phone pinged, and she glanced at the incoming text. "That's Cassie," she told Wyatt. "Dave is getting off duty now. I'll wait a few minutes to give her time to get him into the break room, and then I'll go in."

The Sheriff's Office was all lit up. Though, at nearly eight in the evening, the visitor parking lot sat empty. Cool air drifted through her open window. She zipped up her gray hoodie and reached across the seat for the dinner she'd brought for Cassie. Her prop, or rather *excuse*, for coming to the Sheriff's Office.

"Showtime," she said.

Wyatt had been quiet all day. More quiet than usual since the whole *I love* debacle. She must have freaked him out because after they'd made the long trip back from Jackson Hole, he'd dropped her off at her place, spinning the wheels on the truck as he lit out of there. Okay, so maybe the spinning his wheels was a bit of an exaggeration, but it didn't feel like much of one.

"Hey," Wyatt said as she went to disconnect the call. "Be careful. If something feels off, if you change your mind, it's all good. We'll find another way."

But there wasn't another way. Not that either one of them could see. She needed to do this not only for the case but for Caleb as well. She didn't think she would ever sleep soundly until she found out why Caleb had drawn on Wyatt. And if that helped Wyatt get to the bottom of the Nightwalker murders, then all the better.

But she said, "I will," to appease Wyatt if nothing else.

Geneva walked the lighted pathway to the front doors and stepped inside. The door buzzed, announcing her arrival, and she waited in the entry until somebody walked down the hall to the front desk.

It was Melinda. One of the senior volunteers who manned the desk at times when the deputies were stretched too thin. She was heavy on weight, short on body, and always had a smile on her face and a kind word.

Geneva held up the take-out bag. "Cassie left her dinner, so I'm bringing something by. She's so forgetful I swear if her head —" Geneva cut herself off as her sentences ran together in her nervousness.

"You're such a good friend," Melinda said. "Go on back. I think I saw her headed to the break room."

"Thanks." Geneva headed down the brightly lit hall. Offices on either side of her lay dark, their doors closed. She rounded the corner and spilled out into the bullpen where the deputies gathered and got their updates before their shifts.

She took the short hall off the bull pen and turned into the break room. Dave McMahon's back was to her, but those were Cassie's arms draped over the Deputy's neck. Geneva would recognize those colorful bangle bracelets anywhere.

"Oh, excuse me!" Geneva slapped her hand to her chest, hopefully not *too* dramatically, "I-I'll..."

Dave's head popped up, and he shoved away from Cassie as if he'd just discovered an IED taped to her tonsils. "Uh, I was... We were..."

He turned an interesting shade of magenta that Martha Stewart could market the hell out of.

"I gotta go." He wiped his mouth on the back of his hand and shoved past Geneva.

Cassie looked a little flushed, too, but it wasn't from embarrassment. Geneva eyed her friend, and the realization hit. "Oh, my God. You liked kissing him."

Cassie cocked a hip and raised her hands in surrender, though one hand had folded into a fist. Geneva assumed she held the keys. "Trust me, no one is more surprised than me. Here I was thinking I was taking one for the team and then, *vroom vroom*, Mr. Deputy-who-may-still-live-with-mom, has got serious skills."

Then her eyes got that impish glint. "If Dave's that good at kissing, I wonder how good he is in the sack. I can overlook an attached-at-the-hip momma's boy for—"

Geneva grabbed her friend by the shoulders and gave her a shake hoping to rattle some of the crazy loose. "*Focus.*"

"Have you and Wyatt..." She bobbed her eyebrows in a come-on-you-can-tell-your-bestie manner.

"*Cass!*"

"Okay, okay," Cassie conceded. "But you have to promise to tell me later."

"I'll do no such thing."

"Bullshit."

"You're right, but now's not the time. You uh…" Geneva glanced around the break room. There were two tables with six chairs each. A refrigerator, microwave, sink with a few cabinets above and below. Basic, standard-issue governmental stuff. She scanned the ceiling, but as Cassie had said, there were no cameras in the breakroom.

Geneva's stomach churned as the reality of what they were about to do hit. "So did you—"

"Hey, Cass," one of the female deputies popped in and yanked open the door of the refrigerator. "Oh, hi, Gen." She was quick to turn her attention back to Cassie. "What did you do, offer Doofus Dave a blowjob? I've never seen him so flustered."

Cassie boosted herself onto the counter. "Counter sex, actually. You know, I think I might have underestimated him."

The deputy took a sip of her red sports drink and, by the way her eyes narrowed when she looked at Cass, she couldn't decide if Cass was joking or not.

"With Doofus Dave?" The deputy backed out of the break room. "I seriously doubt that."

After the deputy left, Geneva tossed Cassie the bag of food, and Cassie threw Geneva the keys. She fumbled the catch, then snatched them up off the linoleum and stuffed them deep into her front pocket.

Geneva gave her friend a thin smile, as the butterflies in her stomach morphed into bats. She wasn't cut out for a life of crime. "Thanks, I owe you one."

"You'd do the same for me."

"Sure," she said as she backed through the doorway.

A Mack truck slammed into her from behind and almost knocked her to her knees, wait no, that was Dave. A frantic, half-crazed expression on his face.

"Have you seen my keys?" Dave said.

"They're in your hand."

"No, the station keys."

"Search me," Cass said with an inviting bite of spice and sauce.

Dave made some sound of exasperation and glanced at Geneva.

"Don't look at me," Geneva said. The lie wouldn't have gotten past Wyatt, but Dave wasn't a detective and way too frantic to focus on her.

Cassie jumped off the counter, her feet hitting the floor with a slap, and linked her arm through Dave's and led him toward the bullpen. "Come on. I have a few minutes before my break is over. I'll help you look."

14

WYATT RATTLED THE PEN BETWEEN HIS THUMB AND INDEX FINGER, making a *ratta-ratta-ratta* sound as it bounced against Massey's desk. Massey's hand came down on his, stilling the incessant beat.

"Sorry." Wyatt tossed the pen onto the desk.

"Relax. Geneva said she'd text when she got out of there."

"That should have been ten minutes ago. You think it went okay? Maybe Cass couldn't get the keys, or she got the keys and got caught and—"

"*Dude.*" Massey cut him a look.

"Fuck. Sorry."

Wyatt heaved himself out of the chair and paced Massey's computer room, one hand wrestling with the tight muscles at the base of his neck.

Maybe she got in an accident on the way home. He whipped his phone out and started dialing.

"She's fine, Wy. Have a little faith in your woman."

"Is that what she is?" Wyatt asked as he met his friend's annoyed gaze. "My woman?"

Massey shrugged. "I don't know. What would *you* call her?"

"I honestly don't know."

Turning back to the computers, Massey said, "All I know is if I had someone who made me groan that loud while having sex—"

Wyatt huffed out a laugh. "Seriously? You're going there?"

"Hey, not my fault. I gave you fair warning about the walls. What you did with that information was up to you."

"Screw you," Wyatt said, but he couldn't put any heat behind it.

"I'm just saying, I wouldn't want another man screwing—"

"It's not like that." And why the hell was he saying anything to Massey about his relationship? Went to show how stressed he was that he'd allow this conversation in place of sinking deeper into that rabbit warren of worry.

Massey's office chair squeaked as he spun around. "Then, how is it?"

Jesus, was he really talking about this? Out loud? Bad enough, Wyatt had heard it all in his head. "She's different. There's the physical chemistry, sure. But it's much more than that. She's the first woman in a long time that makes me question my motives and makes me want more than a boat on a pond in the middle of Wyoming. She has a huge heart. She's compassionate... with a forgiving spirit that—" Wyatt's voice cracked.

That makes you want to forgive yourself? Say it. Say it out loud. I dare you. Wyatt opened his mouth and, "She told me she loved me," dropped out.

"No, shit? She just up and said—"

"Not exactly." Wyatt's capillaries heated, and he shoved the window up and propped it open with a piece of two-by-four cut to the appropriate length. "When are you going to fix this damn window?"

"Don't change the subject." Massey turned back to his

keyboard. He tapped keys and right and left mouse clicked, but Wyatt wasn't fooled. Massey was listening.

Wyatt grumbled to himself. Massey wouldn't let the subject drop until Wyatt spilled. Why had he opened his big mouth? "She said she loved my macabre sense of humor, but the way she said it... I don't know. It sounded like she was about to say she *loved me*. She knew it. I knew it. It got awkward from there."

"Why?" The way the word came out, Massey was utterly flummoxed. Like he couldn't comprehend quantum physics, which was a joke because the kid understood quantum physics just fine. Kid was stupid smart.

But in this one instance, Massey was clueless, so Wyatt spelled it out for him. "I. Killed. Her. Husband."

"No shit, but that doesn't explain why—"

Wyatt's phone rang—praise the gods of the freaking universe—and he punched the answer button. "Where the hell have you been?"

"Excuse me?" Her words were part amusement and part exasperation—heavy on the amusement.

He wasn't trying to be funny.

"I'll be there in ten."

Wyatt waited the ten minutes on the front stoop, straddling That-A-Way's back and scratching behind her ears as she lay blocking the front door. It beat facing Massey's verbal firing squad.

That-A-Way burped up a wad of cud and chewed away, and her big brown eyes closed as she leaned her head into Wyatt's scratching.

Finally, Geneva's headlights swept the driveway. He dismounted the bovine and was yanking on the Prius' door before she'd even shifted into park.

"Well?" He tried not to take his irritation with Massey out on her. He held out his hand to help her out of the car. She plopped the keys to the evidence room in his hand.

Her hand shook, and when he held it, her palm was sweaty against his. "How'd it go?"

"When I left, Cass was helping Dave look for his keys. He freaked, but lucky for him, Cass liked the way he kissed so he might get laid when it's all said and done. All in all, a win for the deputy, I guess."

"Laid?" Wyatt helped her step over That-A-Way. If That-A-Way kept sleeping at the house, he'd have to bring her pad over for her to lay on. "Why would—"

Geneva shook her head, exasperation welling up like the storm surge from a hurricane. "It's Cass. Better not to ask."

He led her into the kitchen, where he got himself some coffee. His bed was already calling, and it would be an exceptionally long night before they got the chance to sleep. "You want any?"

Her hand went to her belly, and she scrunched up her nose. "I'm not sure the caffeine would play nice with the nerves and the fear. Threesomes never work well, unless you talk to Cass. She has a different take."

Wyatt chuckled. "Your friend is..." Running on little sleep, his brain failed to drum up an accurate descriptor.

"Unique," Geneva supplied. "And ballsy and brave and holy pickpocket Batman you should have seen how cool-headed she was. I could have hooked her up to the ECG, and I bet her heart rate never spiked. You would never have known she'd committed a crime. I'm convinced her talents are wasted as a dispatcher."

Wyatt pulled down another travel mug and filled it for Massey. It was easier to clean another mug later than walk back and forth to the computer room and refill his.

Geneva took Massey's coffee and followed Wyatt to the

computer room. She took one look at the desk covered in dirty paper plates, candy wrappers, and empty travel mugs with dregs of coffee congealing at the bottoms, and took hold of the back of Massey's chair and rolled him away from the desk.

"What the fuck?" Wyatt and Massey said at the same time.

Geneva stepped between Massey and the desk, her arms crossed over her chest. "When was the last time you got any sleep? Or had a meal that didn't look like a twelve-year-old fixed it or one that won't induce diabetes?"

"I'm working," Massey's tone came out flat, and Wyatt could see Massey's wheels spinning—the mental ones, not the ones on his chair—as his friend tried to puzzle out a way to get past Geneva without resorting to force.

"No. You're taking a break and a shower because I'm not sitting in the truck with you for a couple of hours with you stinking of squirt cheese, oven fries, and Ding Dongs."

"But I just got some info on the cabins in the area."

"What?" Wyatt said.

"Nope." Geneva made a twirling motion with her finger, indicating Massey needed to turn his chair the hell around and leave the room. "Shower first. Then a meal that your good friend here and I are going to fix, *then* you can tell us."

"But," Wyatt and Massey said at the same time.

Geneva raised her brows and her chin in a way that said *you boys seriously don't want to test me.*

Wyatt got a serious woody and had a difficult time keeping the smile off his face and not tossing her over his shoulder and taking her to bed. Screw the evidence room and screw—

"Go," she ordered.

"Fine," Massey grumbled as he wheeled out of the room, "but I take back all the nice things I said about you."

———

At one in the morning, Wyatt pulled his truck behind a short row of shops a couple of streets over from the Sheriff's Office. They'd chosen the spot because of the lack of security cameras, and it wasn't readily visible when driving down the street. They didn't want to risk one of the deputies on night duty seeing the truck and getting suspicious.

Geneva and Wyatt sat in the front seat of his truck while Massey sat in the back with his laptop, wand scanner, and portable printer, ready to do his part when they brought him the sealed evidence bag. After a shower and a good meal, Massey seemed recharged and ready to go another thirty-six hours straight.

Wyatt was a crappy friend. Not because he'd pushed Massey so hard. He hadn't. Massey was that kind of guy who wouldn't, or couldn't, rest until a problem was solved or the question answered. But Geneva had been right. In that situation, it was up to Wyatt to police his friend and make sure he took care of himself.

Now all they had to do was wait for the all-clear text from Cassie letting them know it was safe for them to move in.

They waited and waited and waited with the windows cracked for some much-needed ventilation as the tension in the truck spiked to an all-time high.

Geneva's knee bobbed up and down as if it were the only pump jack trying to supply the world with oil, while Wyatt chewed on the tidbit of information Massey had provided them back at the house around mouthfuls of jar spaghetti and meatballs—and a salad, because Geneva didn't consider it a real meal without a veg—information that had his guts twisting and his thoughts swirling.

On the massive list Massey had created of cabin owners that fit the description Desiree had given, one entry had stood out. The Light Group. It had taken Massey some serious digging, but he'd finally been able to drill down and find the names of the group members that owned the cabin.

A group of prominent men from the community.

Several of whom matched Caleb's journal list of initials.

And of those, two stood out, churning the acid in his stomach until it felt like the juices had eaten a hole in the lining rivaling the depth of the Mariana Trench. Those names? Jed Day and Larson Lambert.

Wyatt couldn't believe Day would be involved. Rodriguez wouldn't believe Lambert would be involved.

Could it still be someone else?

Possibly. But of all the other people on the list, those two were the most powerful, the most influential, the men with the most ability to scare witnesses silent.

He pressed the illumination button on the dial of his watch. A minute and a half had passed since he'd glanced at it last.

If he only had twenty-four hours to live, he wanted to pass it in his truck while waiting to commit a felony. It would feel like years.

Geneva's phone *bleeped*, and she said, "All clear."

He popped his door latch, and so did she. "You're staying here, remember?"

"Massey and I decided you needed the extra set of eyes more than he did."

Wyatt eyed his friend in the rear-view mirror. They'd turned off the automatic dome lights, but the light from a distant streetlight filtered in enough for him to see the shine of his friend's eyes and the flash of traitorous teeth.

Wyatt didn't want Geneva involved. If he got caught, he might be able to talk his way out of it, despite Rodriguez saying that Day wanted complete deniability of Wyatt's involvement in the investigation. It would be near impossible to explain Geneva's presence away.

But she had that look on her face. The hard set of her jaw. The you-don't-wanna-mess-with-me furrow between her brows. Short of cuffing her to the steering wheel, there was little he could do to stop her besides try to talk her out of it, and they didn't have that kind of time.

"Fine," Wyatt said, putting enough mustard on the word to indicate it wasn't in the least bit *fine.*

On the walk to the Sheriff's Office, they kept to the dark back alleys, more concerned about a passing patrol car than being caught as a grainy image on security footage. Though to be careful, they kept their heads down and wore baseball caps to make any possible identifications that much more difficult.

They reached the back door of the Sheriff's Office and, with the duct tape over the door latch, slipped inside without incident. Ten steps inside the back entrance was the door to the evidence room. With gloved hands, Wyatt pulled the keys from his pocket, and within seconds they were inside.

He locked the door behind them and only then turned on his penlight. With only an opaque roll-down window for deputies to pass the evidence through, Wyatt had little concern that anyone walking down the hall would notice if he turned the overhead light on, but there were also security cameras in the evidence room and between the penlight and the ball caps tugged low on their heads, Wyatt hoped that even if someone discovered the break-in and checked the footage, that it would be impossible to identify their faces.

Wyatt searched the stacks of evidence boxes. His light flashed over dates and case numbers until he found Caleb's. "Over here," he whispered.

Geneva stumbled over a box left on the ground, and he caught her arm to keep her from falling. She held onto his arm, well past the time she was steady on her feet again.

She shined her light on the box. The light shook. "This is it?"

"Looks like." Wyatt handed her his light and worked the box free from the tight space on the rack and set it on the ground. He pulled the lid, squatted, and rifled through the evidence. Mangled pieces of lead with slashes of red—the slug removed from Caleb's body, no doubt. Casings ejected from Wyatt's gun. A bloody shirt. A thumb drive.

Geneva was unusually quiet. He couldn't even hear her breathe. He stood, the thumb drive in his hand. "Shine the light over here." He waited a beat, two, still no light.

He glanced up at her, the flashlight's spillover glow high-lighting the hollows in her cheeks and the faint bruising under her eyes from lack of sleep. "Gen?" Even though he'd kept his voice low, it cut through her stupor.

She shook her head. "What?"

"Light?"

"Oh, yeah, sorry." The light wavered, and it was like he was trying to read the evidence tag beneath the sparkle and flash of a disco ball. He placed a hand on her arm to steady the light. He read the label.

Bank of the Rockies—security footage.

"Hold this," he said as he handed her the evidence bag with the thumb drive. He replaced the lid and stored the box. "You still with me?"

She came back to herself, back to him. "Yeah. Let's get out of here."

GENEVA AND WYATT WAITED IN THE TRUCK WHILE MASSEY worked his magic, copying the thumb drive to his computer and printing out the new chain of custody tag after scanning the old one. Under the truck's dome light, the labels looked almost identical.

"I don't know if it would hold up to forensic scrutiny," Massey said, "But it should pass a cursory inspection if no one suspects foul play."

They placed the copied thumb drive in a new evidence bag, applied the sealing tape, and affixed the new chain of custody sticker and were out the door and back at the Sheriff's Office with Geneva running on autopilot.

She tripped over a curb and went down, scuffing the palms of her leather gloves and banging her right knee.

"You okay?" Somehow, Wyatt managed not to add a tone of *what the fuck* to those simple words. *Something else she admired about him.*

Maybe she should have stayed in the truck. In her present state, she was more of a liability than an asset. She straightened and brushed herself off, pain pulsing across her kneecap. "Sure."

With each step, her knee throbbed, but it kept her in the here and now, not focused back on the box of evidence, of her husband's dried blood on the *Sox* T-shirt she'd given him their first Christmas together.

They made it back to the evidence room and replaced the evidence bag with no trouble. Wyatt had his hand on the knob of the door of the evidence room, about to open it when Geneva's phone vibrated in her back pocket.

Wyatt turned the handle, the latch clicked.

"Hold up," Geneva hissed. A text came though. One word. "Incoming," she read aloud. "Do we hide?"

"Nowhere in here to hide. We're gonna make a run for it."

Loud voices hit the squad room. As long as no one came down the hall...

Wyatt opened the door and shoved her out in front of him. She hit the back door, and Wyatt caught it before it slammed closed. Behind them, someone said, "You lock him up, I'll put this down the evidence chute."

At the last second, Wyatt stripped the duct tape off the latch. With no time to spare, he took it with him instead of replacing it on the edge of the door. When the latch closed, it clanged, and in the relative silence of the early morning, it sounded like it echoed for miles.

Wyatt's face fell. "Run."

She didn't need him to elaborate. She took off sprinting with Wyatt on her heels. It had to be fifty or sixty feet to the end of the building. She was fast, but not fast enough to run that far when someone entering the back hall only had about twenty steps to traverse to get to the back door. Adrenaline heated her blood and sent flames licking through her veins, scorching, searing. The breath in her lungs came quick, and her legs felt concrete heavy as she ran down the back alley.

No way were they going to make it around the side of the building.

Wyatt caught up and snagged her arm, yanking her with him behind the dumpster. She crashed into him, her hip slamming into the pavement. She bit down on the curse words that tried to fight their way out. At the last second, she tucked her feet to her butt so they wouldn't stick out into the alley.

The back door opened, and wan light from the hallway spilled out into the night. Geneva covered her mouth with her hand, trying to muffle the harsh sound of her panting.

"Brian? Zeke?" A man called out. Working so close to the Sheriff's Office not only in building proximity, but she came into contact with them daily as a first responder, she knew many of the deputies, but couldn't put a face to the voice.

She counted to ten. Twenty. Thirty. The door clicked, and the light disappeared, and she collapsed against Wyatt.

His head fell against the metal container with a dull thud, but he smiled. "That was close."

"What about the keys?"

"Dave's a smoker. I dropped the keys right outside the back door when we ran."

"You think the coast is clear?" She set her hand on the pavement. It landed in something sticky. She tried wiping it off on her jeans, but it had a viscosity between honey and whale vomit. Though whale vomit, if whales did vomit, might have smelled better.

"The sooner we get out of here, the better." Wyatt shifted and looked through the few inches of space between the dumpster and the building. "All clear."

He scrambled to his feet and helped her to hers. They speed-walked back to his truck, keeping their heads down and angled away from the security cameras on the backside of the fire station and some of the retail buildings. The last thirty yards, when they could no longer be seen from a road, they broke out into a jog.

They jumped into the truck, and Wyatt had the engine cranked over and was backing up before Geneva had her door closed. But he wouldn't get any complaints from her.

They were halfway back to the ranch when Massey sniffed and said, "What's that smell?"

———

By the time Geneva had showered, thrown her smelly jeans into Massey's washer, and slipped into a pair of Wyatt's sweatpants, Wyatt and Massey were already in the computer room seeing what they could do with the file of the security footage.

With a cup of coffee in each hand and a travel mug tucked under her arm, she turned the corner into the computer room just as the video version of Wyatt drew his gun and fired.

Caleb fell.

Geneva crumpled.

She woke up flat on her back in the doorway, staring up at Wyatt's face as he kneeled beside her, mopping her forehead with a damp rag.

Massey had a giant wad of paper towels soaking up the spilled coffee as he tossed pieces of the shattered coffee mugs into a dustpan.

"You're back," Wyatt said.

She tried to sit up and put her hand in a not yet cleaned up puddle of cold coffee. Wyatt grabbed her forearm and helped her scoot over and prop herself against the door jamb.

Nausea rolled in her belly as what she'd seen on the screen flashed through her mind, again and again, her own personal horror channel on an infinite loop. "Hey." She said the word, but it sounded like it had come from someone else's body.

Wyatt felt the back of her head.

She winced. "Ouch."

"Let me see that." She leaned forward, and Wyatt parted the hair on the back of her head. "Gonna need some ice for that goose egg."

"I want to see it."

"Ah, kinda hard, but I can see if Evie has a hand mirror."

"Not my head, the video."

"*Gen...*" Wyatt sat hard, resting his shoulder against the wall beside her. He scrubbed a hand over his face and looked at her. Written on his expression, Geneva read his need to apologize. That need to ask forgiveness. But she'd shut him down so many times already, he didn't even try to say the words. "Maybe that's not such a good idea."

"I need to see it." She got to her hands and knees, attempting to stand. Her arms shook with the effort, and her knees wobbled, but she made it to her feet. Wyatt scrambled to his and caught her around the waist when she took a faltering step.

He grabbed the closest chair, which happened to be the

wheelchair, and plopped her in it. He squatted in front of her, the color gone from his face. A solid vertical line formed between his brows. "Think about what you're asking. I don't know if—"

"Massey? Would you replay it for me? Please?"

He glanced up from the floor where he'd made a pile of all the coffee-soaked paper towels, his eyes cutting to Wyatt's first. "If that's what you want."

Her stomach took up residence around her feet as her heart bled out into her chest, each drop making her chest tighter and tighter until it took conscious effort to breathe. "It is."

Wyatt muttered a curse. "*Mass*," but the word came out more in resignation than warning.

Massey held onto the arm of the wheelchair and grunted at the effort it took to stand. To Wyatt, he said, "Can you hand me my crutches?"

"You can have your chair," Geneva said.

When she went to get up, Massey placed a staying hand on her shoulder. "The crutches are fine."

Wyatt handed over the crutches from where they had been leaning against the wall all week, and Massey slipped the cuffs over his arms and stepped over to cue the video. "Where do you want me to start?"

"The very beginning."

Wyatt rolled her to the desk, taking the chair beside her. He linked his fingers with hers and held on tight.

Massey clicked on the triangle icon and said, "I'll be in the kitchen."

The video played, and Geneva watched. Caleb showed up at the mouth of the alley. A few minutes later, the man in the suit did as well, but in the dark, with the lighting poor, if she hadn't already known it was Caleb, she wasn't sure she would have recognized him from the footage.

There was no sound, of course. The two men talked. By the rigid body language, and halting hand gesticulations, they argued. Caleb shoved the man in the suit, his hands on the man's lapels as he propelled him backward until Caleb had rammed him up against the side of the building. The man's head cracked against the brick wall, and even on the grainy video, Geneva saw the man's knees buckle before he caught himself.

Caleb certainly didn't look like the good guy. Not in his scruffy jeans and ratty jacket with his hands all over another man.

Her fingers in her left hand went numb, and she almost needed the Jaws of Life to extricate her hand from Wyatt's grip. "Sorry," he mumbled as he held her closed fist and kissed the back of her hand.

He paused the video and said, "This is where I come in. I saw the scuffle and announced myself."

Wyatt clicked play, the screen reanimated, and Geneva sucked in short, shallow breaths. Her heart breaking in her chest all over again as she watched the deaths of the two men she loved play out frame by grainy frame.

Yes—two men—*loved*. One died a physical death. The other a spiritual one. As much as Wyatt had tried to hide it, as much as he'd thought he'd moved on, there was no doubt in her mind he was merely the ghost of the man who'd walked this earth prior to those fifteen long, agonizing, soul-crushing seconds.

Caleb's head turned as Wyatt walked into frame, Wyatt's left hand raised, his right at his side.

"I'm holding up my badge. That's where I identified myself."

Geneva covered her face with her hands, peeking out between her fingers. Not wanting to see, but needing to. Her heart hammered and adrenaline shot through her veins, knowing what was coming, but unable to stop it. The video played out the exact way Wyatt had described, but her mind slowed the frames down.

She saw the moment when Caleb hesitated, then drew. Wyatt's right hand went for his gun. A spit of white from Caleb's muzzle. More white from Wyatt's. Caleb going down. Wyatt running toward him.

Her vision blurred, and she blinked, but it did no good. Stars formed in her peripheral vision, then started to tunnel. He stopped the video.

"Breathe, Gen." Wyatt cupped her face, and his fingers threaded into her hair at the back of her head. His voice thick, his eyes watery.

She took in a breath. And another and another until only her tears marred her vision. "Play it," she said, her words as fractured as her heart.

He sighed but resumed the video. Video Wyatt slammed a hand in the center of Caleb's chest as her husband writhed on the ground. He hadn't died quickly. He hadn't died easily. Wyatt tore off his jacket and used his shirt as a compress as he dialed his phone with the other hand.

"You tried to save him."

He didn't answer for a while, and she thought he hadn't heard her. Then he said, "I never wanted him to die."

Minutes passed. Three or four interminable minutes. Wyatt maintaining pressure. Caleb's movements growing weaker. The front end of an ambulance came into frame as Caleb grabbed Wyatt's wrist with both hands. Wyatt leaned over, putting his ear to Caleb's mouth.

Then the paramedics pushed Wyatt away, and she watched as her husband died, and the man she'd grown to love collapse against the building. Wyatt's elbows went to his knees, his head in his hands, and the man she'd spent more than a year hating, the man she'd spent more than a year vilifying, the man she'd spent a short time loving, shattered.

Her throat bobbed, the pain searing as the words ripped from her throat. "That's enough."

Wyatt fumbled with the mouse and clicked pause.

Everything Wyatt had told her had been the truth. But he hadn't told the whole story. He hadn't told her that Caleb had shot first. Hadn't told her how it must have felt to have another man's blood on his hands, how it must have smelled and hurt and crushed and—

As her tears fell in streaks down her face, she glanced over at him. His chin lay on his chest, his body silently shaking.

"Wyatt..."

Slowly, he raised his head and met her gaze, his eyes red-rimmed, his cheeks wet. He held his hands out to her. "Come here."

She crawled into his lap and curled up against his chest. He wrapped her tightly, tucking her head beneath his chin, and they both wept.

She cried not only for Caleb but for the lost future with her husband. The laughs they would never laugh, the fights they would never fight, the kids they would never wrangle.

"I'm sorry," Wyatt said. "I'm so, so sorry."

He pressed kiss after kiss to the side of her head, repeating *I'm sorry* over and over again as they clung to each other, not sure who comforted who.

He rocked her in his arms until their breaths stopped hitching, and their eyes stopped leaking. But even shattered, there was a piece of her soul that was whole again—a piece brought back into place by the unimaginable power of forgiveness.

Drained, physically, mentally, Geneva wiped her cheeks with the heels of her hands, pressed her forehead to his, and gave Wyatt her most precious gift. "I forgive you."

Wyatt took a shuddering breath and swallowed hard, holding on tighter.

They sat silent for a long while, mopping up their emotions, and drawing strength from each other. Her mind went back to the video, to Wyatt leaning over her husband as Caleb whispered something into Wyatt's ear.

"What did Caleb say to you?"

Wyatt didn't even pretend not to know what she was talking about. Geneva didn't know what she'd expected Wyatt to say. Maybe something along the lines of, "Tell my wife I love her." Instead, Wyatt said, "He said, 'I win.'"

Geneva leaned back to see his face. "What does that mean?"

"Wish I knew."

Before she could think of another question, she yawned. Big and wide. Her jaw popped.

Wyatt patted her thigh and said, "What do you say we get you out of these coffee-stained sweats and catch a few hours of sleep?"

Geneva glanced out the window at the gray dawn that was giving way to the first pinks of a new sunrise. "It's already morning."

He glanced out the window, one corner of his mouth tipped up in a sad smile. "So it is."

"But catching a few hours of sleep will do us both some good."

She climbed off his lap and helped Wyatt to his feet. She tugged him along in search of Massey to let him know they were crashing for a few hours.

They found Massey standing in front of the coffee pot when they came into the kitchen, most of his weight resting on one crutch as he poured himself a cup of coffee. He leaned back against the counter, the drink almost to his lips when he saw them. He looked from her to Wyatt, then back to her, and held out the cup. "Take it. You look like you need it more than I do."

With her nerves shot, drinking coffee would be about as much help as trying to put a Band-Aid on roadkill, but she took the mug, needing the warmth more than the caffeine. "Wyatt and I are going to catch a few Zs."

Wyatt stole the mug and slurped a sip of her coffee, and to Massey said, "You should too."

"Are you kidding me?" His voice went up like a high school cheerleader who'd been told she couldn't cheer at the championship football game. "We just got the footage. I took a nap on the couch, and now I've got my second wind. Besides, I can sleep when I'm d—"

Massey's eyes rounded, and he amended his sentence. "Later. I can sleep later."

Wyatt made an exasperated sound at the back of his throat, but before he could say anything more, the house phone rang.

The cordless sat in a cradle on the wall next to Wyatt's head, so he snatched it up. "Yates residence." He listened. Color drained from his cheeks, and his face fell.

He held out the phone to Massey, "It's the hospital. Something's happened to Evie."

15

———

Geneva lay curled beside Wyatt in the ICU waiting room of the hospital in Murdock. The nurses had taken Massey up to see Evie more than two hours before, but so far, Wyatt and Geneva hadn't heard any news.

Wyatt flipped through a magazine that should have been thrown away back when Nixon was in the White House, but it didn't matter how old the magazine was, it wasn't like he was reading it anyway. He just needed something to do, and since Geneva had her head in his lap, pacing wasn't an option.

The door to the waiting room opened. Wyatt glanced up, expecting to see a doctor or nurse or Massey. Instead, Rodriguez strode in looking raw and beat, like ten pounds of over tenderized meat.

"Hey, buddy," Wyatt said, careful to keep his voice low, but Geneva stirred and sat up anyway.

The dark cloud over Rodriguez's head darkened, and his jaw sawed back and forth as he looked from Geneva to Wyatt. "I need to talk to you."

Wyatt put an arm across Geneva's shoulder. "Whatever you have to say, you can—"

"No, Wy," Rodriguez said through tight, clenched teeth. "I can't."

"Go on." She picked up Massey's computer tablet, the one he'd insisted on bringing to the hospital, the one with a copy of the security footage on it. "I've got some stuff to work on."

He squeezed her hand, then followed Rodriguez down the hall and out onto a balcony with a few scattered tables and chairs. A place for people to smoke or take a break while they waited for news on their loved ones, but that early in the day, Wyatt and Rodriguez had the area to themselves. Overhead, thick, gray ominous clouds hovered, reflecting Wyatt's mood.

Rodriguez pulled out a seat for Wyatt. "Sit before you fall."

Wyatt sat. Just what the doctor ordered. "How did you know I was here."

Rodriguez held up his phone.

Of course, the fucking locator app. "I don't know why you didn't delete that back when Day fired me."

"You had me worried, buddy. Especially in those early days after the shooting. I wanted to keep my eye on you."

"You thought I was going to eat my gun?"

Rodriquez shrugged. "You were a mess. The drinking got bad. Honestly, I wouldn't have put it past you."

Wyatt didn't bother denying it. They both knew that would have been a lie, because the truth was, after killing Caleb, the thought had crossed Wyatt's mind too many times to count. But they weren't here to talk about his questionable mental stability back then. "Is this you coming to tell me the Feds are going to bring me in for questioning over the fingerprints?"

Rodriguez hesitated, his gaze calculating. "You screwing her?"

Wyatt barked out a laugh. Hard and cold as Alaskan steel. He shoved a chair out with his foot for Rodriguez to take. When his ex-partner sat, Wyatt said, "You come all the way out here to ask me that? You couldn't wait for me to update my status on social media?"

"Sadly, I don't think 'fucking a potential witness to murder' is one of the relationship status options yet." Rodriguez didn't look all that broken up about it. "Just answer the damn question."

Wyatt made sure he enunciated clearly. "I don't see where that's any of your business."

"It is when you're working for me."

Interesting choice of words. Wyatt raised a brow.

"Day," Rodriguez corrected. "Working for Day."

Anger burned bright, but Wyatt refused to let Rodriguez see that he'd scored a direct hit. After all, what did that say about Wyatt's objectivity? "She's not a witness." *Of course, you would say that.*

Because she wasn't.

Wyatt hadn't murdered Desiree. No matter what his fingerprints on the lamp suggested.

But she'd been privy to his investigation every step of the way. What if she was playing him? What if she'd known all along what was in Steele's journal? What if she'd been playing him to get what she wanted?

No. She wasn't that good of a liar.

Like she wasn't playing you, trying to get what she wanted, when you took her home from the bar? Then later when you knew who she was and you almost couldn't keep it in your pants?

Rodriguez snapped his fingers in front of Wyatt's face. "Hey, where'd you go?"

"What? Nowhere." He scrubbed his hands down his face. His mental reserve tank had run dry hours ago. Hell, there weren't even any fumes.

"Look, say what you came here to say."

Rodriguez leaned back in his chair and crossed an ankle over a knee. He wore black slacks with a long-sleeve gray dress shirt. The cuffs buttoned at the wrists. Red tie. Polished shoes. The only concession to his current state of sleeplessness was the wrinkles and lack of starch in his shirt, as if he hadn't been home to change in a couple of days. "Where were you last night?"

"Is this my friend asking, or is this the Sheriff's Office asking?"

"Your friend... for now."

Wyatt shook his head in mock disbelief, even as the pulse thumped at his temple. Had someone seen them? Had someone been curious enough and gone over the security footage and recognized Wyatt? No. He didn't believe that. There was something else on Rodriguez's mind more important than a break-in at the Sheriff's Office.

More important than Rodriguez's best friend committing multiple felonies?

"I was at home."

"Alone?" Rodriguez asked it, but by the way his chin hitched up, he knew the answer and was waiting to catch Wyatt in the lie.

Wyatt didn't appreciate being on the defensive. Never had. Never would. "What's this all about?"

"Candy Lane."

Wyatt didn't say anything while he waited for the punchline.

"You know the name." It wasn't a question.

"She's one of the women present the night Alexa Martinez was strangled."

"And you didn't think it was important that you tell me that? This was why Day hired you. To find this information, then feed it to me. Not run off to Jackson Hole half-cocked."

Wyatt couldn't believe his ears. "You followed me?"

"Don't be ridiculous. I didn't follow you."

At Wyatt's look of *what the royal fuck then*? Rodriguez added the piece de resistance, the icing on the cake, the shit thrown at the fan. "I saw your location on the app."

Wyatt laughed. It was funny how fucked up this was all becoming. He made an *out with it* motion with his hand. "Come on, don't keep me in suspense."

"Teton County Sheriff's Office called this morning. Candy Lane was found dead in her condo at the Cedar Creek complex."

"You don't seem too torn up about it," Wyatt noted.

"Actually," Rodriguez said on a long, exhausted exhale, "I'm relieved in a way. I think these murders are covering up for the Martinez murder like we'd suspected. We still got a long way to go to catch this bastard, but I also think this ends the escalating body count, at least."

"Strangled?"

"Shot." Rodriguez had a smile on his face, twisted with irony. "With what appears to have been like your gun. We'll know better once we check the serial number."

The air whooshed out of Wyatt's lungs. "Of course, she was." *Fuckity, fuck, fuck, fuck.* "I reported that gun stolen."

"So, you said," Rodriguez's words came out even, but the accusation rang through them.

Wyatt stood and planted his hands on the table as he leaned across it, pissed at the unspoken allegation. "Excuse me?"

Wyatt considered telling Rodriguez about the sheriff's deputy's vehicle caught on Evie's security camera the night his boat had been vandalized but stopped himself at the last moment. He was still unsure how that played into what they were dealing with. Now that his gun had possibly been used in a murder, the simple vandalization-slash-robbery looked a whole lot more like a setup.

And yeah, even in his current limited mental capacity, the scenario sounded a whole lot paranoid.

His brain reeled at the ripple effect that little tidbit of information wreaked. But he didn't have the bandwidth to focus on that now.

Rodriguez raised his hands, not so much a surrender as *don't shoot the messenger.* "That's the Feds talkin' anyway."

Wyatt slammed his fist on the table. The red ashtray bounced, and a cigarette butt jumped out. "Let me get this straight. The Feds think I used the lamp at the Delight Inn to strangle Desiree. Then they think I tracked Candy Lane to Jackson Hole and used the gun I reported *stolen* the night my boat was vandalized to kill her?"

"About sums it up."

Wyatt came around the table, his fists clenched. Rodriguez stood, and Wyatt got in his face.

Rodriguez didn't back down. He wasn't that kind of guy. "Do you have an alibi for last night or not?"

If he said yes, that he might have video proof that he was stealing evidence—*borrowing evidence*—when Candy was killed, that would bring a shit-show of trouble on Geneva's, Massey's, and Cassie's heads. Trouble they would not be in without him. "No."

"You should go," Rodriguez said.

What? Wyatt stepped back. "What are you trying to say?"

"A little inside tip from me to you, buddy. If you weren't at home last night. If you don't have a credible alibi. If you were respons—" Rodriguez put his hands on his hips and glanced out over the mountains and the thick curtain of rain marching their way. Without looking at Wyatt, Rodriguez said, "I'm saying maybe you should hire a good lawyer before it's too late."

THE ICU WAITING AREA WAS DEATHLY QUIET. NOBODY TALKED. Nobody slept. Nobody snored. The handful of people scattered around the room sat there with silent tears on their cheeks or dazed expressions on their faces.

Geneva had her socked feet on the edge of her chair, her knees bent, Massey's tablet resting on her thighs. She'd already watched the security footage several times, from the time the guy in the suit showed up to the time he disappeared down the alley after the shots were fired.

Then she switched modes and watched the video frame by frame. As long as she stayed focused on the unidentified man and didn't let her concentration drift to Caleb, she was fine. Mostly. She sniffed and grabbed a tissue from the box on the table beside her, and added it to the growing pile in her lap.

"What the fuck?" Oops, that was out loud. Everyone's head turned. Geneva winced. "Sorry. Sorry."

Her heart tripped and stumbled a spattering of beats. She sat up straight and went thirty frames back, focusing on the man's left hand as he waved it in the air at Caleb.

There. Right there.

Was it just the play of the light? A trick of the shadows?

She clicked back one frame. Forward one. Back. Forward.

Wyatt stepped into the waiting room, and Geneva jumped up, tablet in hand. "I think I've found something."

WYATT ONLY HALF-HEARD GENEVA WHEN SHE TOLD HIM SHE thought she'd found something, not only because of the news Rodriguez had laid on him, but because before the door to the waiting room closed behind him, it opened again, and Massey crutched his way in. He looked about to drop, but he'd been in such a hurry to get to the hospital, he'd told Wyatt to leave his wheelchair behind.

Massey swayed. Wyatt caught his arm and helped him to one of the chairs. Wyatt sat on one side of him, Geneva, on the other.

Acid ate away several more layers of his stomach lining as he waited for Massey to speak. "How's Evie?"

Massey sucked in a long, considering breath. "Been better. Evie threw a blood clot to her lungs, a pulmonary embolism, the doctors called it. She couldn't breathe. But they caught it fast, got some good drugs in her that are breaking up the clot. She's not out of the woods, but her color is better, and she's breathing easier." Massey rubbed at his eyes, then to Wyatt said, "She's asking to see you."

"Me? Um, yeah, sure. Gen?"

"Go." Geneva patted the tablet on her lap. "This can wait."

The ICU nurses directed Wyatt to Evie's cordoned off area. Her curtain lay open, the lights dimmed, and he wrinkled his nose at the smell of antiseptics.

Evie looked frail in a bed that could have easily held two of her. Her eyes were closed, her chest rising and falling in steady, if not deep, breaths. The heart monitor pulsed silently, a ribbon of green light across a black field.

He sat in the chair next to her bed and brushed the back of her hand, careful not to tug on the IV or dislodge the thingy clipped to the end of her index finger. Her eyes fluttered open at his touch.

"Hey, beautiful." Wyatt brought her hand to his lips and kissed her cool skin. "Your hands are freezing. You want me to find you another blanket?"

She smiled. Weak, but there. She patted his cheek. "You've always been so good to us."

"You and Massey were the ones who took me in when no one in that town wanted anything to do with me. I'm the one who's grateful."

"I... I wanted to give you something." The strength in her voice faded the longer she talked.

"It can wait. You need rest and to concentrate on getting better."

Her eyes fluttered closed, and when he thought she'd fallen asleep, she spoke. Wyatt had to lean in to hear her say, "Take my medal. I want you to have it, just in case..."

In case I die.

She didn't have to finish the sentence. Wyatt's throat went tight, and his Adam's apple bobbed painfully.

Her right hand went to her neck, where her Saint Jude's medal hung from a thin gold chain. The patron saint of lost causes.

Of lost souls.

Fuuuck. Wyatt couldn't remember a time when she didn't wear it. "I can't take that."

But then she grew agitated and started pulling and tugging on it until he feared she'd break the chain.

"Okay, okay. Hold on a sec."

His thick fingers fumbled with the delicate clasp, but she finally held still long enough for him to remove it. He held the charm in his hand, the metal warm from her skin—the metallic relief of St. Jude worn from her regular touch over the years.

"I got that after my husband died. I was so lost. It gave me comfort. You and I... we are very much alike."

Wyatt wasn't sure he liked the implication that he was somehow broken, but she was a kinder, gentler person, *better* person than he'd ever be, so he appreciated the comparison even if it was a fallacy.

"How about I just hold onto this for you for a while?" Wyatt glanced down at her when she didn't answer. Her heart monitor continued its rhythmic squiggles, and her face had relaxed as peace and sleep overtook her.

He slipped St. Jude into his front pocket and placed a light kiss on her forehead before returning to the waiting room.

Geneva waved him over with enthusiasm as soon as he walked into the room. While he'd been gone, the waiting room had cleared out, and Massey and Geneva were the only two people left. She moved over and patted the seat between her and Massey.

"Evie's sleeping comfortably," he reported.

"That's encouraging," Massey said.

Geneva offered a sympathetic smile. "I'm so glad."

"I think Geneva found the smoking gun. So to speak." Massey plopped the tablet in Wyatt's lap the second he had sat down, his friend's *holy shit* vibe cranked up to ten.

Massey hit play, and the video moved forward one frame at a time.

"There." Geneva pointed at the screen. "Watch this guy's fingers."

Massey went back a couple of frames, zoomed in on the hand, and played it again. And Wyatt saw it. Five fingers on the left hand then one frame, *one single frame* where the man had four fingers.

An index finger. A middle finger. A ring finger.

No pinkie.

"*Lambert.*" Wyatt glanced at Massey for confirmation.

Massey's eyes held a light Wyatt hadn't seen in days. "This footage has been doctored. I'll have to examine it with another program on my computer at home to be sure, but I'd bet the entire ranch and one gassy bovine that I'm right."

"This only adds to the questions, though," Geneva said, "Why was Caleb meeting Lambert in the middle of the night? Does this tie the Senator to the murdered women?"

"Oh, my." Geneva pointed to the flat screen mounted in the

corner of the room. She walked over to the TV and turned up the volume.

On the screen, Wyatt's mentor, Sheriff Jed Day, stood at a podium in the bullpen of the Sheriff's Office, a full bank of microphones in front of him. In the corner of the screen, played a short video on infinite loop of Wyatt leaving the courthouse after he'd been cleared of any wrongdoing in Caleb's death, with the reporters crowding in and Rodriguez running interference as they made their way to the cars.

"Though not a suspect at this time, former Bison County deputy, Wyatt Wolfe, is a person of interest in the Nightwalker murders that have plagued our county. If you see him—"

Geneva pressed mute, the TV went silent, and all Wyatt heard was his heart beating. Behind Jed, Rodriguez stared at the camera, as he spoke. No, not just at the camera. *At Wyatt.*

I'm saying you should hire a good lawyer before it's too late.

The Feds didn't know where he was. But Rodriguez knew, and he was covering for him, risking his career, again, *for him.* Rodriguez's little visit to the hospital was more than a warning to get a good lawyer. It had been his friend's way of telling him to run while he had the chance.

Geneva placed a hand on Wyatt's forearm. "What's going on?"

His stomach cratered and his entire abdomen burned. Maybe that acid had finally eaten all the way through. "Rodriguez came by to tell me Candy Lane was found murdered this morning. Shot. With the gun that I'd reported stolen. Between my fingerprints on the lamp, and my gun used in a murder? I'd be pointing the finger at myself, too."

"But you were with me last night," Geneva said.

"And me." Massey had this look on his face, refusing to be left out.

"What did Rodriguez say when you told him you had an alibi?"

Wyatt fished his keys out of the front pocket of his jeans and handed them, plus his cell phone, to Geneva. His truck and his phone would only make it easier for the Feds to find him. "I didn't."

"*What?*" Geneva's voice went shrill at the same time Massey's went equally flat when he said, "Not cool, dude. Not cool."

"You have to tell them!"

"Look," Wyatt said to them, "I'm not implicating you two in a crime—"

"You're not the only one who made that decision with their eyes op—"

"I don't want you losing your job over this," and to Massey, Wyatt said, "And your grandmother is going to need you when she gets out. Besides, I need you two on the outside, feeding me information, not stuck at the station being questioned by the FBI."

"But—"

He grabbed her forearms and planted a hard, quick kiss on her lips. He meant it as an *until later,* but under the circumstances, it felt a whole lot more like a *goodbye.* "Stay by a phone. I'll get a burner and be in touch."

Geneva grabbed a fistful of his shirt. "Wait, where are you going?"

"To find some answers while I'm able."

He turned to leave as a nurse came into the waiting room. Geneva went and turned off the TV probably because the newscast still had Wyatt's ugly mug plastered on the screen. But the nurse didn't seem to notice.

"Is everything okay?" Massey asked as Wyatt and Geneva stepped aside so the nurse could pass.

"Routine paperwork," the nurse said, handing Massey a clipboard with a pen and some paperwork.

"What's this?"

"On patients of your grandmother's age, we have the medical guardian choose whether or not to sign DNR papers."

"DNR?" Wyatt said.

"Do Not Resuscitate," Geneva supplied. "In case—"

"Yeah, I know what the hell it means." Wyatt hit the nurse with a look meant to batter and bruise. "Before the car accident, Evie was a happy, healthy, seventy-eight-year-old. And she's going to be that again." Wyatt grabbed the clipboard and thrust it against the nurse's chest on his way out the door. "Fuck your DNR."

———

A FEW HOURS LATER, CASSIE LET HERSELF INTO GENEVA'S HOUSE and walked into the den. She took one hard look at Geneva, at the empty candy bar wrappers strewn over the couch cushions and the tub of ice cream in Geneva's lap rapidly turning to soup, and pulled her Sasquatch-sized bottle of pepper spray out of her purse and said, "That bastard. I'm going to kill him. No, wait, that's too good for him. First I'll take him by the balls and—"

"Whoa, whoa, whoa." Geneva tossed the packet of cookies and tub of cream ice cream onto the coffee table and stopped Cassie at the front door, slamming her hand against the door before Cassie could escape and cause Wyatt, she assumed, great bodily harm.

Wyatt might laugh at Geneva trying to protect him from Cassie, but if he knew the pissed off, protective side of her friend the way Geneva did, he'd run for the mountains, and even then, he wouldn't be safe.

"Outta my way, Gen. I know you've fallen for this guy, but shit, hon, you deserve better than—"

Geneva grabbed Cassie's shoulders and gave her a shake. She'd hate to have to resort to a Three Stooges face slap. "Cass. *Stop.*"

"You always see the good in people, but sometimes there's no good to be had."

"This isn't sophomore year, Cass. I don't need you riding in on a dark horse to slay my relationship demons."

Cassie's lip went up. "So, he's your boyfriend now?"

"What? No."

"So just a fuck-buddy then? That's still not okay that he—"

"Cass, Wyatt didn't *do* anything."

"He didn't? He didn't break up, or break your heart?"

"No." Geneva led her back to the couch and handed Cassie the ice cream and an extra spoon.

Cassie waved her spoon in a circular motion to encompass all the junk food wrappers lying around. "Then why the *my relationship has ended, and no one will ever love me* binge?"

"It's not." Geneva took the tub back and scooped another spoonful into her mouth even though her blood sugar level had probably spiked to death-defying levels, and she'd wake up in the morning fifty pounds heavier. "It's my... *boyfriend,*" she decided, because fuck-buddy didn't quite cover it, "*is going to risk going to jail for murder because he won't implicate me in a crime* binge."

Cassie's eyes went all dreamy, and Geneva could practically see little puffy red cartoon hearts bubbling around Cass as she reached for the tub. "Awh, that's *so* sweet."

"Sweet? Cassie! Did you not hear me? Did you not see the news? See Wyatt's face plastered across the state? Sheriff Day is saying he's a person of interest in the Nightwalker murders.

Another woman was found dead this morning in Jackson Hole. Shot. They're saying it was with his gun."

"Well, he does have a history of shooting pe—"

Geneva cut her a look that shut Cassie up and had her friend digging in for a frozen chunk of cookie. "Wyatt was with Massey or me the whole night. It couldn't have been him."

"Then, who?"

"That's what we're trying to find out." Geneva stole the ice cream back and almost panicked when she saw the bottom of the container until she realized she had an emergency pint of mint chocolate chip in her outside freezer.

Cassie's phone rang, and Geneva went to get the other ice cream. When she returned, Cassie held the phone out to her and said, "It's for you. It's Wyatt."

How had he known to call Cassie's phone? Geneva set the pint carton on the coffee table and wiped the ice crystals off her hands with the leg of her pink flannel pajama bottoms with the flying hippos.

"Where are you?" As angry at him as she was, she had a hard time keeping the vinegar out of her words.

"Someplace safe," he said. "I just wanted to let you know I'm going to lay low for a few days, try to figure this thing—"

"No. We're in this thing together. Me and you."

"I don't want you taking the fall—"

"It's not considered taking the fall if I did the crime, Wy. We broke into that evidence room *together*. I'm not going to sit back and let you go to jail for a *murder* you didn't commit."

"I'm not going to jail."

"Yeah, and how are you going to manage that? You don't even have a car."

"Evie has an old Continental in her garage I can borrow and the other... I'm working on that, too. I need you to have a little faith. Oh, and Gen?" There was a softness to his voice as it dipped down a couple registers, the way it had after they'd had sex.

Her breath caught, and her body automatically heated. Damn the man. "Yeah?"

She thought he was going to tell her that he loved her. And if not exactly that, then something along those lines. Outside, car doors slammed. And instead of Wyatt's profession of love, she got, "Heads up, the Feds are at your door."

16

Geneva broke out into a cold sweat when the knock came at her door. A heavy pounding that echoed through her entryway.

"Who could that be?" Cassie asked around a mouthful of mint ice cream.

Wyatt had to have been close by to warn her that the Feds had pulled up. Geneva tamped down on the urge to look out her front blinds and see if she could spot him. He had to be close by if he could see her driveway, but she was afraid to do anything that would look suspicious. She had to trust him to stay safe and out of sight.

"The Feds," Geneva mouthed and made a shoo-ing motion with her hands. The last thing she needed was to worry about what Cassie would accidentally say in front of members of law enforcement.

Cassie spat the mouthful of ice cream back into the bucket. "Feds?" she squeaked, wiping the drip of ice cream off her chin. "How do you know?"

"Wyatt," she whispered and wiggled Cassie's phone. He must have bought that burner phone.

When the knock came again, Geneva put her hand on the knob and worked her head from side to side, deciding upfront she wasn't going to lie.

She opened the door. On the other side stood a man who reminded her of Agent K from *Men in Black* except this guy was slightly taller, years younger, infinitely more handsome, and ten degrees more severe than Tommy Lee Jones. Behind him stood Deputy Dave McMahon from the evidence room. Mr. MIB must be throwing the poor guy a dry, splintered bone if he was bringing him into the field.

Geneva opened the door all the way. "Can I help you?"

"Agent Finn, FBI. And this is—"

"Yeah, we know," Cassie said as she stepped through the door with her purse on her shoulder. "Find your keys, deputy?"

Dave turned an unusual shade of green but nodded.

Cassie waved her goodbye, and Geneva invited the pair inside. She scooted in ahead of them, quickly snatching up the empty wrappers and tubs of ice cream and headed for the kitchen.

The two men trailed after her. Over her shoulder, she said, "Can I get you two some coffee?"

Agent Finn said, "Yes, thank you."

Gonna take longer than you thought. Her stomach sank, and she added an extra scoop of coffee into the coffee maker. The extra hit of caffeine warranted she'd need to get through the questioning.

After the pot finished brewing, she poured three mugs.

When she turned around, Dave sat on the far side of her table with his back to the wall. She passed him a cup, and he muttered his thanks.

Finn accepted his coffee, and Geneva pulled out a chair for him and went back for her cup. "Have a seat."

"I prefer to stand," the agent said.

Dave shifted uncomfortably and scooted the stack of decorating samples to the edge of the table as if nervous he'd done something tactically wrong by sitting, but it was too late to fix his mistake.

To give herself some breathing room, Geneva boosted herself onto the counter and took a fortifying gulp. *Shit. Hot. Hot. Hot.*

She sucked air over her scorched tongue and said, "What can I do for you, Mr. Finn?"

"*Special Agent* Finn," he corrected.

Piece of work. Geneva inclined her head at Mr. By the Book. Oops, her bad… *Special Agent* By the Book. He probably didn't just follow it, he probably wrote it. In triplicate. By hand.

"We're looking for Wyatt Wolfe."

Okay, so also not the type for small talk. All the better. She didn't want these men hanging around any longer than necessary. "He's not here."

"When's the last time you saw him?"

As much as she wanted to lie, Rodriguez knew the two of them had been together that morning, and she had promised herself to tell the truth. "This morning. At the hospital. We were visiting a friend. He left after Sheriff Day's broadcast. I haven't seen him since."

"Do you know where he is or where he's going?"

"No." She brought her mug to her lips, remembering to blow on it this time before she took her sip.

"Describe the nature of your relationship with Mr. Wolfe." Finn didn't shift or shuffle his weight. He didn't even lean a shoulder against the door jamb or a hip on the table. Maybe two-thousand-dollar suits didn't do well if creased.

As she tried to come up with the correct descriptor for what she and Wyatt meant to each other, Finn said, "Your relationship has been described as amorous."

Amorous? Did real people still use that word? She didn't even try to hold back the snark when she said, "By who? Mother Goose?"

Dave's smile faded with a glare from Finn, but the carefully controlled Finn-facade didn't crack. He held her gaze. *Ugh. Fine.* She rolled her eyes. "I guess you could call it that."

"The two of you went to speak with the decedent, Ms. Cartwell, in Jackson Hole. Why?"

"We did. We were looking into circumstances surrounding my husband's death. We thought she might have some useful information. Unfortunately, she didn't."

"How was she when you left?"

"If you're asking if she was alive, then yes, she was very much so."

"Did Mr. Wolfe have reason to go back. Later?"

"No."

"Were you home last night?"

"No. I was at a friend's house. With Wyatt."

"Doing what?"

Geneva raised a brow. Finn raised one back. Okay. He'd asked for it. "Fucking."

Okay, maybe she'd allow herself a bit of a white lie.

Dave coughed and fiddled with the kitchen samples. A muscle beneath Finn's right eye twitched.

"Do you need an affidavit stating how many times I ca—"

"That won't be necessary, Ms. Steele." Finn cut Dave a look, and the deputy stopped rearranging paint samples.

Finn placed his untouched coffee cup on the table. "If Mr. Wolfe was with you last night, why didn't he give that information to Detective Rodriguez?"

"Apparently, chivalry isn't dead."

"But five women are, Ms. Steele."

Finn's mask fell, a momentary slip. An emotional bobble and

Geneva saw the fatigue, the frustration, and most surprising of all, that he truly cared. Aaah. There was a human being in there, after all. Perhaps he was someone she and Wyatt could trust. But she also believed Finn wouldn't hesitate to arrest Wyatt on sight. Oh, it might all get cleared up eventually, but in the meantime, the real killer would be getting away with murder.

And begrudgingly, she appreciated the fact Finn had referred to the dead as women. Not prostitutes or whores.

Women.

Finn reached over and with his index finger, slid a paint chip, a cabinet piece, and a granite sample together in the corner of the table. The same three Caleb had chosen. Why was she not surprised?

He took out his business card and placed it on top, then looked up at her. "If he contacts you, I would appreciate it if you would give me a call."

Geneva didn't reply, which went along with the whole not-lying bit. Finn turned to go. Dave stood.

Geneva jumped off the counter. "Aren't you even going to ask me if he did it? If he's capable?" Isn't that what they do in the movies?

Finn was slow to turn back. "I know what he's capable of." A bit more of his human side slipped in. He looked her in the eye and said, "I think you do, too."

———

BETWEEN THE PISSING RAIN AND THE LONG, CIRCUITOUS WALK through the ass crack of Murdock trying to avoid being seen by the sheriff's deputie's cars patrolling the street, Wyatt stepped into Cruisers Bar wet and boiling for a fight.

Looked like he'd come to the right place.

Getting to Geneva's house and Cruisers had taken a lot of

walking and a little bit of hitchhiking giving him sufficient time to think. About the dead women, Caleb's journal, the jointly owned cabin, possibly linking both Day and Lambert to the scene of the first murder.

And then there was the Feds at Geneva's door to worry about as well.

He was more concerned she would get caught up in a lie than her spilling any potential information that would lead to him.

As far as being concerned that people would recognize him from the local news broadcast, it wouldn't be a problem at a place like Cruisers. If the TVs were on, they were set to the sports channels, and even if they weren't, Cruisers didn't attract the type of clientele that called the Sheriff's Office. The people here were the ones that ran from the law.

Wyatt wasn't considered one of them, but being labeled a cop killer had kinda changed his reputation around town. Those who weren't afraid of him were in jealous awe. It made him sick.

The bartender glanced up, bar rag in hand as he dried a beer glass. A guy at the end of the bar, complete with tatts, beard, leather, and beer gut, watched him with bored, disdainful curiosity. Maybe Wyatt had arrested the guy at some point. The other handful of people paid him no mind.

Wyatt walked toward the restrooms and the payphone. Luckily, in a town with limited cell service, you could still find the occasional public landline. He'd picked up a burner phone, but didn't want to risk the number getting out to authorities. Wyatt wiped the sticky receiver on his wet shirt, thumbed some change into the slot, and punched in Rodriguez's number.

It rang and rang. Water pooled at Wyatt's feet from his rain-soaked clothes. But in that place, where things were held together with rust and grime and duct tape, he didn't think it mattered much. Besides, with all the pitting in the old concrete, a little water wouldn't be much of a slip hazard.

As Wyatt went to replace the receiver, he heard Rodriguez's voice on the other end. "Detective Rodriguez." The words came out fast and clipped—heavy on annoyance and light on patience.

"Hey," Wyatt said.

Rodriguez muttered a curse and said, "Hang on."

Wyatt heard the familiar sounds of a busy Sheriff's Office. The many voices, the cussing, the laughing, the general buzz, and the distant blare of a siren as someone was sent out on call. The voices faded away and were replaced with the hum of street noise.

"Where are you?" Rodriguez's words were barely audible over the sound of the country song playing on the bar's jukebox.

Wyatt plugged his ear with a finger. "You got a minute?"

"I don't know. I'm kinda busy looking for a murder suspect at the moment."

"C'mon, man. I know you don't believe I had anything to do with those murders."

The silence stretched out, except for the burr of the wind over the line and the swoosh of tires on pavement and the hiss of tractor-trailer brakes.

"Rodriguez?"

"I'm not sure what I believe anymore. Maybe if you could alibi yourself..."

"I have one, buddy. Just not one I can share at the moment. Give me a little more time. I think I'm close to blowing this thing wide open."

"Then spill."

Wyatt wasn't ready to divulge all of his information, especially since he didn't have all the answers, but he'd throw his old partner a meaty bone to gnaw on. "The way those last two women were murdered shortly after we located them makes me think you have a leak at the office, and…" What he had to say next would gut his friend as much as the news had done to him.

"Leaks didn't put your prints and your weapon at two different crime scenes."

"It's obvious someone is trying to frame me."

"You sound a little paranoid, buddy."

Wyatt had withheld this next tidbit of information waiting for the right time. At this point, it was important for Rodriguez to know.

Because without an alibi, he doesn't believe you. Not a hundred percent. So much for friendship and partnership and loyalty and—

"The night my boat was vandalized, a Bison County sheriff's car was caught on Massey's security camera. Can you check the log and see who had pool cars that night?"

"Why didn't you say anything?"

"At the time, I wasn't sure what it meant, but whoever tossed my boat, stole my gun."

"Quite the conspiracy."

"Hear me out. Besides the leak, I think Lambert and Day may somehow be involved."

Rodriguez blew out a long breath. His laugh stressed and strained, sounding near the breaking point. "Having a leak has been at the back of my mind. But Day? I know you two are on the outs—"

"This isn't a personal vendetta. Day and Lambert and some other town officials own a cabin in the mountains in the general area I think the five women were taken the night Alexa Martinez was strangled. Ownership hidden behind a couple of shell corporations. Did Lambert ever mention a cabin to you?"

"Not that I recall," Rodriguez said. "And so what if they do? A lot of people have cab—"

"There's more." Wyatt waited while the beard from the bar

shuffled by to take a piss. "Caleb had a journal. Initials with dates. Initials that correlate to prominent members of the county and state. With Caleb working undercover for the DEA as a pimp, I can only think the journal has to do with drugs or sex work. Maybe both. Who the hell knows. But my gut says, prostitutes."

"You can't just come out and accuse these men of wrong-doing without any real proof. Initials in a book mean nothing if you can't back that up with other evidence."

Wyatt rubbed his damp forehead, thinking about how a shot of good whiskey could ease his tension headache before it hit Mt. Vesuvius proportions. "Trust me. I'm working on it. But all those rumors of a cover-up? Looks like there may be some truth to that after all."

"Some of those rumors involved you if memory serves. You trying to shift blame?"

"This you playing devil's advocate, or are you just being an asshole?" Rodriguez didn't reply. It wasn't a rhetorical question. "You *know* me."

"And you think I don't know Lambert? Hell, he's... he's like—"

A father to Rodriguez. The same way Day was like a father to Wyatt.

Was.

"Yeah, I know what he's like, buddy, but if these guys are involved, no matter what they've meant to us, no matter who they are or what positions they hold, we can't look the other way. It's our duty."

"*We. Our.*" Rodriguez laughed again, but it came out harsh. "Looks who's sounding like a deputy again. Give me the *Reader's Digest* version of your theory."

"Day and Lambert and the others use the cabin for drinking and drugging and women. A little somethin' somethin' for them and their buds. But then one day, things get out of hand. And one of the women winds up dead."

"And all the other deaths?"

"Those men did what everyone does when there's a mess. Call someone in to clean it up. No witnesses mean no one to testify against you."

"It's a little farfetched," Rodriguez said, raising his voice over some asshole honking. "Besides, Day isn't the man he used to be. I doubt he's strong enough to drag dead weight a hundred yards from a road over rough terrain."

"Maybe, but I bet that thirty-six-inch belt used to strangle the first victim would fit Lambert like a glove."

"I'm not sure I like what you're implying."

"Neither do I, buddy, neither do I. There's more, but I want to confirm a few things before I say anything else."

"Probably for the best." Rodriguez was seething. He didn't yell or scream or holler. Instead, his voice went flat and tight. But Wyatt knew his friend well enough to know he hadn't liked what he'd heard. "Oh and, Wy, you might want to get the hell out of Cruisers before my deputies show up."

Those sirens Wyatt had been hearing weren't coming over the phone anymore. They were coming from outside. Still a minute or so out, by Wyatt's estimation. But they were coming. Wyatt must have given the guys at the bar, or Rodriguez, too much credit.

The beard came out of the john, and Wyatt pulled fifty dollars out of his wallet and held it out to him. "This is yours if you'll meet me out back with your bike and a helmet."

———

WYATT HAD THE BIKER DROP HIM ON A SIDE ROAD TWO MILES from Massey's ranch as the crow flies. The rain had stopped, and the ride from the bar had helped dry out his clothes some, but he still had a long hike overland back to Massey's house.

His socks squished in his boots, and his damp jeans made his legs feel ten pounds heavier, especially after all the hiking he'd already done that day.

He kept inside the tree line, not wanting to risk anyone from a neighboring ranch seeing him.

If he kept a steady pace, he should make it to Massey's right as the sun set. A light breeze kicked up, tree limbs shuddered, and prairie grass in the fields swayed. His stomach grumbled, and his tongue stuck to the roof of his dry mouth.

He pressed on. The muscles in his legs burned. His heart churned. As the last of the light faded, the back of Massey's house became visible about three hundred yards in the distance. From his vantage point, he couldn't see any cars out front, so he circled around, adding about another quarter of a mile to his hike. He ended up where the thinning trees came within fifty yards of the back of the barn.

He ducked low and sprinted across the open area and into the barn. The horses spotted him and cantered over to greet him. Great, if he got caught because of the horses...

Their stall doors opened up into the pasture, and they ran into their stalls and skid to a stop. He gave them treats through the bars and took a second to scratch them behind the ears.

He swiped a bottle of water out of the mini-fridge in the tack room. Drained it. Grabbed another and crept up to the closed doors at the front of the barn. The old sliders didn't close all the way, and he peeked through the two-inch gap between the heavy doors.

He stared out over the yard in front of the house. Geneva's Prius was gone, and his truck sat out front all alone. No deputy vehicles, no unmarked Fed cars. Even the short turn out up the road, where Geneva had parked to stalk him not so long ago, was clear.

The authorities either hadn't made it to Massey's house yet, or they'd already come and gone. He pocketed a couple of alfalfa cubes from the feed room and jogged across the open expanse to the house.

That-A-Way had bedded down near the front door. He tossed a couple of cubes on the grass in front of her nose, and she gave him a muffled moo. After a quick pat, he bolted through the front door.

"Massey?" he called out. No answer.

He did a quick run through the house, but definitely no Massey. No doubt, he was still at the hospital with Evie.

Wyatt couldn't believe it had just been that morning since the hospital had called. It felt like it had been days since they'd gotten the news Evie had had a setback.

He stripped in the laundry room, desperately needing a shower, but knowing he couldn't spare the time. He threw his wet clothes in the dryer, turned it on, and hurried to the guest room to throw on some dry clothes.

He paused in his room where Geneva's scent lingered. A subtle scent that almost had him reaching for the phone and calling her. But the best thing he could do for her was stay away.

Sitting on the edge of the bed, he put on his running shoes. Exhaustion hovered like a ghost, waiting to take over his body when he wasn't looking.

He stood before his body revolted and said, "screw it" and crawled beneath the covers and checked out of life for the next twelve hours. As much as he needed the rest, he couldn't do that until he was someplace safe.

He grabbed another bottle of water from the fridge, and clamped a leftover fried chicken breast between his teeth and beat it for the garage and Evie's old Lincoln Continental—a whale of a car that rarely saw the light of day except for when Wyatt took it out to keep the battery charged.

No light came on when he flipped the switch in the garage, and he added replacing the bulb on his mental To-Do list.

Using his free hand, he felt his way around to the driver's side. The hinges on the driver's side door creaked and popped as he opened and closed it.

He dug the keys out of the cup holder, the engine kicking in on the second try. He idled for a minute, letting the old engine warm then mashed the button on the garage door opener before the exhaust fumes got too heavy.

As the door rolled up, he kept his eyes glued to the rear-view mirror, half expecting a line of deputy cars to pull in the driveway, tires skidding, and sirens blaring.

But the driveway was dark and quiet. Did he have Rodriguez to thank for that?

He started inching out of the garage even before the door was fully open. Seconds later, he accelerated down the two-lane road, away from home and Murdock.

He scanned his mirrors every few seconds, but no headlights approached from either behind or ahead.

Could he be in the clear? The muscles in his jaws ached, and he realized he had the chicken breast clamped between his teeth. He tore off a bite and swallowed.

He drained the water bottle and finally started feeling more human. As the minutes passed and the miles increased, the target he'd felt on his back shrank two sizes and the hair on the back of his neck laid down.

He reached over to turn on the radio and heard, "Are we almost there? I really need to pee."

———

WYATT STOMPED ON THE BRAKES. GENEVA MADE AN *UMPH* SOUND as she slammed into the back of the front seat. In the rear-view mirror, his eyes went wide.

She caught her breath and scrambled over the seat, rubbing at her right shoulder.

Should have seen that coming.

Yeah, but what was the best way to announce yourself after you'd stowed away inside a dark car at night? A polite throat clearing?

Wyatt sat silent, shaking his head as if the motion would re-engage his brain. Didn't seem to help.

The car sat crosswise in the road. Behind them, the road stretched out long and straight with no cars coming, but not too far ahead was a blind curve. She pointed up ahead. "Maybe we should get back in our lane."

"What are you doing here?" He eased his foot onto the gas pedal and maneuvered out of the way of oncoming traffic.

He didn't seem nearly as happy to see her as she thought he'd be. *Liar.* Okay, so maybe she'd had the slightest, teeniest, tiniest inkling that he would not be too thrilled to see her. But like Cassie liked to say, tough patootie.

Geneva buckled up. "Where we going?"

"*Jesus Christ.*" He shook his head again, but the corner of his mouth twitched up a fraction.

Considering the circumstances, she took that for a Chiclet-tooth wide grin. And yay, he didn't turn the car around and take her back or drop her off on the side of the road. But she'd known all along that wasn't something he could risk. He of all people knew it, too.

"Hand me your phone." When she did, he tossed it out the window.

"Hey, I—"

"We can't take the chance that the Feds will decide to track your phone."

"Where to?" she asked again at the same time he said, "How'd it go with the Feds?"

"You first," they said in unison.

Geneva waited him out until he said, "Rodriguez has a hunting cabin in the mountains about ten miles from here."

"He doesn't look like the type to hunt."

"He doesn't, but sometimes in our line of work, it's nice to go somewhere where you can check out for a couple days."

"But won't that be the first place he looks?"

"He's the only one who would know to look there. Right now, he's looking the other way."

"For how long?"

Wyatt shrugged. "We'll be safe. For now." He waited a half-beat, then rushed on and said, "Tell me about the Feds."

Geneva gave him a brief rundown. There wasn't much to tell. "Honestly, I expected them to be more exacting in their questions. Instead, they lobbed a few easily answered or blocked questions. Like a sparring match instead of a real fight."

"A fishing expedition. Nothing more. You were not under arrest and had no obligation to speak to them. You could have stopped answering questions and asked them to leave at any time. Finn was well aware of that."

Wyatt slowed and turned onto a dirt road. The Lincoln's tires slid and spun in the fresh mud, then gained traction.

About twenty yards in, the road narrowed, and the overgrown brush and trees scraped and slapped at the windshield and the sides of the car. They bumped over deep ruts, and Geneva grabbed onto the dash to keep from being tossed around.

Finally, they broke into a clearing, the headlights sweeping across an old-style log cabin, not much bigger than a one-car garage.

"Home, sweet home," Wyatt said.

They both climbed out. Tall grass brushed against the backs of Geneva's thighs and got caught in the car door as she pushed it closed. Wyatt left the headlights on until he found the hidden key and unlocked the front door.

Geneva went around and popped the trunk.

"What are you doing?" Wyatt asked as he turned on the cabin's lights. Knowing it had electricity gave her hope the cabin would also have indoor plumbing.

"I packed a few things for us. I didn't know where we were going or for how long or what."

He met her at the back of the car, the trunk light illuminating an expression she couldn't quite read. She reached for the cooler, but he took it from her hands and set it back in the trunk.

"Hey—"

"I want to yell," he said, with a soft and contradictory tone. "And holler, and throttle your pretty little neck."

He brought a hand to her face, cupping the back of her neck and brushing a thumb across her cheek, her jaw, her lips.

With a hand on her hip, he stepped closer, touching his lips to hers, his eyes closing as he breathed her in.

It was the lightest, faintest, tenderest, briefest of touches. A giving, not a taking.

A promise.

An apology.

It wreaked havoc on her heart and tore pieces from her soul.

"I'm not quite sure what I ever did to deserve having you in my life," he said. "In fact—"

She shut him up with a kiss of her own, taking it deeper,

giving back, giving in, refusing to let him demean himself, to say he wasn't worthy.

She was the unworthy one.

While she'd been driven by hate, he'd been driven by his sense of truth and justice.

She loved his integrity, his perseverance, his loyalty, his... him. She loved *him*.

"I love you." Unguarded, her words escaped.

He smiled, but his eyes had no spark. And instead of hearing the words she wanted to hear, he kissed her on the forehead and said, "I never meant for any of this to happen."

She laughed. Rueful. "I guess it's too late to take my words back, huh?"

Taking a step away, she slung the duffel over her shoulder and grabbed the cooler and shuffled to the door. Wyatt slammed the trunk, killed the headlights, and caught up with her at the porch, stripping her of the items and carrying them into the house.

He closed the door behind him and dropped the cooler and the bag at his feet. "Look, Gen—"

She turned on him, her heart hurt, her temper flaring. "No, you look. I. Forgave. You. And if that didn't sink home when I said it, let me say it again. *I forgive you*. And it's about damn time you forgave yourself."

"I killed—"

"It was self-defense! Caleb drew on you! Hell, he fired the first shot."

The irony that she was defending Wyatt against himself wasn't lost on her, but she'd seen the video with her own eyes. Wyatt hadn't been looking to gun down anyone. "And what he told you, 'I win'? What did that mean anyway?"

Before she and Caleb moved to Murdock with Cassie not far behind, she'd been a paramedic in a bigger city. Suicide by cop wasn't unheard of. Was that what Caleb had wanted? "Did he not want me anymore? Were our lives so terrible that he saw no other way out than—" Her throat closed, her knees buckled, and the room spun.

Wyatt caught her as she crumpled, and settled on the ground with her in his lap. Her chest so constricted the sob couldn't escape.

He held her as the tears flowed not only for the man she'd lost but for the man she could never have. It didn't matter how much she loved Wyatt if he wouldn't—or couldn't—love her in return.

Wyatt picked her up and laid her on the bed in the single room cabin, stretching out beside her and pulling her against his chest, tucking her head under his chin, his hand stroking her hair.

As the sobs slowed, her brain kicked back in and swept all the broken pieces under a thick carpet of denial. They didn't have time for this shit. They had murders to solve before the law caught up with Wyatt. And since she was aiding and abetting, before the law caught up with her.

She sat up. Tried to find a smile. Couldn't. Wyatt sat up, too, his hand rubbing her back.

"Sorry," she said.

He pressed a kiss to her temple and stood. "For what it's worth, when Caleb said 'I win,' it came across as sad, not vindictive. That in winning, he's also lost something very dear. I don't think those words had anything to do with you, at least not in the way you think."

The tightness in her chest eased, and that time she did manage a brittle smile. And because she couldn't think of anything else to say, she asked, "You hungry?"

He smiled. "Starved."

THEY SAT AT THE TWO-TOP TABLE. DINNER WASN'T A GOURMET meal. But after three servings of weenies, bread, and cheese nuked in the microwave, at least Wyatt's stomach quit complaining.

"You going to finish that?" He pointed to the last bite of Geneva's hot dog, and the lone pear slice at the bottom of a can they'd found in the cupboards.

Geneva pushed her plate and the can his way. "Have at it."

Wyatt watched as she glanced around the cabin, her gaze landing on the wood-burning stove in the corner. The full-sized bed. The apartment sized fridge with a sink and microwave.

Just the bare basics for Rodriguez. No pictures on the wall. No curtains. No nick-nacks. But at least he'd installed a tiny bathroom tucked into the far corner. She'd done a happy dance when she'd seen that.

Wyatt finished eating and rinsed their dishes in the sink.

"What are we going to do, Wyatt? How are we going to find the real killer?"

"Killers." Wyatt returned to the seat at the table. "One who killed Alexa Martinez—the kink gone awry—and whoever is getting rid of witnesses or trying to throw investigators off the trail, making everyone think we have a serial killer on our hands. If so, it worked. At first. And even with the rumors of a police cover-up, I was still thinking serial killer until we found out the second and third victims were witness to the first murder."

"Do you think Senator Lambert was The Suit Desiree told us about? Do you think he was the one with the fetish?"

Wyatt didn't want to admit it, more because he knew it would gut Rodriguez if it were true.

The same way it would slice and dice you if you found out Day was killing and covering up for Lambert? But who would be in a better position to cover up the crimes if not the sheriff?

But what motive did Day have besides friendship and loyalty? That would be a lot to ask.

How is that different than Rodriguez covering your ass?

For one, Wyatt hadn't killed anyone.

The hot dogs churned in his stomach, and he swallowed down a sour burp. "It's looking that way, though with the eyewitnesses dead and no real physical evidence besides a thirty-six-inch belt, short of a confession, I'm not sure how we'd pin it on him."

"Not all of them are dead. The driver who took the women up there, he might have seen something. And if he didn't, he certainly knew he brought five women up to the cabin, and only four came back down."

"I'll talk to Rodriguez. With his connections to Lambert, I'm sure he can find out who the driver is."

"You don't think that's a conflict of interest. Having Rodriguez check into it?"

"Rodriguez and I have had each other's backs way longer than the time we've been together with the department.

"I know what kind of man he is. The job comes first. If Senator Lambert is involved, Rodriguez will hate it, but he'd be the first one to arrest Lambert if he thought the senator had killed anyone."

"How can you be so sure?"

"Because his relationship with Lambert is similar to my relationship with Day. Or how my relationship *was* with Day. And if the rumors are true, if Day is covering for Lambert, or killing for him, I wouldn't hesitate to slap the cuffs on him either."

Seriously, you'd arrest your own father?

Wyatt's throat clogged. Day *was not* his father.

No. Day meant more to Wyatt than that worthless shit of a sperm spewer that was his bio-dad.

"So how are you going to find out if Day's involved?"

Wyatt cleared his throat. "I'll ask him."

The chair scraped on the wood floor as Geneva scooted back. "Not alone, you're not."

"You're not coming with me."

Geneva jumped up. "I'm not staying here alone."

Wyatt stood. The frustration building, like a pressure cooker set on high. How the hell did she expect him to keep her safe if she wouldn't listen? "Maybe you should have thought about that before you stowed away in the car."

She laughed. The way her lips twisted, it must have tasted bitter on her tongue. "You didn't seem so concerned about that when you were chowing down on the food I brought. Besides, you don't even have a gun. How do you expect to protect yourself?"

"You don't happen to have yours with you?"

She shook her head. "Sorry. It's locked in my gun safe. I'm not used to carrying it everywhere."

"It's okay. Jed won't shoot me." Arrest him? Very likely, but Wyatt now knew he had to take that risk. If Day wasn't involved, he'd trusted Wyatt enough to hire him to investigate—even if it was off the books—then Wyatt had to trust Day would have enough faith to give him a little leeway.

It hit him then that as much as he wanted to protect her, he couldn't leave her behind in a cabin with no landline, no cell service, no car to get back to civilization if Day arrested him.

Wyatt went to the cabinet above the refrigerator and pulled out a Sig Sauer P938. Rodriguez's old backup for his ankle holster. It held seven-shots with the extended mag if he carried a round in the chamber. "There. I'm armed. But I assure you, I'm not going to need it."

Hopefully.

He reached into the cabinet for ammo and extra magazines. As he removed the box of 9mm rounds, a thumb drive dropped on top of the refrigerator.

He brought the thumb drive, the gun, and the ammo to the table. He checked the weapon and thumbed rounds into the extra magazine.

Geneva picked up the thumb drive. "What's this?"

"Maybe it's Rodriguez's porn stash."

"Wouldn't put it past him," Geneva said. Wyatt cut her look that said *get real.*

She'd never come right out and said she didn't like Rodriguez, but she didn't have to. Her not liking Rodriguez would definitely put a strain on their relationship if she and his best friend didn't get along.

Relationship?

Distraction. Geneva was a wonderful, amazing, caring, *forgiving* distraction.

She's a woman. Who loves *you. Despite what you've done.*

He hadn't been looking for a relationship.

Funny what can happen when you let your guard down.

Geneva snapped her fingers in front of his face. "Hey, where'd you go?"

He returned his focus to her. She'd had her hair pulled back into a messy ponytail and didn't have a lick of makeup to mar her beautiful face. Right then, right there, he wanted to forget it all and let nothing consume him but her.

Her body, her softness, her strength, her love.

Snap, snap. "*Hel*-lo? I was asking how you expected Rodriguez to watch his kiddy porn without a TV or computer."

"I didn't say kiddy porn, and you know I was teasing."

She waggled the thumb drive in front of his face. "Still doesn't answer the question of what's on the thumbdrive. It's not for entertainment if he doesn't have anything to play it on."

"He probably brings his laptop when he comes."

"Why do you sound so defensive?"

"I'm not defensive." And yeah, when he responded that fast, with *that* tone, he sounded even more defensive. "Rodriguez isn't your favorite person. He's an acquired taste. I get that. But don't get all suspicious and read anything into a stray thumb drive just because you don't like the guy."

17

"Sorry." Geneva slumped in the Continental's seat as a car drove by.

Wyatt sunk as low in his seat as he could get, but with his long legs, there was only so much squishing down that he could do. "You don't have to whisper. Day's not home yet, and even if he were, we're two blocks away. I don't think you have to worry about being overheard."

Wyatt killed the engine. He'd parked in a vacant corner lot with a direct line of sight to Day's house between two cars with *For Sale* signs stuck to their windshields. In this area of town, where the neighbors looked out for each other, he couldn't park on the street without being noticed.

"What are you apologizing for anyway?"

"I'm sorry I don't like Rodriguez. And I'm sorry I've let that cloud my judgment." She spoke louder, but not by much.

"No worries," Wyatt said. "I'll make sure we have poker nights at his house."

Which kind of implied that the non-poker nights they'd be at his. Or hers. Or at least together. Geneva did a double-take, and he couldn't quite tell what she was thinking. The silence stretched out awkward and still.

"Uh… I better get going. I want to be there before Day shows up. Could be a while." Wyatt handed her his burner phone and popped the door but didn't get out. "He'll have to pass by here to get to his house. So give me about thirty minutes from the time he drives by before doing anything. If I'm not back by then, go home."

"I'd feel better if you had a phone or—"

"I'll be fine. I'd rather know I have a way to get hold of you if I have to."

He wanted to lean over, to kiss her, to turn on the engine and head north or south or east or west.

Anywhere that wasn't there.

Anywhere their pasts couldn't follow.

Anywhere where they could make a life for themselves… together.

Instead, he threaded his fingers through hers and pressed a kiss to the back of her hand and said, "See you in a few."

The moon sat high and bright and made his ability to skulk unseen through the shadows nearly impossible. So Wyatt boldly walked down the sidewalks like he belonged, all while keeping an eye out for patrol cars or Day's truck.

In Day's neighborhood, not all the houses had fences, so as soon as he got the chance, Wyatt slipped between houses and eased over to Day's backyard. He slapped his hands on top of the old chain link and hurdled Day's fence.

At the back door, he listened for movement. A light shone in the kitchen, but in Wyatt's experience, Day rarely shut it off. Using the punch pad, he unlocked the back door, let himself in, and disarmed the alarm on the wall by the refrigerator.

"Jed?" Wyatt called out, just in case.

No answer. Wyatt wandered into the den and plopped into Day's old recliner. The frame creaked as he sat.

Rodriguez's Sig dug into the small of his back, and an old spring squeaked as he adjusted his position. In the dark room, he rested his head against the cushion, closed his eyes, and waited for the chug of Day's diesel truck.

In the kitchen, the refrigerator whirred, and the ice maker *clunk-clunked* as the tray emptied into the bin.

But even as exhaustion caught up with him, Wyatt was far from falling asleep. His fingers drummed on the armrest, and adrenaline seeped into his system, warming his veins and tightening his muscles in readiness.

Over and over again, he considered how he'd confront Day. Should he come right out and ask, 'Are you killing for Lambert?' or should he start with a simple conversation starter, such as 'Did you know one of your deputies was using the evidence room as his personal pharmacy?'

Headlights flashed, and the front window vibrated from the low grumble of the old diesel engine. Then the driver's door slammed, and boots clomped on the front porch.

Wyatt leaned forward. Silent. Ready.

The front door opened. The security pad didn't beep. Day froze, his hand went to the butt of his service weapon, and in that instant, Wyatt realized that in his exhaustion, he'd made a serious, possibly fatal, miscalculation.

He'd be lucky to get a word out before Day got a shot off. He shifted his weight, the recliner creaked.

He opened his mouth to yell 'don't shoot' as Day spun around, his gun raised, the badge at his waist flashing in the moonlight coming through the open front door.

Wyatt dove over the side of the recliner. The muzzle flashed. Day's .45 *boomed*. Pain erupted in Wyatt's side.

"What the *fuck*, Jed!" Wyatt hollered from the far side of the recliner.

The overhead light flicked on. "Wolfe? That you?"

"Jesus Christ, don't shoot." Wyatt raised his hands over his head and peeked over the top of the armrest, Day's .45 still pointed at his forehead. "Would you put the damn gun down?"

This wasn't how it played out in the movies. In the movies, the mysterious guy in the chair in the darkened room got a chance to speak before the exchange of gunfire. Day may be getting older, but his wits and reflexes were Wyatt Earp sharp.

The portable radio on Day's duty belt squawked. "Sheriff," the dispatcher said. "Your neighbor Ms. Erma said she heard a gunshot and that it sounded like it came from your house."

Day lowered his gun and thumbed his mic. "'S okay. Shot a snake is all."

"Roger that."

"Get the hell up." Day turned and closed the front door. "And for Christ's sake, put your hands down."

Wyatt lowered his hands and clamped one to his side. He hissed as pain spiked across his abdomen and radiated over his ribs. His hand came away soaked in blood. "You fucking shot me."

Day reholstered, and turned toward the kitchen. "Want some coffee?"

Wyatt watched Day's retreat, glanced at the recliner, at the .45 caliber hole in the back cushion right where his chest had been and followed him.

As Wyatt stepped into the kitchen, Day tossed him a cup towel. He caught it with one hand and pressed it to his side.

"What happened to knowing what you're shooting at before you pull the trigger?" Wyatt asked, the pain making it impossible to keep the overwhelming annoyance out of his voice.

"Someone tries to sneak up on me in my house in the dark,

I'm shooting first. Sit," Day said over his shoulder as he prepped the coffee maker. When he finished, he turned around and said, "You owe me a new recliner."

Wyatt laughed. "Ouch."

Day bumped his chin toward Wyatt's side. "Let's see."

Holding up his shirt, Wyatt twisted and looked at his side. Day stepped closer, taking the cup towel and dabbing at the wound.

"*Fffffft*." Wyatt sucked in a breath through his teeth. "Easy!"

Day clucked his tongue and placed Wyatt's hand and towel back on the torn flesh. "It's just a flesh wound." The way Day said it, *Monty Python* played in Wyatt's head.

Wyatt glanced up at his mentor. If Day had been trying to be funny, you couldn't tell from his stoic expression. The same expression Wyatt had known Day to strap, tape, and clamp on when shit went sideways.

After Day poured the coffees, he sat across the table from Wyatt and slid a cup over to him.

They sipped quietly for a time. Day looking like an older, tougher, smarter version of Sam Elliot, but with grayer hair and bushier brows. The word *manscape* would never be in Day's vocabulary.

"How have you been, son?"

Wyatt huffed out a laugh and sat back. "I've been better." He pulled the towel away. Though it felt like he'd been hot branded, the bleeding had slowed to a trickle.

"Whatcha doing here?"

"Look, I let myself in because I know you don't want to be seen talking to me. I know I'm supposed to give my reports directly to Rodriguez. I get that, but..."

Day's expression shifted from interest to mild curiosity to what-the-hell as his bushy brows met a the furrow above his eyes.

"What the hell are you talking about, boy?"

"The Nightwalker investigation. You don't have to play dumb. I won't tell anyone you you wanted me—"

Wyatt cut himself off.

If Day didn't authorize Wyatt's investigation it meant Rodriquez had his own agenda. Wyatt's stomach twisted and turned until acid scorched the back of his throat. He coughed up fire and chugged his coffee to douse the flames.

The slow, steady flow of adrenaline hit critical mass, dulling the pain in Wyatt's side even as he jumped out of the chair and started pacing. "You've no idea what I'm talking about, do you?"

Day didn't hesitate. "Not a clue."

Day hadn't been at the helm. Rodriguez had.

Then all the things that didn't make sense in the investigation started falling into place. The deputy car the night his boat had been vandalized, Desiree's murder right after they'd found her, his missing gun used to shoot Candace.

And Rodriguez hadn't been unofficial backup the night he'd talked to Scout, Rodriguez had been following him.

The same way Rodriguez must have followed him to Desiree and Candace.

That fucking app.

Rodriguez hadn't needed him to find the witnesses to catch the killer. He'd needed Wyatt to find the witnesses so he could silence them, and frame Wyatt in the process.

Rage. Red. Hot. Incendiary. A nuclear bomb of emotions. The timer counting, counting, counting down, a deafening drum in his ears until...

Ka-boom!

Wyatt slammed his fist into the refrigerator door, again and again and again. Until his knuckles bled and his fingers went numb, the shock of the blows shooting up his arm and exploding in his shoulder.

He grabbed the handle of the refrigerator door, set to rip it from its hinges when Day's arms came around him, pinning Wyatt's arms against his ribs.

His side throbbed in time to the trill and thump of his pulse racing through his veins.

But all of that was nothing compared to the breath sucking, soul-breaking agony of his heart being ripped from his chest.

Of all the people in the world, the one person he'd trusted the most, the one person who'd always had his back, the one person he'd have gladly given his life for had betrayed him in the most despicable, heinous way.

And he'd never seen it coming.

Like stepping off the curb and being slammed by a bus.

Or a bullet to the back of the head.

One minute you're living your life and the next... *nothing*.

Day dumped Wyatt in the chair and went back to the refrigerator and grabbed a couple of beers. Apparently this called for something stronger than coffee. He kicked the door closed with the heel of his boot. The stainless-steel skin dented, the hinges bent, the seal not sealing.

Twisting off the tops, Day handed him the beer and took a sip of his own. He leaned back and said, "You owe me a refrigerator, too."

Wyatt chugged the beer, draining half in four long swallows, his lungs billowing, harsh, raspy pants.

"Wanna tell me what this is all about?"

"First, I need you to put your gun out of reach and answer a question."

Day held his gaze for what seemed like five minutes, but that was probably just the thump, thump in his side counting out the seconds in triple time. "You first."

Wyatt twisted—*ouch*—and pulled the Sig from his waistband, unloaded it, and slid it out of reach at the end of the table.

Day tugged his .45 from his holster, did the same, and placed it next to the Sig.

Day took a sip of his beer and said, "Go on."

Wyatt hesitated, wanting to savor this last moment where Day could still be the stand-up man Wyatt had always known him to be. Without proof, he couldn't fully believe Rodriguez was the killer, but right then, it made the most sense. But could Rodriguez have pulled it off without Day's help?

"You gonna say something or are you going to make me guess? Because, at sixty-three-years-old, I don't have that kind of time."

Wyatt puffed up his cheeks and blew out a lungful of stale air. "Did you kill those women?"

The beer Day'd been sipping caught in his throat, and he spewed the liquid onto the table and down the front of his shirt. Slow and considering, Day wiped his mouth with the back of his hand, ignoring the rivulets of liquid running down the front of his tan uniform shirt. "Rodriguez said you'd been slipping. Drinking. Acting paranoid since I let you go."

"Let me go?" Wyatt's incredulous laugh echoed in the kitchen. "You didn't *let me go*, you showed me the door, and when a boot up my ass wasn't enough to get me to leave, you used a cattle prod."

"As much as I don't like it, being sheriff is an elected position. I had an obligation to my constituents—"

"Fuck your constituents. I was *cleared*. I didn't do anything wrong. All I wanted was my job and for things to go back to the way they were before. But you didn't want me there. I could have sued—"

Day's chin went up. "Is that what this is about? You want to sue me to get your job back?"

Wyatt tossed the blood-soaked cup towel onto the table and dug the heels of his hands into his eye sockets, but the sharp pain behind his eyes didn't ease. He hadn't come here to talk about his job. He'd come here for answers.

"I don't want to sue. I want you to answer the question."

"No." Day's reply came out calm, steady, bored almost. As if Wyatt had asked Day if he'd seen the TV remote. "But your life could be in question if you don't tell me what the hell is going on."

A smile tugged at the corner of Wyatt's mouth. He'd missed the old bastard.

Wyatt told Day everything. From Rodriguez 'hiring' him on behalf of Day to investigate the murders, to the clues in Caleb's journal, to how his prints ended up on the lamp used as a murder weapon, to his now suspicion of Rodriguez in the vandalization of his boat and the stealing of his gun to frame him for murder, to the paper trail that led to the jointly owned cabin by Lambert and Day, and finally to the video evidence of Lambert at the scene of Caleb's shooting.

Conveniently, Wyatt left the whole felony breaking and entering at the station off the list. Day already had a lot to absorb.

Deep in thought, Day retrieved two more beers. Wyatt polished off his first and twisted off the cap to the second.

Instead of focusing on the murders, Day came back with, "And you believed Rodriguez when he said that I wouldn't speak to you. That all communication and updates would go through him?"

Okay, so now it seemed a bit odd, but— "You haven't exactly been beating down my door to open the lines of communication this past year, or even go so far as to acknowledge me on the street, so, yeah, at the time, it wasn't far outside the realm of possibility."

"And you really thought I was capable of murder?" Day's

voice dropped as incredulity crept into his words, making him sound like the one who'd been wounded.

"I would never have thought Rodriguez would be either. But it's looking like I could be wrong about that."

"Say what you're saying is true. That Rodriguez killed the witnesses and used his position as lead detective to keep the cases unsolved. What is his motivation?"

"Loyalty," Wyatt said without hesitation.

Day scoffed. "*Before…*" Wyatt knew Day meant *before he'd shot Caleb.* "Before, if the situation had been reversed and I had accidentally killed someone, would your loyalty have had you covering up for me?"

"No. Maybe it's the power, then," Wyatt added with a little more reluctance. "If Lambert makes it to the White House, he'd take Rodriguez with him. And for the record, I'd come fully prepared to arrest you if you'd been involved."

"You don't have that kind of authority." Day spoke without anger or animosity, only an observation.

"I'd have found a way."

Day smiled, wide enough for Wyatt to see the gleam of the discolored filling on Day's left upper incisor. He held his bottle up to Wyatt, and they clinked the necks. "That's my boy."

Wyatt tried to ignore the tightness in his chest at the pride in Day's voice. Wyatt was an adult. Day's opinion of him shouldn't matter anymore.

But even after all these years, and after what Wyatt had endured after the shooting… it sure as hell did.

———

Geneva let herself in through Sheriff Day's back door, leaving the car in the vacant lot as Wyatt had instructed.

Her eyes immediately went to the splotches of blood on the white linoleum.

"Who's been shot?" Geneva joked.

Wyatt and Day sat at the kitchen table with three empty beer bottles between them. Wyatt tossed his head back, draining the last of his beer and raised a couple fingers half-heartedly. Make that four empty beers.

Geneva rushed to him, peeling his hand away from the blood-streaked towel he held to his side.

"Are you freaking kidding me?" Geneva peeked at Wyatt's bullet wound. *Bullet wound. WTF?* Then pinned Sheriff Day with a scorching look. "You *shot* him?"

Day mumbled something along the lines of 'Wyatt shoulda known better.'

Then she nailed Wyatt with a similar look, only adding a heaping helping of you-are-*so*-dead. "You said he wouldn't shoot you."

"*Ouch*. Jesus. Take your frustration out on me, not my side."

She let up on the overzealous wound blotting. Though clotting, every time Wyatt moved, sections bled again. "Hold still, or the whole thing is going to start hemorrhaging again. You need to go to the hospital and get stitches and antibiotics."

"No." Wyatt and Day said at the same time.

"Look, I know the hospitals have to report gunshot wounds, but he's the one they'd report it to." Geneva jabbed her thumb over her shoulder at Day in case there was the slightest confusion as to who would get the report. Even though it didn't look like Wyatt had lost that much blood, it was apparent he wasn't thinking too clearly.

Day didn't have that excuse.

"You're a paramedic," Day said. "Can't you just..." He waggled his hand in a get-it-done motion that Geneva took to mean 'do your paramedic-y thing.'

She booted Day out of his chair and moved it closer to Wyatt and sat. Glancing at Day, she said, "You got any first aid supplies? Because I didn't count on this being a professional call."

Day went out to his truck and came back with a first-aid kit. He dumped it on the table, and she rummaged through it until she found the disinfectant, some steri-strips, and bandage material.

Geneva tugged at the bloody waistband of Wyatt's jeans. "Pull your pants down."

Wyatt complied, unfastening his pants and shoving them down until she was staring at half of the most perfect ass cheek. *Eyes on the prize. Ehr... the wound. Eyes on the wound.* She was a professional. She saw asses and much more every day. This was nothing.

Hah. Nothing *had never looked that good.*

As she cleaned the wound and closed it with six steri-strips, she said, "So does this mean he's not arresting us?"

"Us?" Day's brow went up.

Wyatt gave her an almost imperceptible shake of his head.

"You," she amended.

No one said anything.

She looked up after she taped the gauze pad over the steri-strips. Wyatt stared at Day. Day stared at Wyatt.

"No, he's not," Day said at last. "But I also can't call off the Feds without taking a chance Rodriguez will get word."

"Is that why I had to walk here? So no one would see the Continental in front of your house?"

"I like her," Day said to Wyatt as if she weren't there. "Don't fuck it up."

Geneva coughed. "There's noth—"

"I'm trying my damnedest not to," Wyatt said.

Geneva gaped.

Wyatt winked.

How was she supposed to take that? Did that mean Wyatt wanted something more than the sex? She cleared her throat. "Uh... you can pull up your pants now."

Wyatt did, careful to keep the waistband below the bandage to prevent the band from rubbing against the dressing.

Geneva gathered up the blood and Betadine-soaked gauze pads, and the empty wrappers, and tossed them in the trash.

"So how are we going to catch Lambert and Rodriguez?"

"Give Jed the thumb drive we found."

Geneva pulled it out of her back pocket. Day left and returned with his laptop. Together they watched what turned out to be the unedited version of the security footage of Caleb's shooting. Wyatt had a tight grip on her hand, and she felt him flinch when video-Wyatt fired.

Wyatt moused over the rewind button until it got back to where you could see the man in the suit's, or rather Lambert's, hand. Without Massey's ability to enlarge a point of interest in the video, it was harder to see, but if you looked carefully, Lambert's left hand clearly lacked a pinky finger.

"This was hidden in a cabinet at Rodriguez's cabin."

"Rodriguez has a cabin?"

"Go figure, right?" Geneva said. "I pictured him as more of the spa and mani-pedi type."

"He manipulated the footage. Or had someone manipulate the footage, and entered the new thumb drive into evidence."

Day stilled, his gaze assessing, missing nothing. "How would you know that?"

Wyatt swallowed. "Is the 'how' really important right now?"

Day could have pressed, but he didn't. *Phew.* Geneva took that as a small victory. She didn't buy into the whole *Orange Is the New Black* thing. It clashed with her skin tone.

"But what does Caleb's shooting have to do with the

murders?" Day ejected the thumb drive and shut his computer down.

Watching the shooting again still upset her, but this time, she felt more removed. More disconnected. That man in the video wasn't her husband. The man she'd loved wouldn't have shot at Wyatt, a fellow officer, after he'd identified himself. It was a side of Caleb she'd never experienced and didn't recognize.

"Clearly," Geneva said, "that was an argument he and Lambert were having. And there are indications in Caleb's journal that he was involved in his own side investigation into Alexa Martinez's murder. I think Caleb somehow had made the connection and was confronting Lambert."

Wyatt absently picked at the label on one of the beers with his thumbnail. "And from what Desiree said, I think the cabin you bought with your friends may be where Alexa Martinez was murdered. Ground zero, so to speak."

"My cabin." It was neither a question or a statement.

Wyatt shifted in his seat, and he winced. "Anything look out of place there, anything suspicious?"

Sheriff Day shrugged. "I haven't been there in a year, at least. Being sheriff doesn't afford me a lot of free time."

"Why are we sitting here? Why aren't you guys going out and arresting Rodriguez?"

"We've got nothing solid on him," Day said.

"And besides him lying about Jed hiring me to help with the investigation, we have no physical evidence or witnesses that tie him to any of the murders."

"Hell, we don't even have enough probable cause to get a warrant. Especially with a county judge who's good friends with Lambert."

"Then what do you need?" Geneva was ready to wrap this up. She wanted all this behind her. She wanted her life to go back to normal, or at least as close to her new normal as she could get.

"A confession," both men said at the same time. Wyatt chuckled. Day shook his head.

Geneva stood. "Then let's go get one."

Wyatt snagged her wrist and sat her back down. "It's not that easy, and you know it."

"We need to get him alone." Day rubbed his hand across the short stubble on his jaw. "Without notifying the Feds or alerting anyone else in the department. We don't know if he has anyone else on the inside working with him."

"And we need back up. At least one more person would be nice. Someone we can trust." Wyatt looked to Day. "What about—"

"My sister." Why hadn't Geneva thought about her before? *Maybe because you haven't spoken to her since the funeral?*

"You have a sister?" The surprise on Wyatt's face might have been comical under other circumstances. "You never mentioned you had a sister before."

"We aren't exactly close." All because her father had picked Geneva to live with him after their parent's divorce. It wasn't Geneva's fault. It wasn't like she'd had a choice in the matter. Like either of them had had a choice. "And you never asked. But she's a cop with the Rock Springs PD. She wouldn't have any ties around here."

"You think she would help?" Wyatt seemed skeptical.

"All I can do is ask."

Geneva excused herself and went into the den for a little privacy and followed the blood trail back to the recliner. White fluff stuck out of a hole, midway up the back cushion. Her hand shook as she stuck her finger in the bullet hole. That could have been Wyatt's chest.

She gagged on the rising bile and swallowed it down. She couldn't lose Wyatt. She couldn't lose another man she loved.

Her knees buckled, and she plopped onto the recliner before she fell, the faintest scent of gunpowder still lingered in the air. Her fingers fumbled with the phone. Hopefully, her sister hadn't changed her number, because it was the only one for her she remembered by heart.

Her heart thumped against her sternum as she pressed the *call* button. Becca answered on the first ring.

"H-Hey." Geneva cleared her throat. "It's me." *Duh.*

"Thought you'd lost my number," Becca said with a taste of fuck-you in her voice. Maybe this was a bad idea.

But Geneva powered through. "I could really use your help."

———

When Geneva returned to Day's kitchen, her steps slow, her face pale enough she could have been the one who'd lost blood instead of Wyatt.

Wyatt stood and helped her to a chair. He scooted his chair over and laid his arm—*ouch*—across her shoulder and kissed the side of her head.

After a moment, she said, "I knew I wasn't my sister's favorite person, but... but I'm pretty sure what she feels for me goes beyond a strong dislike."

"It's okay," Wyatt said. "Day and I can handle Rodriguez. It just would have been nice to have the extra hand in case it turned into a cluster."

Geneva glanced up at him, a mixture of emotions flitting across her face, and he couldn't even begin to fathom what she was feeling. "Oh, she's helping. No idea why. But I guess that doesn't matter. She has the early shift in the morning, but she can be here by six tomorrow night."

"That'll work," Day said. "Gives us a chance for me to get a warrant for the wire for you to wear and for us to pick a meeting location."

"Rodriguez's cabin." Because his side ached, Wyatt lowered his arm and linked his hand with Geneva's on top of the table. Day's eyes darted to their joined fingers, but he didn't say anything. "It's isolated. Geneva and I are already there. We can prep the area, and there's a rocky outcropping on the edge of the property that overlooks the road going in. Geneva can watch with binoculars from there and radio us if it doesn't look like he's alone. From that distance, it would give us enough time to bug-out the back and through the trees, if need be."

At first, Day didn't say anything, and from Wyatt's experience, his mentor was going through all the scenarios in his head —the mental list of pros and cons and Murphy's long list of all the shit that was likely to go wrong. "You know he's going to try to kill you, right?"

Geneva flinched, and she squeezed the blood out of his fingers. "Maybe this isn't such a good idea."

He raised their joined hands and kissed the back of her hand. "I'm counting on Day and your sister not to let that happen." With a little effort, he'd managed to keep the doubt out of his voice.

Geneva cut him a look. But dealing with just Rodriguez would be infinitely better confronting him in a semi-controlled environment, than out there on the streets.

Wyatt would take his chances at the cabin with Day and Geneva's sister as backup any day. "Now, all we have to do is figure out how to lure him up there."

"Tell him you want to turn yourself in. But only to him," Day said.

Geneva's grip got even tighter, and Wyatt no longer concerned himself with the lack of circulation in his hand as much as her not crushing his bones to powder. He pried his hand free. "That should work."

Geneva just shook her head over and over again. "There's got to be a better way."

"Sweetheart, this is the better way. Look me in the eye and tell me there's another person out there that you know, I mean *know* one hundred percent, is not working with Rodriguez that has the skill set to help us."

She didn't have an answer for him. He hadn't expected that she would.

Day slapped his hand on the table with a resounding finality. "That settles it then. Meet me behind Cruisers about noon. I'll bring you the wire, a couple of radios, and a little more firepower than that pea shooter you got there." Day indicated the Sig with a tilt of his head. "You can call Rodriguez from the payphone there. I'll make sure the Feds keep him busy, so he doesn't show up at the cabin early."

Wyatt reloaded the Sig and stuffed it in the holster in his waistband. Geneva stood, and Wyatt pointed to the refrigerator spilling cold air into the kitchen. "Sorry about the refrigerator."

Day waved him off. "Sorry about the slug to your side."

"Bullshit." Wyatt chuckled and grabbed his side. *Damn, that hurt.*

Together, Wyatt and Geneva slunk back to the car. The moon had gone behind the clouds, and they were better able to stay in the shadows. Geneva insisted she drive. Wyatt didn't protest. And even though he worried about getting to the end of tomorrow night without another hole in him, his eyes drifted closed as fatigue called him home.

Geneva patted his thigh. "Wake up. We're here."

Wyatt shook himself awake. It felt like he'd been asleep two seconds, not twenty minutes. He struggled with the door, his side having stiffened up on the ride up.

"Hang on. I'll come—"

"'S all right. I got it." Wyatt shifted until he got his boot against the door and shoved.

Geneva muttered something about him being stubborn and hard-headed, and something else that didn't quite sound complimentary. She waited on the top step of the porch, her hands on her hips as he slowly made his way around the Continental's long front end.

When he made it to the top step, he ducked his head and kissed her. The evening temperature had dipped, and even that short period of time outside had stolen a hint of the heat from her lips.

She kissed him back, and in an instant, his body became immune to the cold. All he felt was this inferno burning inside him for this fierce, trusting, amazing woman. He didn't think these next twenty-four hours would be his last, but if they were, he sure as hell wasn't going to waste a minute.

He walked her backward and let them into the cabin. He closed the door and pressed her against the solid wood—the muted light from the cloud-covered moon shining through the back windows, the only illumination.

But he didn't need light to see. All he needed were his hands, his lips, his di—

Geneva pulled his shirt over his head, her breath coming in quick pants that revved his heart and sent his libido into overdrive.

She slid her hands down his sides. Her left stopping just above the bandage. "I guess you taking me against the door with my legs wrapped around your waist is out of the question."

Wyatt groaned, deepening the kiss and grinding against her. He ran his hands down her curves and cupped her ass, wanting nothing more than to feel her ankles lock behind his back. How much would it hurt anyway? If they were care—

Geneva broke the kiss. "Don't even think about it."

"We could—"

"Nope." She took his hand and led him toward the bed. In the span of about five seconds, she'd dropped his hand, her shirt, and her bra. Her boots went next.

"You on top, then." Wyatt sat on the edge of the bed and unfastened her jeans and let them drop to her ankles.

She stepped out of them. "My knee could tear your bandage off."

He huffed out a frustrated breath as he wrapped his arms around her waist and trailed the tip of his tongue up her midline. Her hands fisted in his hair. Truth was, as much as he wanted her, his side screamed like a bitch, and he didn't think he was physically up for anything too strenuous.

Which pushed a couple of other fine ideas out of the running.

"Vanilla may be all I'm up for." He relieved her of her panties, and she kicked them, as well as her jeans, away.

"Somehow, I—*Jesus*." Her breath hitched as he cupped her breasts and brushed his tongue over one of her peaked nipples. "I-I don't think having sex with you could ever be considered vanilla, no matter the position. And if you're hurting, we don't have to do this."

He released her left breast with a resounding *pop*. "Yeah. We do." His tone left no room for argument or the slightest hint of doubt.

Pulling her down onto the bed, he stood long enough to retrieve a condom from his wallet and lose the rest of his clothes.

She scooted over and made room for him, not bothering to get between the sheets. He stretched out beside her, and she plucked the condom from between his teeth. "You know," she said as the tips of her fingertips brushed past his belly button and into the curls at the base of him, "me and the um..." Her hand slid further down until she'd wrapped her hand around his cock. "...the Wolfe cub never got formally introduced."

A strangled laugh escaped him, and his hips surged into her hand as he pulled her tight against his chest. "Wolfe cub, huh?"

She didn't answer. Instead, she slid down his body and settled between his legs, wasting no time putting her mouth on him. And just like that, Wyatt no longer cared that she hadn't answered. She could call his cock anything she damn well wanted as long as she didn't stop whatever the hell it was she was doing.

He pulled out her hair tie and ran his fingers through her silky hair, then cupped the back of her head. She stroked him with her hand, her tongue, her mouth. The slightest scrape of her teeth had him bucking, the tip of him hitting the back of her throat.

She pulled back, running the tip of her tongue across the ridge of his head, then licking across the slit. "Mmm... definitely doesn't taste like vanilla." She practically purred her appreciation.

He chuckled, but it came out choked. And as much as he didn't want her to stop, now or ever, he also wanted to be balls deep, taking what she offered, giving what he could.

"Come here," Wyatt said as he eased her up until she laid on his chest.

She found the condom by one of the pillows and handed it to him. "Don't keep me waiting."

He ripped the wrapper, and she scooted over long enough for him to cover himself. His side shouted out a complaint as he rolled Geneva onto her back and settled between her legs.

With his weight on his hands, he ducked his head, covering her mouth with his. Their tongues dueled, and he tasted himself on her. *Holy hell, that's hot.*

She broke the kiss, nipped at his chin. "I'm still waiting."

"Impatient."

"I just know what I want."

He reached between them, brushed the tip of his cock at her slick entrance. He balanced above her, teasing, taunting—and by the way she writhed—driving her mad. "That what you want?" Then he slicked his thumb and circled her clit. "Or do you want this?"

"Both."

Wyatt smiled. He loved a woman who knew what she wanted. She ran her hands over the curve of his ass and arched her hips and took him in one smooth stroke.

He hissed in a breath as his head dropped to her chest. "Jesus Christ, you feel good."

Arms trembling, he could no longer hold himself above her. He pinned her with his weight, his arms sliding beneath her shoulders, bracing himself, his hands cradling the back of her head. "This okay?"

"The only way it's not okay is if you stop."

He grinned. "That's not going to happen."

Geneva lay there on the bed in Rodriguez's cabin, Wyatt's weight pinning her down, him filling her. He started to move, and she pressed up against him. Loving the slow, languid strokes the position demanded, but also wanting more.

And she didn't mean harder or faster. She wanted more. Of him. But she was afraid that it wasn't going to happen tonight, or perhaps any other night.

She'd forgiven him.

She'd told him she loved him.

But still, he held on. Held back. Refusing, or unable, to fully give himself over to her. Whether or not it was his guilt for killing Caleb or some twisted sense of chivalry that told him that she shouldn't or couldn't belong to him, she didn't know.

But until he got past that, it didn't matter how much she loved him, they had no future.

And that's if they got through the next twenty-four hours in one piece.

Her chest tightened, and it was more than Wyatt's weight that made it difficult for her to breathe. As the sting came to her eyes, she tore her thoughts away from the what-ifs. She refused to cry during sex. No matter what was at stake.

And she refused to let the uncertainty of tomorrow take away what they shared tonight.

He stilled. Pressed a kiss to the tip of Geneva's nose and raised up on his elbows. "Hey. You okay?"

That close, even in the dark, she could see the worry in his eyes. Not just for her, but for the danger they'd face tomorrow. She cupped his face, so he couldn't look away. "I love you, Wyatt."

His expression softened, and the sad hint of a smile tilted his lips. Did he love her? She thought so. Would he ever admit it?

She didn't know.

But he lowered his mouth to hers, laying soft, gentle kisses on her lips as he began moving inside her. Her hands went to his ass, wanting him harder and deeper, but he stayed with the same slow, sensuous strokes. His body telling her what his heart couldn't.

The tension built, but instead of rushing toward it, she held back, not wanting it to ever end. But the peak grew near, and there was nothing she could do to stop it.

He pressed hot kisses under her jaw, nipped at the soft skin between her neck and shoulder. He braced his weight on his arms, driving harder and faster.

Goosebumps skittered across her skin, her blood racing, racing. The *whoosh* behind her ears sounded like waves crashing on the shore in the heart of a hurricane. His breaths became harsh pants as their bodies slicked with sweat.

He reached a hand between them, teasing her to the brink as she met him stroke for wicked, sweet stroke. He groaned, his rhythm becoming erratic. Wyatt rose on his haunches, splaying her wide, teasing and taunting the tight bunch of nerves.

Then he tipped her over the other side, her muscles clamping around him as he threw his head back and howled. He gripped her hips, pumping, straining until he'd emptied himself.

He fell forward on his elbows, still grinding gently against her as they met on the other side. He buried his head in her neck as their breathing slowed. Before he pulled away, before he pulled out, he pressed his lips to hers.

The touch light.

The emotion sharp.

"Gen," he said, in that low, growl of a register his voice sank to after sex. "You matter to me. A lot."

He paused, and though she didn't question his sincerity, she heard the big fat *but* roaring around the corner like a freight train bent on ego-demolishing destruction.

She pressed a finger to his lips, and he gently caught the pad of her finger between his teeth. "Leave it at that," she said, tossing in a smile that cost her dearly. "No qualifiers. I'll take it as it is. And I'll take you as you are."

And because he looked doubtful, she added, "You're a good man, Wyatt Wolfe. You've made me believe it. It's past time you believed it as well."

18

Those words should have made Wyatt proud. Instead, as he and Geneva lay under the covers with her head on his chest, all he felt was shame and guilt.

Caleb should be lying in his bed with Geneva in his arms.

Caleb should be making plans for the future with Geneva by his side.

Caleb should be grinning madly as Geneva's belly bulged with his child.

Instead, Caleb got dirt and dust and an eternity without her.

And you got Geneva.

He stared up at the rafters, his eyes bleary from lack of sleep, but his body too keyed up to rest. With care, he extricated himself without waking her and sat on the edge of the bed, rubbing his eyes with the heels of his hand. He reached for his clothes and dressed in the dark. It would be another couple of hours before the sun rose, but he couldn't lay still any longer without going mad.

He wanted to prep, to prepare, but there wasn't much he could do until he met Day in town and got the wire. He retrieved the holstered Sig from the floor by the bed and clipped it to his belt at his hip, feeling more in control just being armed. He reached into his front pocket, and brushed his thumb across Evie's medal. He would take all the strength he could get.

He went to grab a bottle of water out of the refrigerator when he caught a flash of light in his peripheral vision. The hair on the back of his neck spiked, and Wyatt rushed to the front window in time to see a pair of headlights disappear as a car backed down the driveway.

Rodriguez. It had to be.

This is it.

Adrenaline spiked—releasing a hormone tsunami that surged through his system. Fatigue vanished, leaving readiness in its churned wake, every sense on high alert. He took one calming breath, knowing what was coming. This was all part of the plan. Only it had arrived early and without backup.

The part he hadn't counted on was Geneva being here when it happened. In his plan, Geneva would have been at the ridge. Out of sight and, more importantly, out of harm's way.

"Geneva." He hurried to the bed. When she didn't respond, he shook her shoulder. "Geneva. Wake up. Rodriguez's here."

She bolted upright, and he gathered her clothes and shoved them into her lap. "What? What's going on? He's here?"

Wyatt returned to the window, peeking out from the side while he kept his body hidden. Though he didn't quite know what the point of that was. Rodriguez would have seen the car in the driveway and known someone was there. He had to assume it was Wyatt.

At least Rodriguez didn't know Wyatt was onto him yet.

Geneva pulled on her pants and slipped her feet into her boots, pushing the hair out of her face. "You saw him?"

"Saw a car. Backed away when the Continental came into view."

Geneva strapped on her bra and pulled her shirt over her head. "Maybe someone's lost."

Wyatt didn't buy it. "You saw the road in. This isn't the type of place that people stumble on. You pretty much have to know it's here. Which leaves Rodriguez."

Her boots clomped on the wood floor as she stomped her feet home. "I'm dressed. Let's get out of here then."

Wyatt tore his focus away from the window. He wished it were that easy. Just because they weren't fully prepared didn't mean Wyatt wasn't ready. This needed to end. Now. "Take the burner phone. Go out the back door and get to the tree line. Follow it east. It will take you to the ridge. You should be able to get enough of a signal to call Day from there."

There was a back way off the mountain, down a ravine, treacherous enough in the light of day. Nothing short of deadly at night. She'd be safer on the ridge.

She stared at him, her jaw working from side to side. One of the things he loved about her was the way she thought through a situation. "There's no cell signal on the ridge, is there?"

With a quick shake of his head, he admitted, "No."

She stepped up beside him, took his hand, and tugged. "Come with me."

"Even if I wanted to, I can't. He knows someone is here. If I'm not at the cabin, he'll start looking, and I don't want to take a chance he'll find you. I need you to go. I need to know you're safe."

"What am I supposed to do? Sit out there on the ridge and wait for him to kill you, too?"

"He's not going to kill me."

"You said the same thing about Day not shooting you."

He brushed his thumb across her jaw. "Go."

Her body slumped a fraction, and Wyatt knew she'd leave. She reached into her back pocket and handed him the burner phone. "Take it. The batteries are low, but they should last. Put it on record and hide it somewhere. Without a wire, it's the next best thing."

As he leaned in for a kiss, he caught a shadowed movement at the edge of the clearing. He took the phone and ushered her to the back door. And suddenly there was so much he wanted to say. So much that he wanted her to know. Yeah, she mattered, but the way he felt about her was a whole hell of a lot stronger word than *matter*. The way his throat tightened and the way his guts churned, it felt a whole lot like love. He opened his mouth to tell her, but the only word that came out was, "Hurry."

Geneva slipped out the back door, and the latch clicked, too soft and too quiet to carry. Though he hated to take his eyes off Rodriguez for too long, he watched out the back window until she'd made it safely to the tree line, no more than a dark shadow at the base of the trees.

The shadow hesitated, then vanished.

Wyatt found the voice record app and placed the phone on the floor next to one of the bed frame legs, then went back to the front window, trying to pick up Rodriguez. When he saw no movement there, he moved to the window by the fireplace.

There. Behind the woodpile.

Wyatt shifted from window to window, watching Rodriguez's progress. With it being darker inside the cabin, Wyatt had the advantage, but he still ducked beneath the windows as he passed.

After a full circuit around the cabin, Rodriguez approached the porch with his gun raised. Wyatt's heart didn't spike. He didn't fear Rodriguez would try to shoot him. Yet. As far as Rodriguez knew, no one knew his involvement in the murders. The only thing Rodriguez knew for sure was a strange car was on his property, and he was taking the same precautions Wyatt would have under similar circumstances.

But he also didn't want a repeat of what had happened at Day's house. Rodriguez's shoes scuffed on the porch, and Wyatt sat at the table with the gun in his lap and said, "It's me."

"Wolfe?"

The front door creaked open, the barrel of Rodriguez's gun preceding him over the threshold. Rodriguez flicked on the light, and they both squinted at the sudden brightness. Wyatt blocked the glare with one hand, careful to keep his gun hand on his lap and hidden beneath the table.

Rodriguez relaxed and holstered his gun. "Hey, man. Thought it might be you. You know you got a lot of guys looking for you, right? You ever think about turning yourself in? I'm sure we can get the whole thing straightened out."

"Is that what you would do?" Wyatt asked, knowing full well it wasn't. "Or maybe I should rephrase that and say, maybe *you* should turn yourself in."

Rodriguez froze for a microsecond before reanimating. The first flicker, the first hairline fracture in his facade as Rodriguez realized there could be a problem. But Rodriguez was the consummate, cocky game player.

"You're a funny guy for someone who has almost every branch of local, state, and federal law enforcement after him." Rodriguez stepped closer. "The APB lists you as armed and dangerous. You get someone who's trigger happy, and they're likely to shoot on sight. Do us both a favor, and let me bring you in. I can protect you. We'll find you the best lawyer. I don't know why you did it. Don't know if I want to know. But you're still my friend. You're still the kid that's had my back since high school."

At that point, the all-points bulletin was the least of Wyatt's worries. He wanted to laugh and cry at the same time. Instead, he stared in disbelief at the man who had single-handedly pulled him through the dark days of hell after he'd killed Caleb. The man who'd been there for him through the grind of the department's internal investigation, through the sidelong looks from his so-called friends. Through the grief and the guilt and the gut-wrenching self-doubt. The man who'd put his life on the line for Wyatt on more than one occasion.

The man who lied to him with a straight and guileless face.

The man Wyatt didn't recognize. Didn't know. Perhaps never had.

"What are you doing here?" Wyatt asked.

Rodriguez cracked a smile. It frayed at the edges. "I think that's my line."

"You know why I'm here."

Rodriguez glanced around the cabin. Sniffed the musk in the air. "Where's that pretty piece of tail you've—"

"Answer the question." Wyatt kept his finger indexed along the gun's barrel, but he so wanted to reach for the trigger. Luckily for Rodriquez, he had more self control than that.

Rodriguez stepped over to the refrigerator and grabbed a cold beer. Wyatt turned in his seat. No way was he letting Rodriguez out of sight. After twisting off the top, Rodriguez took a long sip and studied Wyatt over the upturned bottle. He swallowed and lowered the beer. "I needed to get something."

"At four in the morning?"

"I couldn't sleep." Rodriguez's tone shifted. Wariness crept in. If Wyatt hadn't known Rodriguez as well as he did, he would have missed it. Wyatt tightened his grip on the Sig.

Rodriguez reached up and opened the cabinet above the refrigerator, feeling around with his hand even though Rodriguez was tall enough to see the cabinet was empty.

A hundred emotions flicked across Rodriguez's face. Wyatt shifted and Rodriguez clocked the gun in Wyatt's lap. A quick mental calculation. With the beer in Rodriguez's right hand, Wyatt had the advantage. Wyatt knew it. Rodriguez knew it.

Even with the gun at Rodriguez's hip, Rodriguez couldn't clear his holster before Wyatt got a shot off.

"You coming to destroy the thumb drive to protect the senator, or keep it for blackmail?" Wyatt asked.

"Insurance."

"How's this going to play out?" Wyatt asked. Because Rodriguez couldn't draw on Wyatt, Rodriguez settled for taking another drag of his beer. "We shoot it out? Last man standing gets to tell his version of the truth? Or are you going to let me take you in for murder so I can take the senator down and clear my name?"

A muscle ticked by Rodriguez's right eye. He didn't deny anything. Not a single. Damn. Thing. *Bastard.* When had his friend left, and this shell of a human taken his place? Or had there never been a human there from the beginning? Just twenty years of lies and deceit and subterfuge.

"Was it worth it?" Wyatt's words dripped with disdain.

Rodriguez shook his head. Not in response to Wyatt's question as much as in disbelief. "*You* are judging *me*? You're the one who killed the cop."

"This from the man who killed four innocent people."

"Whores," Rodriguez spat. "I killed four worthless, drugged up—"

"*Women.*" Wyatt stood and stepped into Rodriguez's personal space. Tactically, it was the wrong move getting so close to Rodriguez, but he trusted his reflexes to keep him safe. "Four daughters and sisters and mothers—"

Rodriguez threw his head back and barked out a laugh. "Look who's all high and mighty. Don't forget you're the one Day pulled off the streets as a kid. Day might have turned you into a cop, but hell, back in high school, you weren't any better than any of those hookers. Stealing, selling drugs, selling yourse—"

Wyatt fisted Rodriguez's shirt in his hand and shoved him

against the counter. "I did what I had to do to *survive*. I didn't grow up with a silver spoon or daddy's Ferrari or kissing ass or sucking the senator's co—"

The beer bottle shattered as Rodriguez slammed it against the counter. The blow came fast. Wyatt jigged when he should have jagged. The shattered end of the bottle sliced the skin above Wyatt's brow right before Rodriguez's fist slammed into his jaw.

Wyatt staggered back, blood running into his left eye, a flap of filleted skin just visible in his peripheral vision, the pain in his jaw searing as he worked it side to side. Not broken then.

Rodriguez's Beretta was in the hand where the broken bottle had been. The barrel steady as Wyatt's best friend took aim at center mass. "You shouldn't have made me do that, man."

Even with the Sig still in Wyatt's hand, Wyatt had already lost. He'd never win in a shootout. Not with a gun already pointed at his chest. He had to find a better way.

Wyatt raised his hands out to his sides in mock surrender. "Hey, now. You don't want to do that." He took a step back and then another. And another. The more distance he could get between him and Rodriguez, the better the likelihood Rodriguez might miss.

Fat chance.

But hope was all Wyatt had. Plus, some fast-talking.

Rodriguez motioned with the barrel of the gun. "Put the gun on the table and step back."

Wyatt hesitated.

"I'm not going to shoot you, Wy. I just want to talk."

Talking was good. Talking bought Wyatt time. Heart thumping, blood dripping down his face, he complied. The gun thunked and clattered against the tabletop. Then there was that flit of a thought that went through Rodriguez's mind. Wyatt watched it play out on his friend's face. That flicker of *I can get away with this.*

Wyatt waited for the boom. The rent in the silence as gunpowder exploded. The pain that would bloom in his chest.

But nothing came.

Instead, Rodriguez said again, "I don't want to shoot you, Wyatt."

Not the complete truth. Wyatt had seen the urge to kill that Rodriguez had suppressed. But now wasn't the time to call Rodriguez out on the lie. "What do you want, then?"

Rodriguez lowered the gun to his side and tossed Wyatt the dishcloth that hung from the handle of the refrigerator. Wyatt pressed it to his forehead and used the ends to wipe the blood off his cheek and lips, smelling copper and tasting iron.

"Sit," Rodriguez ordered. Wyatt eyed the gun on the table, and Rodriguez added, "Don't get stupid."

He sat. Rodriguez sat and tossed Wyatt's Sig onto the mattress. It disappeared behind a rumple of disheveled covers.

"Where is she?"

No sense in pretending. "I sent her to the ridge to call for help."

"There's no signal."

"She doesn't know that," Wyatt lied. Sounded natural enough.

"You love her?" Rodriguez sounded more like Wyatt's old friend, but Rodriguez's lip twitched. A hint of a sneer.

Wyatt refused to let Rodriguez's vileness taint something so pure. "No."

"You may be able to fool her, or even yourself, with your lies. But you can't fool me."

Wyatt's side throbbed, his forehead stung, and the teeth in his jaw ached. Rodriguez had about run Wyatt out of patience.

Wyatt wasn't about to discuss his love life with him. "Geneva's off the table."

"Fair enough."

Wyatt eyed him, from the scruff on his face, to the bags under his eyes, to the rumpled clothes, to the sweat stains under his pits. "You look like shit, buddy. Working cases, tying up loose ends, trying to stay ahead of the Day and the feds and me all while trying to pin the murders on me. Takes a toll. Even on a man like you."

"You kept me busy," was all Rodriguez would allow. "No one said the climb to the top was easy."

Wyatt stared at him. Rodriguez stared back, each waiting for the other to make a move.

Rodriguez shifted. "The way I see it, we can both come out of this a winner."

Wyatt laughed. How could he not when Rodriguez was living in some parallel demented dimension? Leaning back in the chair, Wyatt settled in to listen to the fucked-up fantasy Rodriguez was about to spin.

"I bring you in. You have your girl alibi you."

"I'm pretty sure perjury is not at the top of her bucket list."

"Hey, what's a little lie when her man is facing the death penalty? Use that charm. I'm sure you can talk her into it."

"Say that she agrees, what then?" If he wanted any chance of getting out of this mess without landing on death row, he needed this conversation recorded before the battery on the burner phone died. If it hadn't already died.

"Then we find someone else to pin this on. Your cousin maybe. No love lost there. Plus, his truck was used to move the first victim. He knew where you lived. Knew you had a gun."

Wyatt's veins turned to ice, his blood slowing, cooling. Rodriguez had been planting seeds, implicating him from day one. Nothing had been left for chance.

Rodriguez could have stolen any truck to move Alexa Martinez's body, but he'd chosen Wyatt's cousin's truck to bring Wyatt's involvement into question, starting the rumors of him being a bad cop.

And even though Wyatt's cousin probably deserved to be in prison for any number of things he'd likely gotten away with, ramrodding an innocent man for murder wasn't an option. "You're pretty good at that, aren't you, buddy? Covering your ass."

Rodriguez must have taken Wyatt's response as a *no go* because then he came back with, "Or we clear you. Continue the investigation. Follow leads that go nowhere until the case goes cold. With you on my side, there are no more loose ends. The murders stop. And people forget."

Did Rodriguez really think Wyatt would fall for that? "Until the senator kills another."

"That was a one-off. Larson assured me it wouldn't happen again."

Wyatt had the urge to pull on a pair of hip waders because the bullshit Rodriguez was slinging was getting mighty deep. "So the case goes cold, then what?"

"Then, when Larson gets the presidential bid, he takes us with him to DC. To the top." Rodriguez laughed. Giddy almost—like a girl getting front row tickets to her favorite boy band.

Over Rodriguez's shoulder, Wyatt caught movement out the back window over the bed. Not a wayward moose or a bear. Something much worse.

Geneva.

His scalp tightened. What the hell was she doing? He gave Rodriguez an exaggerated shake of his head, hoping Geneva would see it and understand that whatever crazy-ass idea she had cooking in her head, she needed to forget. He had this under control. "You know I've always preferred the country."

The burner phone made a quick series of beeps—the low battery warning— even though he'd silenced it before setting it on the floor. At least he'd thought he had.

But now that was the least of Wyatt's worries.

Rodriguez scrambled out of his chair, his aim unwavering in the center of Wyatt's chest. "What the hell was that?"

Wyatt didn't answer.

Rodriguez slowly backed away, giving himself some space so he could search for the source of the sound without any danger of Wyatt rushing him. The phone chimed again, and Rodriguez quickly located it by the bed's leg.

"What's the code?" Rodriguez glanced up from the lock screen.

If Rodriguez deleted the recording, Wyatt had no idea if the tech guys or Massey could recover it. He couldn't take that chance. Wyatt stood.

"Stop." Rodriguez turned his back to the window and aimed the gun at Wyatt's head.

Smaller target to hit, but infinitely more lethal.

Wyatt stopped.

"The code."

With a gun aimed at his head, Wyatt had little choice. The most important thing at the moment was not provoking Rodriguez. And staying alive. "One, one, zero, five."

Rodriguez lowered the gun and, with one eye still on Wyatt, thumbed in the numbers. Wyatt tensed, his muscles ready to dive out of the way of a bullet if need be.

When Rodriquez realized which app Wyatt had been using, Rodriguez's face fell and landed somewhere between dismay and disbelief. "You were recording us this whole time?"

Funny how Rodriguez didn't see what he'd done to Wyatt as a betrayal.

Rodriguez's face flushed, and the gun came up again. "This whole fucking time?"

The window behind Rodriguez shattered. Wyatt dove for cover, and the Beretta went *boom*.

———

Geneva jumped on the bench on the back porch and dove through the window she'd broken, landing on the bed, her hands fumbling around through the shards and rumpled folds of the blanket searching for the Sig she'd seen Rodriguez toss there.

Wyatt grunted. Geneva glanced up in time to see Wyatt shove off the floor and ram his shoulder into Rodriguez's stomach as the man scrambled for his dropped gun.

Glass bit into her fingers and sliced into her palm, but that didn't slow Geneva down. Then her fingers closed around the barrel of the gun. She rolled off the bed, her boot snagging in the covers and taking her to her knees.

She kicked free and clamored to her feet, Wyatt's gun raised in her hand, her aim unsteady as she panted, trying to catch her breath. "Freeze," she yelled.

But Wyatt and Rodriguez didn't freeze. They grappled and rolled on the floor, exchanging punches and elbows, filling the air with grunts and groans and cuss words.

Rodriguez landed a wicked blow to Wyatt's throat that left him writhing and gasping for breath. Rodriguez crawled free from Wyatt's hold and slapped a hand over the loose gun.

Aiming at the floor a few feet from Rodriguez, Geneva fired. The gun kicked in her hand, but not nearly as bad as Caleb's .45 she'd shot at the range. Her ears rang, and her words sounded dull when she hollered, "Don't do it, Rodriguez."

He froze for a half-second, giving Geneva time to retake aim.

Rodriguez gripped the gun and rolled onto his back, pointing the barrel at her.

Wyatt yelled, "No!" A hoarse, strangled, shattered word.

Geneva dove to the side, closed her eyes, and fired. The *boom* of the gun battered her eardrums, leaving them ringing. Her shoulder crashed into the floor, knocking the gun from her grip. She scrambled to her hands and knees and picked it up.

Wyatt was already stripping the gun from Rodriguez's hands. He tossed it aside, well out of reach as he applied pressure to the left side of Rodriguez's chest, where red bloomed brightly.

"*Aaah!*" Rodriguez hollered, his face screwed up in agony. "Mother *fuck*—" His words cut off as Wyatt pressed harder as the blood pooled beneath his hands.

What had she done?

She dropped the gun on the floor and rushed to the bed, stripping the top sheet free. "Here, use this."

She balled up one corner and handed it to Wyatt. He released the pressure just long enough to shove the balled-up wad of material against the wound.

Rodriguez grabbed Wyatt's wrists and coughed. Blood bubbled and splattered Rodriguez's lips and chin.

Wyatt glanced up at Geneva. Blood from the wound above his eye had rained down over his eye and cheek, coagulating on the left side of his face, the flap of skin dangled over his brow. But that wasn't what made him look so grim.

"Find his car. There's a blowout kit in the trunk."

Blowout kit. The special first-aid kit that everyone in the department carried to treat gunshot wounds in the field. She should have thought of that.

"Don't let me die, Wy."

"I'm not letting you off that easy."

But as the sheets absorbed more and more blood, and as Rodriguez's breaths became increasingly labored and his color drained, Geneva went into paramedic mode. She shoved her emotions aside and ran for the kit, knowing Wyatt may not have a say in whether or not Rodriguez lived or died.

GENEVA AND WYATT WERE BACK AT THE TRAUMA HOSPITAL IN Idaho Falls, where Life Flight had taken Rodriguez. They sat in a private waiting room while they waited for Rodriguez to come out of surgery. The past eight hours had been filled with medical exams and treatments and questioning by the sheriff, as well as the FBI. They'd confiscated the burner phone hours ago to retrieve the recording and, with Day vouching for them, managed to not be placed under arrest.

But the officer Finn had posted outside the waiting area made it clear they weren't exactly free to leave either.

Geneva's saliva dried up, and she re-read a paragraph in one of the outdated women's magazines, something to do with getting a man or keeping a man or trapping a man. After another read-through, she still wasn't sure what the article said. She dumped the magazine on a side table and sighed.

"How's the head?" she asked Wyatt.

"Can't complain." He reached a hand up almost reflexively to the bandage on his forehead covering the fifteen stitches it had taken to put him back to rights. "You?"

She had a bandage across the palm of her right hand and various nicks and scrapes, but nothing that needed more than a good cleaning. "I'm good." Her voice didn't carry. Maybe because deep down, she didn't believe the words that came out of her mouth.

He reached over and took her hands, his thumbs brushing the inside of her wrist. Her pulse thrummed beneath his touch. Even almost eight hours post-shooting, her skin felt too small, like taking that shot had changed and shaped her until she was no longer the same person she was before. Her stomach knotted with a powerful mix of emotions she couldn't name or tame.

She swallowed hard and had to clear her throat before speaking. "Does it ever go away? This... this gnawing at your soul, this..." She tapped a fist against her sternum, not knowing how to describe the giant void in her chest and the *wrongness* of it all, even though she knew in her head Rodriguez hadn't given her any choice but to shoot.

And for good or bad, she now had a much greater understanding of what Wyatt had gone through, what he'd lived every day of this past year and a half. As guilty as she felt, at least Rodriguez hadn't died. Yet.

"I wish I could tell you it gets better. It changes. I'm not even sure it gets easier as much as it gets *different*. But Rodriguez didn't give you a choice. He brought it on himself. It's not your fault."

"Do you hear yourself?" Geneva turned his words against him. She knew how much he continued to blame himself for Caleb's death, but she'd seen the video with her own eyes. Caleb hadn't given Wyatt a choice either.

"That's different."

"No, Wyatt. It's *not*."

He gave her a sad smile as if humoring her, but it fell epically short. How could she convince him that Caleb held blame in his own death?

Before she could try again, the door opened, and Day and Special Agent Finn stepped through.

Wyatt stood and, despite what Rodriguez had done to him, to them, Wyatt's concern for his friend had etched themselves into the worry lines on his face. "How is he?"

"In recovery," Day said. "He's asking for you."

Wyatt turned his attention to Finn. "Am I free to go?"

Finn rested his hands on his hips. "You both are. Tech made a copy of the recording, and we've issued a warrant for Lambert's arrest. He's speaking at a rally in DC, so as soon as the DC guys are in place, they'll take him into custody. Good work, by the way."

"It's over?" Geneva couldn't believe it.

At the same time, Day said, "Not exactly," Finn said, "It's just the beginning."

"We'll need you to come in for more questioning as well as testify when the time comes, but for now, you're free to go," Finn said. She couldn't tell for sure if letting them go displeased him. He wasn't an easy man to read.

"And the APB you had out on me?" Wyatt asked.

"Canceled," Day said. "As soon as Lambert's in custody, we'll make an official announcement that you're in the clear at a press conference along with information about Lambert's and Rodriguez's arrests."

Wyatt wrapped an arm around her shoulder and pulled her closer as some of the tension left his body. He was a long way from repairing the damage to his reputation, but having an official announcement to the press that would play over and over again because of the senator's involvement and notoriety would go a long way toward correcting that.

"Go see Rodriguez," Geneva said, well aware that Wyatt should see Rodriguez while he had the chance.

His arms slid down her back, and he took her hand. "Come with me."

The post-adrenaline-rush shakes she'd been battling intensified again, and she hid her free hand in her front pocket. Geneva tried to step away, but Wyatt held firm. She shook her head, unable to face the man she'd nearly killed

"I think it will help." He took a step toward the door, and she allowed him to tow her along behind him. He gave Finn and

Day a firm nod as he passed. Geneva said nothing. Her palms started to sweat, and her skin prickled and itched as if she'd rolled naked in poison oak. What do you say to the man you tried to kill?

———

"Hospital policy is one visitor in ICU at a time," the nurse said. He was short. Could have probably been a jockey if the nursing thing hadn't worked out for him. But his face was kind, and behind the words, the compassion rang true. "But…" The nurse glanced behind him, and when he saw no other hospital personnel around, he said, "Come with me."

The nurse led Wyatt and Geneva to one of the ICU bays, a couple spots down from where Evie had stayed. Wyatt made a quick mental note to call Massey when they finished and check on Evie.

The nurse glanced at his watch. "Make it quick. My supervisor is due back from a break in ten."

Wyatt held out his hand and shook it. "Thanks, man."

Geneva trembled like a rabbit caught in a snare. Wyatt almost let her go scurrying back to the waiting room, but he felt it was important for her to see Rodriguez alive and awake, especially if there were any life-threatening complications later.

Wyatt and Caleb hadn't been lucky enough to have that opportunity.

He pulled her into his chest and whispered in her ear. "You've got this."

She nodded into the crook of his neck. He took a step back and held the edge of the curtain. "Ready?"

Working her neck from side to side, she wiped the emotion from her face, and he watched in fascination as she painted the warrior on.

Oh, man. His heart tripped. "I love you," he said. So in awe of her strength and resilience, the words came out before he had a chance to censor them. That wasn't how he'd wanted to tell her. Not here. Not now.

She glanced up, her gaze fierce, and her smile slow. "I love you, too."

Before he could lean in and kiss her, she opened the curtain and stepped inside.

Rodriguez lay on the bed, with tubes and bandages and machines making noises. Rodriguez's hand reached for the bed controls, and he raised the head of the bed a bit, his focus on Geneva. "Come to finish the job?"

Geneva huffed out a laugh even though it didn't sound like Rodriguez was joking. "I thought I had come to apologize."

Rodriguez didn't say anything. There was a 'but' coming, and he waited for it.

"But seeing you again, seeing the unapologetic defiance on your face, I don't think I can. You're the one who needs to apologize, not me."

Rodriguez's eyes fluttered and drifted closed. When they thought he'd drifted back to sleep, Rodriguez lifted his hand and made a motion with his finger, urging her closer.

Geneva leaned in, her ear near his mouth. "Don't look at me like I'm the devil," Rodriguez said, his words dark with disdain. "Your husband was no saint, either."

Clenching Rodriguez's forearm, Geneva said, "What are you saying?"

When Rodriguez slid his eyes to Wyatt, Wyatt's stomach blubbed and gurgled and sank as if someone had yanked out the transom plug. What had Wyatt missed?

Geneva turned her attention to Wyatt. "What does he mean?"

Wyatt stepped in front of her. His eyes fixed on Rodriguez.

"Don't listen to him. He's drugged and delusional and trying to get back at you any way he can."

Rodriguez held Wyatt's hard gaze, and though his ex-partner's lids were at half-mast, there was a clarity in them that had Wyatt questioning all that he knew about the case. Before Wyatt could ask another question, the nurse came back in and told them their time was up.

Geneva didn't need to be told twice.

Rodriguez held up a weak finger to the nurse, and to Wyatt said, "So you haven't figured it all out yet? Guess the case isn't over then."

Another nurse came in, she was tall and lean and frowning. To the male nurse, she said, "The patient's heart rate has spiked, and he's thrown extra beats. I'll call the attending. You get these guys out of here." The woman left to fetch the doctor, Wyatt supposed.

The nurse put his hand on Wyatt's shoulder, urging him to leave. "Come on, man. Do me a solid."

"Was it all bullshit? Huh, Roddy?" Wyatt took a step back, shaking his head as Rodriguez's childhood name fell from his lips. "All those years of friendship. Did it mean nothing?"

Rodriguez's eyes drifted closed again. Not so much as if he were sleepy. More as if he was tired of the conversation. "We both got what we wanted out of the relationship." Then he opened his eyes as the nurse pushed Wyatt past the curtain. "No hard feelings, huh?"

No hard feelings.

Wyatt couldn't help the bitter laugh as he turned to go. He'd thought Rodriguez would apologize. Thought he'd ask for forgiveness. But even shot up and lying in a hospital bed with a lifetime of prison or possibly execution staring him in the face, Rodriguez had no remorse. So yeah, *hard feelings.*

"Come on, man," the head nurse called out, "I told you to get them out of here."

The male nurse pushed Wyatt out of the ICU bay. "Dude, you're going to get me fired."

Wyatt mumbled an "I'm sorry" to the guy urging him to leave and shoved through the ICU's double doors with a focused determination he hadn't felt in a long time.

He needed Caleb's journal, and the rest of the case notes so that he could find the truth once and for all.

19

———

WYATT WALKED THROUGH THE FRONT DOORS OF MURDOCK'S Sheriff's Office, and the receptionist promptly took him back to Day's empty office. After five minutes, when Day hadn't returned, Wyatt sat in one of the chairs facing the desk. After seven minutes, he was on his feet again, pacing the room, checking out the framed photos on the bookcase—Day with various members of the community or state officials. A candid of Wyatt with his fishing pole mid cast on the banks of the Snake River, taken a few months after Day had pulled him in off the streets.

The cast hadn't gone more than fifteen feet. Wyatt had been long and lean and gangly, and more uncoordinated than he'd liked to admit. In the picture, you could tell his technique was all wrong, but he'd had a huge smile on his face. For a kid that had little to smile about most of his life, that was telling.

A knock sounded on the jamb, and Wyatt looked up. Deputy Westin. Jeff. They used to be friends. Before.

"Hey, uh..." Westin glanced away. Ever since Rodriguez's arrest, Wyatt had been getting a lot of that lately. Former friends and associates trying to make amends, but at a loss as to how to go about doing it. "You wanna grab a beer sometime?"

Wyatt almost glanced behind him to make sure Westin was talking to him.

Day walked up and clapped a friendly hand on Westin's back. "Don't you have someplace you're supposed to be?"

"I was just leaving." Westin raised his brows at Wyatt, waiting for an answer. Usually, the invitations had been more rhetorical, but Westin seemed sincere. "How's Friday at Bullchips?"

"Sure." Wyatt found himself saying. Westin turned to leave, and Wyatt called out after him. "Stay safe."

Day landed hard in the old leather chair behind the desk. The springs squeaked, and the cushion hissed. "Good to see you making friends."

"This isn't the first day of kindergarten. You don't have to worry about me being the lonely kid on the playground. I have plenty of friends." Only he didn't. Not really. But he had Massey and Evie who were more like family.

And he had Geneva.

That's what mattered.

"So why did you call me in here? If it's about my breaking into the evidence room…" Wyatt had told Day everything, including 'borrowing' the tape from the evidence locker, conveniently leaving out the part implicating Cassie, Massey, and Geneva. By the sour look on Day's face when Wyatt had told him, Day had known there was more to that story, but for reasons Day had kept to himself, he hadn't asked.

That short stint of having law enforcement's hot breath on the back of Wyatt's neck wasn't something he'd relished, and he'd confessed to Day because he didn't want to look over his shoulder any longer. If there were consequences for what he'd done, he'd pay them.

Day leaned back in the chair, his forearms resting on the gun and taser on his duty belt. "I figure you did me a favor. Pointing out some security issues and reopened my eyes to what was going on around me. Besides, after the inventory check, all evidence in Steele's case has been accounted for. And McMahon confessed to stealing drugs out of the evidence room. So I'll call it a win all the way around."

"Then why am I here?"

Day stood and came around his desk and extended his hand toward the chairs, an expression on his face somewhere between consideration and constipation as he hooked a leg over the corner of his desk. "Have a seat."

That didn't sound good. Wyatt stifled a sigh and sat.

"I wanted to apologize."

Wyatt stood back up and looked over Day's left shoulder, not quite able to meet his mentor's eye. Wanting to hear the apology, and actually hearing it, were two different things. He didn't want to live in the past any longer. Not when his future looked so bright. "Apology accepted. If that's all you brought me down here for..."

Day sat on the corner of his desk and folded his arms over his chest. "Wolfe. Sit."

He sat.

"I was wrong. I was too worried about appearances and the next election to stand up for you, and it's one of the choices in my life I think I'll regret the most. You'd been loyal to me, to the department, from day one. And I let other people's opinions sway me. I thought I was better than that. But as I said, I was wrong."

Wyatt cleared his throat. He'd been wrong, too. He'd *needed* to hear the apology, more than he'd realized. "I appreciate that." An awkward silence descended. Wyatt tapped his fingers on the arm of the chair. "Well, if you don't have—"

"There's one more thing." Day rounded his desk, unlocked the bottom drawer, and laid Wyatt's service weapon and badge on top of his blotter. "I'd like to offer you your job back."

Wyatt leaned forward and picked up the badge. The leather holder smelled of saddle soap, and the badge shined like new. There was a heft to it, a weight he'd missed. Not just for the object, but the weight of the responsibility as well. This was what he'd wanted since the minute he'd been forced to surrender it.

But now he wasn't so sure.

"Thanks." Wyatt laid the badge back on the desk and stood. "Can you give me a couple days to think about it?"

Day flinched. He'd obviously expected Wyatt to jump at the chance.

"Uh, yeah. Sure."

Wyatt extended his hand, and Day gave it a firm shake. "Take whatever time you need. It will be here when you're ready."

Another knock on the door jamb and Finn strode in, gave Day a nod, and extended his hand to Wyatt. "CNN get hold of you yet?"

Wyatt shook his head. "I don't want any part of that circus. I don't ever want to watch the news and see my mug plastered across everyone's screens again."

"Fair enough."

"How's the case?" After leaving Rodriguez at the hospital, through Geneva's urging, they had turned over Caleb's journal to the FBI in the hopes that it, along with what information they were getting from Senator Lambert, would help solidify the case against Rodriguez. Turns out, Rodriguez had picked the wrong man to give his loyalty to.

Lambert gave up Rodriguez like a virgin offering to the rain gods after a ten-year drought. Though there was no doubt Lambert would spend time in prison on reduced charges for his cooperation with the investigation, he wouldn't be getting out any time soon. Given Wyoming's mandatory twenty year sentence for murder, for a man Lambert's age, that could be a life sentence.

Finn looked from Wyatt to Day and then back again. "Day didn't tell you, did he?"

"Tell me what?"

"The night of Steele's shooting, according to Lambert, you interrupted their argument. Steele was drunk and pissed off, threatening to kill Lambert for Alexa Martinez's death."

"I never understood why he cared so much about her death."

Day cut in. "Apparently, while undercover, Steele was the pimp who sent the women to Lambert. He blamed Lambert for her death but sounds like he blamed himself even more. Steele told Lambert that when he went, he was taking Lambert with him."

The ligaments in Wyatt's knees must have disintegrated because Wyatt plopped back down on the chair as his legs gave way beneath him.

Maybe Wyatt had misunderstood. "Take Lambert with him?"

"He was going to end his life, and his guilt, once and for all," Finn said. "But then you came along."

Wyatt scrubbed his hands over his face, and glanced between Day and Finn, still not believing his ears. "Suicide by cop? Is that what you're telling me?" Wyatt of all people knew the suffocating weight of guilt. How it choked the brightness and joy out of each day until anything, even a bullet, seemed like a better option.

"That's what we're thinking. Steele had planned to die, one way or another."

Something in Wyatt's chest broke free, and for the first time in a very long time, it felt like he could take a full breath without feeling the suffocating squeeze of guilt. Then his mind shifted to Geneva. "Does Geneva know?"

"I caught her at the fire station on my way over here and informed her," Finn said.

Anger boiled inside, and Wyatt jumped up. "What the fuck, Finn? You told her at work? You couldn't wait until I was there so she wouldn't have to face that news alone?"

Finn opened his mouth and then closed it without speaking. He hadn't thought that through. But Wyatt didn't have time for Finn to find an empty platitude. He needed to find Geneva. Now.

Wyatt bolted out the door and jogged over to the fire station only to be told that Geneva had been called out to a multi-vehicle accident and wasn't expected back at the station any time soon.

———

Four hours later, Geneva found Wyatt at the hitching rail on the backside of Evie's barn, scrubbing a rubber curry comb over the dips and valleys of That-A-Way's rear haunch.

"Hey there," Geneva said as she came through the barn aisle, a beer in each hand.

He took the one she held out for him and took a long, solid pull and dove headfirst into a conversation he didn't want to have but knew he must. "Finn said he spoke with you."

In answer, she asked, "How are you?"

"Me? How about you?"

Geneva scratched her fingers over That-A-Way's swirl in the middle of the bovine's forehead while the cow's wet nose poked in Geneva's pockets for a treat. She shrugged and took a sip of her beer. "It's been a hell of a day."

Wyatt handed her a soft bristle brush and said, "Tell me about it."

While he brushed and spit-polished That-A-Way, Geneva told him about the ups and downs of her day, from her realtor calling and telling her she had an offer on her house, to her revealing conversation with Finn, to the multi-car accident where a young mother had lost her life, but they'd been able to save her baby. "The whole time we were extracting the baby from the wreckage, all I could think was how precious each day we are given is. How you never know when a day will be your last. Except Caleb. Caleb knew."

Geneva fell silent as he took long, soothing strokes with the brush down That-A-Way's top-line, the dirt and hair clouding the air between them as she flicked her wrist. Wyatt turned his head and sneezed. That-A-Way startled, but it didn't seem like Geneva even heard. She stared off into near space, her thoughts turned inward.

Her hand landed on his, stopping it mid-stroke. He glanced at her. Her eyes held a fierceness he'd only seen in a bear protecting her cub. "You've got to let it go," she said, and she wasn't talking about the brush in his hand. He knew she was talking about his guilt.

"I'm working on it." He extricated his hand from hers and kept brushing, working doggedly at a patch on the cow's shoulder caked with dried mud.

Geneva dropped her brush and stole his from his hand and tossed it aside. She ducked under the halter rope and stepped in close, her hand going to his face. She smelled of disinfectant and dust and cow, and it worked for her. "That's not good enough. As much as I loved and love Caleb, I will never forgive him for forcing you to make that choice. Caleb's death rests on his shoulders, not yours. One hundred percent."

And then Wyatt let loose with a truth he'd promised himself

he wouldn't lay at her feet. "I can't help but feel like I've stolen you from him. If I hadn't taken that shot, you wouldn't be in my arms right now."

"Maybe not," Geneva conceded. "But by forcing you to take that shot, he put me here. *He* put me here. And for that, I'm forever grateful. I love you, Wyatt. You aren't the big bad wolf of my nightmares. You're the man of my dreams."

———

Four months later, Wyatt stood in the doorway of Sea-Celia's head and tried for the third time to correctly tie the knot on his tie. For a guy who lived on a boat, you wouldn't think knots would be a big deal, but this wasn't any old knot he wanted to tie. It was *the* knot.

As in marriage.

The ring box lay heavy in the pocket of his new suit. He'd called Geneva at work, told her he was taking her out. He had seven o'clock reservations at the fanciest restaurant in Alpine, and if she didn't hurry up and get home, they'd be late.

Home. Well, the boat. Even before her house had sold, Geneva had been practically living on his boat. It wasn't set up to handle two people living aboard, but you wouldn't find Wyatt complaining. He glanced around. The dinette cushions had been fixed, and with the mattress in the berth having been replaced, it almost seemed luxurious. Slowly, life was getting back to normal, if you could call having bras and panties drying in his shower normal.

Again, not complaining.

But as much as he loved the boat, he knew as soon as he popped the question, they'd have to look for another place to live. As much as he hated to move, he loved Geneva more, and though Geneva hadn't said anything, Wyatt knew Sea-Celia wasn't a long-term option.

He pulled the St. Jude's medal Evie had given him out of his pocket and hung it on the knob of his medicine cabinet. He wasn't a lost cause anymore. With Geneva's love and forgiveness, he'd been found.

That-A-Way moo-ed and eyed him through the porthole. Since Evie had been home, recovered from her accident, she'd replaced the old dock. It was bigger and stronger with a wide area for a table with an umbrella and chairs, and a comfy spot for That-A-Way to lay. Wyatt had tried to talk Evie out of it, knowing he may not be living on the pond much longer, but she'd insisted. It was her way of thanking him, she'd told him, for watching out for Massey while she'd been laid up. Even though it was Massey who'd been an invaluable help to him and Geneva.

But that's what family did. They looked out for each other.

Wyatt heard the crunch of gravel under tires and stepped up on deck, his stomach tying in a better knot than what he'd done with the tie around his neck. But as soon as he heard the engine, he knew before the car came into view that it wasn't Geneva in her Prius.

Climbing out onto the dock, Wyatt met Finn at the head of the gangway, "What can I do for you?"

Before Finn could answer, Evie's front door opened, and she came out with a glass of lemonade in each hand and started heading their way. Evie had missed so much while laid up in the hospital, she had been making up for lost time ever since. Wyatt smiled.

Finn reached into the front pocket of his suit coat and pulled out a sealed envelope and handed it to Wyatt.

"What's this?"

"The reward money."

"Good one." Wyatt laughed. "Geneva said you didn't have a sense of humor. She won't like hearing that she's wrong."

Evie stepped up and handed a glass to each of them. Wyatt leaned forward and planted a kiss on her weathered cheek. "Hey, beautiful."

Evie blushed while Wyatt made the introductions, but the first thing out of Evie's mouth was, "What's this about a reward?"

Wyatt stuck his finger under the flap and tore the envelope open. "Finn was just jerking my chain. He's tired of the FBI and is giving stand-up a try."

Finn didn't say anything. Instead, he took a sip of his lemonade and rocked back on his heels while Wyatt pulled out the piece of paper and unfolded it. A strangled laught escaped when he saw the number of zeros on the check after his name.

"I don't understand," he said. "What's this for?"

Finn took another long sip before he replied. "It's the reward for information that led to the indictment of the Nightwalker killer. The father of one of the women killed owns a big cattle operation about fifteen miles outside of Murdock. He put up a bunch of the money."

"The rewards are for civilians."

"Which, since Rodriguez had no authority to hire you, you were at the time."

"Ah...Day offered me my job back. I don't think I can take this."

"Doesn't change anything. The money is yours."

Finn polished off the rest of the lemonade. Evie snatched the check out of Wyatt's hand and gasped so hard Wyatt thought she might swallow her dentures.

"Well, ain't that something."

Finn handed Evie back her glass and thanked her. He was halfway to his car before he turned around and asked, "What did you tell Day? About the job. You taking it?"

"Haven't decided yet. Geneva and I have a few things to sort out first." He reached into his pocket and palmed the velvet box. And speaking of his uniformed devil, Geneva's Prius turned into the driveway.

"Well, if you decide against it, give me a call. Your team impressed us. We could use a group like yours in special cases. Our own kind of mercenary confidential informant."

His team? His group? Hmm. He and Geneva and Massey did work well together. But as Geneva pulled in, Wyatt had more critical questions on his mind, like 'Will you marry me?' "I'll think about it."

Finn waved and drove away. Before Geneva got out of the car, Evie said, "I can't wait to see her face when she sees that ring."

Evie called out when Geneva opened her door. "Hurry up, young lady, your man's got something for you."

"Hush, now," Wyatt said, trying to sound stern but failing, "you're going to give it away."

"Don't worry, child. The old bat knows how to keep a secret." She went up on her tiptoes and kissed him on the cheek and whispered in his ear. "Good luck. Nobody deserves this more than you two."

His shirt collar got too tight, and Wyatt had to pop the top button to breathe. Evie took the two empty glasses and toddled away, waving at Geneva as she headed to the house.

Geneva stumbled onto the dock, looking more exhausted than he'd seen in a long time after working extra shifts the past week. He caught her arm and pulled her up against him.

"You don't want to do that," she said as she wiggled free. "Busy day. There's no telling what kind of bodily fluids I have on me. I don't want to mess up your suit."

"I don't care about the suit."

"Hey, Wy." Geneva wrinkled her nose the way she did when she had something to say that she didn't think he would want to hear. "I know we have reservations tonight, but do you think we could stay home? Cook hamburgers on the grill? We could lock That-A-Way in the back pasture, so she won't be offended."

Wyatt deflated, even though there was nothing that said he had to ask her to marry him tonight. They had plenty of time. They had their whole lives ahead of them. He kissed her on the forehead and tucked her under his arm and led her back to the boat. "Whatever you want is fine with me."

Twenty-five minutes later, Geneva and Wyatt had both changed into casual clothes. Wyatt in jeans and a sweatshirt. Her in sweatpants and a T-shirt and light windbreaker. The sun would hit the top of the mountain range in about another forty minutes, and the delivery crew was running out of daylight.

"You taking medicine?" Wyatt turned from the grill, his scraper in hand as yellow-red flames rose from freshly lit coals. The smell of smoke and lighter fluid filled the air.

"No, why do you ask that?"

"Because that's the third time in the last fifteen minutes you've looked at your watch. Hot date then?"

"No, I just—"

The *hooonk-hooonk* of a semi-trailer pierced the air and Wyatt tore his gaze from the fire. "What the hell?"

His jaw dropped and he glanced back at her. "Gen, what have you done?"

Her stomach somersaulted. *What have you done?* Geneva had been asking herself the same question ever since she signed her name on the check. What if this wasn't what he wanted?

What if *she* wasn't what he wanted?

He'd said he loved her. And as much as she wanted to spend the rest of her life with this man, that didn't mean she hadn't been presumptuous. But as Caleb used to say, you can't go through life wishing for what you want. You have to go out and get it.

So she had.

"*Gen.*" Wyatt tugged her out of the chair, a goofy grin splitting his face.

"Sea-Celia is great, but I think the Lone Wolf will suit us better."

"The Lone Wolf?"

Geneva tossed him a smile. "Seemed like fate."

As the semi with the loaded down trailer crossed the cattle guard, the house boat's name, emblazoned across the stern, came into view.

Evie and Massey came out of the house, and Massey gave the driver directions to the pond.

"How long have you been planning this?"

"A while," was all she'd admit to.

"And the dock?"

She grinned. "That was all Evie. But still, part of the plan."

Three hours later, the delivery crew packed up the last of the spotlights. After a lot of fancy maneuvering and cussing and jockeying, they managed to launch the Lone Wolf and tie her up to the new dock with Sea-Celia tied to the Wolf's starboard cleats.

Evie and Massey had gone in for the night, and That-A-Way sniffed around the dock, the coals in the grill having long grown cold. Geneva collapsed onto one of the galley chairs, and her stomach let out a long, low growl.

Wyatt turned around from his inspection of all the cabinets and cubby holes. "I still can't believe you did this."

Geneva scrunched up her face. "You like it?"

"Like it?" Wyatt stepped over and pulled her to her aching feet, wrapping his arms around her waist. "Two bedrooms. A small office. A covered rear deck and a salon with almost more room than all of Sea-Celia put together. What's not to love?"

"I know how much Sea-Celia means to you. How your grandfather gave it to you. I wasn't sure you would want to move."

"What I want is you. I would have moved wherever made you happy but to have you understand what I love about living on the water, and how much that means to me, makes it that much more special."

He leaned in, pressing his lips to hers. She stepped closer, locking her arms around his neck, but before she could take the kiss any deeper, her stomach growled again.

"I never did feed you, like I'd promised." Wyatt stepped back, her hands slipping down his chest. "Wait here."

Wyatt exited through the sliding glass door and disappeared over the side of the boat, scrambling onto Sea-Celia. Geneva waited. And waited some more. What was taking him so long? She didn't require a gourmet meal. At this point, she'd take a bowl of Goldfish crackers and a microwaved bowl of mac and cheese.

She stepped out onto the deck as Wyatt hopped back on board, dressed in his suit, a bottle of champagne tucked under one arm with two flutes in one hand and a basket of food in the other.

To Geneva, Wyatt looked good all the time, but something about the way he filled out a suit made her hungry for more than food.

She took everything out of his hands and set it all at their feet.

"Hey, what—"

She snagged his tie and brought his lips down to hers. "Suddenly, I have an appetite for something else."

Wyatt smiled, and it might have been the glow of the porch

lights, but the smile looked green around the edges. Her somersaulting stomach landed with a splat. "What's wrong?"

Wyatt caught her hands. "I have something I want to say, and then I have two questions for you."

Sweat broke out on his brow, and Geneva looked around for a chair before her legs gave way, but there was no furniture on the back deck yet. Whatever he had to say couldn't be good.

He pressed his forehead to hers, took a deep breath, then lifted his head and held her gaze. Her stomach grumbled with fear, not hunger.

"I don't know how the worst day of my life has turned out to also be the best. Those months after... those months after were *dark*. I'm not going to lie. And then I met you." He brushed his thumb over her cheek, and she was surprised there was moisture there. "And the more I got to know you, the more I got to know Caleb through you, my world got darker and lighter at the same time. You've shown me there is life on the other side, you've shown me a forgiveness I couldn't find for myself. And even after all you've lost, after what I'd taken, you're that beacon that shines through the densest fog, lighting my way."

He pressed a kiss to her lips, breathtaking in its lightness, so dark and devastatingly tender. Everything Wyatt was, he poured into her, giving more than he took like he always did. Filling her with his love and devotion.

Breaking the kiss, he reached into his pocket and pulled out a small box. "I love you and want to spend the rest of my life with you." He opened the box toward her. "Gen, will you be my partner in crime?"

A strangled sound ripped from her throat, part sob, part laugh, all love. "Yes. There's no one else I'd rather be shackled to for the rest of my life."

His eyes lit, and he hugged her tight, then fumbled with the ring as he pried it out of the box. Geneva reached over to remove Caleb's ring, but Wyatt stopped her. "Don't take it off."

Geneva glanced at him, confused.

He slipped the ring on, and it fit beside Caleb's ring, a platinum band with a string of diamonds each one lining up perfectly with the space between the diamonds on the gold band Caleb had given her.

"I had the band specially made. I'm not trying to replace Caleb. I could never do that. He's part of our lives. Part of our story. I don't want to ever forget that. The wedding band is designed to fit on the other side of Caleb's band. Not holding us apart, but keeping us together."

Geneva's heart tripped, ripping out that last bit of tissue that had scarred and locked it down, allowing it to beat free for the first time in a very long time.

Some women were never lucky enough to find their one true love. How on earth had she been fortunate enough to find two?

Geneva dried her cheeks with her hands and tucked the champagne bottle under her arm and grabbed the stems of the flutes. With her free hand, she snagged his tie and led him to the main cabin. "Come, Mr. Wolfe. We need to huff and puff and blow this house down."

With a wicked grin, Wyatt kicked out of his shoes and shucked his suit coat, shirt, pants, and briefs. Leaving a trail of discarded clothes in his wake. By the time they'd made it to their bed, he was naked—besides the tie she held firm in her grip— and most assuredly aroused.

He set the champagne and flutes on the bedside table and backed her against the bed, stripping her out of her clothes. He tossed them over his shoulder one by one. Gripping his hands around her waist, he picked her up and threw her on the bed. When he moved to crawl onto the mattress, she pressed a foot to his chest and stopped him.

"What is it?" He held her foot, trailing his fingers up her calf.

"You said you had two questions. Will you marry me was one. What's the other?"

A delectably feral look settled in his eyes, promising a wild ride. He removed her foot and settled between her legs, kissing his way between her breasts, down, down to her belly button. He nipped her on her hip bone. "Vanilla..." then he turned her on her stomach with a warm chuckle that melted her insides. He bit her on the ass cheek and said, "...or chocolate?"

A LETTER TO MY READERS

Dear Reader,

I hope you enjoyed Wyatt and Geneva's journey to love and forgiveness. Don't worry, there is more excitement coming to Steele-Wolfe Securities. In the mean time, you can catch their cameo in Cowboy, Unbridled, or start where it all began in this world with Cowgirl, Unexpectedly. You won't be sorry you did.

Your next adventure starts here:

ROMANTIC SUSPENSE

Lazy S Ranch Series
Cowgirl, Unexpectedly (Book 1)
Must Love Horses (Book 2)
Hot on the Trail (Book 3)
Cowboy, Undercover (Book 4)
Cowboy, Unbridled (Book 5)
Cowgirl, Unbroken (Book 6 Coming soon!)

Wright's Island Series

Don't Look Back (Book 1)
In Her Defense (Book 2)

Steele-Wolfe Securities
Wyoming Confidential (Book 1)

CONTEMPORARY ROMANCE

Rockin' Rodeo Series
Luck of the Draw (Book 1)
Photo Chute (Book 2)
Reined In (Book 3)
Rockin' Rodeo Series Collection (Books 1-3)

MM ROMANCE

Black Stallion Studios Series
One Shot (Book 1)
Key Grip (Book 2)
Best Boy (Book 3)

Valley Boys
Art of Love (Book 1 Coming soon)

ABOUT THE AUTHOR

Vicki Tharp makes her home on small acreage in south Texas with her husband and an embarrassing number of pets. When she isn't writing, you can usually find her on the back of her horse—avoiding anything that remotely resembles housework—smelling like fly spray and horse sweat.

Join my newsletter at: http://eepurl.com/croJgz
Join my street team and receive free Advance Reader Copies of my upcoming books at: http://eepurl.com/cWhXbD
You can find my website at: www.VickiTharp.com
I love to hear from readers. You can email me at vwtharp@VickiTharp.com

Or you can stalk me at:

facebook.com/VickiTharpAuthor

instagram.com/author_Vicki_Tharp

bookbub.com/authors/vicki-tharp

amazon.com/author/vicki_tharp

twitter.com/vwtharp

9 781948 798266